Praise for

JEANETTE
BAKER

RITA® Award-winning author of *Nell*

"Baker is an excellent storyteller."
—*Romantic Times BOOKclub*
on *A Delicate Finish*

"Baker is a fantastic writer with talent to
spare…a storyteller, plain and simple."
—*Amazon.com*

"Delivered with thoughtful exposition and
flawless writing…a provocative book."
—*Publishers Weekly* on *Blood Roses*

"Baker is a forceful writer of
character and conflict."
—*Publishers Weekly* on *Nell*

"It grips the reader from first page to last."
—Diana Gabaldon, author of
the *Outlander* series, on *Irish Lady*

Also by JEANETTE BAKER

A DELICATE FINISH
CHESAPEAKE TIDE
THE DELANEY WOMAN
BLOOD ROSES

Watch for

ONE HOT SUMMER

Coming June 2007

JEANETTE BAKER

The Lavender Field

MIRA

ISBN 0-7783-2311-0

THE LAVENDER FIELD

www.MIRABooks.com

Printed in U.S.A.

ACKNOWLEDGMENTS

A very special thank-you to Janet Gardner and her gorgeous warmblood, Prime Suspect, for inviting me to The Dressage Center to view a competition. Although I changed a few details, I used this beautiful center in the heart of Moorpark's horse country as the setting for my story.

Also, thank you to Steve Kipper and Vladimer Tom Valter at the Jdon Andalusian Farms in Somis, California, for answering every question I could think of, and then some. The weather and the scenery couldn't have been more perfect.

The story of Alois Podhajsky's valiant rescue of the Lipizzan stallions with the help of the United States Army's 2nd Cavalry, under orders from General George S. Patton and carried out under the direct command of Colonel Charles H. Reed, is well-documented, so much so that Walt Disney was inspired to make a movie of the subject. These are truly gallant horses. That part is fact.

The fiction begins with Franz Kohnle bringing a strain of Lipizzaners to America, and with the hypothetical Navicular Disease. The man never existed and the disease has never, as far as I know, afflicted any of the Spanish Riding School's famous Lipizzaners.

As always, my appreciation for Valerie Gray, my editor at MIRA, her lovely colleagues and, of course, my agent, Loretta Barrett, and Nick, Gabriel and Allison at Barrett Books grows with every book.

Thank you, Steve, for your immutable support. Thank you, Jean, Pat and the Bills for years of professionalism and friendship.

Prologue

Vienna, Austria, the Spanish Riding School

Seated behind the balustrade, Dr. Werner Pohl, sixty-nine years old, director of the Spanish Riding School, tall and spare as a riding crop, fixes his penetrating gaze on the lead horse in the arena. It is dress rehearsal and he is watching the final movement of the haute école. Adolphus, one of the finest stallions ever bred at the Piber Stud, moves with quiet pride, his neck arched, his hooves spurning the raked sand. His rider, uniformed in the rust-colored livery of the bygone Hapsburgs, sits still as stone, back straight, hands firm, eyes intent on the fluid perfection of his performance. Seven horses follow. The violins of Bizet's *L'Arlésienne Suite* play sweetly in the background.

Pohl watches the superb precision of the stallion's movements and his heart thuds with relief. So far, everything has gone perfectly. Perhaps he is mistaken and the limp he noticed earlier never happened. More than likely it is a figment of his imagination, a result of too little sleep and the demands of an exhausting schedule. Some of the tension leaves his shoulders.

Pleased that he has nothing negative to report, he is about to turn away when something catches his eye, a movement, flawed, out of place, definitely unrehearsed, so quickly recovered that it seems as if it never happened. But it has. This time there is no doubt. Once again, his star stallion, Adolphus, shortens his stride, stumbles and is pulled back by his rider.

Leaning back against the red velvet balustrade, Werner Pohl closes his eyes. Pain, searing and complete, consumes him. Another one down. How many more to follow? It is a rhetorical question. He is a trainer, an instructor, not a veterinarian or a breeder. He will consult with Heinz Lundgren at the Piber Stud.

Piber, a nine-hundred-year-old village fifteen miles from the hub of Graz, has been home to the Stud since the end of World War I. Lundgren, a slight man in jodhpurs and wire-rimmed glasses, manages a staff who provides for approximately one hundred and fifty Lipizzaners.

Pohl finds him in the pasture surrounded by mares and their foals. They are nuzzling his pockets, hoping for carrots or lumps of sugar. He waves Lundgren to the road, waiting impatiently until he climbs through the fence and stands beside him. Pohl doesn't mince words. "Adolphus has symptoms. This is disastrous. Something must be done."

Lundgren leans against the fence and whistles through his teeth. "Are you sure?"

"If you mean has he been diagnosed, no. But he stumbles. His gait is unsure. He rests with his weight on the toe."

"How many is that now?"

"All of them, Heinz, every stallion over twelve years."

Lundgren looks at the ground. Werner Pohl is a legend when it comes to training and showing Lipizzaners. He can feel the older man's pain. "What can I do to help you, Dr. Pohl?"

"We must make this stop. We must infuse new blood. We cannot train a stallion for eight years and have him ruined before his prime."

"New blood is possible," Lundgren says slowly, "but it will take time. We don't know if the problem is inherited, or if it is due to conformation."

"Both are the results of inbreeding."

Lundgren frowns. "I wish I had an immediate solution. But these are Lipizzaners. Of course they are inbred."

"We've eliminated the ram head. We can eliminate the caudal heel."

"The ram head was eliminated by selection within the race," Lundgren reminds him patiently. They have been down this road before. "It is a visible characteristic. Caudal heel doesn't show up for years. Where will we find trained Lipizzaners, ten years and older, who haven't been a part of our breeding program?"

Both men are silent. Each knows what the other is thinking.

Pohl breaks the silence. He speaks grimly. "We have been very patient with Franz's son. I think it is time to remove the gloves."

"We should leave politics to the diplomats," suggests Lundgren. "Perhaps the ambassador can be enlisted."

Pohl grins. "I've heard that California is lovely in the spring. Don't you trust me, Heinz?"

Heinz Lundgren fights his rising panic. Before the

First World War, every court in Europe had a classic riding school. Now there is only one. The reputation of the Spanish Riding School must be maintained. This is a matter of the utmost delicacy. Pohl can be arrogant and gruff. He is a horsemaster, not a politician. Deciding it is worth the risk to stick his neck out, he speaks. "The ambassador will serve us well, Dr. Pohl. You are needed in Vienna."

One

Whitney Benedict, only child and sole heir to Whitney Downs, Boone and Pryor Benedict's Thoroughbred farm, reread her notes and frowned. The involuntary gesture formed a small vee in the space between her eyebrows. It was her third perusal of the draft she'd composed and she was committing it to memory. She always read her drafts three times, the first for content, the second for changes and the third to edit the changes. It was a habit she'd picked up in law school and kept throughout her twelve years of practice. Not much escaped a third read. Not much escaped Whitney.

Carefully she aligned her pencil with the other two on her desk so that the erasers faced up and the points down. Then she stacked her papers, all nine sheets, neatly on top of one another and placed them in the righthand drawer of her desk. She had exactly four minutes before her meeting with Everett Sloane, senior partner of Barnaby & Sloane, and Robert Kincaid,

United States senator and chairman of the Foreign Relations Committee. She would put those minutes to good use.

Leaving her desk, she strode purposefully across the gleaming hardwood to her private bathroom, soaped her hands for precisely fifteen seconds before rinsing and drying them, sprayed mouthwash on her tongue, massaged her gums and reapplied her lipstick. Her hair, a sophisticated twist at the back of her head, her suit—navy, severe, expensive—and her immaculate pumps needed no adjustment. They were flawless.

It was time. She was ready. Smiling at her secretary, she walked toward the boardroom, her heels clicking sharply on the priceless cherrywood floors. Her gait was confident, her expression serene. What would follow was a challenge she'd prepared for. Whitney welcomed challenges.

Everett Sloane was seated behind his enormous desk. The senator faced the window. Both men rose when she entered the room. Robert Kincaid looked at Whitney and his jaw dropped. She pretended not to notice, but behind her cool smile, annoyance curled into life.

"My, my," the senator said in the good ol' boy voice that won him the state of Kentucky in the last election. "Are you sure a pretty thing like you is old enough to practice law?"

Not by the flicker of an eyelash did Whitney's expression change. "I'll give it my best shot," she said smoothly, taking the chair across from him. "Please, sit down, gentlemen."

The two men resumed their seats. "Whitney's specialty is international law," Everett Sloane explained. "She's the best there is. If she can't get the job done, no one can."

Kincaid rubbed his fleshy hands together. "Well, then. What's the plan?"

"The *plan*," Whitney replied smoothly, "is to remind Mr. Mendoza that not only will he become a millionaire many times over, he'll also be contributing to a timeless legacy."

"What if that doesn't work?"

Whitney allowed a small, superior smile. "It will."

"He didn't rise to the bait before," Kincaid said slowly. "What's different now?"

Whitney's eyes met those of her colleague. She shook her head slightly.

Everett Sloane leaned forward. "We're not at liberty to say, Bob. It's a matter of confidentiality. You'll have to trust Whitney on this one. If she says Mendoza will take the money, he will."

"Hell, I say we just confiscate the damn horses," said Kincaid. "Who is this guy, anyway?"

Sloane stood and walked around his desk to the fully equipped bar. "Care for a splash, Bob?"

The senator grinned. "If it's bourbon, I won't say no."

"Whitney?"

"No, thanks. I've got a few more hours to put in after this." She nodded at Robert Kincaid. "To answer your question, Senator, the Lipizzaners belong to Mr. Mendoza. He is their legal owner. The last of the stock brought over by Franz Kohnle died long ago. Gabriel Mendoza is under no obligation to sell his horses. The ball is in his court. I'd like to proceed cautiously."

"Whose side are you on, young lady?"

No one on the receiving end of her charming smile would have guessed that it was calculated. "The winning side, Senator. That is the point, isn't it?"

Robert Kincaid sampled his bourbon and sighed.

"Mighty good, Everett, mighty good." He turned his piercing gaze on Whitney. "If Everett chooses his employees the way he chooses his liquor, I'm sold."

"Whitney is a partner, Bob," Sloane reminded him gently, "not an employee."

"I don't care if she's Sherman's granddaughter, as long as she brings us those horses. I need all the positive strokes I can get, if you know what I mean." He shifted his eyes to the senior partner. "Do we understand each other?"

"We do."

Kincaid drained his glass and stood. "Well, then, I'll be on my way. Keep in touch, Everett. I'll expect updates."

"You'll have them."

Whitney watched him leave. "So much for southern gentlemen."

Everett chuckled. "He's one who still believes a woman's place is in the home."

"He's insufferable."

"He's not the issue. I don't have to tell you what it means to the firm to do this one right. I'm sorry about your vacation, Whitney, but I meant what I said to Kincaid. You're the best we've got. We're counting on you."

She stood. "You won't be sorry.

"Has Mendoza gotten back to you?"

"We have an appointment on Tuesday."

"Good luck."

"Thanks." Whitney closed the door behind her. Luck had nothing to do with it. Luck wasn't reliable. Hard work, research and the right price were her preferred negotiating tools. They hadn't let her down yet.

Whitney Downs Thoroughbred Farm

When, precisely, did Whitney turn difficult? I think back, recalling her formative years, and still it escapes me.

I'm her mother. I should have seen the signs. Not in my wildest dreams would I have believed my agreeable child would grow up to be the cause of such frustration.

Pryor Benedict dispassionately studied the words she had written only yesterday on the first page of her journal. It was one of those lovely leather-bound ones with the gilt edges, the kind only the best stationery stores offered. Pryor didn't believe in using a computer. There was something about the process of actually forming the letters with a black fountain pen and watching the words take shape on thick, cream-colored paper. In her opinion, people used computers far too much. What was wrong with handwriting or books, for heaven's sake? What could be more satisfying than curling up on the couch, turning pages at one's own pace, lingering over a particularly fine passage?

Seated on a spindle chair in front of the eighteenth-century secretary that had originally belonged to one of her ancestors, she stared out the window into the blue twilight. Fireflies seeking refuge from a sudden burst of blood-warm rain swam around the smeared gold light of the porch lamps. They were early this year. She loved watching them flit about, awed by the amazing resilience of the little bugs whose lives were spent over the course of a single day. They were indigenous to Kentucky, to home, just as much as the sight of spring foals munching on summer bluegrass, their legs so long and delicate and bone-thin that it didn't seem possible they could hold their own velvety weight.

Pryor was proud to admit that she was a homebody. Her heart never failed to lurch when, after a day of shopping or volunteering at one of her endless charities, she turned down the long, dirt-packed road bordered with white rail fences and lined with ancient oaks that led first to the house, then to the barns of Whitney Downs. The Thoroughbred stud farm had been her family's lifeblood for more than a hundred years, ever since the first Whitney crossed the Kentucky state line, smelled the loamy dark earth, rich with lime and carpeted with blue-tinted grass, and dreamed of raising horses.

Pryor didn't consider herself a horsewoman. Not that she was afraid of horses. No Whitney had ever been afraid of them. Growing up, and in the early years of her marriage to Boone, she spent most of her time helping out in the barns. She still rode, of course. There was nothing like an hour or so in the saddle every day to keep a woman lean-hipped and flat-bellied. But ever since middle age had crept up on her, she no longer had any interest in mucking around the stables, even those that housed Thoroughbreds valued in the millions. She wanted time to relax a bit, lunch with friends, take up golf and spoil her grandchildren, if only Whitney would come up to scratch.

Pryor had put off beginning her memoirs for quite some time now. There was no need for haste. She was only fifty-eight and of sound mind and body. But she'd always believed that one shouldn't delay something important until the final moment. When better to start a journal than when one had something to say? And Pryor certainly had something to say, although she would rather eat dirt than voice the words she had just written about her much loved daughter. There was no point in hurting the girl's feelings. After all, Whitney didn't work at being difficult. But it didn't seem quite fair to Pryor that her only daughter, a child who'd never caused anyone even a hint of trouble from conception through her eighteenth birthday, should have turned out the way she had. No. It simply wasn't fair.

Once again, she read the words she'd written. The sentiment was true, but the tone wasn't completely accurate. She made it sound as if Whitney was a failure or something close to it. Pryor prided herself on accuracy. No one in her right mind would consider Whitney Benedict a failure. *Disappointment* was a better word. That was it. Whitney had disappointed her, and not for the first time. It was a condition that occurred with more regularity than it should have, considering the fairly typical circumstances of her upbringing. She'd been such a biddable little girl, so sunny and sweet-tempered, with her Alice in Wonderland looks and gracious manners. If only she hadn't been gifted with such a remarkable intelligence quotient.

Pryor wasn't one of those old-fashioned mothers who thought that a smart girl would never catch a man. On the contrary. It was essential that a young lady be properly educated. How else would she meet the *right* man? Heaven forbid that her daughter should marry someone unacceptable. Pryor shuddered. They'd been down that road before, and she would rather Whitney stay single for the rest of her days than have her subject to the likes of Wiley Cane. She remembered to thank God every day of her life that the Whitney name still meant something in Lexington, Kentucky, enough to have her daughter's brief, terrible marriage annulled before it went on too long.

Thankfully, Whitney had never given her that kind of trouble again. In fact, it was just the opposite. The girl was so discriminating in her tastes that she couldn't seem to find a man to suit her. If only she wasn't so— Pryor searched for the right word. *Rigid* came to mind.

Whitney was rigid to a degree that caused Pryor to lie awake at night and worry. Could it be healthy for a young woman to be so consumed with order?

She was beginning to wonder if she would ever cradle a grandchild of her own on her lap. Her daughter was thirty-seven years old. If she didn't get busy quickly, it would be too late. Pryor pushed away the terrifying thought that thirty-seven might already be too late.

Boone was no help, either. "Leave her alone," he always said. She couldn't count on Boone when it came to Whitney. All he thought about were his precious horses. They were actually Pryor's horses, but after she married him, he fell into the family business so seamlessly that no one remembered how far up he'd married.

That suited her just fine. Horses weren't her first priority. What she was concerned about was her daughter, her only child, who'd turned her back on the family business to become a lawyer with the killer instincts of a piranha, one of those fish who could strip the flesh from a hundred-and-fifty-pound manatee in less than sixty seconds, and then refused to settle down and produce a family. And now this final insult, after Pryor had gone to such trouble to arrange the getaway cruise, and Whitney had promised. To have it all come to nothing was enough to make a grown woman cry, or at least begin venting in her journal.

The phone rang. Pryor glanced at the caller ID window. It was Whitney. Her heartbeat accelerated. She composed herself and answered on the second ring. "How are you, sugar?"

"Hi, Mama. I'm fine. I wonder if you wouldn't mind collecting my mail while I'm gone?"

"Of course, dear. How long do you think you'll be away?"

"I'm not sure. No more than a few days."

Pryor sighed. "Whitney, are you sure you have to go on this business trip? Isn't there anyone else the firm can send? The cruise would be so good for you. Besides," she reminded her, "you promised."

The silence on the other end of the phone meant Whitney was annoyed and that she was taking a second or two to collect herself and compose a rational argument. The Benedicts did a lot of that—collecting themselves, that is—but no one would ever call them rational, except for Whitney, and she was only part Benedict.

"I'm sorry, Mama," Whitney replied, "but if you recall, I didn't actually promise. I said I would try. I appreciate your concern, but in all fairness, you have to remember that I didn't plan on this trip. I didn't even know about it until last week. Sometimes it isn't possible to rearrange my schedule. We've already gone over this. I've been given the case because of my background. There's no one else."

Pryor took this to mean Whitney's specialty in international law and her experience with horses. She knew all along that it was pointless to try, but she couldn't resist a final argument. "What would they do if you had an accident, God forbid, or if you didn't exist at all?"

"But that isn't the case," Whitney said slowly and patiently. "A singles' cruise isn't exactly in the same league as a debilitating accident, is it?"

Pryor didn't answer. Sometimes she felt as if she were the child and Whitney the mother.

"C'mon, Mama," Whitney prodded her. "Is it?"

"No," Pryor conceded. "I guess it isn't."

"Thank you."

"Will you at least come for dinner?"

"Tonight? It's late already."

"Why not? You have to eat."

Another silence and then a slow, deep breath. "All right, Mama. I'll be there for dinner."

Immediately Pryor felt better. "See you at eight, sugar. Wear something pretty."

It wasn't until after she hung up and thought about her mother's parting words, did Whitney suspect an ulterior motive. Who was her mother inviting this time? Could she have found another eligible man, one Whitney hadn't already met, who was available for dinner on short notice?

She decided against changing. Her navy-blue suit with the skirt that hit the top of her knee was exactly what the occasion warranted. If she was wrong, and it was only family, she would shuck the jacket. If not, the severe blue tailoring was enough to send her mother's latest candidate running for the hills.

Whitney tapped her nails on her desk blotter. Her mother was certainly tenacious. Whitney's single status was like a red flag being waved in front of a bull.

It wasn't that she didn't want to get married. It just wasn't an impending need. Occasionally, on her birthday or when someone asked her age and then raised a dubious eyebrow, she would feel a slight twinge. But the truth was, it didn't bother her as much as it did everyone else. Whitney was quite happy with her single state, especially after the devastating consequences of her brief and only foray into married life. She had a challenging job, plenty of money, the independence to spend it any way she pleased, intellectual stimulation, too many invitations on her social calendar, a luxury apartment with a view of the river and, when she wanted it, male companionship. What she didn't have, as her mother pointed out in nearly every conversation, was a child.

Pryor wanted to be a grandmother, but Whitney wasn't really sure that she wanted to be a mother. Children were an enormous responsibility. It wasn't the money or even the effort that Whitney begrudged, it was the mess. Children meant frequenting restaurants with high chairs, and high chairs meant crumbs under the table and gummy fingers and embarrassing scenes where waitresses with thin, disapproving lips pretended it didn't matter that your little darling had overturned her spaghetti for the third time. Whitney shuddered. Raising a child, hers or anyone else's, meant that she would never be completely alone again, not for another twenty years. For a person who valued her solitude, the idea of someone always there, needing her, was terrifying. She was responsible enough, far-sighted enough and selfless enough to understand that a child needed parents who were fully, unwaveringly committed. Children, in Whitney's world, should come first.

She checked her watch. It was after seven, barely enough time to sew things up here in her office and make the drive out of the city to Whitney Downs, her namesake, the Thoroughbred farm where she was born and raised and which she couldn't seem to put behind her, no matter how hard she tried.

She pulled into the driveway at the same time her father emerged from the foaling barn. Whitney leaned against the car and waited until Boone caught up with her.

He slung an arm around her shoulder, pulled her against him and kissed her forehead. "What a nice treat. I didn't expect you tonight. How's my girl?"

"I'm fine, Daddy. Mama invited me at the last minute. She's stressing over my not going on the singles' cruise she planned for me."

His eyes crinkled at the corners. "She'll get over it. All she wants is the best for you, honey. We both do."

Whitney changed the subject. "How's Cinnamon Stride? Is he still Derby material?"

"You betcha," her father said emphatically. "We're clocking him regularly now and he keeps gettin' better and better."

"Will you enter him at Saratoga?"

"I haven't decided yet."

Whitney frowned. "He's closing in on three years old. If you don't give him some running experience, he won't be ready."

Boone hesitated.

"C'mon, Daddy. If you can't trust your own daughter, who can you trust?"

"Promise you won't say a word, not even to your mother. When she gets involved in the running of the place, everybody tenses up."

"I promise."

"He's skittish coming out of the starting gate. I don't want to push him. We haven't had a Derby winner in a long time. I think this one has what it takes, but if he gets spooked early on, we've lost him. He needs gentle handling." Boone glanced at his daughter. "Are you interested?"

She shook her head. "You know that isn't possible."

"Just checkin', honey. It doesn't hurt to ask." He opened the front door and stepped back, allowing her to precede him. "Shall we?"

She stopped before walking inside. "Are you worried, Daddy? Is everything going all right with the business?"

"Everything's fine," he said heartily. "But it wouldn't hurt for us to have a winner. You know how it is."

Whitney knew exactly how it was, which was why she wanted no part of a profession in which too much was out of her control. Whitney Downs wasn't one of those fancy stud farms where horses had e-mail addresses and barns had mahogany doors and stained-glass windows. It was a working farm where one good virus, a plague of caterpillars or a few slipped foals could run it into bankruptcy.

Pryor's high-pitched, breathy voice called out from the living room, asking questions and issuing orders in that fist-behind-the-velvet-glove way she had of getting what she wanted. "Is that you, Boone, honey? Where have you been? Hurry and clean up, we have guests for dinner. Whitney's coming and Drew Curtis dropped in, so I invited him, too."

Boone chuckled. "Give me a few minutes," he called out. He lowered his voice. "She never gives up." Then he glanced at his daughter's face. "Don't be upset, sweetheart," he said soothingly. "It's only Drew. You can talk circles around him."

"That's not the point," she retorted. "Why should I have to entertain Drew Curtis? I've worked all day. I leave tomorrow on a business trip. I want to relax, watch the news, read a good book and finish packing. Mama knows that, and she also knows I haven't been the least bit interested in Drew since the junior prom, even if he hadn't taken up with Teri Cooper and had two kids with her before she dropped him." She would have continued but she was out of breath. Inhaling deeply, she asked, "Why does she keep doing this to me?"

Boone dropped a light kiss on his daughter's nose. "You know it isn't as bad as all that. You're so independent we hardly see you anymore. Cut your mother some slack. Now, if you'll excuse me, I'll shower and shave and be back to rescue you before you're into your second bourbon and branch."

Whitney watched him climb the stairs two at a time, refraining from reminding him that she didn't drink bourbon and branch. Then she looked into the beveled mirror that took up most of the long wall leading to the rest of the house, buttoned the top button of her severely tailored jacket and walked into the living room.

Drew and her mother were seated across from each other on identical cream-colored sofas. They both stood when she entered the room. Pryor, elegant as usual in tailored pants, pearls and a cashmere sweater, held out her arms.

"Whitney, honey, isn't it nice that Drew could be here? He stopped in unexpectedly, and since he hasn't eaten, I invited him." She kissed her daughter's cheek.

Whitney raised one skeptical eyebrow. "Really?" She looked at Drew and noted the wave of color rising from his neck. He was one of those unfortunate redheads who blushed easily and never tanned, definitely not her type. "Were you in the area?"

"Well, I—"

"Now, Whitney," her mother chided her. "You're not in the courtroom anymore. There's no need to interrogate a dear friend." She sat down and patted the seat beside her. "Sit down."

Whitney sat. "How are the kids, Drew?"

He grinned, obviously grateful for the change of subject. "They're just fine. Tommy's the star of his Little League team and Sammy is the terror of her kindergarten class. I only wish I saw more of them. Now that Teri's remarried and moved to Louisville, I'm odd man out."

Whitney nodded sympathetically. "It must be hard."

Pryor shook her head. "How long has it been since your divorce?"

"Two years."

"Two years." She fluffed out her artfully streaked hair with a manicured finger. "My, my. Where does the time go? It seems like only yesterday that we attended your wedding. Do you ever wish for a crystal ball?"

Whitney struggled against the acerbic comment hanging on the edge of her tongue. Had her mother always been this obvious? "Mama," she interrupted. "You haven't offered me a cocktail."

"Since when do you need an invitation to help yourself to the bar in your own house?"

"Cocktail?" Boone's voice cut in. "Did I hear someone say cocktail?"

Whitney released her breath. Her father was here. There would be no more talk of soured marriages and crystal balls. "I'll have a gin and tonic," she said.

"How about you, Drew?" her father asked. "Does your drink need freshening?"

"No, thanks. I'm doing all right with this one."

"Pryor? How about you?"

"No, darling."

Boone handed Whitney her drink and seated himself beside Drew. "So, buddy, long time no see. How's the foaling going?"

"We're okay this year," Drew said slowly, "but most of our mares haven't delivered yet and you know what happened last time."

Boone nodded. "It's heartbreaking to lose 'em when they're full term. I'd cut off my right arm to stop it from happening again."

Pryor cleared her throat. "Drew was telling us about his children."

"Is that so?" Boone pretended a polite interest.

"It must be so lovely for your parents to have grand-children," Pryor began.

Drew nodded. "They don't see as much of mine anymore."

"Drew is one of four children, Mama," Whitney reminded her. "The Curtises have several grandchildren."

Boone's thick eyebrows knitted together. "I wouldn't mind a grandchild or two, Whitney. Maybe one of 'em would join me in the business. It gives a man something to work for when he thinks he's leaving a legacy."

Whitney drained her drink and surreptitiously checked her watch again. Twenty minutes had passed since she'd walked through the front door and they were already on grandchildren. The night promised to be a long one.

Two

Ventura, California

Gabriel Mendoza pulled the blanket from the tack room and tossed it to his stepson. "Be sure to cover Othello after you've rubbed him down." He grinned. "You've done a terrific job today, Eric. I appreciate it. I'll tell Juan and Carlos to call it a night, if you think you can handle closing up on your own."

The teenager nodded and looked away. "I was hoping to see a little extra money in my paycheck this time."

Gabe fought back the tension that never failed to knot his stomach whenever someone asked him for money he hadn't counted on spending. "Is there a reason?" he asked calmly.

"Prom is in two weeks. I wanted to ask Sandy to go."

Gabe relaxed. "I suppose that's a good-enough excuse. You've worked harder than two people this week."

The boy's face lit up. "Thanks, Dad. I didn't think—"

Gabe clapped him on the shoulder. "It's okay. I know it's not easy asking me for money. Be patient. I'm working on it."

Eric bit his lip, opened his mouth as if to say something, decided against it and disappeared into the tack room. He came out carrying a grooming brush.

Gabe headed out the door. "I'll see you at dinner."

"Have you heard anything from Mom?"

Eric's question, uttered in the slightly defiant tone of a sixteen-year-old bringing up a forbidden subject, stopped him. He turned around slowly. "Not in a while. What about you?"

The boy shook his head. "She keeps in touch with Emma. I think she sent something for her birthday. I guess *The Dead* are more important than us."

Gabe didn't miss the sarcasm or the pain in the teenager's voice. "Maybe she thinks you're still mad at her," he offered.

"I am still mad at her. Aren't you?"

Gabriel was mad as hell, but he didn't think telling Eric would be a good idea. "She's your mother," he said instead. "You only get one mother in this life."

"How come she doesn't feel the same?"

"I don't know, Eric. I never could figure her out. That was the problem. It's the reason she left." That, and two difficult daughters, the older one wildly out of control, the younger completely devoid of emotion. Asberger's syndrome, *borderline autistic,* the experts said. Those elements, along with a struggling dressage center, a mother-in-law whose boundaries were so loose she saw nothing wrong with sprinkling her advice like the lavender seeds she cultivated, too little money for luxuries and a husband stretched so thin it was impossible to take even a weekend vacation, were enough to make a woman far more grounded than Kristen wonder if the hand she was dealt had been stacked against her.

Logically, Gabe understood why she left. Emotionally, he resented her with every waking breath. Forcing himself, he smiled. "Don't be too late. Your grandma's making enchiladas."

Eric laughed and the mood lightened. "Tell her I'm on my way. I wouldn't miss those for the world."

Gabe made his way from the barns, through the purple haze of the blooming lavender field, across the dirt-packed courtyard, the greenbelt lined with olive trees where the kids played soccer, the wide velvety lawn with its flower beds of more lavender, Mexican sage, impatiens and yellow roses, up the porch steps lined with brick pavers and through the brightly painted red door, his mother's concession to her latest fad, feng shui.

"Touches of red are necessary for harmony, *mijito,*" she'd said to him when he questioned the authenticity of a red door at the entrance to her Mexican hacienda, now a renovated B and B. He let it go immediately, partly because he really didn't care what color she painted her door, but most of all because he'd learned a long time ago that arguing with Mercedes Mendoza was as pointless as growing orchids under Ventura County's relentless sun.

Moving back into his family home had been a mistake. Gabe admitted that now. But when it became clear that their younger daughter, Claire, would consume all of Kristen's time, it didn't make sense for him to live so far away from where he worked, and work was the dressage center his father had founded with the Lipizzaner horses he'd rescued from Austria after the Second World War.

When considering the move, Gabe had thought no further than the convenience and how it would lighten his schedule and Kristen's, but he'd forgotten what it was like growing up with his mother. Mercedes's intensity for life and movement, for food and drink and music and color and pleasure, was overwhelming, if not embarrassing, in its hedonism. Not that she didn't mean well, or care about the kids, or do her share. Far from it. She accomplished more in a single afternoon than Kristen had in a week. It was quite simply that the power of her relentless energy, her sloppy casualness, her rule-flaunting, her lack of precision, her tendency to speak her mind, her complete disregard for convention, eventually sucked the spirit out of all but the heartiest of survivors.

Kristen wasn't a survivor. She'd lasted eighteen months at the hacienda, and then, during a rare evening of casual conversation over her margarita and his beer, she'd told him that she'd pulled exactly half the money from their retirement account and purchased a trailer to travel the country and fulfill her lifelong dream of touring with *The Dead,* as the re-formed *Grateful Dead* were now known, as a backup singer.

At first, Gabe laughed. Kristen's voice was decent enough to harmonize with the church choir, but no one in his right mind would pay her for using it. He stopped laughing when she left her unfinished drink to walk out of his life that very night, leaving him with three children, her two and their one. He hadn't laughed since. He was done with laughing. His life had never been a picnic, but he couldn't remember when it had ever been this hard.

A combination of dinner smells—cilantro, cooked beef, chili and onions—wafted from the kitchen down the long, white-walled entry to where he stood, undecided as to his next move. His stomach rumbled. Pulling off his boots, he carried them in one hand and crossed the tiled floor to the stairs. With luck, he would fit in a shower and a quick look at the bills before anyone knew he was home.

Gabe reached the top of the landing when he heard the steady knock-knocking against the wall that never failed to kill his mood and fill him with despair. Setting his boots on the floor, he walked down the hall to the second bedroom and looked in on his daughter, eight-year-old Claire. She sat on the floor, legs straight in front of her, and methodically, without emotion, banged her head against the wall.

His hands balled into fists. As always, the education he hadn't used rescued and soothed him.

O thou foul thief, where hast thou stowed my daughter? He shoved his hands into his pocket. "Hi, sweetie," he said softly.

She ignored him.

Every instinct told him to grab her, pull her off the floor into his arms and demand that she speak to him. Once, he would have. Now he knew better. Keeping his voice consistently gentle, he asked, "Did you miss me?"

Again, no response, just the knock-knock-knocking of her delicate little head against the plaster wall.

Gabe gritted his teeth, counted to ten and tried again. "I have a surprise for you," he said, and waited for her reaction. Autistic children were slow processors. Was she slowing down or was it wishful thinking? Slowly, he approached her and knelt down on the floor. "Macbeth has learned the capriole," he said. "He did it three times today, each one better than the one before."

The back of Claire's head rested against the wall.

Encouraged, Gabe maintained his flow of conversation, not knowing or caring what she understood as long as it stopped her destructive behavior. "I think he'll be ready to perform before long." He reached out with his index finger and stroked the back of his daughter's hand. "Would you like to see him do it tomorrow? We can go together, tomorrow afternoon. Nearly everyone will be gone then."

Painfully, as if the brief movement required agonizing effort, the little girl turned her head. He looked into the thickly lashed blue eyes and his heart lurched. They were Kristen's eyes, even down to the Siamese-cat tilt at the corners. The spattering of freckles on her golden cheeks was Kristen's, too. So were her floating curls and the delicate cant of her bones. The only traits she'd inherited from him were her hair, Mendoza dark, the olive cast to her skin, the graceful slimness of her brown hands and limbs and her love of anything with four legs. Gabe was quite sure he had never seen anything so breathtakingly beautiful in all his life as this eight-year-old child, even if she was missing her two front teeth.

"Can we really go tomorrow?" she asked.

He released the breath he hadn't realized he was holding and nodded. "We'll go right after you finish school."

She settled her hand in his. "I wanted you today."

"I wanted you, too, sweetheart."

"I didn't feel like seeing Mrs. Cook. Grandma made her go away."

Gabe sighed. "She's a good teacher."

Claire stared at him. She spoke carefully, choosing the words, as if she had all the time in the world. "I like it when she reads to me. But sometimes we have too much to do and she doesn't."

"I'll ask her if she'll read to you every day if you promise that you'll do what she says."

Claire tilted her head on her impossibly long neck and appeared to consider his question.

Suddenly he felt a tingling at the base of his spine.

They weren't alone. He turned. Emma, his fourteen-year-old stepdaughter, stood in the doorway, dressed in chains and black leather. He swallowed. Once, it had been so easy to love Kristen's daughter. "Hi, hon. Is dinner ready?"

"How should I know? I've been up here doing my homework."

Gabe highly doubted it. "Don't you think you should change? Grandma Lynne will be here."

Emma shrugged and her blouse slipped down over one shoulder. He was about to change his polite question to a not-so-polite command coupled with *wipe off the makeup,* when he saw her eyes narrow.

"Why do you think she's coming?" Emma asked.

"To see her grandchildren. What else?"

"Are you sure?"

"Of course I'm sure. What are you worried about?"

Again the nonchalant shrug. "Nothing, I guess. What's going on in here? I heard pounding."

Gabe stood. "That's all over now. If you two will excuse me, I need a shower. I'll meet you downstairs in ten minutes."

He waited outside the door for an instant. He wasn't quite sure of Emma anymore.

"Do you want me to brush your hair?" she asked Claire.

Comforted by his stepdaughter's soft voice, he walked into his bathroom and turned on the shower.

Fifteen minutes later, shaved and dressed in a clean polo shirt and Dockers, he walked into the kitchen. It was a large room with long windows, lots of counter space and plants, bright with Mexican colors: red, yellow, turquoise and hot pink. His mother loved color.

She stood at the center island chopping cilantro, a

woman in her mid-seventies carrying a hundred extra pounds dispersed proportionally over her five feet eight inches, with glossy dark hair, except for the dramatic gray wings framing her face, glowing skin, enormous black eyes and a wide mouth filled with straight white teeth. Breathtaking in her youth, Mercedes Mendoza, was still arresting enough to stop traffic.

He came up behind her, wrapped his arms around her soft middle and kissed her cheek. "Hi, Ma."

"Gabriel!" Waving her knife in the air, she pirouetted, graceful as a dancer, and grabbed his cheeks with her hands. "*Mijito,* you're here early. I'm so glad. You can set the table, unless you want to mix the margaritas. Or, maybe you want beer." She stopped and tilted her head, an unaccustomed wrinkle forming in her forehead. "Kristen's mother is in the living room. She says she doesn't want anything. Maybe you should check again."

"If she said she doesn't want anything, she probably doesn't." He frowned at the ice-filled tumbler sitting on the counter near his mother's workspace. "What's that?"

"It's sangria, *mijito.* You know, a little wine, a little sugar, a little fruit, a little lavender. I have it every day."

"Not everybody needs alcohol every day."

She brushed his words aside and turned back to her task. "A glass of wine is good for the heart and the soul."

Gabriel eyed the sixteen-ounce glass. "A glass means four ounces."

Mercedes shook her head and continued her chopping. "I don't know what's gotten into you, Gabriel. Ever since you married that woman you've become such a prude. I've always had a drink or two in the afternoons and here I am, a healthy, seventy-six-year-old woman who can still turn heads. Your father never minded my habits. If he didn't, you shouldn't."

"I'm no longer married," he said shortly, pulling cloth napkins and placemats from the cupboard. "Kristen has nothing to do with this, and Dad's dead."

Mercedes looked up, her magnificent eyes brighter than usual. "I know you're not married. I think about it every day." She set down her knife and clasped her hands together. "I've decided to do something about it."

He turned and stared at her. "What are you talking about?"

"You know how you're always telling me I should learn the computer?"

"Yes."

"I decided to take your advice. I'm on e-mail."

"No, Ma," he corrected her. "You're online and you have e-mail."

"Whatever." She beamed. "Aren't you proud of me?"

"Certainly," he said cautiously, "but what does that have to do with what we were talking about?"

"I joined Matchmaker.com."

His jaw dropped. "You're kidding. Isn't that a dating service?"

Her eyes flashed. She dug her fists into her ample waist, a movement that jiggled the undersides of her arms. "Why should I be kidding? Are you saying that no one would want to go out with me?"

"Of course not. I'm surprised, that's all."

"Your mother is too old and too unattractive to find a man. Is that it?"

"No. That's not it at all," he protested. "But it's been ten years since Dad died. Why now?"

"Why not? Sometimes it takes a long time to heal. I loved your father very much. We were happy. We had four children. They're all happy, except for you, our only son."

His lips tightened. "I don't want to get into this."

"It's been nearly two years since Kristen left. You should get on with your life. You're not getting any younger."

He leaned against the counter. This was an old argument. "She's been gone eighteen months, not two years."

"What's the difference? She's gone. You need to find someone else. You're still young, and if you'd smile now and then, some might even call you handsome."

He grinned. "You're prejudiced."

"Not at all. I included it in your profile. Tall, dark, handsome man with blue eyes, seeking woman who likes children and horses."

He froze. "What did you say?"

"I joined Matchmaker for you, not me. You're forty years old, Gabriel. This is the modern world. How else will you find a woman?"

"Jesus Christ! Ma." He shook his head. "I'm not looking for a woman. I have enough to worry about. I've got the kids and the horses, and this place. I don't have time for a relationship. That's what ruined it for Kristen and me. She said I never had any time for her."

"Don't swear, *mijito*. Kristen wasn't right for you, not from the beginning. I knew it. Your father knew it. Everyone knew it but you. She's a woman who deserted her children. What kind of a woman does that?"

"That's beside the point. She's gone."

"Good riddance is what I say."

"Cancel my profile."

"What?"

"I said, cancel my profile. I'm not going out with anyone you find online. When I feel the need for female companionship, I'll do it on my own. I can't imagine why you would think I'd want another woman around here, anyway."

Mercedes sighed. Deliberately she picked up her glass and drank deeply.

"I think I'll say hello to Lynne."

"You're a sorry case, Gabriel," Mercedes said out loud to his retreating back. "I love you very much, but you're a very sorry case."

Three

Lynne Chamberlain had never been comfortable visiting the Mendozas. She couldn't put her finger on exactly why, but she felt deep in her bones that they weren't her kind of people. Mercedes was too loud, too familiar, too earthy, too sensual, too—*ethnic* was the word Lynne was looking for, although she wouldn't admit it. It sounded bigoted and Lynne prided herself on her lack of bigotry.

Ask anyone. She'd lobbied for funding for the new Bower's Museum wing, the one featuring Hispanic art, and in the last election, she'd voted to support affirmative action. Her internist was Vietnamese, her gardener Japanese and her accountant African-American. Ethnic minorities made up the majority of the population in California. She had no objections at all when Kristen declared she was going to marry Gabriel Mendoza. Not that Lynne considered Gabriel the least bit ethnic. He didn't speak Spanish and his father was Austrian. No, it wasn't Gabriel who made Lynne uncomfortable, or his three sisters, all of whom were far more accomplished than her own daughter. It was Mercedes she didn't want to rub elbows with.

The woman didn't behave the way an elderly woman should behave, at least in public. First of all, she was too large, too loud and too present. It wasn't just her girth. In a world where women counted their carbohydrates, attended Pilates classes and worried about cholesterol, Mercedes, dressed in a garish muumuu, her arms jiggling, served up purple margaritas in salt-dipped glasses and appetizers piled high with melted cheese, guacamole and sour cream. When she laughed, she tipped her head back and, from somewhere deep in her throat, emitted a loud braying sound that turned the heads of everyone within fifty yards. She drank too much, asked personal questions, left vulgar tips in restaurants, struck up conversations with homeless people and store clerks. She favored colors like red and hot pink and lime green. Her hair, although quite beautiful, was too long, and jewelry swung from her ears and her wrists in gypsy-like abandon. She harvested and distilled her own lavender, which wasn't really all that bad, but then she actually rented a booth at the farmers' market on Tuesdays and *hawked* it to passing strangers. Most embarrassing. The woman had no boundaries. She couldn't possibly be a good influence for her grandchildren.

Lynne considered Mercedes to be the primary reason Kristen left her family. No Chamberlain had ever abandoned her responsibilities in such a way. It must have been Mercedes. Kristen simply couldn't cope with her. Although it was the last thing on the planet she wanted to do, Lynne saw it as her duty to rescue Kristen's children. There was nothing she could do about Claire, of course. Claire was Gabriel's daughter, too, and no court on earth would remove a child from her natural father, especially one so devoted to her well-being. Besides,

Claire required a different kind of care, an energy that Lynne, a woman in her seventies, no longer had to give.

"Hello, Lynne."

Startled out of her thoughts, she turned and saw her former son-in-law. "Gabriel. I'm sorry. I was deep in thought. How are you?"

He came farther into the room and sat down in the chair across from her. She noticed that he made no move to embrace her, or even shake her hand.

"I'm fine, thank you. It's been a while," he said. "I'm glad you could make it."

"Well, yes." Deliberately, she kept her hands still in her lap. "I've been meaning to come for quite some time. I wanted to talk with you about the children."

"The children?"

"Eric and Emma."

Those piercing blue eyes regarded her steadily. When it came to good looks, Gabriel Mendoza, with his blade-sharp features, lean height and cool blue eyes, had been fairy-touched at birth. He didn't smile enough, but Lynne would never hold that against him. A serious man would take life seriously, she remembered telling her daughter.

She knew from the minute Kristen brought him home that there was no point in trying to talk the girl out of marrying him. Gabriel was one of a kind, a hybrid, taking after neither parent. Claire was the same, the best of both her mother and father. Lynne wasn't superstitious, but sometimes she wondered if there wasn't some kind of master scale weighing checks and balances to assure that a child approaching perfection bore some type of adversity. Her youngest granddaughter was beautiful and intelligent, but there were times when she slipped behind a cloud so dark and impenetrable that those who loved her were moved to levels of quiet desperation.

When Gabriel didn't respond, she prodded him. "My grandchildren, Eric and Emma?"

He nodded. "Two of your grandchildren. You have three."

She flushed. "I'm aware of that, Gabriel. I love all of them, equally. They're all my daughter's children. But I'm here because of the two who aren't yours."

"I don't think of them as not mine."

"Nevertheless, you know the saying, 'blood will out.'"

He frowned. "What does that have to do with anything? Being a father is more than sharing a gene pool."

"I won't argue with you about that."

"Why are you here, Lynne?"

She'd pushed him too far. She smiled tentatively. "Do you mind if we have dinner first? I'd like to share a meal with the children without animosity. Can we do that, Gabriel? Please?"

He looked surprised. "Of course. You're always welcome here, Lynne. I hope you know that."

"Yes. Thank you. It's just that since Kristen left—" She left the sentence unfinished.

"It's awkward. I know. However, you don't have to visit with them here if it makes you uncomfortable. Make whatever arrangements you want with the children. Take them to lunch or keep them overnight. Whatever you'd like."

"I appreciate that, Gabriel, because that's exactly what I had in mind."

Emma poked her head into the room. "Gran said to tell you dinner is ready."

Lynne smiled. "Come in, darling, and say hello to me. I didn't realize you were home."

Slowly, Emma slunk into the room, still dressed in chains and leather. Gabe closed his eyes briefly.

Lynne looked at her granddaughter, her glance moving slowly over the torn blouse dipping over one shoulder, the tight, low-waisted leather pants that left a significant part of Emma's midriff bare, and the silver chains hanging from her belt to her knees. Her mouth dropped. "Why are you dressed like that? Are you going to a costume party? What on earth did you do to your hair?"

"I dyed it."

"But why?"

"Hair grows, Grandma. It's temporary. I needed a change."

"Do they let you go to school like that?"

"Yes," Emma said briefly. "Now, if we're done talking about my clothes, can we eat? I'm starving."

Lynne didn't move. "Do you approve of this attire, Gabriel?" she asked.

From across the room, Emma's eyes challenged her stepfather.

"I think Emma's natural hair is more attractive," he said slowly, "but I remember what it's like to be a teenager. Hair grows, and as long as she isn't piercing anything or coming home with tattoos, and as long as it's acceptable at school, I'm not going to forbid her to dress the way she wants."

Lynne felt the blood rise in her cheeks. This was worse than she thought. Gabriel either couldn't or didn't want to control Emma. "I don't think—" she began.

Mercedes, resplendent in yet another colorful, flowery shift that hung from her shoulders, appeared in the doorway. "What's the matter with you people? Dinner's ready. What does it take to get you to come to the table?" She laughed to show she wasn't really annoyed.

Lynne closed her mouth, picked up her purse and preceded Gabriel into the dining room.

"Your purse is safe here, Lynne," Mercedes whispered into her ear. "I can guarantee the help are honest."

Flushing again, Lynne turned back to the living room to hang the offending bag on the hall tree.

Eric and Claire were already seated when she joined the others in the dining room. Eric stood to kiss his grandmother. "Hi, Grandma," he said. "How are you?"

"I'm fine, Eric. I've missed you." She looked at Claire and summoned a bright, artificial smile. "Hello, darling. How have you been?"

Claire stared at her and then looked down at her plate.

Mercedes sat at one end of the table. She lifted her glass, once again filled to the top with ice and wine. "Here's to good health and good company."

Obediently, the others followed suit.

"What are the children drinking?" asked Lynne. She wouldn't be surprised if Mercedes had spiked their sodas.

"Milk," said Eric. "We always drink milk at dinner."

Mollified, Lynne sipped her drink. She wrinkled her nose. Another one of Mercedes's sweet concoctions. She would have a raging headache tomorrow morning. The food, however, was delicious: enchiladas and rice, refried beans, salad and a chicken dish, just spicy enough for interest but not so much that it was difficult going down. Even Claire was eating, Claire who didn't eat more than a mouthful at a meal.

Lynne cleared her throat. She addressed the children. "Do any of you hear from your mother?"

Their stricken glances smote her. She almost wished she hadn't asked the question.

Mercedes picked up the conversation. "Funny you should mention that. Do you have a computer, Lynne?"

"Yes, I do."

"Are you familiar with Matchmaker.com?"

Lynne was confused. "No, I don't think so."

"It's an Internet dating service."

"Really?" Where was the woman going with this?

"Yes. I've sent in Gabriel's profile. I think it's time he started dating. What do you think?"

Lynne stiffened. "I don't think it's any of my business."

"You must have an opinion." Mercedes served herself an enormous helping of beans and salsa. "My thinking is this," she continued conversationally. "There's no reason for Gabriel to be alone for the rest of his life. He's still young, he's handsome and, most of all, he's a good man. What do you think, Lynne?" She looked at the woman's plate. "Have more beans. They're good for you, unless you're flatulent. Are you flatulent, Lynne? So many of us are at our age."

Lynne's hands shook. "Certainly not. And I think Gabriel should do whatever he feels is best."

"I'm so glad you agree." Mercedes beamed. "See, Gabriel, even Lynne wants you to find someone else, resume your life and provide a mother for these children."

Gabriel glanced at his children. Eric looked stricken, Emma mutinous and Claire oblivious. His jaw tightened. "That's enough, Ma," he said. "I have everything I need right here."

"Now that you mention it," said Lynne, "I was wondering if Eric and Emma wanted to stay with me for a while. After all, I am their blood relative and it can't be easy raising two additional children who aren't yours."

The children, except for Claire, stared at her open-mouthed.

"I've been raising them for eleven years," Gabe reminded her.

"Circumstances have changed. Kristen is gone."

Gabriel's eyes slanted to slits of brilliant blue. "Thank you, but I'm declining your offer."

Lynne set down her fork, lifted her napkin, dabbed the corners of her mouth and readied herself to do battle. "Maybe it would be best for the children."

"How would it be best," he said evenly, "for two teenage children to have a woman in her seventies raise them?"

"Isn't that what Mercedes is doing now?" countered Lynne. "She's also running a B and B. At least I don't have that to contend with."

Mercedes opened her mouth.

Gabriel lifted his hand and she closed it again.

"*I'm* raising the children," he said. "My mother helps out when I need her."

Lynne refused to retreat. "Why don't you ask them what they want?"

Gabriel pushed his plate away. "I won't do that."

"Why not?"

He stood. "If you're finished, I'd like to continue this conversation in private in the living room."

Pushing her chair away from the table, Lynne stalked out of the room.

Mercedes eyed her son. "Don't lose your temper, Gabriel."

Gabe looked at his ex-wife's children. "I'm sorry," he said calmly, "but there is absolutely no way I am giving you to her."

"Why not?" Emma asked.

"I love you," he said simply. "I don't want to lose you."

"What if we want to go?"

"Emma!" Eric's strangled gasp rose up out of his throat.

She looked at her brother. "I was just asking. What's wrong with that?"

"Sometimes you're so stupid."

Emma glared at her brother. "Shut up, Eric. In case you haven't thought about it, maybe we'd hear from Mom more often if she could call Grandma's house instead of having to reach us here. It's got to be hard for her."

"Hard for her!" Eric's pale skin was nearly purple. "If leaving her husband and kids wasn't too hard, a few phone calls now and then should be a piece of cake."

Mercedes pounded on the table with her spoon. "That's enough. Let your father handle your grandmother and the rest of us will finish eating."

Emma threw her napkin on her plate and ran out of the room.

Claire continued to eat as if nothing had happened.

Eric's eyes met Gabe's. "I'm sixteen. I can decide where I want to live."

Gabe nodded. "I'm not giving you up without a fight."

Eric relaxed. A slow smile began at the corners of his mouth. "Do you want me to come with you?"

"I think I can handle your grandmother."

Eric picked up his fork. "Go for it."

Lynne sat on the edge of a chair. She wore her jacket and her purse was on her lap. She started in immediately. "I don't want to have to make this legal, Gabriel, but I will."

"You can do whatever you please, Lynne, but understand this—I'm not going to allow the children to live with you. Neither will I ask them if they want to live with you."

"Why on earth not?"

"Because they have already lost their mother. She made a choice and they came in last. In their minds they are already unworthy of their mother's love. I'm not going to have them believe their father doesn't want them. I'm going to fight for them. I'll fight for them with every breath and every dollar I have. Do I make myself clear?"

"Have you considered that the reason Kristen left might be you, not the children?"

"I'm sure you know much more about that than I do, since she left without any explanation at all. However, the fact remains that she left them. That's the bottom line. That's how they see it. To give them to you would be washing my hands of them. I won't do that. If you want to hire a lawyer, so be it. The ball is in your court."

"I always liked you, Gabriel. I hope you know that. I don't condone my daughter's actions."

He smiled. "I know your heart is in the right place, Lynne. I'm renewing my offer. Whenever and wherever you want to see the children is fine with me. You're their grandmother. As far as I'm concerned, the more people who love them, the better off they are."

"You're a good man, Gabriel," she said at last. "I don't know what I'm going to do next. I'm seriously worried about Emma. The choices she's making could land her in serious trouble. I do believe she'd be better off with me. Your mother—" She stopped.

Gabriel's jaw tightened. "My mother isn't your concern, Lynne."

Their eyes met. "I think I'll leave now," she said. "You can say goodbye for me."

He stood. "I'll walk you to your car."

Four

Whitney tapped her foot on the marble floor. The desk clerk of the Hyatt Regency hotel looked apologetic. "I'm terribly sorry, but the conference room is being used until tomorrow. There is no record of your reservation."

"I see." Whitney's blood pressure rose. She checked her watch. "How long does it take to drive to Moorpark?"

"An hour or so, depending on traffic."

"I need to rent a car."

Relief lit the young man's face. "That won't be a problem. Would you like to see your room first?"

"No. I'm in a hurry."

Whitney pulled out her cell phone and punched in the phone number of the Mendoza residence. She waited impatiently for the lengthy greeting to end and then left a brief message detailing the changes of their appointment. Neutral territory would have been the optimal setting in which to present the offer, but under the circumstances it couldn't be helped. A successful outcome was the only outcome. One small glitch wouldn't derail her.

Twenty minutes later she clutched the steering wheel

of her rented Chevy Impala, the knuckles of her hands clearly defined beneath her skin. Her heart pounded and she kept one foot hovering over the brake pedal, the other resting on the gas. Once again, she reduced her speed as yet another driver in a shiny sports car cut across four lanes of traffic to insinuate himself into the nearly negligible gap between her rented car and a very large utility vehicle.

A big rig obstructed the freeway sign. Whitney was too hemmed in and the traffic moving too slowly for her to go around it. Not that she would even think of attempting a lane change on this terrifying death trap of a freeway. She'd never seen such gridlock or such intrepid, foolhardy drivers who harbored a casual disregard for the relationship between speed, momentum and the time it would take for a two-thousand-pound automobile to come to a complete stop.

She'd been on the road, the 101 North, for nearly ninety minutes and the odometer registered an unbelievable fifteen miles. All around her drivers were drinking coffee, talking into cell phones, applying lipstick or mascara and fiddling with buttons on dashboards. Loud music boomed from speakers. Billboards advertised gentlemen's clubs, whiskey, home loans and auto insurance rates. Neon signs flashed the world's lowest prices, the most competent Realtors, the best value for a night's sleep or a hot meal. She was lost in a world of concrete without even a hint of green to mitigate the smell of diesel fumes, the din of angry drivers sounding their horns and the frightening yellow-brown haze hovering at the edge of the horizon.

Whitney wrinkled her nose, trying not to breathe too deeply. She'd seen London, Paris, Brussels and New York, but nothing, *nothing,* had prepared her for Los

Angeles, this parking lot of a freeway and the tense, angry hostility emanating from its trapped commuter population. She couldn't wait to leave. She would conclude this project, go home and take her mother up on whatever long, slow and peaceful singles' cruise Pryor wanted to plan for her.

The road sign was completely hidden by the rig in front of her. Taking her life in her hands, she maneuvered into the exit lane, noted the unfamiliar street names, and pulled back behind the truck. Immediately a blinking red light appeared in her rearview mirror. Her stomach churned. A police cruiser was bearing down on her. She looked for a spot to pull over, but there was no shoulder and the next exit was nearly a mile away. A loud amplified voice boomed in her ears.

"Pull over immediately."

Whitney panicked. Mentally, she weighed the merits of pulling over onto the nonexistent shoulder and risking instant death, or facing the officer's ire at her lack of response to his command. She pulled over. Heart pounding, she waited while the cruiser parked behind her and the officer approached her passenger window.

"The right lane is the exit lane, miss. The law says you need to be in the merge lane three hundred yards before the exit if you're not going to turn off."

Whitney reached for her purse, pulled out her license and handed it to him. "Sorry," she said.

"Registration?"

"It's a rental." She opened the glove compartment and handed him the paperwork.

He glanced at it. "Where are you from?"

"Kentucky."

"You're a long way from home."

She nodded.

"I'll be right back."

Whitney popped an antacid into her mouth, leaned back against the headrest and closed her eyes, hoping that none of the drivers of the endless river of oncoming cars would be momentarily distracted and sideswipe her vehicle.

After what seemed like an eternity, but was actually only ten minutes on her watch, the officer was once again at her window. He handed back her paperwork and a clipboard with a ticket. She signed it.

He pulled out the yellow copy and grinned. "Welcome to California. By the way, your right rear tire is low on air."

"Thanks," replied Whitney, taking her ticket.

"No problem."

Nearly two hours and several antacids later, the junction leading to Highway 23 loomed ahead. Whitney breathed more easily. Traffic had thinned out and the concrete warren of skyscrapers had turned into beige housing developments, an occasional strip mall and then, as she neared her destination, tilled fields of strawberries, tomatoes, lettuce, corn and, finally, the tiered horse country of Moorpark, nestled between Highway 118 and 23. She followed the signs, noting the different horse properties dotting the hills before turning south on Madera Road and then right on Tierra Rejada. The road was well paved but only two lanes. Finally she saw it, the white sign with black letters indicating the Mendoza Hacienda and Equestrian Center.

Pulling her Impala around to the small parking lot in the back, she turned off the engine and stared at the house in disbelief. She hadn't expected this. It was unbelievably perfect, so much a part of the landscape, so charming in its genteel disrepair. This was old California, when the Spanish dons ruled from the tip of the Baja to the borders of Canada, a picture-perfect movie set complete with weeping bougainvillea, white stucco walls, a red-tiled roof and long windows that opened onto a circular patio with low chairs and small tables, lush plants and colorful flowers. All this set smack in the middle of what must be at least two acres of gently waving stalks of fragrant lavender. A large woman wearing a flowery yellow dress, a wide-brimmed straw hat, and carrying a basket of blooms, was bent over one of the rows.

Opening the window, Whitney sat for a minute, closed her eyes, breathed deeply and opened them again. The pungent, herbal smell of ripe lavender stung the sensitive membranes of her nose. She didn't know California was capable of nurturing such foliage. Her image of the golden state, west of the mountains and east of the Pacific Ocean, was an irrigated desert where cars, designer clothing and film contracts vied with movie-star politicians, tract houses and an obscene amount of votes, enough to sway elections.

She'd never considered herself a plant person. She wasn't home enough to cultivate a garden. Her apartment contained a few bedraggled specimens that she forgot to water and would eventually have to be thrown out. But for some reason, the lavender field called to her. Her nail-biting freeway experience seemed far away. She wanted to walk beside the plants, touch the blooms and inhale their perfume. Climbing out of the car, Whitney hitched her briefcase to her shoulder and slowly walked toward the purple sea.

The woman straightened, saw her and shaded her eyes against the sun. She was even larger than Whitney thought, tall with shining black hair and striking features. She smiled as Whitney approached. "What a pretty girl you are," she said in faintly accented English. "But so tired. Come. Sit down and relax with me."

Whitney shook her head, startled by the familiarity and the unexpected concern. She hadn't expected southern manners in Los Angeles. "I—no. No, thank you." She collected herself. "I'm looking for Gabriel Mendoza."

"He'll be around soon. Come." She walked through the field toward the house and Whitney followed. They came to a vine-covered patio with low chairs and small tables. "Sit down and rest your feet," said the woman. "I'll get you something nice to drink." Her eyes flickered over Whitney's figure, assessing the sweetly fitting flesh and the small, slender bones underneath. "Maybe something to eat, too." She tucked a sprig of lavender into Whitney's lapel. "Wait here. I'll be right back."

"Please," Whitney said. "Don't go to any trouble. If you'll tell me where I can find Mr. Mendoza, I won't bother you any longer."

"I'm Mercedes Mendoza, Gabriel's mother," the woman said. "He's at the dressage ring working with the horses. You look very tired, *mijita,* as if you've been moving for a long time."

"Actually, I have. I flew into Los Angeles from Kentucky. The traffic here is unbelievable."

Mercedes eyes widened. "Kentucky. I had no idea they would send people from so far away. Isn't the Internet amazing?"

Whitney frowned. "I suppose it is."

Mercedes beamed. "I have a wonderful margarita mix all made up, or maybe you'd like a glass of wine? You look like the wine type to me."

"A margarita will be fine." Whitney glanced at her watch. At this rate she wouldn't get to her hotel until well after dark. Sighing, she set her briefcase on a table, sat down in one of the low chairs, crossed her legs and leaned her head back, grateful for the peace surrounding her. She must have dozed. When she opened her eyes, her head rested against a pillow. A light blanket had been draped over her knees and a foaming margarita sat on the table. It was purple. Mercedes occupied the chair beside her.

The woman smiled and pointed to an artfully arranged platter of grapes, yellow and orange cheeses, breads and crackers. "I thought you could use some food."

Suddenly Whitney was ravenous. She cut off a slice of cheese, sandwiched it between two crackers, and washed them down with a sip of her drink. She smiled approvingly at Mercedes. "This is wonderful. I've never had a purple margarita. What's in it?"

"I have my own margarita recipe," the woman confided, "and I use lavender."

"Will you share it?"

Mercedes appeared to consider the matter. She looked sideways at Whitney. "Possibly." She nodded. "Quite possibly. Have you ever been married?" she asked abruptly.

The woman was blunt, but Whitney was intrigued rather than offended. "How do you know I'm not?"

Mercedes's smile faded. "No ring. And you wouldn't be here if you were married, I hope."

Whitney thought back over their conversation. Something wasn't right. "I think we may have a misunderstanding. My name is Whitney Benedict. I'm a lawyer with a firm representing the Austrian government. Mr. Mendoza and I had an appointment. I left a message." She pulled her business card from the side pocket of her purse and handed it to Mercedes. "I'm here to make your son an offer for his Lipizzaners. Didn't you get my message?"

"Sometimes I forget to listen. I'm not good with machines. You're not from Matchmaker.com?"

Whitney's lips twitched. "I'm afraid not."

"I was hoping you were. You're exactly what I asked for."

"Asked for?"

Mercedes sighed, pushed away her drink and settled back into her chair. "I'll have to explain everything."

"Please do," said Whitney. It was already too late to worry about the time and she was more than a little interested.

"My son lives to work," began Mercedes. "His wife left him two years ago and since then he's been unhappy. Mind you, Kristen wasn't anything to smile about. I didn't like her much. I never interfere with my children, but I thought Gabriel could do better, and her circumstances certainly weren't the best. She had two young children whose father couldn't be bothered with them." Mercedes waved her hand as if to move on to the next scene. "Gabriel took them in hand. Then he and Kristen had a baby. That was eight years ago. Claire has—" Mercedes hesitated "—problems. They were too much for Kristen. She left him with all three children." The woman leaned close to Whitney. "I think he needs someone. I sent in his profile to Matchmaker.com. I thought they'd sent you. You're very nice. Why aren't you married?"

Whitney laughed. "You sound like my mother."

Mercedes's liquid black eyes continued to regard her. "That's no answer."

"I don't know, really. I suppose it's the usual reason. I never found anyone I wanted to be around that much."

She didn't mention Wiley Cane. Once, she'd wanted to be around him very much indeed and look how it had turned out. *That* was a piece of ancient history she didn't want resurrected.

"That's not good."

"It's not so bad, either."

"Do you want to grow old alone?"

"There are worse fates."

"Such as?"

"Growing old with someone you no longer respect and aren't attracted to. Having someone control your time and your money. Constantly compromising." Whitney picked up her drink with shaking hands and swallowed a good portion of it. What was the matter with her? She hadn't meant to divulge so much to a complete stranger.

The older woman shook her head. "My goodness. Where do you get such ideas?"

"I've seen it. Can you honestly say that you know of anyone, married more than ten years, who is really happy all the time?"

Mercedes thought a minute. Then she leaned forward. "Are *you* happy all the time? What has being married got to do with happiness?"

Whitney stared at her. "I've never considered it that way, I guess." She set down her drink, folded the blanket on her lap and stood. "This has been lovely, but I really need to speak with your son. Otherwise, I'll never stay awake long enough to make it back to my hotel."

"I'll point you in the right direction, but please, stay with us. I have five guest rooms and tonight they're all empty. There's no sense in battling the traffic during rush hour. Besides, I don't know anything about you."

"I appreciate the offer, Mrs. Mendoza, but I really—"

She stopped. A dreadful thought occurred to her. "Are you saying that what I just came through *wasn't* rush hour?"

"Rush *hour* is just an expression," Mercedes explained. "The roads aren't fit for traveling until after nine o'clock."

"Good Lord."

"Think about it," Mercedes said. "The offer stands. Now, let me direct you to the barns. Claire will be there with Gabriel. It's just across the field. Normally I would tell you to walk. It's faster. But you'll want to drive the back way because of your shoes."

Five minutes later Whitney was on the road again. She couldn't remember when she'd been so firmly routed. Her mother could learn from this woman, a terrifying prospect, and one that Whitney was determined to avoid.

For a brief quarter mile, the double-lane highway twisted through dusty, shrub-covered acreage dotted with an occasional giant oak or copse of black-trunked olive trees. Cocoa-brown trails cut into spring grass, winding question marks into sage-covered hills. The wind was up. A flurry of leaves, crackling like parchment, round and brilliant, the size and color of gold coins, eddied around the car. A wrought-iron sign signaled the equestrian center.

Whitney maneuvered the car past the business office, past the pipe corrals on one side, the silver-roofed stalls on the other, past a barn stacked with bales of hay, three small meticulously raked training rings, three tack rooms, three trainers' offices and a dressage arena circled by a white split-rail fence. Narrow strips of grass separated the rings, and tiered stone benches bordered with roses looked out over the performance arenas. In the distance, against the rolling hills, she could see the junction of the two highways from where she'd come, the cars miniature and soundless, a direct contrast to the aura of calm purpose and the breathing, glistening animals all around her. She drew a deep breath and was immediately engulfed in the familiar smells of equestrian country: plowed earth, sweet hay, sage, dry wind and horse dung blended with foliage she'd never encountered before.

Whitney pulled the car close to one of the barns and, stepping carefully through the dirt, made her way over to the training center.

Inside one arena, a young woman sat astride a white warmblood held on a guide rein by a trainer. The gelding trotted in a circle while the woman, using neither stirrups nor reins, sat him as lightly as a leaf. Occasionally, at the bark of the trainer, the rider would rotate her arms in paddle-wheel fashion, fold them across her chest or hold them straight down. No matter what her position, her balance never wavered, nor did her back slump.

Whitney called out. "Can you tell me where I can find Gabriel Mendoza?"

The trainer glanced at her and shrugged.

In the middle of the same arena, a man was schooling a young horse between the posts. From a padded halter, two short straps ran to the wooden pillars; the horse, urged on by his trainer, performed his exercises in place. Whitney recalled her old dressage days when she'd exercised her mare in the same way to strengthen the horse's haunches and render her muscles more supple. She walked around the ring to where he could see her. The heels of her designer shoes sank down into what she hoped was merely mud.

"Are you Gabriel Mendoza?" Whitney called out.

"Gabe's in the last ring," he replied.

Whitney glanced down at her shoes. The expensive taupe leather was irreparably stained, a stone had lodged somewhere in her heel and the beginnings of a headache flickered in her right temple. Her temper flamed. She fought it back and walked to the farthest arena.

Backlit by the late afternoon sun, a man led a spectacular white stallion through a set of complicated maneuvers that Whitney hadn't seen outside old videotapes. She watched in disbelief as the horse extended his legs in the famous Spanish Walk, found his tempo, leaped into the air and, at the height of elevation, kicked out violently with his hind legs. Whitney gasped in appreciation. The old war moves of the famous Lipizzaners were nearly obsolete in modern dressage.

Anger firmly suppressed, she made her way to where a small girl watched from the side. Nodding at the horse and rider, she breathed deeply. "I've never seen anything so perfect."

The child turned her head, looked at her for a minute and then looked back at the intricate performance.

"I don't remember what that's called," Whitney continued. "I know it's part of the Airs Above the Ground, but I'm not sure—" She stopped talking to concentrate on the scene in front of her.

"It's a capriole," the girl said. "It's very hard to do. Macbeth just learned it yesterday."

"Is that your dad?"

The child nodded.

"Did he teach her?"

"It isn't something you can teach," the girl said. "The horse already knows how to do it from when his ancestors were fighting horses. Mostly stallions do it, but not all of them. My dad made Macbeth remember."

The child was remarkably self-possessed. Whitney looked at her, paying more attention this time. She was strikingly lovely with those light eyes, dark hair and olive skin. "What's your name?" she asked. She'd already guessed, but she wanted to hear the child speak.

"Claire Mendoza."

"It sounds as if you know something about horses."

The child shrugged. "What's your name?"

"Whitney Benedict."

"That's a man's name."

"Yes, it is."

"Did your dad want a boy?"

Whitney nodded. The admission no longer bothered her.

"You know something about horses, too," Claire said. "Most people don't know about Airs Above the Ground."

Whitney smiled and pulled a strand of hair out of her mouth. "I know about training racehorses and breeding them. I grew up on a breeding farm. Do you know what that is?"

The girl nodded. "We're a breeding farm, too. We breed Lipizzaners."

"Do you sell them?"

"Not the purebreds." She looked at Whitney. "Are you here to take lessons?"

Whitney shook her head. "No. I'm here for another reason." She nodded at the man in the ring. "Do you think your dad'll be finished soon?"

"Pretty soon. He doesn't like to overwork Macbeth. He's not patient."

"I see." Whitney laughed. "It's a good thing we are, isn't it?"

Reluctantly, Claire smiled, revealing a gap where

her front teeth would grow in. "I don't mind waiting. I like to watch."

"Me, too," said Whitney.

Deliberately, Gabriel focused on the movement, forcing himself to relax, to ignore the car and the woman who stood beside Claire, watching and occasionally talking. Horses sensed tension and Macbeth was particularly sensitive. If Gabe's legs didn't lie like two wet rags against his sides, if his weight wasn't firmly balanced in the saddle, if his head wasn't up and his back straight, the stallion would feel it and try to correct, resulting in a poorly executed move. Gabriel wanted the maneuver to be perfect, for Claire's sake, and for his own. Macbeth was his experiment, a stallion beautifully trained but labeled too touchy for traditional dressage. Gabriel hadn't agreed. He accepted the challenge.

Once again, Macbeth lifted his head, found his tempo, one, two, three, four steps, leaped into the air, drew his forelegs in and kicked out with his hind legs. Gabe released his breath. Well done. Not perfect, but very well done.

Allowing the stallion to take the bit and stretch out, he circled the arena two more times before dismounting. Patting Macbeth on the neck, he led him out of the gate to where Claire and the woman waited. "What do you think?" he asked his daughter.

"It was really good, Dad. Whitney thinks so, too."

He looked directly at the woman. Her eyes were the color of rain. *For to withstand her look I am not able, yet can I not hide me in no dark place.* "Whitney?"

"Whitney Benedict."

Her accent surprised him. So did her clothes. Her shoes were ruined. She either had no idea what she was getting into, or she knew nothing about horses. Gabe held out the reins to his daughter. "I'll walk with you while you take him in. You can help Juan wipe him down. Then the two of you can turn him out until he's cooled off, twenty minutes or so."

A rare smile crossed Claire's lips. She took the reins confidently and led the horse toward the barns.

Gabe nodded at Whitney. "If you'll excuse me for a minute, I'll be right back."

Whitney nodded.

He was back in less than five minutes. "What can I do for you, Ms. Benedict?"

"I'm here on behalf of the Austrian government to make you an offer. We had an appointment today in Los Angeles."

"We did?"

Mentally, Whitney counted to ten.

"Yes."

"Are you sure it was me you talked to?"

"I'm here, Mr. Mendoza. I've crossed three time zones, as well as your infamous Los Angeles freeways, to meet with you."

His dismay was genuine. "I'm really sorry. The drive must have killed you."

"That part wasn't your fault. We were supposed to meet at a hotel near the airport." She waved her hand. "Never mind. It's a long story."

"Are you a government official?"

"I'm a lawyer."

"But not from Austria."

"From Kentucky."

Gabe frowned. "Did I miss something?"

Whitney sighed. His apology had disarmed her. "I'm not doing a very good job of this. I'm still in awe over your performance. I've never seen anything like it. I didn't know moves like that were done anymore."

"They aren't," Gabriel said shortly. "Modern dressage doesn't incorporate the traditional moves anymore."

"Then why are you training your horses to do them?"

He grinned and something in her chest that she hadn't felt in a very long time turned over.

"I'm a dinosaur. Do you know anything about horses?"

Directness obviously ran in his family. "Only race-horses. I've done some event riding in the past, but that was long ago."

"A different ball game entirely. These animals play until they're three and a half. They begin training when they're four and aren't completely finished until they're eight. At twenty-five they're still star performers."

She nodded. "Completely different."

He looked at her, a quick, brief assessment that apparently satisfied him. "Let's go back to the house," he said. "I'll get cleaned up. My mother will offer you dinner and a place to sleep. We can discuss your offer tomorrow."

"Tomorrow? What's wrong with tonight?"

"This is a family-owned business. I can't sell without permission from my mother and sisters. I'll have to call them tonight."

Her heart pounded. "But you have power of attorney. I would have contacted all parties otherwise."

"My family has to agree," he said firmly. "I wouldn't feel right making a decision like this without their okay." He stopped and looked at her. "I don't want to waste your time, so I feel I should warn you that it isn't going to happen."

"Because of your mother and sisters?"

"No. I'll be the one dragging my feet." He frowned. "I really don't remember making an appointment with you. I must have been completely focused on something else."

Whitney refused to feel discouraged. "After I present the offer we can go over the pros and cons."

Gabe continued to look at her. "Fair enough," he said after a minute. "We have guest rooms. You're welcome to stay."

"Your mother has already offered me food and a bed, even after she found out I wasn't from Matchmaker.com."

He winced. "Good God. I hope not."

Whitney stopped. "That wasn't very complimentary."

He looked at her, taking in the woman's wheat-colored hair, clear eyes and spiky dark lashes, her long, long legs and the finely drawn features sprayed with a light sprinkling of pale freckles across her cheekbones. "Somehow, I don't believe you'll be shattered if I don't compliment you," he said dryly.

She swallowed. The camaraderie was broken. For a minute she'd almost thought—Whitney straightened her shoulders. It didn't matter what she thought. She was here for professional reasons, and nothing more.

Five

"Are you sure you won't stay for dinner?" Gabe asked. "There's always plenty of food."

"No, thank you." Whitney pulled the car key from her purse and unlocked the door. "I'd like to settle into my hotel room and look over a few things. I'll phone you tomorrow and we can discuss when would be a good time to meet with all of you."

"Fair enough. Any time after nine would be good."

Gabe stepped back and watched her back out of the driveway. She waved and would have moved forward, but he motioned her to stop. She rolled down the window. "What is it?"

"Your right rear tire is flat."

She groaned. "What next?"

"It shouldn't be a problem. I'll change it for you and you can be on your way in fifteen minutes, tops."

"Are you sure? I can call the rental company."

"It's after five. The only location open is at the airport. It's no trouble. Pop the trunk and we'll see what we've got."

She climbed out of the car and walked to where he stood. "I really appreciate this."

"It's the least I can do, except—" He set her bags on the ground and pulled up the vinyl backing on the floor of the trunk and ran his hands over the entire area. "You're not going to believe this."

"What?"

"You don't have a spare."

"That's impossible," she said flatly.

He gestured toward the empty trunk and stepped aside.

Whitney stared at the pristine emptiness and lifted a hand to rub her forehead. "I don't believe this is happening."

Gabe closed the trunk and picked up her bags. "What you need is a drink, one of my mother's spectacular meals and a good night's rest, all of which you'll find right here. Follow me."

Whitney watched helplessly as he carried her bags up the porch steps and into the house. What was the matter with her? She was behaving completely unlike herself. Why didn't she take charge, demand that he leave her bags where they were and insist on calling a taxi? She looked down at her shoes. They were her favorite, Louis Vuittons, beautifully crafted and undeniably ruined beyond repair. Taking a long, deep breath, she followed Gabe into the house.

It was mid-April and warm enough to eat outside. Whitney, completely recovered after a shower and a glass of wine, was dressed comfortably in loose pants, sandals and a rose silk blouse with wide, floppy cuffs. Making her way downstairs, she marveled at the weather, the patio sparkling with tiny white lights, the hanging plants, gold placemats. The table was set with rust-colored cloth napkins, gleaming silver, sparkling goblets, and she caught the heady, delicious smells of roasting meat, cinnamon, coffee and other spices she couldn't identify.

She followed her nose to the kitchen. Mercedes was sprinkling something green over a platter of chicken. "May I help you?" she asked.

"I hoped someone would show up," the woman said. She held out the chicken. "You can carry the food to the table and fill the water goblets. Gabriel should be down in a minute. I don't know where the children are. They always disappear until I've finished cooking."

Whitney laughed. "That isn't unusual. I did the same thing when I was their age."

Mercedes looked at her. "Can you cook?"

Whitney thought a minute. "I'm not sure. I don't very often. It's not really worth cooking for one person."

"Gabriel needs someone who can cook," his mother said.

"That," said Gabriel from the door, "won't interest Ms. Benedict at all, Ma."

Whitney didn't react. "Please call me Whitney," she said, bypassing him with the platter of food. "'Ms. Benedict' reminds me of my mother."

Gabriel picked up the bowl of salad and followed her to the patio. "You wouldn't happen to be affiliated with Whitney Downs, Boone Benedict's Thoroughbred farm in Kentucky, would you?"

"I grew up there, but it belongs to my parents. Boone is my father. My specialty is international law. I have nothing to do with the farm anymore."

"Do you have a big family?"

Her fingers closed over the back of a chair. "I'm an only child."

He looked at her thoughtfully. "Do you have something against horses, Whitney?"

She frowned. "What an odd question. Of course I don't. I'm very fond of horses, but not enough to make them my life. I wanted something different for myself. I like the freedom of my work."

"Freedom?" His forehead wrinkled. "I'm curious. Would you mind explaining that?"

"Not at all." Her words were spoken crisply and clearly, as if she'd practiced her reply. "When I feel like it, I can arrange my schedule to take a vacation without worrying about the feeding and care of my animals. I'm not awakened in the middle of the night because a horse has colic and needs a vet. I'm not out of pocket thousands of dollars because the horse I'd counted on winning has broken a leg or, after I've spent even more thousands of dollars in stud fees, one of my mares gives birth to a stillborn foal, and more recently, I haven't gone nearly bankrupt because of an epidemic that's wiped out an entire generation of Kentucky Thoroughbreds."

He looked at her thoughtfully. "You know something about horses, don't you?"

"A bit."

He pulled a book of matches from his pocket and lit the candles on the table. "I wonder why you're so bitter."

She ignored his comment and changed the subject. "Is this all for me, or do you eat like this every night?"

"My mother believes in making meals worthwhile. We don't always eat on the patio, but it's usually quite a spread."

"How fortunate for you to be able to sit down every day to such beautifully presented, wonderful food."

Gabe grinned. "Why do I get the feeling you don't really mean that?"

Whitney lifted her chin. She refused to be trumped by a horse breeder from California. "When will you be contacting your sisters?"

"Tonight, after dinner." He looked directly at her. "Just for the record, I'll say it again. I have no intention of giving up my horses. They aren't for sale and I don't like wasting your time."

"I don't consider being here a waste of time," she said coolly. "No matter what happens with the offer, I've enjoyed meeting your mother, staying in your lovely home and sharing your hospitality."

"Are you ever ungracious?"

She looked startled for a minute, then she laughed. "I'm southern, Gabriel. We're bred and raised on graciousness, no matter what the circumstances."

They were interrupted by Mercedes shouting from somewhere down the hall. "Eric, Emma, Claire, dinner's ready. Wash your hands."

Gabe's eyes met Whitney's. They both laughed. "You won't find a lot of gentility here at the hacienda," he warned her.

The children filed onto the patio with Mercedes behind them. They glanced, surreptitiously, at Whitney. After they were seated, Gabe introduced them. "Whitney Benedict, these are my children, Eric, Emma and you already know Claire."

"Hello," Whitney said politely.

"Hi," said Eric.

Emma stared at her throat. "Your jewelry's cool. Where did you get it?"

Whitney's hand moved to the aquamarine at her neck. "Thank you. It's a gift from my mother. I don't remember where she got it. I can ask, if you'd like."

Emma shrugged. "It doesn't matter."

"So," Eric said politely. "Dad says you're from Kentucky."

"That's right. Have you been there?"

Emma snorted. "Hardly. Who'd want to go to Kentucky?"

"Emma," Gabriel admonished her. "That isn't polite."

Whitney ignored him and addressed the sullen teenager. "Sometimes I agree with you, Emma. Kentucky isn't the most exciting place in the world. I like it, but I was born there and my family lives there. I imagine it wouldn't do for a Californian."

"Whitney is a lawyer," Mercedes announced. "She's here to talk to your dad about the horses."

"What kind of lawyer?" Eric asked.

Whitney swallowed a forkful of salad before answering. She wasn't sure how much Gabriel would want her to reveal. "I specialize in international law."

Eric looked at his father. "Is this the Austrian thing?"

Gabe nodded.

Whitney was confused. She looked at Gabriel.

"This isn't the first time Austria's made an offer for my horses," he explained. "Usually, they send polite letters which I ignore. You're the first person they've actually sent. It won't make a difference."

"What are you talking about?" Emma asked.

"The Austrian government wants to buy the Lipizzaners, the ones whose bloodlines go back directly to those my father brought from Austria, from the famous riding school," Gabriel explained.

"Why? Don't they have their own horses?"

"I'm not sure why." Gabe looked at Whitney. "Do you happen to know why they're so persistent?"

"Not really," she replied. "It's possible they take the

defection of the horses very seriously and want to reclaim what they consider belongs to them."

"Now, wait a minute!" Gabriel's eyes narrowed to blue lines in the brown planes of his face. "My father rescued those horses at the request of the Austrian government with specific instructions to return with them if Germany won the war. If they didn't, he was to stay here. They didn't and he did. Hell, he did more than that. He kept the line pure. He trained the horses and he passed his skill and knowledge down to me."

"Calm down, *mijito*," his mother said. "Don't kill the messenger. You asked her a question. She answered it. Relax. Have a little wine. Enjoy this marvelous food that I have prepared for you."

Some of the tension left Gabriel's face. "My mother's right. I apologize."

Whitney smiled. "Apology accepted."

Emma stood and leaned across the table for the salsa.

Mercedes frowned. "Emma, we have a guest. Don't forget your manners."

Emma ignored her. "Is the Austrian government rich?" she asked Whitney.

"Probably. Why do you ask?"

"How much will Dad get for the horses?"

The child was incorrigible. Whitney was quite sure she had never met anyone with such awful manners. "I imagine he'll get what they're worth," she hedged.

"It's none of your business what they're offering," Eric spoke up. "Dad isn't selling."

"What if it's lots of money?" Emma replied. "We never have enough money. Maybe this would solve all our problems."

"That's enough, Emma," Gabe said. "Some things have nothing to do with money."

"Everything's about money," the girl persisted. "You wouldn't be grouchy if we had enough. Gran wouldn't have to rent out rooms in this house." Her cheeks were darkening as she spoke. "Mom would still be here if we had money instead of this stupid horse farm."

Claire, who hadn't said a word for the entire meal, looked up nervously. Whitney's heart ached for her. How could these two children be related? She would have given up a considerable percentage of her fee to have a look at Gabriel's ex-wife.

Mercedes frowned. "Emma is our drama queen. We believe she has great potential."

"I'm sure she does," Whitney said softly. "I agree with you in part, Emma."

The girl's black-rimmed eyes widened. "You do?"

"Yes." Whitney helped herself to more chicken, added salsa and wrapped both in a corn tortilla. "Life is easier when you have money," she said between bites. "It cushions a great deal of unpleasantness, but there are some things it can't do."

"I know what you're going to say," the girl said scathingly. "Money can't buy happiness."

"On the contrary, it buys a great deal of happiness." Whitney was conscious of five pairs of eyes assessing her. She focused on Emma. "What it can't buy is health or youth or life. It can't make people love you, although some would disagree with me, and sometimes, too much of it destroys motivation."

"I bet you have lots of money."

Whitney considered her answer. "I'm certainly not wealthy, but I have enough to keep me happy. What I'm most proud of is that I've earned it myself. No one gave it to me. In fact, I've worked hard all my life. Everyone does on a breeding farm. You probably already know that." She could see that the girl was losing interest. "This is delicious," she said to Mercedes. "I can't remember when I've had a better meal. Thanks so much for inviting me."

"You're welcome." Mercedes looked at Whitney's plate approvingly. "You've a healthy appetite for a small girl. That's good. I don't go for all this carbohydrate-diet nonsense."

Gabriel cleared his throat. "I'll bring out the coffee."

Mercedes waited until he was gone. She looked around the table making eye contact with each of the children. "Don't bother with the dishes tonight. I'll do them. Go upstairs and finish your homework."

"That's okay, Gran," Eric said. "We don't mind. Do we, Emma?" He looked at his younger sister. "Claire, how about it?"

"Speak for yourself, Eric-the-perfect," replied Emma. "I don't want to do dishes. Gran wants to do us a favor. Why can't you just say thank you?"

"Gran works hard all day."

"And we don't?" his sister countered.

Claire remained silent.

"Go on, children. Stop arguing." Mercedes waved them away. "I want to talk with Whitney for a while."

Eric looked unconvinced. "We could help you, Gran. I feel bad about this."

Mercedes reached over to pull his shaggy head down and kissed his forehead. "You're a good boy, Eric." She looked darkly at Emma. "You could learn something from your brother."

Emma ignored her and flounced from the room. Reluctantly, Eric followed. Claire didn't move.

Mercedes spoke to her. "Come here, my baby, and give your grandma a kiss."

Obediently, the little girl left her seat and walked around the table. She stood beside Mercedes. The woman kissed her cheek softly. "Run along now. I'll be up to see you later."

"You mentioned earlier that Claire has problems. May I ask what's wrong with her?" Whitney asked when they were alone.

"She's always been that way," Mercedes answered. "It's called Asberger's syndrome. You've heard of it? No?"

Whitney had heard of it. She couldn't reconcile Gabriel's beautiful little girl with that terrifying condition. "Is she in school?"

"She has a home teacher. A regular classroom didn't work for her. Her disease isn't severe, but there are times when she can't be with others."

"I'm so sorry. She seems normal. I didn't realize."

Mercedes nodded. "It's very sad. Kristen couldn't deal with her. Gabriel says no, but I believe it's the reason she left."

Whitney was silent. There was nothing left to say. Her mind, attuned to succinctly sizing up a situation, had assessed this family—Eric, the pleaser; Emma, the rebel; Claire, cut off from her emotions; Mercedes, the instigator; and Gabriel—Gabriel was the most troubled. It didn't take a genius to figure out exactly why. The responsibility of three children without a mother and a business that was obviously just making ends meet would be enough to send anyone over the edge. All of which should further her cause.

"Let's go into the living room," Mercedes suggested. "It's chilly and I'd like to ask you something."

They settled opposite each other, Mercedes in the chair-and-a-half and Whitney on the couch.

The older woman didn't waste any time. "This offer must be very important to have sent you here."

"It is important. I think it will be very good for all of you if you accept."

Mercedes nodded. "It affects our lives, Gabriel's most of all."

"He told me that you and his sisters have an interest in the business."

Mercedes waved her hand, dismissing the notion. "Gabriel makes all the decisions. He always has. The girls have their own lives. They have little interest in horses. Whatever Gabriel wants is the way it will be."

"Why do I have the feeling that I'm missing something?"

Mercedes nodded. She lowered her chin to her chest and thought a minute. "Is the Austrian offer a good one?"

"Very good."

"Would it be enough for Gabriel for the rest of his life?"

Whitney nodded. "More than that. He would have the capital to start another business and live comfortably, if that's what he wants."

"I would like my son to accept your offer."

"Shouldn't you be telling him that?"

"If only it was that easy."

Whitney leaned forward. "How can I help?"

"Stay a while with us. Convince him to see things your way."

"You would have more influence than I. You're family."

Mercedes's black eyes danced. "It's no wonder you aren't married, Whitney Benedict. You know nothing at all about men."

Gabriel appeared in the doorway carrying a tray with three cups of coffee and a pitcher of cream.

"Come in, *mijito*," said his mother. "We were just talking about you."

He took one look at Whitney's face and decided against asking the obvious. He offered her a cup. "This is Mexican coffee. It's flavored with chocolate, cinnamon and sugar."

"Thank you," she said, avoiding his eyes.

"Whitney is considering staying with us for a while," his mother announced. "She needs a vacation and she's fallen in love with California."

Gabe sipped his coffee. Over the rim of the cup, his eyes met his mother's. "Is that so?"

Whitney choked and set her cup down on the table. "I haven't decided yet," she said quickly. "Any word from your sisters?"

"They'll be here at eight-thirty. Does that work? I know it's early."

"I was born on a horse farm. Eight-thirty is mid-morning for me."

Mercedes was a believer in fate. She looked first at her son and then at the young woman who'd come into their lives at exactly the right time. Smiling, she leaned back in her chair, content to watch and wait.

Six

Whitney surfaced into consciousness the following morning. Keeping her eyes closed, she sniffed appreciatively. The smells of rich coffee, frying bacon and something laced with a healthy portion of vanilla wafted up the stairs, seeping into the space between the floor and the bottom of her door. This was a house where breakfast was given its due, where children were sent off to school and people needed fuel for hard physical labor.

Back home, Whitney considered herself fortunate if she remembered to stock her refrigerator with sugarless bran muffins and juice from the convenience store around the corner. Coffee purchased from the local Starbucks rounded out her meal that wasn't really a meal and bore no relation at all to the breakfasts of her childhood, or to the wonderful repast no doubt awaiting her downstairs in Mercedes's kitchen.

Lazily, she stretched her right arm over her head, pulling the muscles taut, holding the position for exactly fifteen seconds before repeating the movement on her left side. Then she opened her eyes, looked around the room and smiled. The architecture and decor were splendid, like nothing she would ever find outside of the Southwest. Colorful prints of California missions and terra-cotta courtyards awash in brilliant flowers covered the stark white walls. The heavy, dark wood of the head-board, bookshelves, the dresser and desk was a sharp contrast to the red-and-white quilt, the woven rug, the table runners, the lush flowers on the dressing table and the glorious autumn sunlight spilling through the U-shaped window. On one side of the room, French doors opened to a small patio with a lounge chair, a table, climbing plants and a western view of the sway-ing blooms of purple lavender. On the other side, a door led to a fully appointed bathroom decorated with hand-painted Mexican tile, more dark wood, thick red-and-white towels and a shower with a freestanding door.

It occurred to Whitney that Gabriel might need some-thing more than money to be tempted by the offer she'd been instructed to make. She picked up her cell phone to check the time. The three-hour difference had con-fused her inner clock. It wasn't even seven yet and her meeting with Gabriel was scheduled for eight-thirty, plenty of time to drink some of Mercedes's delicious Mexican coffee and have a look around.

Less than fifteen minutes later, dressed in slim-fitting black jeans, boots and a crisp white shirt, she was seated at the island in the kitchen making her way through a healthy portion of mixed fruit and *machaca*—scrambled eggs, chilies, ground beef, cheese and spices.

Mercedes, busy chopping tomatoes and cilantro, smiled approvingly. "You have a wonderful appetite. Did you sleep well?"

"Very well," Whitney replied between bites. "The room is perfect."

"Can I get you anything else?"

Whitney dabbed at her mouth and leaned back in her chair. "I can't remember when I've eaten this much food in the morning. I didn't even realize I was hungry."

Mercedes nodded, looked up from her chopping and tilted her head. "A woman who enjoys her food enjoys life. I have no patience with people who constantly watch their calories. It isn't natural to be so disciplined."

"I don't know about that," said Whitney, "but you certainly are a wonderful cook. Your family is incredibly lucky. I wonder if they appreciate you."

Mercedes laughed. "They should be down any minute. You can ask them yourself."

Just then Emma, dressed in skintight jeans and a peasant top, sauntered into the kitchen, followed by Claire, who stopped suddenly when she saw Whitney.

"Good morning, my darlings," Mercedes said. "Would you like eggs or cereal for breakfast?"

"Nothing for me," said Emma. "I'm on a diet."

Mercedes sighed. "You're always on a diet. It isn't good for one so young to worry about food."

Emma rolled her eyes. "It isn't good to be overweight, either." She glanced at Whitney. "Is it?"

Whitney sipped her coffee, enjoying the bite of cinnamon and something else on the tip of her tongue. Could she really be tasting lavender in her coffee? She kept her eyes on Claire. The child's thick, curly hair stood out around her head like a nimbus. She looked to be on the verge of flight. "I've heard," she said noncommittally, "that people who eat grains for breakfast, even white bread or pastry, are better at keeping weight off than those who eat nothing at all."

Emma eyed her suspiciously. "Where did you hear that?"

"Prevention Magazine."

Emma slid into the chair beside Whitney. Her jeans, cut just high enough in front to cover her pubic bone, slid down in the back, revealing the cleft in her bottom, her cheeks divided by a bright red thong. "I'll have cereal and no eggs," she said to her grandmother.

"What about you, Claire?" Whitney asked gently. "Would you like cereal, too?"

The child didn't answer. Whitney noticed that neither Mercedes nor Emma appeared to regard her behavior as unusual. Maybe her frightened-deer look would go away if everyone ignored her.

Whitney turned back to the older girl. "What grade are you in, Emma?"

"Eighth."

"In Kentucky, eighth grade is the last year before high school."

"It's the same here."

Mercedes poured two bowls of cereal and added milk. "It's cold this morning, Emma. You know I never interfere, but don't you think you should cover up your behind?"

"I'm not cold."

Mercedes shrugged. "Suit yourself." She patted the empty chair. "Sit down, Claire. If you hurry you'll have time to visit the horses with Whitney before your teacher comes. You'd like that, wouldn't you?"

Whitney held her breath. She hadn't intended to walk out to the dressage center, but she wasn't about to disappoint this fragile child.

Slowly, like the unfolding of a flower, the little girl moved toward the food. It wasn't until she'd picked up her spoon that Whitney felt she could safely draw breath.

"You know, Emma," continued Mercedes casually, "Saint Isadora's requires uniforms."

"So?"

"I thought you might want to remember that."

The girl raised her eyebrows. "Why should I?"

"No reason."

The teenager frowned. "There better not be. I won't go to a Catholic high school. Dad wouldn't do that to me."

Mercedes lifted her eyebrows. "You know him better than I do?"

"Has he said I'm going to Saint Isadora's?" she demanded.

"Not in so many words."

"What, then? Why are you bringing it up?"

Mercedes poured juice into two small glasses. Then she cut up a banana and scraped half into each of the girls' cereal bowls. "Two teenagers came to the house yesterday selling candy for a fund-raiser. They were dressed in school uniforms. Gabriel mentioned how nice they looked."

Emma snorted. "They probably look like nerds."

"He told me he thought you would look very nice dressed the same way. Of course I said you wouldn't be caught dead in plaid pleats." Mercedes wrinkled her brow as if deep in thought. "I can't be sure what came next, but it sounded something like, 'Maybe she won't have a choice.'"

Whitney stifled a smile. Rarely had she seen the act of manipulation played out so masterfully outside the courtroom.

"Maybe I'll go live with Grandma Chamberlain."

"That won't solve anything. She wasn't happy about the way you looked the other night at dinner, especially your hair."

"I like my hair," the girl said indignantly. "It isn't any of her business what color my hair is."

Mercedes's eyes twinkled. "Be sure to tell her that when you move in."

Emma pushed her cereal away. "I have to go or I'll be late for school."

Claire, who appeared oblivious to the entire conversation, looked up. "Can I go with you, Emma?"

Emma opened her mouth to issue a stinging retort, caught her grandmother's eye and closed it again. "Not today, Claire," she mumbled before stalking across the kitchen and out the door.

Whitney stared at the space Emma had just vacated. She'd witnessed something here, an interchange, both painful and intimate, and so subtle she'd nearly missed it. She wanted to reach out, stop the clock and reflect long enough to understand what had just happened.

Mercedes broke the spell. She sighed and sat down in Emma's chair. "You do go to school, Claire. Mrs. Cook comes every day to teach you."

"Mrs. Cook comes here. I want to *go* to school."

"I know, *mijita*." The woman took the child's hand in her own. "Maybe, someday soon."

Once again, in the space of a minute, Whitney was touched by the personal tableau. The child's problem couldn't be solved by preparation, logic or an articulate closing argument. This was something poignant and hopeless, a victim with no perpetrator, unless one counted a few twisted brain synapses.

Suddenly, Whitney *had* to do something. "What time does Mrs. Cook come?" she asked.

"Nine o'clock," Mercedes replied.

"That gives us about an hour, plenty of time to walk to the dressage center, have a look and come back. I'd love to have you show me around, Claire. Will you do that?"

The little girl's face was completely still, but behind the blue eyes Whitney saw a flicker. Her mind was moving, processing the information. Finally, slowly, as if something in her head connected, she nodded.

Whitney swayed slightly, gripping the edge of the counter. Waves of relief passed through her. "I'll drink the last of my coffee while you finish your cereal."

The dressage center on a working morning bore no resemblance to the quiet, almost dreamlike place Whitney had visited the evening before. A lemony spring sun hovered over the Ronald Reagan Library to the east, illuminated the silver rooftops of the stalls and colored the hills and grassland a lush, Crayola-box green. To the west, fog swallowed the dark trails, strangling the peaks of low hills, settling over the canopy of trees that bordered the highway, turning the lavender field into a blanket of smoke. The white-fenced rings were once again turned over and beautifully raked.

In all three performance areas, horses trotted and cantered in breathtaking precision, their riders in boots, breeches and helmets. Trainers, walkie-talkies in hand, issued commands from John Deere golf carts. Men in red shirts tossed bails of hay from a flatbed to a massive storage barn. Two mares with glistening coats chased each other around the turnout and another two were being lunged in the outside ring. The office door was open and a rich coffee smell emanated from the room.

Claire pointed to the open door. "Daddy's probably in there."

Whitney nodded and rubbed her arms. No one had told her California mornings were cold. "We can stop in and say hello, if you like. But I'd really like to watch the riding."

"Me, too." Claire ran ahead. "Look! Mary's riding Zinfandel. She's a good one to watch."

Whitney followed, catching up with the little girl at the fence. Less than ten feet away, a woman with a sun-lined face and dry, streaked hair sat in a golf cart, wrapped in a black shawl, issuing commands. She smiled and waved at Claire without missing a beat. Whitney strained to hear her.

"Less half halt and give, pick up the rein, pick it up! Good, now half pass, tighter—tighter! Damn it, Mary, I said tighter! You can do better than that. What's the matter with you? Straighten up! You look like a sack of potatoes tied in the middle! There. That's it. Good impulsion. Now, move forward and don't forget to salute."

Whitney ached for the rider. The gelding was beautiful, a lovely silver-gray Andalusian. An animal like that was worth a fortune and so, obviously, was the woman who could afford him. Typically, trainers with little formal education felt justified in verbally abusing educated professionals who swallowed their pride in order to ride. It was the same in Kentucky as in California, and probably everywhere else in the civilized world, where people had an urge to manipulate the natural instincts of a two-thousand-pound animal.

Beside her, Claire sighed. "She's so pretty."

Whitney looked down at her, recognizing the worshipful look on the little girl's face. She was no expert, but Claire didn't behave like a child with autism. She was far too responsive. "Do you ride?"

Claire nodded. "I had my own horse. Her name was Seville's Rose. But she was old and she died."

"That's too bad. When did it happen?"

"A while ago."

"Will you get another one?"

Again Claire nodded. "My dad said I could ride Lorelei to see if she's good for me." She looked at Whitney. "She's one of ours."

Whitney didn't answer. Unless she was mistaken about Claire's expression, Lorelei was a pure Lipizzaner, one of the horses the Austrian government wanted returned to them. She stared out over the hills, coming alive with color from the morning sun. Why couldn't anything ever be simple?

"Good morning, ladies," a voice said from behind them.

Claire turned. "Hi, Daddy."

Whitney swung around to face Gabe. He wore jeans, a dark plaid jacket with a fur collar, boots and no hat. He removed his sunglasses. His eyes were remarkable. Flecks of green shot through the blue turned his irises a brilliant turquoise. She swallowed. "Good morning."

"I thought we had a meeting at eight-thirty."

"Mercedes thought it would be a good idea for Claire to start her morning this way, instead of watching the others go off to school." She hoped the message in her answer was clear. Apparently it was.

He relaxed and nodded at the rider in the ring. "You're watching Mary Worth on Zinfandel. What do you think?"

"I wouldn't presume to comment on the riding," she said diplomatically. "I've been away from it too long. The horse is outstanding, though. I remember enough to know that." She rested her hand on Claire's head. "I understand this one rides as well."

Gabe smiled. "She's a natural. Sometimes I forget she's only eight and overestimate her strength. I had the perfect mare for her, but she died recently. I'm thinking she'll be able to handle Lorelei."

"I hope it works out."

He checked his watch. "I'll give you a tour later on if you want, but I think Mrs. Cook is due to arrive soon and she runs a tight ship."

Whitney looked at Claire to see the child's expression, but her face was impassive.

"It's time to go, sweetheart," her father said gently.

Claire sighed. "I know."

He tugged her hair. "I'll meet you back at the house, unless you want to ride with me."

The little girl tilted her head, apparently considering her choices. Whitney was reminded of a small, vivid bird.

"I'll go with Whitney," she decided.

For an instant, something flickered in Gabe's eyes, and then it was gone. "All right, then. See you there."

Whitney delivered Claire at the same time Gabe pulled into the lot. A young woman with an armload of books was standing beside one of four parked cars.

Gabe introduced them. "Whitney Benedict, this is Sheila Cook, Claire's teacher."

Whitney liked the young woman instantly. She was casually dressed in a slim denim skirt and a colorful, patchwork vest. Her thick, dark braid hung down her back, and when she smiled her gum line showed.

She hugged Claire. "Good morning. How are you?"

"Fine."

"Good." She smiled brightly. "I'm sorry I'm late. There was an accident on the freeway."

Whitney shuddered. It didn't surprise her. She wasn't looking forward to the drive back to the airport. "Do you live far from here?" she asked.

"About twenty miles," Sheila Cook answered. "But twenty miles could take fifteen minutes or an hour, depending on the condition of the roads. Usually, I'm lucky." She looked curiously at Whitney. "Do I detect a southern accent?"

"I'm from Kentucky."

"Ah, more horse country." Her hand grazed Claire's head. "This one is horse crazy. It's all she talks about." She smiled and spoke directly to Claire. "So, how about it? Are you ready for school to start?"

The little girl nodded.

Mrs. Cook held out her hand. Endless seconds passed while nothing happened. Whitney's nerves were stretched to the breaking point. She felt like screaming, or at least stepping in to smooth over the silence. Why was the little girl responsive one minute and the next nearly comatose? What triggered her reactions?

She glanced at Mrs. Cook. The woman kept her hand out, never faltering. Finally, finally, Claire's small hand reached out and slipped into the outstretched one in front of her. Whitney heard Gabe exhale at the same time she did. She waited until Mrs. Cook led Claire into the house and then leaned limply against the car and closed her eyes.

She opened them to find Gabe's eyes on her face.

"Tough, isn't it?"

She nodded. "How do you do it?"

He looked somewhere over her shoulder. "It's not as if I have a choice."

"I guess not."

"She's better around the horses. They help her somehow. Do you have children?"

"No."

"Ever been married?"

For an instant she hesitated. The question always stumped her. Then she would remember that an annulment meant there had never been a marriage. "No," she said.

"Why not?"

She shrugged, annoyed. "Why is that the paramount question on everyone's mind when it comes to me? Why doesn't anyone ask why I chose international law or whether I like to read, or if I've been to the Galapagos? Why always the marriage question?"

He laughed. "All right. I'll bite. Why all of those things?"

If they were anywhere else, if the two of them had met for any other reason, she might have succumbed to that laugh. She might even have satisfied his curiosity. "I think we have other matters to discuss that have more to do with you than me," she said, instead.

He studied her for a minute, the blue-green eyes veiled against her. "Have it your way." He waved his hand to encompass the small parking lot. "My sisters are here and they're on time. Given that they're all gainfully employed, they must have considered this important enough to put everything on hold to hear what you have to say."

"Should I be worried?"

"Relax, Miss Benedict. They'll all be on your side."

"I take it that your mind is made up."

"Completely. I told you from the start."

Whitney stood her ground. "I didn't come here to make things difficult for you. I'm here to present a very generous offer. You can do pretty much what you want if you accept."

"I'm doing what I want." He squinted into the sun. "Maybe that's difficult for a high-priced city lawyer to understand, but that's the way it is."

She held on to her temper and nodded toward the house. "Shall we?"

"After you."

Seven

Mercedes pulled the last of the steaming tamales from the pot, set it on a platter with the others and ladled the spiced applesauce into a large bowl. She glanced at her three daughters seated around the table drinking cups of scalding, cinnamon-laced coffee, speaking in low, secret voices. No one who didn't know them would believe they were related. Maybe that was the way it was when children were hybrids from two such dramatically different nationalities.

Where had they learned to talk that way, in those refined Anglo tones? Possibly from their father, although Franz had never been much of a conversationalist. They certainly didn't get it from her side. Mexican families didn't relate to each other calmly. They shouted at each other across crowded rooms, describing intimate details of their personal lives, bank accounts and bodily functions without regard for privacy, sensibilities or humiliation. Spanish was a language meant to be spoken rapidly and loudly without pausing for breath, the intent to eliminate anyone from interrupting the speaker.

She couldn't hear what her children were saying and

it annoyed her. She didn't like it when they left her out. Mercedes clapped her hands. "Luz, *mijita,* stir the beans. Ramona, set the table. Pilar can help me carry out the food."

Luz uncrossed her slim legs and walked over to the stove, where she gave the simmering beans a perfunctory stir with a wooden spoon. Ramona and Pilar, opposite ends of the color palette, looked at each other and remained seated.

"It's a little late for breakfast, Mother, and too early for lunch," said Luz. "You don't have to serve a spread like this in the middle of the morning. Coffee and some muffins would be fine."

"We have a guest," said Mercedes. "Besides, your brother will be hungry. He's been up for hours."

"So have we, Ma," said Pilar. She tucked a strand of tawny hair back into the twist at the back of her head. "I had an important meeting this morning."

Mercedes frowned. She handed the plate of tamales to her youngest daughter. "So, you had a meeting. Do you think I would have called you if this wasn't important? You can't give up a morning to help your brother?" She lifted Pilar's chin. "What's that on your face? It looks like dirt."

Pilar flushed. Her skin, pale like her father's, colored easily. "It's bronzer."

Mercedes snorted. "Bronzer?"

"Yes," replied Pilar. "It's the newest product in our fall line. It gives cheeks some color, but it's more natural than blush."

Pilar was an executive for a cosmetics line Mercedes could never remember the name of. Why someone like Pilar needed makeup was something her mother couldn't understand. Blessed with black eyes and lashes, fair skin and hair the color of warm toast, she was drop-dead beautiful the minute she rolled out of bed in the morning. "*Mijita,* you're pretty all by yourself. You don't need bronzer."

"Makeup enhances natural beauty, Ma," Pilar replied patiently, with the long-suffering air of someone who'd tolerated this conversation before. "If you'd let me, I could show you some tips. You've been wearing the same color lipstick since I was born."

"What's wrong with my lipstick? It works."

Pilar sighed. "Nothing's wrong with it, Ma." She nodded at the plate in her hand. "I'll take this into the dining room and come back for the rest."

Ramona, a female version of Gabriel down to the blue eyes, jumped up. "I'll set the table."

Mercedes pinched her cheeks as she walked by. "You're very thin, Ramona. I worry about you. Why don't you eat some of those desserts you make for everyone else?"

Ramona grinned. "I'm healthy, Ma, and I still haven't lost my last ten pounds since the twins were born." She squeezed her mother's ample waist. "You could lose a little bit yourself."

Mercedes laughed. "I'm seventy-six years old, *mijita,* too old to diet." This irreverent daughter never failed to coax a laugh out of her. Ramona was her child of light. No day was too gloomy, no problem too difficult. A pastry chef by trade, she had a heart like the warm butter she whipped into her delicious creations. She had given her father a scare for a few years in high school when she gathered boyfriends like rose petals and refused to take her teachers or her grades seriously, but the phase dissipated with maturity. The mother of year-old twin boys, she had settled into marriage and a career quite comfortably.

Ramona was the one Mercedes never worried about, not that she spent much time worrying about any of them. It was pointless, really. She had tried to explain to Franz that by the time children were thirteen or so, they had absorbed everything parents could teach them. From then on all you could do was hope and roll with the punches. Mercedes was good at rebounding. She had lived long enough to know that most of the time children turned out very much like their parents. Franz wasn't so sure. Fortunately, he'd lived long enough to see that, for the most part, she was right. What he would say about Gabriel and the offer from the Austrian government, she didn't know.

Luz leaned against the stove, her arms crossed against her narrow chest. She was dressed in her usual no-nonsense style: black boots, slim-fitting black pants, a gray cashmere turtleneck and a pair of half-carat diamond studs in her ears. Her hair was pulled back so severely from her face that her dark, almond-shaped eyes tilted up at the corners. Like the others, she was long-legged and very slim. Mercedes often wondered where she had come by such thin children. It wasn't natural.

Luz was a real estate agent, a very successful one. She and her husband, John, a certified public accountant, rattled around in a house made for children but, so far, none were forthcoming. Mercedes had given up asking. Again, it was against her inclination to spend time on a lost cause. She never interfered. Luz would get around to having children, or she wouldn't. Mercedes had enough grandchildren to keep her happy. If only Luz wasn't so serious. To Mercedes's dismay, she'd turned out to be the antithesis of her name. Luz meant light. The girl had absolutely no sense of humor. It was as if she'd been born old, like Gabriel.

No, not like Gabriel, she corrected herself. There was a time when Gabriel laughed frequently and appreciated a good time like anyone else. It was Kristen who'd changed him. Kristen with her sharp tongue and her everlasting complaints and her drama queen personality had wrung out every drop of joy he was born with. She didn't even have the decency to leave him when it was first obvious she was unhappy. Instead, she'd dragged him to marriage counselors and support groups and family therapy, insisting he behave one way and then another until he was so afraid of doing something wrong that he never got anything right.

Mercedes felt Gabriel's pain as if it were her own. She had been sincerely sorry for his loss, but she couldn't help but give thanks the following Sunday in church, sink to her knees and light a candle when the woman finally left him. Mercedes had been a nervous wreck until the divorce papers were finalized, hoping and praying Kristen wouldn't change her mind. Maybe, in time, Gabriel would heal.

She smiled tentatively at Luz.

Luz did not smile back. Her voice was crisp and clear and disapproving. "Mother, what is this all about? You know perfectly well we agreed not to interfere with Gabriel's decisions."

"This is different."

"I don't see it that way."

Mercedes sighed. "Miss Benedict said the offer was a very good one, too good to refuse. It could mean a different life for your brother and for all of us."

"What do you mean by a *good* offer?"

"That's what we're going to find out."

Luz's eyes were huge dark pools in her face. Mercedes was struck by how pretty she was. Not only were her girls thin, they were strikingly exotic. Again, it was probably their hybrid Mexican-German mix.

"Do you really think there's anything we can say that would make him sell?"

"I don't know, *mijita*," her mother said softly. She knew how much Luz loved Gabriel. Every one of his sisters would gladly offer up much of what they had if it would bring him happiness. "We can only try."

Luz bit her lip. "What if it isn't right? What if he won't be happy doing anything else?"

"He doesn't have to do anything else," her mother reassured her. "He can start over with enough capital to make himself comfortable. Lipizzaners aren't the only horses in the world."

"Why doesn't he see that?"

Mercedes wondered, not for the first time, how to explain to this daughter who was selling lemonade on street corners by the time she was seven that, sometimes, it wasn't about money. "Because he's Gabriel," was all she said.

Pilar returned for the rest of the food. "Gabe's here," she said, "and the woman with him is gorgeous. She reminds me of the little girl in *Tom Sawyer,* except she's grown up and obviously sophisticated. What was her name, anyway?"

"Becky Thatcher," replied Luz automatically. She and Gabriel shared a love of classic fiction. She looked at her mother. "Is she part of the plan?"

"Don't be ridiculous, *mijita.* You know I never interfere in my children's lives." She picked up the coffee carafe. "Shall we join the others?"

Pilar's eyes met Luz's, a question in them. Luz shrugged and followed her mother.

* * *

Mercedes patted Whitney's arm and sat down at one end of the rectangular dining room table. "Where's Gabriel?" she asked.

"He went to clean up," Whitney replied. Her eyes widened at the generous repast spread out before them. "I couldn't possibly eat another thing, not after my enormous breakfast."

"Don't worry," Ramona soothed her. "Nobody expects you to. For Ma, everything has to include food. It's her way of smoothing the waters. Unfortunately for us, it's cultural on both sides of the family." She patted her flat stomach.

Whitney laughed. "You hardly look overfed."

"It's a struggle for all of us. Ask Pilar." She nodded at her sister, who had come into the room bearing a plate of pastries.

"What's a struggle?" asked Pilar.

"Keeping our weight down when Ma expects us to eat ten times a day."

Pilar groaned. "Tell me about it. It's easier now because we don't live at home, but growing up was a challenge." She set down the plate and held out her hand. "I'm Pilar."

Whitney took it. "Whitney Benedict."

Ramona tilted her head. "Any relation to *the* Benedicts of Whitney Downs in Kentucky?"

Whitney looked surprised. "The very same. How do you know it?"

"When you grow up around horses, you end up acquiring information by osmosis. Your stud farm is fairly well known in equine circles."

"Mercedes told me that none of you, except Gabriel, are in the business any longer."

Luz spoke up. "Gabe makes the decisions, Ms. Benedict, but we all have a fiduciary interest in the business, which is why we're here today."

Mercedes introduced them. "This is Luz, my oldest daughter."

"It's a pleasure to meet you, Luz," said Whitney, forcing herself to smile warmly. She detected a definite chill coming from Mercedes's oldest daughter. "I'll run upstairs and bring back the paperwork."

Gabriel was already seated when she returned, and despite his sisters' protestations about their mother and too much food, they were all making a serious dent in the morning meal she'd prepared for them.

"Dig in, Whitney," Gabriel said. "The tamales are delicious. You won't find anything like this in the freezer section of your grocery store."

"I doubt I could find tamales in most of the grocery stores in Kentucky," she said. "I'll definitely sample one, but I ate breakfast barely an hour ago."

Luz nodded at the platter of tamales. "The sweet ones are on the left and the pork on the right. Take one of each." She smiled. "No one will make you clean your plate."

Whitney breathed a little easier. Her first impression of Luz dissolved under the charm of her smile. They were a very attractive family. She sat down in the vacant chair beside Luz and spooned two tamales onto her plate.

Mercedes poured her a cup of coffee. "Why don't you tell us about this offer while we're eating." She chuckled. "My girls always tease me about my food, but I notice it makes things easier to swallow."

"The offer is a generous one. It shouldn't be hard to swallow at all."

"We can go over the details after we finish here," said Gabriel. "But I'd like to hear the basics, if you don't mind."

"Not at all." Whitney unwrapped the husk from her tamale. Sweet corn aromas spiked with an indefinable spice swirled around her. Gently she touched the light, spongy masa. Rivulets of dark red chili sauce gushed from the center. Despite her full stomach, her mouth watered. She wanted to eat, not talk. Taking a sample bite, she chewed slowly. Bursts of flavor covered her tongue and shot up to the roof of her mouth. She'd eaten tamales before, but these, freshly made and still puffed with hot steam, were nothing like the dense, dry, store variety she'd sampled on occasion. She closed her eyes and moaned slightly.

Ramona laughed. "You have a convert, Ma. I have a feeling this won't be the last time we see Whitney."

Mercedes's cheeks were pink with pleasure. "I hope not."

Whitney set down her fork. "You truly are a magician in the kitchen, Mercedes. I've never eaten anything so delicious in my life."

"A true compliment considering you're a girl from the South," the woman teased her.

They were all smiling, except Gabriel.

Whitney cleared her throat. "All right. This is it in a nutshell. I've been instructed by the Austrian government to offer you a very large sum of money for all direct, full-blooded descendants of the Carthaginian stock bred to the Vilano, and the Arab, Siglavy."

Gabriel stared at her for a full minute before speaking. "In other words, all of my pure Lipizzaners."

Whitney bit into her sweet tamale. "If you can call them pure," she said when she could talk again.

"I beg your pardon?" Gabriel's left eyebrow was raised, a sure sign to those who knew him that he was annoyed.

"Well," said Whitney, swallowing what she considered as close to ambrosia as she'd ever come, "from what I've read, the breed isn't really pure. The original Carthaginian stock was bred to the Vilano, a Pyrenees breed, and then to Arab and Barbary strains. After the Moors were expelled from Spain, horses were exported to Denmark, Italy and Austria, with fresh Spanish stock systematically added to the breed to maintain its strength, hence the Neapolitan bloodline. These became the property of the nobility."

They stared at her, forks in midair, as she recited the results of her research.

"In the seventeenth and eighteenth centuries, the Neapolitan strain was brought to Lipizza to mingle with the descendants of the original Spanish line out of Denmark and Germany. There are six significant bloodlines in today's Lipizzaners, dating back to eight stallions." She set down her fork and ticked them off on her fingers. "The Dane, Pluto, the Neapolitan, Conversano, Maestosa, Favory, the Neapolitano and Siglavy. After the fall of the Hapsburgs, the horses were split between Italy and Austria and a privately owned stud farm became a government breeding farm, the Piber Farm, supplying mounts to the famous Spanish Riding School."

Her eyes, which had rested on each of them briefly while she spoke, now focused on Gabriel. "I don't think I need to go on. I'm sure you're very well aware of the role General Patton, Colonel Podhajsky and your father played in saving the horses from the Russians during the Second World War. As I said before, Austria wants the direct descendants of Siglavy, from the stables of Prince Schwarzenberg."

"Surely," said Gabriel, "since you've done your

homework so well, you know that the line my father was entrusted with was entirely out of Siglavy, through the stallion he brought with him, Protocol."

"Yes, and the mares, Madeleine and Perdita."

"That would be my entire stock."

She frowned. "Are you telling me that you've kept the breed entirely pure?"

"No, of course not. But I don't keep foals bred to other lines. They're sold before they're bred. That's how the farm makes its money."

"I thought you were a dressage center."

"The lessons and our boarders bring us a regular income. Everything else, any improvements, machinery, construction, comes from the sale of stock. My father's reputation, and mine, were built on the backs of the Lipizzaners. If they go, this place closes down."

"How many horses do you have?"

"Three stallions, all young, sixteen mares, one not so young, and one foal with another six on the way."

Whitney leaned forward. It was time to lay her cards on the table and make the offer she'd given up the Bermuda cruise for. "The currency will be in United States dollars," she said clearly. "I've been instructed to offer you two million for every stallion, another two million for every mare between ten and fifteen years old, one million for mares under ten years old, five hundred thousand for every pregnant mare and another five million for all healthy foals, collectively, even those in utero."

Someone gasped. Whitney did the math for them. "The offer is for thirty-two million dollars."

She didn't bother to editorialize about generosity. The money spoke for itself. Picking up her plate, she stood. "I'll leave you alone to discuss it. If you don't mind, I'll take these delicious tamales out to the patio and finish eating them. Then I'll take a walk."

No one, not even Mercedes, said a word for a full two minutes after she left the room. Then they all spoke at once.

Eight

Luz's voice, higher and sharper than the others, prevailed. "My God. Thirty-two million dollars. Gabe, is there anything to discuss?"

He didn't answer.

Pilar pushed her plate away. "None of us would have to worry about anything again."

"Do you worry about much now?" her brother asked.

"You know what I mean."

"No," he said, piercing her with his diamond-sharp gaze. "Exactly what do you mean?"

"Ma wouldn't have to rent out rooms, for one thing," she replied. "Ramona could open her own restaurant. You wouldn't be dependent on the approval of your medical insurance to find the best doctors for Claire, and Luz—" She stopped.

"What about Luz?"

"Luz doesn't need anything," his sister muttered.

"You haven't said anything about yourself, Pilar. What do you need?"

She looked at him defiantly. "I'm in some debt, if you

really want to know. Where is it written that the oldest son inherits the family business?"

"That isn't fair, Pilar," Mercedes interrupted. "No one else was interested in working the business except Gabriel."

"It could have been sold."

"You should be grateful he didn't sell it," her mother countered. "Otherwise we wouldn't be entertaining an offer in the millions from the Austrian government."

"If Gabriel *will* entertain it. It's not looking that way."

Gabriel spoke carefully to his sister. "I didn't know you were in trouble, Pilar. If you needed money, you could have said something."

Pilar sighed. "I know that. But you don't have money to give, Gabe. You're always worried about making ends meet. How could I ask you for help when your financial problems are bigger than mine?"

"We have enough to get by."

"Do you?" She challenged him. "Do you really?"

He felt the burn in his chest and cheeks. "If that's how you feel, all of you, then we'll sell."

His mother frowned. "What is it, *mijito,* that you aren't telling us? Why are you resistant even in the face of this opportunity?"

Collectively, they leaned forward, in a gesture of solidarity, to understand him. He felt a rush of love for them: his mother, his sisters, his late father, his first family.

"I'm not sure this will make any sense to you," he began, "because I haven't really thought it through, but I'll try to explain." To give himself another minute, he reached for the coffeepot and poured himself another cup. The truth of the matter was that he didn't know if he wanted to turn down Whitney Benedict's extremely tempting offer. What he did know was that he was bothered by selling off his Lipizzaners even for such an enormous return on his money. He needed time to analyze both sides, but apparently he wasn't going to be allowed that luxury. How often did they get together like this, just the five of them without husbands and children? He had to make them understand.

He looked around the table making eye contact with each one of them. "It's like this. Two of those horses were born the year I went to kindergarten. They're the result of a lifetime of training, Dad's and mine. They're all I have left of him. He died before his time. He was my best friend. I know we all miss him, but he and I had a bond, the only males in the family." He summoned a smile. "I wasn't ready to let him go when he died. Every time I walk into Lorelei's stall, or Damien's, or any of the horses he personally trained, I can picture him there with them." He drew a long, deep breath. "I'm afraid that if I send the horses back to Austria, I'll lose Dad altogether. Maybe it isn't fair to all of you. Maybe six-and-a-half-million dollars apiece is reason enough to move on. I'm not going to make that decision on my own. It's up to all of you, too. Together, if you vote the same way, your interest is greater than mine. Money, no matter how much, isn't worth losing my family. But I have to tell you, six million dollars will be different for you than for me. This is my life. I'm forty years old. I'm too young to retire and I don't know anything else besides horses. Six million will be about what it takes to start over again."

Tears spilled down Luz's cheeks. Ramona's eyes were brighter than usual, and Pilar blew her nose, hard. Mercedes reached out, gripping Gabriel with one hand and Pilar with the other. They were all her children. This was not the time to take sides. "Everyone here feels the same way, Gabriel," she said gently. "We are a family. We'll keep at this until we reach a compromise." She looked around the table. "Is everyone agreed?"

Together, they nodded.

She sat back, satisfied. "I propose that we wait one week and see where we are after we've thought about this. Until then, Whitney will stay with us. We'll assure her that she'll have an answer at the end of the week."

"She's a busy woman, Ma," Gabriel protested. "She isn't going to want to stay here with us. Besides, it isn't necessary. We'll call her when we've made a decision."

Mercedes frowned. If Gabriel didn't want a beautiful, intelligent woman around him for a week, he'd been hurt harder than she thought. Instead of arguing, she shrugged. "You may be right. I'll ask her. She mentioned something about a vacation. Maybe she'd like to explore Southern California."

The girls were uncharacteristically silent. Finally, Gabriel stood. "I have to get back to work. I have a show this weekend." His smile didn't reach his eyes. "Don't stay away too long," he said to his sisters. Then he left the room.

Pilar swallowed. "I guess I was a little tough on him."

Mercedes squeezed her hand. "You told him how you feel. He needed to hear it. We've been walking on eggshells around him for a while now. He'll be fine."

Luz sipped her coffee. She looked thoughtful. "Has he heard from Kristen?"

Her mother snorted. "Her own children haven't heard from Kristen. I say good riddance to that one."

"She was his wife, Ma," Ramona said. "They have a history together. Whatever we thought about her doesn't really matter. Gabe's sensitive. He's not going to get over a marriage that lasted more than ten years as soon as we might want him to."

"It's been two years," replied Mercedes.

"Eighteen months," Luz corrected her. "I think you might be pushing Whitney on him before he's ready."

Mercedes rested both hands on the table. "I'm his mother," she said. "I know him better than anyone. The best cure for Gabriel is for him to find someone else. Whitney is a lovely, accomplished woman. She'll be good for him."

Ramona's eyes widened. "Ma, you've got to be kidding. What would a woman like her want with Gabriel?"

Her mother's eyes flashed. "What's that supposed to mean?"

"You know what I mean. It's obvious. Whitney Benedict has a lucrative career. She's single and childless. Gabe is a terrific guy, but he comes with nearly insurmountable baggage."

"Don't use those big words with me, young lady. What is this baggage everyone talks about nowadays? He has three children. So what? He's handsome, he owns his own business and, if he plays his cards right, he could be a multimillionaire. What's so terrible about that?"

"You heard him, Ma," Pilar said. "He doesn't want to sell." She whistled. "He's crazy. Six million apiece. What I could do with that."

"I also heard him say that he would if we wanted it."

Luz stared at her mother. "You can't honestly believe we'd do something that would make Gabe miserable."

"Thirty-two million dollars isn't something to turn down without very good reasons. I'm not sure sentimentality is enough. Sometimes, we do what's best, even if the person we're doing it for doesn't know it yet." Mercedes stood and pushed her chair in. "I've said my piece.

Stay as long as you like. I have to move Whitney to the room with the balcony. She'll like that one better."

Ramona waited for her mother to reach the second-floor landing before speaking. "I can't believe it. She's doing it again."

"She only wants him to be happy," said Luz. "Pilar's right about the money. He needs it. It's too much to turn down."

Ramona spoke up. "You heard him. After taxes, six million would just cover the cost of starting over again. If Gabe is set against selling his business, I, for one, don't want to make him."

"It might not be so bad," suggested Pilar.

Ramona stared at her. "Just how bad is your financial picture?"

"I'm not talking about the money."

"What, then?"

"Maybe Ma's right about finding someone to replace Kristen."

"No, Pilar." Ramona shook her head vehemently. "Ma can't manipulate people into a relationship when they're not ready."

"That's the point. If they don't connect, there's no harm done. If they do, all the better. People can only be manipulated so far and then it works or it doesn't. Whitney's a nice-enough woman. Gabe could do worse. He did do worse. Why not give it a chance?"

"Gabe could get hurt, that's why. Hasn't he been through enough? What if he falls for this woman and she goes back to Kentucky?"

"Of course she'll go back to Kentucky," said Luz. "Her job is there."

"What difference does that make?" asked Pilar. "People have long-distance relationships. Air travel isn't all that expensive. Maybe it would be a good thing if she didn't live here. Gabe's busy. She's busy. It might give him something to look forward to. You know what they say, absence makes the heart grow fonder."

"More like out of sight, out of mind," said Ramona.

"I'm worried about what it will do to him if it doesn't work out," Luz said.

"At least he'll be over Kristen. Ma's right. No one is really over a relationship until they have a new one."

Ramona was clearly exasperated. "Pilar, you've never had a relationship that's lasted more than six months. You have no experience. Gabe was *married* to Kristen. They have a child together."

"I agree with Pilar," Luz said unexpectedly, "and I've been married for fifteen years. If he and Whitney hit it off and it doesn't work, at least he'll know there's the possibility of finding someone else. I'm not sure he knows that now. Frankly, I'm concerned about his judgment. People don't turn down thirty-two million dollars."

"Does he want to find someone else?" asked Ramona, ignoring her sister's money comment. "What about what Gabe wants?"

"If he's not interested, we'll know in a week. As Pilar said, there's no harm done."

Ramona sighed. "I give up. Count me out. You're all insane. This is going to be a very interesting week."

Whitney followed the pounded dirt road to the edge of the lavender field. Even though she was shaded on both sides by olive trees, the sun was hot on her head. She couldn't explain her fascination with Mercedes's lavender crop. But the color and the aroma surrounded her in a haze of well-being. For the first time in years she felt completely relaxed. Meandering through the fragrant blooms, she occasionally stopped, closed her eyes, lifted her face to the sky and listened. Somewhere in the distance, she heard the faint hum of a plane. Unfamiliar birds called to one another, leaves rustled and a light wind lifted the hair from her shoulders. Bees heavy with pollen ignored her and explored the tiny flowers that made up the tall stalks. The waistband of her jeans felt tight, and very soon she would need to find a bathroom, but right now she felt unusually, utterly calm, as if everything was moving forward as it should.

She thought back to her meeting with the Mendozas. The family dynamics were interesting. First of all, their name was an anomaly. Why Mendoza, after Mercedes, instead of Kohnle, their father's name? What kind of man was Franz Kohnle, other than a risk-taker willing to give up all he knew to smuggle priceless horses out of Austria and begin all over again in a country hostile to his own? How much had he influenced his children? Where did Mercedes fit in and why had her three beautiful daughters chosen fields outside the family business?

Various possibilities occurred to her as she walked alone in the temperate, golden Southern California morning, thick with the smells of lavender, sage, gorse, wild mustard and horses, always horses. Whitney smiled as she checked her watch and reluctantly turned back to the house. Somehow, she always found her way back to her roots. She wasn't at all sure how she felt about that.

She found Claire sitting alone on a swing in the back of the house, not really swinging but dragging her feet back and forth over the bare patch of ground below her. Not wanting to scare her, Whitney circled around to the front so the child could see that she was approaching. "Hello, there," she said, smiling. "Are you taking a break?"

Claire glanced her way briefly and then, with a sweep of her magnificent eyelashes, looked down at her feet.

"Would you like me to push you?" Whitney asked.

Again, the child didn't respond.

Whitney sat down in the second swing and, using her feet, propelled herself backward. Then she lifted her feet from the ground and swung forward. She glanced at Claire. Obviously, the child was lonely. How much fun could it be for a little girl to be taught at home with no one to play with? Why didn't Gabriel send her to school? Surely there were schools for children like Claire.

She bent her knees as the swing moved back and straightened them on the forward glide. Unconsciously she repeated the motion again and then again until she was fairly high off the ground.

Suddenly she heard a peal of laughter. Claire was pumping with her legs, gaining on Whitney until they swung in tandem. Intense in their concentration, they moved together until Whitney's full stomach protested by turning queasy. Reluctantly, she relaxed her legs until her swing slowed.

Claire, her cheeks glowing, skidded to a stop beside her. "That was fun," she said. "Where did you learn to do that?"

"I was a kid once. When I was little my dad used to push me on the swings in my yard."

Claire nodded. "So did mine."

"Is your teacher gone for the day?"

"No. She's talking to my grandma. I'm supposed to be taking a little break."

"How long have you known Mrs. Cook?"

Claire shrugged and looked away. "A while."

Her mood had definitely changed. It was clear that

Claire no longer wanted to communicate. But Whitney refused to be put off. "Do you like having her come out here to teach you?" she persisted.

Minutes passed before the child answered. "I like her," she finally said.

"She seems nice," Whitney agreed.

Claire stared at her feet.

Searching for something, anything, that would bring the little girl to life again, Whitney looked around. The three cars that belonged to Mercedes's daughters were no longer there. "Your aunts were here this morning." She didn't expect a response. "I wonder if you had a chance to see them, or maybe you were too busy with Mrs. Cook. They're all very nice." She looked appraisingly at Claire. "I think you look the most like your aunt Ramona. She has the same blue eyes, but your eyelashes are longer. Where, I wonder, did you get them?"

She would have gone on in the same inane vein but Sheila Cook stepped out on to the porch. "Claire," she called out, "it's time to come in."

Whitney waited until Claire was on the porch with her teacher before releasing her breath. Why did a little girl with a handicap, a little girl she barely knew, make her so edgy?

Leaving the swing, she walked around the house to the back patio and sat down in a lounge chair. Tilting her head back, she closed her eyes and concentrated on the source of her unease. She knew it had to do with Claire's disability. Something wasn't right. Whitney didn't have a strong background in neurological disorders, but Gabriel's daughter didn't fit the picture of an autistic child. Certainly there were times when she appeared sullen and nonresponsive, but it appeared to

Whitney that Claire expressed herself the way any child her age would under the circumstances.

Deliberately, she pushed her thoughts aside. Claire Mendoza was none of her business. Whitney was here on behalf of her client, and as soon as the Mendoza family came to a decision she would be on her way home.

The back door opened and Mercedes stepped out on the patio. She sat down beside Whitney.

"You're not going to offer me food, are you?" Whitney teased her.

Mercedes laughed. "Soon, but not quite yet."

Whitney breathed a sigh of relief. She wasn't as uncomfortable as she'd been an hour ago, but she most definitely was not ready for more food. She smiled. "Don't keep me in suspense. What have y'all decided?"

Mercedes shrugged. "Nothing."

"Nothing?"

"Gabriel doesn't want to sell and the rest of us do."

Whitney was quiet for a minute. "Does that mean it's a no?"

"Not necessarily. I've talked him into thinking it over."

"For how long?"

"One week."

Whitney grimaced. Could she put the Austrian government off for a week? They had already waited years. Maybe another week wouldn't matter. She would have to work it out. "There is one more thing." She hesitated.

"Go on."

"I'm curious. Why would someone give up the chance to be independently wealthy? I'd like to be able to give my client a reason, but I'd like to know, too."

"It's his father," explained Mercedes. "He feels that the horses are all he has left of him."

"Is that true?"

Mercedes stared at the horizon line where green hills met blue sky. "Franz was very special," she said in a soft voice. "He was also a very private man, not given to conversation. The horses might have been all they had in common. Gabriel was interested in other things, but he was our only son. Franz needed him in the business."

Whitney studied the profile of the woman beside her. Her instincts told her she had left a great deal unsaid. Mercedes's lower lip trembled.

"I think that Gabriel is fortunate in both his parents," she said softly.

Mercedes smiled. "You're a lovely young lady, and now I'm going to impose upon you. My daughters tell me I do it all the time, and they're right. So, if it's too much, you'll tell me. Okay?"

"Okay."

"Please, stay with us this week. Talk to Gabriel. Explain to him that his world can continue in much the same way without the Lipizzaners, only his money worries will be gone."

Whitney didn't answer right away. Her instincts told her to refuse, that pressuring Gabriel wouldn't serve her cause, but she didn't want to offend his mother, who had turned into an ally. On the other hand, she didn't want to alienate Gabriel. "I'm not sure that's a good idea," she said at last.

"It's a wonderful idea."

"I don't think I'm Gabriel's favorite person, Mercedes. After all, I'm the one rocking his boat. He might see my presence as forcing the issue. It might make him more defensive than he is already."

"I've already told him you're staying."

Whitney stared at her, eyebrows raised. "How could you say something like that without asking me?"

Mercedes shrugged and managed to look innocent. "I told you. It's my way. No one can force you, of course."

"You're shameless."

"Then you'll stay?"

"You haven't given me a good reason," she protested. "I'm afraid I'm going to sabotage the desired result. I'd turn you down in a minute, if only—"

"If only...?"

She couldn't explain it. There was something about this woman, despite her bossiness, and the house and the lavender and the whole Mendoza family. Mentally, she considered the positives. The firm would want her to stay, and she'd never seen California. A week might be too long, but three or four days would work. "I could use a vacation," she said out loud, "and this place is so wonderfully relaxing. My firm would probably encourage it if they thought I was mixing business with pleasure."

Mercedes sighed, content that she'd won. "You've made me very happy, *mijita.*"

"You always say that word. What does it mean?"

"It means, my own."

Whitney was touched. "You've been very welcoming. I appreciate it." She laughed. "I have a feeling you have an ulterior motive and I think I know what it is. I hope you won't be too disappointed when it doesn't work out."

The older woman smiled. "I think you were meant to come here. I have a good feeling about you."

Whitney certainly hoped so. Her client was being billed at three hundred dollars an hour for her professional services. She looked at her watch. As of right now, she would turn off the clock, place a call to her firm and then one to her mother.

Moving inside, she sat in front of the long windows that faced the lavender field and waited for Everett Sloane to pick up his phone. Normally, anticipating a conversation with the senior partner made her nervous. Today, for some reason, it didn't. Where had she heard that the color purple was soothing?

"Whitney?" Everett's clipped voice came through the receiver.

"Hello, Everett."

"What's happening?"

"There's been a slight complication. I need a week or so to sort it out."

"Can you be specific?"

"Apparently this is a family operation. Gabriel is only one of the players."

"How did that get past you?"

"Technically and legally, Gabriel has power of attorney," she explained. "Ethically, he's accountable to his mother and sisters. The good news is, I think they want him to sell. He's the one dragging his feet. However, he's run into a few more complications that have nothing to do with horses. I have a good feeling about this, but I need a week."

"I won't belabor how important this deal is to us, Whitney. We could lose our position as legal counsel for those who count in this state. I know you'll remember that."

"Of course," she said coolly. "I won't let you down."

"Good. Keep me updated."

She heard the click and sighed. Everett Sloane was a friend as well as a colleague. Normally his tone didn't irritate her. Today, it had.

Whitney sat with the phone in her lap for a long time. The scene in front of her was so serene, so perfect in its symmetry of purple stalks and gold hills. Her mind drifted. Her eyes began to close. A nap would be welcome. Immediately the thought snapped her out of her reverie. Whitney never napped. She considered it a serious character flaw as well as a flagrant waste of time to sleep during the day.

Picking up her phone again, she dialed her parents' number. This call would be much more difficult than her previous one.

Nine

Lexington, Kentucky

Pryor Benedict set the phone back in its cradle. A perplexed frown marred the smoothness of her forehead. She leaned back into the couch cushions of her sitting room and stared, unseeing, out the long windows, their view blurred by filmy, sheer curtains.

Twenty minutes later her husband, hoping to talk her into a late lunch, found her in exactly the same position. "Hi, hon," he said from the doorway.

She didn't respond.

He walked in and tentatively sat down beside her. Pryor's sitting room was sacrosanct. She liked her privacy and those who knew her well understood that this room was where she found it. Her stillness and the look on her face convinced him to broach the sanctuary. "Pryor? Are you all right?"

She blinked and looked at him. "Hello, dear."

"Has something gone wrong?"

"Whitney's not coming home."

Boone frowned. "Forever?"

"No. A week."

He relaxed. "That's all right, then."

"Do you know anyone named Gabriel Mendoza?"

Boone stroked his chin. "Sounds familiar."

"He owns a dressage center in California and he breeds Lipizzaners."

"Not too many people breed Lipizzaners."

"These are special Lipizzaners. The Austrian government wants them. Whitney is trying to work out a deal."

Boone's face lit up. "Now I remember. The name is wrong. It's Kohnle, Franz Kohnle. He's an Austrian who brought Lipizzaners into the United States at the end of the war. Rumor has it he was trying to keep them away from the Russians."

Pryor nodded her head. "I don't blame him. But are you sure it's the same one? Whitney said his name was Gabriel Mendoza."

"Franz Kohnle would be over eighty years old by now. Maybe he sold out, or maybe a relative is running the place." He glanced at his wife. "I'm surprised you didn't ask Whitney for specifics."

Pryor sighed. "Whitney isn't the same. There's a wall between us. I try to break through, but she won't have it. She doesn't go out of her way to avoid me, exactly. It's just that we don't have real conversations anymore. She's so unfailingly polite. We barely go deeper than the weather."

"You're pressuring her because she's not married," he said bluntly. "She's sensitive about that."

Pryor nodded. "I know. But I worry about what will happen to her when we're gone." Her eyes filled. "Who will she have?"

"For Pete's sake, Pryor. We're not in our dotage. I'd

say we have a few good years left. The last thing we want is another disaster like Wiley Cane."

"That's not the point. She's gun-shy, Boone. You know perfectly well that all men aren't like Wiley. Our daughter is an only child and she doesn't have a husband or children. Who will she spend holidays with? She's nearly past the age when she can start fresh with someone. Everyone she meets will already have been married with children to support."

"Is that so terrible?"

Pryor shrugged. Her face crumpled. "I guess not. I wanted more for her, that's all."

Boone wrapped an arm around his wife's slight shoulders and squeezed gently. "Whitney's a smart girl. She'll land on her feet. You'll see."

Pryor shrugged off his arm and stood. It was Boone who didn't see. For as long as she could remember, she'd had a vision of how a family was supposed to be. At first, it seemed as if it would happen effortlessly. Whitney was born a year after they were married. There was no reason to assume that more children wouldn't follow. But it hadn't turned out that way. Boone was...easily distracted. It wasn't until Whitney's tenth birthday that Pryor realized with certainty that there would be no more children. Still, she had hopes for the family she'd dreamed of: Whitney's husband and Boone talking intelligently of matters that men talked about; towheaded children with milk mustaches gathered around the Christmas tree opening gifts while she and Whitney looked on, talking and snapping photos.

Embarrassed by her lapse into self-pity, she smiled brightly. "How about some lunch? You're probably starving."

The look of relief on her husband's face was comical. Boone didn't like to delve too deeply. Strong emotion unsettled him, which was exactly why, in Pryor's opinion, he needed a good dose of it on occasion. Boone had been her husband for thirty-eight years. She'd alternated between loving and hating him for twenty-eight of them. It was only during the past ten that she'd truly accepted him for who he was and settled into a comfortable fondness that in some strange way brought out the best in both of them. They had weathered the storms and were heading into their golden years with the deep affection into which all long relationships eventually evolve. There had been a time when she didn't like Boone at all. Thankfully, that had passed. Now, even though he had his flaws, he was her best friend.

"I'd like some of that fried chicken and gravy we had the night before last," he suggested.

Pryor shuddered. "Not a chance. Your cholesterol is over three hundred and you're growing a belly even with all the exercise you get. I'm not having you die off on me before we can retire. It's salad and fat-free cottage cheese for you."

Boone groaned.

She laughed. "C'mon, Boone. I'll have the same lunch you do, just so you don't feel bad. Now, is that love or what?"

"I don't know about that," he sulked. "You like that stuff. That's probably what you were planning to eat, anyway."

"You could take a lesson or two from me when it comes to your diet. Don't you want to live to see your grandchildren?"

"Now, see?" Boone slapped his thigh. "There you go again. No wonder Whitney's cautious around you."

Pryor bit her lip. "You're right. I'm sorry."

"Don't apologize to me. Just watch yourself around Whitney. I'd rather have my daughter come around once in a while than have a passel of grandchildren."

"I'll make an effort," Pryor promised. "Now, I want you to tell me all you know about this California dressage center and Gabriel Mendoza."

Brilliant sunshine flooding through the French doors woke Whitney at six o'clock Pacific standard time. Stretching lazily, she sat up and looked out the long windows at the brush-covered hills, their outlines blurred by low-hanging clouds, the winding roads broken up by plots of pasture and farmland, the silver thread of freeway, the tiny ant-size cars moving in the distance and the gorgeous purple blooms of row after row of maturing lavender.

The sachets filled with dried seeds that she kept in her underwear drawer at home were pale and artificial next to the real thing. What did Mercedes do with it all? There must be at least two or three acres, all blooming at the same time. Whitney inhaled deeply. This was horse country, but not in a way that was at all familiar. Suddenly she felt an ache, not deep or serious but definitely there, for the lush, lime-rich bluegrass of home.

She showered quickly, pulling on riding breeches and boots, and headed downstairs.

Surprised to see anyone in the kitchen so early, Gabriel looked up from the coffee he was pouring into a mug and grinned at Whitney. "What's up?"

"I thought you might want an extra hand today, with the show and all."

He liked the way she talked, the soft, sibilant consonants and that funny little *all* she added to her greetings. "That's not a bad idea. You got any experience?"

She found a mug on the shelf and held it out. He poured the coffee, stopping just short of the rim.

"I can cool and rub down horses, and I've been known to do some braiding of manes and tails in my life. You might even trust me to exercise a few of the regulars and free up your grooms for the contestants."

"I'm sure of it." He didn't want to think about her motives. It would ruin the gesture. He would think of her offer as nothing more than an honest desire to be of service. Besides, he liked Whitney Benedict. In the senses-drowned world of the hacienda, presided over by his overpowering mother and its cast of characters—his three needy kids and, occasionally, his sisters—she was a cool drink of water, all legs and pale hair and clear, rain-washed eyes. She reminded him of moonlight, Yeats's *human child*.

Deliberately he stopped the thought. Poetry was an indulgence, a sensitive pursuit in a world where there was no place or time for indulgences except in the brief few minutes he stole between slipping into bed and unconsciousness. He sipped his coffee silently. It wasn't until he lifted the mug to drain the last of it that he realized she was staring at him, obviously waiting for a response. "I'll put you to work," he said, "unless you'd rather watch the show. Have you seen one before?"

She laughed. "I'm from Kentucky. We have horse shows every weekend in every city. I've seen quite a few, with the exception of a real Spanish Riding School performance. Those moves aren't done anywhere in Kentucky. If that's what's going on today, I'd love to watch."

Gabe shook his head. "Typically, they aren't done here, either." He set down his cup and reached for a plate of pastries covered with plastic wrap. He reached under the plastic, pulled out the first one and bit into it. He held the plate out to Whitney. "These are homemade."

She chose a flaky, apple-filled circle and tasted it tentatively. The buttery pastry was half gone before she spoke again. "Why do you train your horses in moves that are obsolete?"

He stared at something over her head, his eyes narrowed and vividly blue. "To keep the art alive," he said slowly. "My father was entrusted with a priceless legacy. I feel that I should keep it going. Does that make sense to you?"

Whitney nodded. "Perfect sense. I'd feel exactly the same way, but—"

"What?"

"You have a chance to make good on that legacy and cash in on a very large amount of money, as well."

He rinsed his cup and left it in the sink. "Why is it so important to you? Your money is earned no matter what I decide."

"True," she admitted. "I didn't really mean to pry. I guess I'm interested in your motivations."

He grinned again, dispelling the tension that rose between them. "Lawyers are interested in facts, Miss Benedict. Maybe you should have taken up writing."

She raised her eyebrows and moved toward the sink, where she rinsed her cup and set both hers and Gabriel's in the dishwasher. "That's a new one. I'll have to think about it. Meanwhile, I don't want to waste your time. Shouldn't we be leaving?"

He checked his watch. It was twenty minutes later than he wanted to be. "Let's go."

They walked in silence, cutting across the thin grass flowing like a river in the light wind, Gabe deep in thought while Whitney stopped occasionally to touch and smell the fragrant lavender. The barn roofs glinted silver in the morning sun.

The day was already beginning to warm up. The center was awake. Soft nickers came from the stalls. Two men threw bales of hay into a barn. In one of the rings, a groom lunged a deep-chested warmblood. Driving a golf cart, a trainer in a baseball cap and heavy jacket positioned herself near the show ring and picked up her walkie-talkie. Her student, sitting deep on a delicate gray Arabian with a black mane and tail, trotted into the circle. The animal's muscles gleamed as he moved to the left and then right, in tunc with commands from the cart. His mouth foamed, an indication that he'd already been worked hard.

In the stalls, horses were nose-deep in buckets of bran, mash and oats. Fragrant straw, a foot deep, carpeted their stalls. Mounted on every door were charts with feeding and exercise schedules.

Whitney greeted the groom she'd met earlier, a wiry man with a dark complexion. "Good morning, Juan."

The groom nodded. *"Buenos días,* Miss Benedict." He spoke in the accented English she was beginning to associate with Los Angeles. "You're up early. Seen enough of the sights?"

"For a while. I thought you could use me today. I'd like to help."

He smiled, revealing a flashing gold tooth. "Always glad of another set of hands."

Gabriel checked his watch again. "If you'll put her to work, Juan, I'll get to the office."

"No problem, boss." Juan fastened the latch on a stall and checked off a box on the schedule. "Come with me, Miss Benedict, and I'll show you how to wrap legs."

"If wrapping for a show is the same as wrapping for a race, I'll save you some time because I already know how to do that. Would you mind if I looked around for a bit first?"

"Not at all. Take your time. When you're ready to start, let me know."

Whitney paused near a pipe stall, admiring a smoke-gray foal nuzzling his mother. Her coat was a pure, unbroken white. So, this was a Lipizzan mare. "Hello, girl." She spoke softly. "What a pretty baby you have."

The mare's ears twitched. She approached the rail and nickered softly.

Whitney reached in and massaged her forehead. How different these horses were compared to the touchy hot-bloods she was familiar with. Only her dad and the vet could come within ten feet of a mare who'd recently given birth.

She looked around. Already the activity around the stalls was fairly heavy. Women, and a few men, in breeches, expensive boots and helmets were saddling horses and riding toward the training rings. Inhaling the familiar smells of hay, mash and horse dung, Whitney walked down the aisles of the first two barns without encountering any questions or unusual looks. Maybe it was normal for strange women to walk through the Mendozas' stables. In Kentucky, strangers did not have access to the training yards or the barns.

The third barn was something different entirely. Horses of the purest white filled the pristine stalls. Whitney caught her breath. Here were the famous Siglavy Lipizzaners bred of the stallion, Protocol. She'd done her research. These were horses worth millions of dollars, but more than that, they had a history of their own. They were the aristocrats, the royalty, the light and nimble dancers, aerialists of the equestrian world. Their distant ancestors from the Orient bore Genghis Khan out of the wastes of Asia to conquer much of the then-known world.

A small, dark-skinned man wearing a baseball cap came up behind her. "May I help you, *señorita?*"

"I'm Whitney Benedict. I'm staying with the Mendozas."

He nodded. "I'm Alejandro. So, what do you think of our Lipizzaners?"

"They're incredible. Where are the stallions?"

"On the other side of the property. I'll show you."

"I'd like that."

"First, we'll stop at the office. Maybe Gabe isn't busy. He's a much better tour guide than I am."

They found Gabriel on the phone. He waved them into two chairs in front of his desk while he ended his conversation.

"Finished already?" he asked.

"I haven't really started yet," Whitney replied.

"Miss Benedict would like to see the white stallions," Alejandro explained.

Gabe grinned. "I'll be happy to show her. Let me straighten out a few things first. Alejandro can direct you. I'll join you in about ten minutes."

"I'd appreciate that," she said warmly, "but I don't want to keep either one of you from your work."

"It will be my pleasure," Alejandro assured her. He held out his arm. "Shall we?"

He led her out of the office toward the stud barn, pointing out various landmarks in the distance.

"How did you get into the horse business?" Whitney asked.

He chuckled. "I was born on horseback. My father was a vaquero on the estate of the descendants of the last Mexican governor, Pio Pico. He had me in the saddle before I could walk. I've never done anything else."

"I don't know much about California history," Whitney admitted, "but surely the last time California had a Mexican governor was over a hundred years ago."

His eyes twinkled. "I'm older than I look, Miss Benedict."

"Whitney," she said automatically. "Please, call me Whitney. You can't be that old."

"The descendants of the early dons are sprinkled throughout Alta California. They've lost much of their land, but not their skills. I was apprenticed on their land." He ushered her into another meticulously kept barn. "Here are the masters, the heirs of the infamous Protocol."

"Did you know him?"

Alejandro nodded. "I was a boy when Franz hired me, but never has a horse left such an impression with me. These are magnificent animals, but none are like Protocol."

Gabriel spoke from behind them. "Don't tell her that. She'll tell her client and Austria will withdraw the offer."

Whitney turned. "Have you decided to sell?"

Gabe nodded at Alejandro. "I'll take it from here."

The groom touched the bill of his hat. "It's been a pleasure, *señorita*. Enjoy your tour."

"I will. Thank you." She waited until he left the barn. "I didn't mean to put you on the spot, Gabriel."

"You didn't, but I would like my family to be the first to know."

"I understand." She gestured toward the muscular stallion in the first stall. "He's an albino, isn't he?"

"Right. They're rare, even among Lipizzaners. His name is Macbeth. So far, he hasn't sired any like him.

White foals are rare among Lipizzaners. Usually they're born black and change slowly through a period of six to ten years, eventually reaching their pure white color. We call the white ones grays. In the days of the Hapsburgs, white foals were chosen to draw the royal equipages. Macbeth, here, was always white with blue eyes. Every one of his foals has been coal black."

"He's gorgeous."

"I think so."

"What about the other two?"

Gabe walked beside her to the next stall, where another massive stallion stood with his nose in a feeding pail. His eyes were liquid black, and when he lifted his head, Whitney saw the smoke-gray color of his nostrils. He snorted and began pacing back and forth in his limited space.

"This is Othello," Gabriel explained. "He's the most sensitive of the three. One of the grooms usually turns him out if I can't get to him. Eric helps me with the others, but he's not up to Othello yet. His temperament requires careful handling."

"And the last one?"

"I'll show you." He led her to the end of the barn where a powerful stallion stood, head erect, ears pricked, tail high. "This is Romeo. We're standing him to stud today. He's our best breeder."

"They're mostly Shakespearean names. Why is that?"

Gabriel shrugged. "No reason, other than I appreciate the classics."

"Really?" Whitney couldn't imagine her father appreciating any such thing.

"Does that surprise you?"

"Yes," she said honestly. "I'm curious. How does a man who reads Shakespeare end up in this line of work?"

"People don't always end up working in their fields of study."

"Was English your field of study?"

"Yes."

Surely she'd misunderstood him. "You have a degree in English?"

"Yes."

She stepped back to study him. "You're more than meets the eye, Gabriel."

"Are you suggesting that in the horse business in Kentucky, no one has a degree in the humanities?"

"I can't think of any right offhand, certainly no one who works in the barns."

"Do your parents work the barns?"

"My father does."

"And your mother?"

"Only when absolutely necessary, but neither has a degree in English. For that matter, they aren't even college graduates. My mother didn't finish and Daddy never started."

Gabriel frowned. "I'm not sure where you're going with this."

"I'm interested in what makes you tick."

"Why is that?"

"Why do you think?"

He shook his head and chuckled. "You never give a man a straight answer, do you? You know, you have a great deal in common with my mother."

"I'm taking that as the highest compliment."

He laughed. "Was it my imagination or did you volunteer to help out this morning?"

"You didn't imagine it. I'm ready."

"Good girl." They walked into another barn. "You can start here with Intrigue. Wrap her legs and then move on to Top Gun next door. They're showing today, but not till later." He checked out her clothing approvingly. "If you're up for riding, I have a few that need exercise. You'll have to use the farthest ring because contestants will be taking up the others. Has it been a long time since you've been on a horse?"

"Not too long. My father usually gets me up on one when I go home."

"Good for him. I won't worry about you. There are saddles in the tack rooms. Use any that are marked with an *M*."

Whitney watched him walk away. Then she turned her attention to the horse. Intrigue was a classic Andalusian, a gray with dark markings around the eyes and nostrils. Her forehead was smooth, her eyes widely set and intelligent, and her temperament gentle. Before even attempting her task, Whitney spent a good ten minutes speaking softly, clucking and rubbing her forehead, sides and legs. When she was certain the horse was comfortable, she pulled up a stool and began to unwind cotton from the skein. Beginning with the front legs, she worked quickly and competently, her fingers finding their rhythm in a task she'd done more times than she could count.

She repeated the routine with Top Gun, a gelding. After rubbing the animal's forehead, she latched the stall. The sun had burned off the morning chill. It was almost too warm. She hung her jacket on a peg in the tack room and went in search of Alejandro.

While she worked, the lot had filled with silver trailers. Men and women in breeches, boots, dark jackets, top hats and gloves milled around the stalls. Most were silent, concentrating on the events to come. Whitney remembered the nail-biting, preperformance twitchiness, the mental exercises and rehearsals that came before a show, and breathed a sigh of relief, grateful it was no longer a part of her life. High school track and swim meets were one thing, controlling a thousand-pound animal was another.

Outside the main traffic areas, she slowed her pace. The weather was incredible. She lifted her face and felt the sun warm her skin. A slight, dry wind rustled the grass and a minty, herbal smell wafted from the eucalyptus trees. The deep blue of the heat-stunned, cloudless sky relaxed her. It was like summer in Kentucky, without the humidity and the clouds of black flies that hovered around swimming holes, walking paths and bass streams, waiting to attack unprotected skin. She could see why residents of California looked beyond their crowds and freeways.

She found herself in front of the exercise ring. A young girl, no more than twelve, was riding a medium bay. Whitney could see that her mount was trying his best to correct his stride, but his weight was on his forehand because of his young rider's flawed seat. She would lose points if her error wasn't brought to her attention.

Whitney ducked under the fence. "Pull him in," she ordered.

The rider, responding to the authoritative voice, slowed the horse to a stop.

Whitney approached the pair, reaching out to grip the bridle. "You're not sitting deep enough in the saddle. Pull up the reins and straighten your back. You have to feel the leather on both sides of your bottom."

The child's dark eyes widened. Her face looked pinched and pale.

"Are you all right?" Whitney asked.

She nodded. "Just a little nervous. I'm up in fifteen minutes."

"What's your name?"

"Debbie Arnold."

"Do you know how to do what I asked you?"

She nodded. "I think so."

Whitney took another long look at the little girl. "I'll tell you what," she said gently. "I'll cross your stirrups and you try to balance without them. It's all in the balance. How about it?"

"Will it work?"

"Every time," Whitney promised.

The child smiled shyly and slipped her feet out of the stirrups. "Okay."

Whitney flipped the stirrups back out of the way. "Now, give it a try."

Debbie clucked lightly and the horse moved forward. Instinctively, the little girl straightened, tucking in her seat and throwing back her shoulders. Like magic, the horse's stride changed. He moved into position and found his rhythm.

Whitney nodded approvingly as Debbie gained confidence and put her horse through his paces, walking, trotting, cantering. Finally, she pulled up and reached down to pat the animal's neck. Her cheeks glowed. "I did it. He's doing everything right, isn't he?"

"Yes, he is."

"Thank you so much. Are you a trainer?"

Whitney laughed. "I'm a lawyer. But I know something about horses. Good luck with your event."

"I'm okay with it now. Thank you."

"You're welcome."

She turned to follow Debbie and her horse out of the gate.

Gabriel leaned against the fence, watching. He'd taken off his jacket and his shirtsleeves were rolled to the elbow. Dark glasses hid his eyes. He nodded at Debbie and waited for Whitney to reach the gate.

"Nice job," he said. "You have good instincts."

"Thanks. It was easy enough to correct."

"Maybe so, but her trainer didn't think of it."

Whitney touched the part on her head. It was tender. She pulled the elastic from her ponytail and shook out her hair. "I'm getting sunburned."

Gabe studied her. "You're changing the subject."

"I thought we were finished with it."

"Why does it make you uncomfortable when people compliment you for having a talent with horses?"

"Does it seem that way?"

"I'm sure you're a very good lawyer."

"Why do you say that?"

"Because of the noncommittal way you answer questions when you don't want to disagree."

"That sounds like a politician more than a lawyer."

"You did it again."

She turned on him, facing him squarely. A muscle flickered at the corner of her mouth. Her voice was low and controlled. "What is it that you want me to admit, Gabriel?"

He looked at her for a long minute. "You're unusual, Whitney Benedict," he said softly. "I apologize if I've offended you."

The tension in her shoulders eased. She drew a long breath. "No offense taken," she replied.

Ten

Gabriel clawed himself out of the thick foggy sleep that weighed him down, pressing him into the comforting warmth of the mattress. Beneath closed lids, his eyes burned with fatigue and his throat felt raw and scraped, as if he'd swallowed a ball of steel wool. It was always this way after a show, exhaustion coupled with aching limbs.

God, what was that sound? It couldn't be the alarm. Not more than an hour had passed since his head hit the pillow.

Once again the piercing ring assaulted him. It was the phone, not the alarm. He blinked, forcing his eyes open. The digital clock read 3:00 a.m. Groggily, he reached for the receiver, fumbling in the dark bedroom, hoping it wouldn't wake the kids. "Hello," he said tersely.

"Gabriel, it's Lynne."

Her voice, like a shot of adrenaline, cleared his cobwebs instantly. "What's wrong?"

"It's Emma. The police have her at the Ventura station. They called me. She was driving without a license. The policewoman said she'd been drinking."

Gabe was already shrugging into his shirt and jeans. "I'll be there right away."

"I won't have this, Gabriel. The girl is out of control. What is she doing out at this time of the morning?"

"We'll discuss it later."

"Gabriel—"

He hung up and turned on the light. It blinded him. Hesitating for a minute, he stumbled across the room to his closet, found his Nikes, grabbed a jacket and ran downstairs in his bare feet. "Damn you, Emma," he cursed softly. "Damn your spoiled little ass."

Inside the truck, his hands shook as he slid the key into the ignition and turned it over. Nothing. Again he tried turning the key, flicking his wrist back and forth several times. The familiar, empty click signaling a dead battery was the only sound in the cold cab.

Rage and fear warred in his chest. He rested his head on the steering wheel. Emma was in police custody. Emma with her flirty smile and her smoke-rimmed Madonna blue eyes and her indecently cut jeans. Christ. She must be terrified. Once again, Gabriel tried the engine, willing it into life. Still nothing.

He was still barefoot. The simple act of putting on his shoes, pulling back the tongue, sliding his feet in and tying the laces steadied him. All right. His battery was dead. He could wake his mother and take her car, but he wasn't up to his mother tonight. He glanced at the white Impala parked beside him and made up his mind.

In a flash he was out of the car and up the stairs. Restraining himself, he knocked softly on Whitney's door. She opened it immediately, her face a mix of curiosity and concern.

"What is it?"

"Emma's being held at the police station. My truck battery is dead. Can I take your car?"

"It's only insured for me," she said quickly. "I'll drive you."

"I don't have time—" he began, but stopped when he saw her reach for her keys and bag. She was dressed in gray sweats and socks.

"My jacket's in the car," she said. "Let's go."

"You need shoes," he reminded her.

"They're in my bag."

She ran lightly down the stairs ahead of him, pulling the silky banner of her hair back and securing it with an elastic band. Less than two minutes after he'd knocked on her door, her shoes were on and they were heading toward the 101 north exit.

Gabriel breathed a sigh of relief and leaned back against the headrest. Her efficiency calmed him. This was a woman who knew how to take charge. *Heavens, how deeply you at once do touch me.* He closed his eyes, absorbing the heat pouring from the vents.

She broke the still warmth with a question. "What happened?"

"My mother-in-law called. She isn't happy. Emma was caught drinking and driving." He shook his head. "One of the above would have been enough. She's underage. This time she may very well have gone too far."

"What's her problem?"

"How should I know?"

"C'mon, Gabriel. You can do better than that. A fourteen-year-old girl doesn't cry out for attention the way Emma does unless there's a problem. What do you think it is?"

Gabriel looked at the profile of the woman beside him. It was austerely clean and honest. Without hesitating, she'd come to his aid. She deserved an answer, even if it meant his pride took some bruising. "She misses her mother," he said simply. "Kristen dumped all of us, the kids and me."

"Does she write?"

"No."

"She has no contact with her children at all?"

"If she does, it's minimal. According to Eric, he's heard from her four times in eighteen months."

Whitney thought of her own mother's cloying interest in her life. Suddenly it assumed a new perspective. "Are you divorced?"

"Yes."

"What are the custody arrangements?"

"She didn't show up at court when the settlement was finalized. I have full custody."

"In other words, you have three children who feel their mother has abandoned them."

That was it in a nutshell. Whitney had a way of dispensing with fluff and exposing the core of the situation. Gabriel wondered if it was all legal training or if her personality wasn't given to superfluous detail. "Yes. The case is classic, isn't it? Emma is testing me to see if there's anything she can do that will make me abandon her, too."

She glanced at him. "You seem to have figured it out. Why are you surprised and upset? This isn't that big a deal. She won't be able to get a driver's license at sixteen and she'll do community service, but that's about it. No one will take her away from you."

"Her maternal grandmother wants to do just that. Emma isn't my biological daughter."

She thought a minute. "My expertise isn't in family law, but if you've been her father for more than ten years, and if her mother has abandoned her, you shouldn't have much to worry about."

"Lynne will hire a lawyer. If she does, I will, too. I can't afford that kind of drain right now."

"I see."

The offer from the Austrian government lay between them, thick and impassable.

"I'm sure you'll work it out," was all she said.

He stared out the window without answering.

The Ventura police station saw its share of activity on a Saturday night. Gabriel and Whitney waited nearly thirty minutes before Emma, escorted by a thin-lipped policewoman, was released to them. She sat on the bench beside Whitney while Gabriel filled out paperwork and spoke to the officer at the desk.

"What are you doing here?" she asked Whitney.

"Your dad needed a ride. He had a dead battery."

"Lucky for him you were still here."

Whitney shrugged. "I suppose so. I imagine he would have awakened your grandmother."

"Why didn't he do that in the first place?"

Whitney looked at Emma, deliberately not answering until she saw a rosy flush stain the girl's chest and cheeks. "Like your other grandmother, Mercedes is an old woman. He didn't want to worry her."

The implication was clear. Emma had already unnecessarily worried one old woman.

"You don't like me, do you?"

The corners of Whitney's mouth turned up. The girl certainly was an original, a blunt one. "I don't know you, Emma," she said honestly, "but that's your intent, isn't it, to behave badly so people dislike you?"

"I don't like you, either."

Again Whitney shrugged, frustrated with the child's disagreeable attitude. "I can handle it."

Gabriel joined them. "You have a court date in three weeks." He reached for Emma's arm. "Let's go."

On the ride home no one spoke for a long time.

Emma broke the silence. "Am I grounded?"

"Yes," Gabriel replied.

"I wasn't really drinking," she began.

"The police report says differently."

The lies flowed easily from Emma's mouth. "I was trying to help Casey. She was the one who was drinking. She couldn't drive home."

"You're fourteen, Emma. You couldn't drive home, either."

"But I wasn't really drinking. I had just a little in my Coke. Honest, Dad. It really isn't a big deal."

"Tell that to the judge and to your grandmother." His composure slipped. Turning around he glared at his stepdaughter. "You're damn lucky that Casey's parents didn't report the car as stolen. What in the hell did you think you were doing by involving Lynne?"

Whitney looked in the rearview mirror. Emma's eyes had the wide, frightened look of a cat caught in the headlights.

"I didn't want to wake you."

Gabe snorted and turned away. "Right, Emma. I really believe that one."

"How long will I be grounded?"

"For the rest of your life."

"That's not fair," she wailed. "You can't make me. You're not my father. I want my mother. I want to live with Grandma Lynne." Tears rolled down her cheeks.

Gabriel opened his mouth, and then closed it again.

Whitney was impressed. Gabriel Mendoza had remarkable self-control.

"I'm the only father you have, Emma, and living with Grandma Lynne isn't an option."

"Why not?"

Whitney watched Gabriel struggle for an answer. Seconds ticked by, and then minutes. Her heart felt hard and tight. Lord, if parenting was this hard, she was grateful she'd never had the opportunity. Mentally, she spoke to him. *Make this right, Gabriel. Whatever you say, make it right.*

She thought he'd decided not to answer and searched her brain for an appropriate filler—the weather, the horse show, anything to fill the tense silence. She was just about to pick up the ball when he spoke.

"Because I'd miss you too much."

The wave of relief that engulfed Whitney was palpable. She needn't have worried. Gabriel was not going to destroy this incorrigible child, who cried out for any kind of attention. She smiled into the night, and then wondered why on earth she should be concerned at all.

Only Claire was awake and seated on the stairs, waiting for them. Her feet were bare and she wore a white, gauzy nightgown without sleeves. With her hair, a cloud around her pale little face, and her too-big eyes, she looked to Whitney like an angel awaiting her wings.

This time Gabriel didn't bother to lower his voice. He scooped the little girl into his arms. "Damn it, Claire, you're freezing to death. What are you doing up?"

"I looked for you," the child whimpered. "You weren't in your bed."

"Emma needed us."

Claire peeked over her shoulder at her sister. "Are you okay, Emma?"

Emma, stricken into silence, nodded.

Whitney looked down at her feet. What was it about this family that affected her so? Everything she witnessed was either intimate or painful.

Gabriel sighed. "C'mon, punkin, let's go upstairs." He turned and looked at Emma, then reached out and pulled her close. "I'm mad as hell at you. Don't you ever do anything like that again. Now, go to sleep, because I'm waking you up tomorrow at nine o'clock. You're going to help me muck out the stalls. Understood?"

Without answering, she ran up the stairs.

Claire laid her head on her father's shoulder. "Will you read to me, Daddy?"

"It's late, Claire. You need to sleep."

"Just one story. Please."

He groaned. "Okay. One story and that's it."

Over her head, his eyes met Whitney's. "I don't think I thanked you for rising to the occasion tonight. I appreciate it."

She smiled. "You're welcome. I have only one favor to ask in return."

His eyes hardened. "What's that?"

"Don't wake me up at nine o'clock."

For a minute it didn't register. He was too exhausted. Then he laughed. "It's a deal. Don't stay in bed too late. Tomorrow's my mother's Sunday brunch. The whole family will be here again after church, this time with husbands and kids. You shouldn't miss it."

"I wouldn't dream of it. What time does she serve?"

"Food comes out at about ten and is replenished until one. We all sort of drift in when we can. Guests come, too, when they're here."

"I'll be there."

He stepped aside. "After you."

She preceded him up the stairs and watched him disappear with Claire into her bedroom.

The light in her own bedroom was still on. She sat down on the rumpled bed, pulled off her shoes and socks and fell back on the pillows. Tonight, Gabriel Mendoza had impressed her. Every other man she could think of, without exception, would have lost his cool and given Emma the tongue-lashing she deserved. Who was she kidding? Every other man would have shipped the child back to her mother, postage due on receipt. At the very least, Emma would be packing her bags and moving in with her maternal grandmother.

Instead, Gabriel had not only kept his anger under control, he'd reassured Emma that she was still loved and wanted, even while he was under extreme duress with very little sleep. There was more to Gabriel Mendoza than met the eye. Whitney liked him. More important, she respected him.

Eleven

On Sunday, Whitney woke to the sound of rain typing irregular patterns on the long windows. Disoriented, with an aching head and heavy eyes, she glanced at the clock. It was already past ten. Groaning, she pulled the covers up to her chin and stretched out on the comfortable mattress. Not until she felt her muscles pull and the familiar surge of energy nudging her brain awake did she roll out of bed and take in the view.

The yellow haze that normally settled against the foothills was gone, replaced by dark, boiling clouds, leaden skies and gusts of rain flung randomly against the windowpanes. The ocean of waving lavender surrounding the house looked grayer this morning, casting a blue filter through which to view jewel-green grass and plowed earth that rolled out carpetlike in rich, dark brown hues. Burlap hills and cloud-studded sky met at the horizon. Everywhere she looked, Whitney could see no sign of another human being, a rarity she hadn't believed possible in Southern California. Maybe residents of the golden state didn't like rain or—more than likely, because they had so little, they didn't know what to do with it.

A shower washed away her headache and fresh makeup restored her mood. Shortly before eleven, dressed in a beige wraparound skirt, a white blouse and loafers, she followed her nose to the Mendoza family dining room. People were everywhere, and once again, a feast, tastefully arranged on platters and in chafing dishes, graced the wide table. Mercedes, rearranging the dishes for a plate of tortillas, smiled when she saw her.

Divesting herself of the plate, she clapped her hands. "Listen, everyone," she commanded. "For those of you who haven't met her, this is Whitney Benedict."

Voices hushed momentarily, and even the black-haired babies standing on unsteady legs, clutching the low coffee table, stared. Then Ramona claimed her, pulling her into the circle of her sisters and two men. "Whitney, you've already met Luz and Pilar. Let me introduce you to the rest of us. You probably won't remember everyone all at once, but this is Luz's husband, John." A slight man with wings of gray at his temples and the features of a Goya portrait smiled and held out his hand.

"Hello, Whitney," he said formally.

"Hello."

Ramona gestured toward a tall, powerfully built man with a ready smile. "This is Danny, my husband, and those—" she pointed to the babies "—are my twins. We're all here except for Eric, Claire, Emma and Gabe. The first two are helping Gabe with the horses and Emma is in disgrace. She refuses to come downstairs. I guess you know all about that."

Whitney ignored her last comment and shook Danny's hand. "I'm pleased to meet you." She looked around. "Do you do this every Sunday?"

"When we can," Pilar answered. "Ma likes it when we all get together." She laughed. "I'm not married, so it's the only balanced meal I eat all week."

"Are you enjoying your stay, Whitney?" Luz was dressed in a calf-length gray dress and black boots. Her chunky silver earrings, bracelet and the barrette that held her hair in place at the back of her head were gorgeous and obviously expensive. "I hear you helped out yesterday at the show."

"I'm learning to appreciate California," she replied honestly. "It's different from what we're led to believe."

Ramona tilted her head. "How so? Tell us."

"Well, for one thing, California isn't all Hollywood Boulevard and the Avenue of the Stars. I love the outlets and your shops are wonderful, but this is really a rural state, isn't it? I mean, I've never seen so much farmland, so many fruit stands and such exotic offerings in my life." Her light-struck eyes moved from one face to another. "Do you have any idea how lucky you are?"

"Sometimes it's hard to appreciate what you take for granted," said Ramona.

Pilar spoke before Whitney could reply. "I don't mean to change the subject, but have you had any luck changing my brother's mind about your offer?"

"It isn't *my* offer," Whitney corrected her. "As Gabriel pointed out, I'm just the messenger. Hopefully, y'all will come to an understanding and a decision will be made before I leave."

"Still, it's Sunday and you've been here since Thursday," Pilar insisted.

"Pilar," Luz said, the edge in her voice unmistakable. "You're pushing."

Pilar flushed. "I asked a simple question, that's all."

Whitney was beginning to feel uncomfortable when

Mercedes clapped her hands. "Everybody, help yourselves," she called out.

At the table, Ramona picked up two plates and handed one to Whitney. "I hope you're not feeling too pressured," she said, filling her own with an egg-and-tomato dish, fried potatoes, beans and fruit.

"Not at all," Whitney lied. "I'm enjoying myself."

Ramona grinned. "From what I heard, you could probably have done with a little more sleep." She nodded at her boys, now navigating the room in their walkers. "Sit beside me. We can talk while they're occupied. Once they're hungry or tired or wet, it's the end of my socializing."

Whitney wondered if it was the end of Danny's socializing, too, but she was too polite to comment.

"I'm sorry you had to get involved last night," Ramona said when they found their seats at the end of one of the couches.

"Don't be. I feel sorry for Emma. It must be hard for a teenage girl to be without her mother."

"That's it, of course," Ramona agreed. "Gabe wanted her to go to therapy when her mother first left, but she wouldn't hear of it. I guess Kristen didn't even say goodbye to the kids. She just sort of sneaked out the back door. I think Eric's handling it, but the girls are having a harder time. For weeks in the middle of the night Gabe would find Claire sitting at the bottom of the stairs in her nightgown waiting for her mother to come home. Every time the phone would ring, Emma would rush to answer it. I guess she keeps hoping Kristen will call. I'm afraid Emma's going to have to come to terms with it herself."

Whitney felt a sudden pang and was no longer hungry. Compared to Kristen, Pryor was looking better and better. "I've heard that she wants to live with her maternal grandmother. Is that a possibility?"

Ramona shrugged. "Anything's possible. I don't think it would last. There's nothing wrong with Lynne's intentions, but she doesn't have a handle on the typical teenager. Apparently Kristen was a model child. Maybe some of her rebellion is long overdue."

"Did you like her?"

"I suppose I did, at first," Ramona replied. "But it's hard to continue liking someone who hurt my brother so badly."

Whitney nodded. "It's obvious that he misses her."

"I'm not sure that's true any longer. I think his hurt has turned into anger." Ramona shrugged. She hadn't touched her plate, either. "I guess that's normal under the circumstances." She smiled at Whitney. "Will you be back?"

"That depends on what your family decides. I'm not sure you're any closer to a decision than when I first presented the offer." She hoped her fishing wasn't obvious. "My firm might find they don't really need me."

"I doubt that." Ramona changed the subject. "Gabe says you're good with horses."

Whitney pushed the food around on her plate. "What a lovely compliment."

"He said you were *really* good. I think his words were, *a natural instinct.*"

"I'm not sure my father would agree with that."

"Did he want you to go into the family business?"

Whitney dabbed at the corners of her mouth with her napkin. "Yes," she said. "He did."

"Why didn't you?"

"It's a long story." Whitney smiled to soften her words. "Next time I come, I'll tell it to you."

The door opened and Claire, followed by Eric and Gabe, walked into the room. "Sorry we're late," Gabe apologized. "I had to call the vet for one of the horses."

"Is everything all right?" Pilar asked.

"For now." He glanced around the room, his gaze settling on Whitney. Something raw and elemental and intensely private passed between them. Shaken, she looked away.

He cleared his throat. "We'll clean up and be down in a minute."

Eric grinned. "Save some for us. Gran never makes enough."

Whitney looked at the groaning table and then back at Eric before she realized he was teasing.

Ramona's husband sat down, both twins squirming in his arms. "They're hungry," he said, handing a baby to his wife. Pulling one of the walkers with its circular tray toward him, he deposited the twin in his arms and reached for the other. Ramona, relieved of her son, spooned a dab of scrambled egg and a few potatoes onto the tray. Then she scooped up more egg from her plate and offered it to the twin in her husband's arms. He ate greedily.

Whitney watched in amazement as the two parents alternated feeding one baby and then the other. They're like birds, she thought, taking turns filling the demanding little mouths of their offspring. She chuckled. "They're adorable." It was true. They *were* adorable, not messy at all. The two little round, dimpled babies, one brown-eyed, the other blue, smiled and babbled and gummed their way through their food.

"Thank you," said Danny, pulling a baby wipe from the bag at his feet and wiping the hands and face of the boy in his arms. "We like them. They certainly are a handful, though. I wouldn't recommend twins the first time around. Do you have any children, Whitney?"

"No."

"Are you married?"

"I'm afraid not."

He grinned. "Well then, I'll spare you the horror stories."

"Danny, that's enough," said Luz from across the room. "First Pilar and now you. What will Whitney think of our manners?"

Across the room Mercedes laughed loudly.

"She'll think we're completely unredeemable," said Gabriel. He walked into the room behind Eric and Claire, who immediately helped themselves to the food on the table.

"Isn't that right, Whitney?"

"Not at all," she replied, trying to be tactful. "I think you're a typical large family. I envy you. It's interesting being around everyone."

"Thank you, ma'am," said Danny.

Suddenly the doorbell chimed. Mercedes rose from her chair, but Gabriel held up his hand. "I'll get it."

He returned a minute later with a young woman. "Ma," he said, presenting her to Mercedes, "this is Antoinette Murray. She said she spoke to you on the phone."

Mercedes's eyes twinkled. "Oh, yes, of course. Please, won't you join us for brunch?"

The woman's eyes flitted around the room, taking in the family gathering. "I don't want to intrude," she said uncertainly. "I think there's been a misunderstanding."

Gabriel frowned. "What kind of misunderstanding?"

"Well, actually—" she faltered.

"There's no misunderstanding," Mercedes said

quickly. "This is Gabriel, my son. These are his sisters and their children. You're very welcome here."

She brightened. "His sisters. Oh, all right. If you're sure—"

"Very sure." Mercedes stood and led the young woman to the table. "Have some strata, dear and a tortilla. The beans are delicious, especially with a little cheese and salsa. Do you like Mexican food?"

"Oh, yes. My roommate and I eat at El Torito all the time."

Mercedes winced, recovered and smiled brightly. "We'll try to measure up." She heaped potatoes, beans and eggs onto the woman's plate. "There now, that should hold you for a while. Go sit beside Gabriel and I'll bring you some coffee." She turned and beckoned her son. "*Mijito,* find Antoinette a seat. No, not over there, beside you." She beamed. "That's it. That's good. You two, have a nice conversation together."

Resigned, Gabriel managed a smile and motioned the woman to an empty chair. Whitney glanced at Pilar. She was staring at her plate. Luz was talking animatedly with her husband, but her face was unusually flushed. Danny and Ramona were silent. Only Mercedes was behaving normally.

All at once, understanding dawned. Whitney choked on her coffee. Her eyes streamed. She pressed her napkin to her mouth while Ramona patted her on the back.

"Are you all right, Whitney?"

"Fine," she managed. "I'll be fine."

"I'll get you a glass of water."

Pilar jumped up. "I'll get it."

Whitney shook her head. "Really, it isn't necessary. Just give me a minute."

Reluctantly the sisters sank back into their seats. Whitney watched their eyes meet for an instant and then, as if in silent communion, they both glanced at Gabriel. Whitney did, too. He was staring at Antoinette Murray as if she'd grown two heads.

The bubble of laughter that started Whitney's coughing fit began to tickle again. If she didn't get out of here soon she would disgrace herself. "Excuse me," she whispered to Ramona, "I'm going upstairs to use the ladies' room."

Ramona nodded.

She'd nearly made it down the hall when she heard Claire's voice, innocent in all it's crystalline clarity. "Are you from Matchmaker.com?"

Climbing the stairs two at a time, Whitney reached the safety of her room. Closing the door behind her, she sat on the bed and erupted into gales of laughter. Poor Gabriel. Poor, poor Gabriel.

It really wasn't funny. She knew it wasn't, but she couldn't help herself. If ever a man didn't need a dating service, it was Gabriel Mendoza. The thought sobered her. Mercedes wasn't stupid. She must know it, too. What was her game? Whitney's mood changed. She stared out the window at the swelling clouds. She would be on a plane home soon. It was none of her business.

She heard a knock on her door. "Come in," she said.

Emma's head appeared in the opening. "It's me. Can I come in?"

Whitney laughed again. She couldn't get away from these people, and she couldn't remember when she'd laughed so much. "Of course. Your family is downstairs. They miss you."

Emma closed the door behind her. Again she was

dressed in the seductive uniform of the modern teenager, low-cut jeans, a wide belt, cropped top and tennis shoes. "They're not really my family."

"Eric and Claire are *really* your family, if you mean related by blood."

She shrugged. "If I was down there with everybody, they wouldn't be able to talk about what happened last night and how awful I am."

Whitney wet her lips and hoped her response wouldn't be taken the wrong way. This child certainly needed to be set straight. "I don't want to offend you, Emma, but I don't think anyone spends as much time talking about you as you might think. Other than your aunt Ramona telling me you refused to come downstairs, no one said a word about you. Is that good news or bad?"

"It doesn't matter what they say or what they think."

"Fair enough." Whitney lay back on her elbows on the bed. "What have I done to deserve your company?"

"I got bored."

"Isn't that the point of being on restriction?"

Emma walked around the room slowly, dragging her finger across the dresser, the bookshelves, the headboard and the walls. "You're a lawyer."

"That's right."

"Do you know anything about divorce and kids?"

"A bit."

"Am I old enough to decide who I want to live with?"

"That depends."

She looked directly at Whitney, her blue eyes even more vivid with their black-penciled rims. "On what?"

"On your parents."

"What do you mean?"

Whitney sighed. "Sometimes parents don't qualify

for custody even though a child wants to live with them. Their schedules don't work or they drink too much or use drugs."

"My mother isn't like that."

Whitney swallowed. "Sometimes parents just aren't up to the task of parenting."

"What about you?"

Whitney wasn't following her. "What about me?"

"I want to go home with you."

For a full minute the room was silent while Whitney digested the child's words. "That's impossible," she said flatly, when she could trust herself to speak again. "I don't even know you. We have no relationship at all. It wouldn't work."

Emma's lip curled. "In other words, you don't want me, either."

"That's emotional blackmail." Whitney was beginning to panic. "You're being ridiculous. Who put such an idea into your head?"

"My grandmother."

"I don't believe you."

"She said people don't have to be related to be family. She said people take in foster children all the time and end up adopting them."

"This isn't the same thing. I'm not a foster mother. I don't have children. I don't know anything about children, especially teenagers. Besides, you have a family who loves you."

Emma ignored her. "You have a good job. You dress nicely. You make a lot of money. Gran says you have good values. You could teach me a lot. I promise to do everything you say."

She was logical. Whitney would give her that.

"No," she said firmly. "The answer is no."

"I want to leave California," the girl pleaded. "I *need* to leave California."

Whitney was caught. "Why?"

Emma brightened. "Does that mean you'll consider it?"

"Of course not."

"Then I won't tell you," she said, and left the room.

In disbelief, Whitney stared at the closed door. What had just happened here? Could she really have participated in such an absurd conversation? What on earth was the child talking about and who should Whitney tell, overextended Gabriel, Emma's stepfather, or Mercedes, her over-the-top step-grandmother? For the first time Whitney began to feel the tiniest stirring of sympathy for Emma's absentee mother. Emma and Claire together might just be too much to handle.

Twelve

Mercedes sat at the kitchen table reading the newspaper and sipping coffee. She liked French roast, piping hot, unflavored and so strong it needed nearly a half cup of pure cream to reach the right color. Two cups a day. That was what she allowed herself for health reasons, although now the nutrition gurus were saying that coffee was good for people, just like wine. She could have told them that. When would they make up their minds? She'd seen every fad that was possible to see. First they touted small amounts of protein, no fat and plenty of grains. Then they switched to large amounts of protein, no sugar, no carbohydrates, lots of vegetables, no fruit and no juice. Now a little fat was okay.

She'd have to be a computer to keep it all straight. Not that she planned to pay attention to any of it. The years when she could fit into a size twelve were long gone, never to be resurrected. There had been only a few of those, anyway, when she was somewhere between twenty and thirty-two. After that, she had Franz and the children, and it was too much trouble to worry about the extra inches around her waist. She'd always been a big woman, tall and large-boned. It hadn't scared away any of the men who'd called on her, either. In her opinion, men didn't like skinny women. They thought they did, but in the end, the ones they brought home were the healthy-looking ones with some meat on their bones. She would have to remember to tell Pilar to eat more or she'd never get herself a husband. Mercedes frowned into her coffee. Maybe Pilar didn't want a husband. Some girls didn't anymore, but there was something to be said for having someone care whether or not you came home at night.

She heard the back door open and footsteps in the hall. Whitney Benedict appeared at the entrance to the kitchen. "Am I interrupting you?" she asked.

Mercedes smiled. "Come in. Will you have some coffee with me? The cups are there on the counter. What have you been up to?"

Whitney hid a smile. Her own mother would have jumped up, set the table, poured the coffee, pulled out the sterling teaspoons, filled the pitcher with fresh cream and fussed until she was sure everything was exactly right. How typical of Mercedes to wave an indolent hand and issue a casual invitation to join her. Whitney chose one of the colorful mugs and sat down at the table. "The dressage center looks like a very successful operation."

"Looks can fool," Mercedes said darkly.

"Oh?" Whitney filled her cup, took a sip and choked.

"I should have warned you," Mercedes apologized. "It's very strong. Shall I make some more?"

"No, please don't bother. I'll just have a little cream. That will round it out just fine."

"The dressage center is operational," Mercedes continued. "It pays the bills, but there is little extra."

Whitney set down her cup. "I'll be honest with you, Mercedes. I can't read Gabriel. I thought I'd have an answer by now. I'm flying home tomorrow. My firm is pressuring me. I'm scheduled for a conference call with Dr. Pohl of the Spanish Riding School and the Austrian ambassador. I need to tell them something. Gabe needs this offer as much as anyone. He's got some serious personal issues. What's going on?"

"He's stubborn, like his father."

Whitney added a little sugar to her coffee and cream. "Do you think he'll refuse to sell?"

Mercedes sighed. "The business belongs to Gabriel. No one in the family will stand in his way. It's up to him."

"What shall I tell the Austrian ambassador?"

Mercedes turned her liquid black eyes on Whitney. "Tell them he'll sell."

"Are you absolutely sure? Has he said that?"

"I know my son. He will do what is best for all of us."

Whitney breathed deeply and changed the subject. "Tell me about the lavender fields. I assume they belong to you."

Mercedes nodded. "The girls and I harvest our crop every year. The plants are perennial, you know."

"I didn't know. We don't grow lavender in Kentucky."

"In the beginning," Mercedes continued, "when I was a girl, my mother would boil water and the plants together in the tub to produce hydrosol, a mix of oil and water soluble plant components. True oil should not come in contact with the skin. That is why we blend it with creams and shampoos."

"You do this yourself?"

"The girls help. I've had my own still for some time now. It's very small, but it's enough for what I need."

"It sounds like an interesting hobby."

"It isn't a hobby, *mijita*. Two acres of lavender produces four gallons of oil and nearly three thousand pounds of flowers. In the summer, after the plants are harvested, I make up lotions, shampoo, soap, body oil and many, many sachets. The money helps," she said simply. "The girls and I do this together. The women of my family have always grafted the soft wood, harvested the field and sold our products. It is our tradition." She smiled. "It is good for families to work together. There are those who say that the lavender field brings good fortune in love."

"Do you believe that?"

Mercedes sighed. "For some, maybe. Not for everyone." She pushed a plate of banana bread toward Whitney. "Have some of this. You haven't eaten this morning."

Whitney chose one of the thinner slices. "Your home is lovely. I've never stayed in a prettier room."

"You're very kind." Mercedes looked around. "I love it here. It was my family home. I've never lived anywhere else."

"Really?" Whitney was intrigued. "What a coincidence. I was born at Whitney Downs and so was my mother. Daddy moved in after they got married."

Mercedes nodded. "It's hard to think it might go to someone else when I'm gone."

"Why should you think that? You have grandchildren."

"No one wants to live here in this dinosaur," Mercedes replied. "Families are small nowadays, and California real estate is worth a great deal of money. It wouldn't be fair to tie up so much capital with just one of the children. It should be divided equally so all will benefit."

"I see what you mean," Whitney agreed. Her own situation was different. She was an only child. Whitney Downs would be hers, but there would be no grandchildren for Pryor. For some reason, with distance between them, she was able to view her mother's position with new clarity.

"You're young," Mercedes observed, "much younger than I am. It isn't something you have to think about now."

"No. I suppose not." Whitney was no longer smiling. "I'd like to do a little exploring."

"Help yourself to the brochures in the entry. There are some lovely spots around here to visit. If you're interested in seeing the ocean, I recommend Ventura Harbor."

"I'll do that." Whitney stood. "Thanks for the coffee and the conversation. You've been very hospitable."

"Enjoy your day." Mercedes waved her away and resumed reading her newspaper.

The drive west wasn't as difficult as she imagined it to be. Ventura was a lovely town with a picturesque marina busy with boats, an ocean walk that featured a spectacular view of the sea and quaint restaurants offering local seafood and an array of ethnic foods. She chose Andrea's Sea Food, ordering at the window and taking her number to a table on the patio facing the ocean.

Boats of every size dotted the water, their white sails billowing like inflated parachutes against the glittering sea. Brown pelicans perched on the pilings and seagulls hovered above commercial fishing boats, their sharp eyes fixed on crews swabbing down the decks.

Whitney leaned back in her chair, removed her sunglasses and closed her eyes. The sun on her head and the crisp ocean air lulled her into a deep, euphoric calm. This was paradise. She wanted to drink wine and eat fish and buy flower-splashed sarongs and Hawaiian shirts in the small shops along the boardwalk. This would be a wonderful vacation spot for her parents, if Boone would leave his precious horses long enough.

The young man with a white apron around his waist brought her order. Fish, chips and wine, overlooking the sea. Why had she never indulged herself like this before? Life was meant to be enjoyed.

Gabriel's excuse for coming home in the middle of the morning the next day was to find his favorite pair of riding gloves.

His mother looked at him from under skeptical eyebrows. "You don't have gloves in your tack room?"

"Not these." He waved the pair in front of her.

"I see." She sprinkled a pinch of cumin into her casserole. "You're in time to help Whitney with her bag. She's leaving now, or maybe you already knew that."

Gabriel felt a wave of heat rise from his chest and turned away. "I'll see if she's ready," he said gruffly.

Mercedes smiled at her son's back. "You do that, *mijito.*"

He climbed the stairs two at a time. The door to her room was open. He stuck his head inside. Her tote and purse were lying on the floor, but otherwise the room was empty. He heard voices coming from the part of the house that had been converted into Claire's classroom and continued in the direction of the sound.

Whitney was leaning over Claire's shoulder, admiring a drawing. Mrs. Cook was erasing the white board.

"Who's this over here?" Whitney asked, pointing to the picture.

"It's my mom," Claire confided. "She's littler than everyone else because she isn't here anymore."

"Why does that make her little?"

"Because she's disappearing. Every day she gets smaller and smaller."

"Is it because you think you'll forget her?"

"No," the child said, her voice a perfect monotone. "I won't forget her, but she isn't a part of anything I do."

Last week, hearing those words from his child would have been like someone kicking Gabriel in the stomach with a heavy boot, but not today. From across the room, he saw a shadow pass over Whitney's face. He cleared his throat.

Claire looked up. A ghost of a smile crossed her lips. "Hi, Daddy."

"Hello, sweetheart. I thought I'd check and see if Whitney needed any help with her luggage."

"Thanks," Whitney said. "I'll take you up on that." Quickly, she kissed Claire's cheek. "Bye, now. It's been wonderful getting to know you." She waved at the teacher. "Goodbye, Mrs. Cook. Thanks for letting me interrupt."

"No problem. Have a good trip."

Gabriel followed Whitney down the stairs.

"Let me say goodbye to your mother," she said. "I'll just be a minute." She handed him her car keys. "Go ahead and put the bags in the trunk."

He was on the porch when he heard her call his name. Gabriel didn't know Whitney Benedict well enough to have seen all her moods, but he knew fear when he heard it. Dropping the bags on the porch, he raced back through the house into the kitchen. His mother was on the floor. Her right ankle was twisted at an odd angle and her face was tight with pain. Whitney handed the phone to him. "I think you should call the paramedics. We can't move her by ourselves. I'll get an ice pack together."

Gabriel looked at his mother's massive bulk, took

the phone from Whitney and punched in the numbers
911. While he gave directions and answered questions,
Whitney found the drawer with the Ziploc bags and
filled one with ice. Carefully, she applied it to Mercedes's swollen limb.

"Are you in much pain?" she asked.

Mercedes nodded, grimacing. "I don't know how it
happened. One minute I was standing and the next I was
on the floor."

"These things happen," Whitney said soothingly.
"Everything will be fine."

"But what about your plane?"

"I'll catch the next one. That's the least of our worries."

She looked around. "What about my house and the
lavender harvest? How will Gabriel manage?"

"Your daughters will help."

"No," Mercedes moaned. "Luz and John left this
morning for their anniversary cruise. Pilar can't leave
her work—she has no benefits—and how can Ramona
come? She has two babies and a new job."

Gabriel hung up the phone. "Don't worry, Ma. We'll
manage. It looks like you may have broken your ankle.
People break bones. The kids and I will help."

His mother threw him a penetrating glare. "When
will you help, *mijito?* In your spare time?"

Clearly he was exasperated. "We'll get through this.
It isn't Whitney's problem." He checked his watch. "You
can still make your plane in plenty of time if you leave
now. There's really nothing more you can do here."

Whitney looked from Mercedes to her son and back
again. The woman's forehead was beaded with perspi-
ration and Gabriel had that glazed look again, the one
he had at the police station when they picked up Emma.
She thought of Eric and Emma and Claire, and Mer-

cedes's lavender field and Ramona's babies, needy as fledgling birds. She swallowed. How long had it been since she'd done something really selfless? Who would be hurt? Not her parents. They would be merely annoyed. Her firm might be inconvenienced, but the partners would make do. She had her computer. A few things would have to be postponed, but she could do everything she needed to right here. There wasn't a single reason why she couldn't stay for another week or so.

She sat down beside Mercedes. "I think I might stay a few more days," she said softly, "just to make sure you can manage. You've been so very good to me. I'd like to repay the favor."

Gabriel shook his head. "It's out of the question. You have a job and a life that isn't here. We're not a charity case."

"Gabriel!" His mother's eyes flashed pure fire. "Where are your manners? How dare you speak to this woman in such a way? She's trying to help us. Are you so filled with false pride that you can't recognize a good deed when it's offered? I'm ashamed of you, *mijito*."

Tight-lipped, Gabriel stood. *O make in me these civil wars to cease.* "I'll wait on the porch for the paramedics."

"You do that," his mother said. She took Whitney's hand. "I apologize for my son. He is not himself to say such things to you."

"No apology is necessary. He's upset and you're right about his pride. He won't accept pity."

"You already know him well."

"I imagine everyone knows that about Gabriel."

Mercedes shifted and winced. "I don't know how this happened," she said again. "I've been walking around this kitchen for most of my life."

"Has it always been the same?" Whitney asked. She

was trying to distract Mercedes from her pain, but she was curious as well.

The woman nodded. "This is a California Historic Heritage property. My grandfather built it in 1876 for my grandmother. She came from Spain. The land grant was given to her family years before, when all of California was a Spanish colony. It was tremendous, over ten thousand acres, but that's long since been sold off. I took care of my father until he died forty years ago. Then Franz and I bought out my brothers. The kitchen has been upgraded, but otherwise not much has changed."

Whitney looked thoughtful. "I was curious about your last name. I wondered why Gabriel and your daughters use your name instead of your husband's."

"The Spanish tradition is to include the mother's name," Mercedes explained. "But that becomes cumbersome after a while. My husband was a man comfortable with himself. He knew who he was. While he never took my name, he insisted that the children carry on the Mendoza family tradition."

Whitney heard the sound of sirens. "I think your rescuers are here, Mercedes. You should be much more comfortable soon."

Claire appeared in the doorway. Mrs. Cook stood behind her. "What happened, Gran?"

"Just a little spill, *mijita*," her grandmother said. "I've sprained my ankle. Nothing serious. Come and kiss me."

Obediently, Claire walked to her grandmother's splayed body and pecked her on the cheek.

Mrs. Cook looked at her watch. "I'm not sure what to do, Mrs. Mendoza. I have another student in thirty minutes."

"Don't worry, dear. Whitney has decided to stay. She'll watch Claire."

"If you're sure—"

"Very sure."

"I'll collect my things." The teacher squeezed Claire's hand. "I'll see you tomorrow, sweetie."

Claire nodded.

Seconds later, six blue-clad medics filed into the kitchen and surrounded Mercedes. Maintaining an upbeat, casual flow of conversation, they asked questions, made notes, wrapped the woman's foot in something cold and inflated, heaved her onto a gurney with her foot elevated and wheeled her out to the ambulance idling in the driveway.

Gabriel leaned over and kissed his mother's cheek. "I'll see you there, Ma. Try not to worry."

"Who's worrying?" she said. "Whitney will be here for Claire and the children and you'll be with me. What more could I ask for? Don't forget my purse."

Expressionless, he waited until the ambulance pulled out of the driveway before turning to Whitney, who was sitting on the porch step with Claire beside her. "You don't have to stay here. We can't depend on you like this."

"Nonsense," Whitney said bracingly. "It's a great excuse to extend my vacation."

"This won't be a vacation, Whitney. I promise you that."

"What would you do if I left, Gabe?"

"I'd take Claire with me."

"What about Emma and Eric? Are you going to leave them alone for however long it takes before you can bring your mother home? What about the people who have reservations here this week? Mercedes said she was expecting guests. You're going to cook, change linen, answer the door and the phone and package lavender sachets while you're running the dressage center?"

"The lavender won't be ready to harvest for a month or so. Besides, it isn't any of your business," he said tersely.

"Be careful," she teased him. "That's hardly the attitude to take when someone is trying to be nice to you."

He turned his back and looked out over the hills.

Whitney whispered something into Claire's ear. The little girl walked over to her father and slipped her hand inside his. Some of the tension left his back.

"Why is it so hard for you to accept favors?" Whitney asked.

He shrugged. "I suppose because it means that at some point they need returning."

"Is that so bad?"

He looked down at his daughter. "Run inside, sweetheart, and work on your homework. I need to talk to Whitney."

He waited until he heard Claire's feet on the stairs. "We're not friends, Whitney. Our relationship is about business. We both know that."

The words stung. She swallowed. "I've been here for nearly a week. Your mother refused to charge me for my room, or for the delicious food she's plied me with. I like your sisters and, until a minute ago, I liked you, too. It's perfectly reasonable for me to stay and help out for a few days. Unless—"

"Unless what?"

"Unless you think I have an ulterior motive."

"Of course not," he exploded.

"It occurred to me that you might think I was staying to put more pressure on you for your horses."

His laugh was completely without humor. "You don't know what pressure is. I've got enough from my family. Compared to you, they're masters of the art."

"But I'm a visible reminder."

"Look, it isn't that." He shook his head. "Never mind. Thank you. I accept your offer. You're very generous."

She frowned. "What's bothering you, Gabe? Surely you can't be this upset over my staying longer unless I've done something to make you dislike me. Please tell me."

"You don't get it, do you?" He sat beside her on the step, his face close to hers. She held her breath. "This week is hardly typical. Claire hasn't acted up. She's behaved normally for once, more so than she has in years. Emma, except for one incident, has been good as gold. We haven't had paying guests. It's been a quiet week, an exceptional week. You have no idea what you're getting into. Normally, this place is bedlam. I fall into bed at night wondering if I can make it through another day."

Whitney looked away, allowed herself to draw breath, and looked back again. "Has it always been this way even before your wife left?"

"I didn't think about it," he said shortly. "It was just the way things were. Kristen was under a lot of pressure. I didn't know how much. I don't blame her anymore. I wish she would have talked to me. That's my only regret."

"What about your mother? I don't get the impression that she's as stretched as you are."

"I mean no disrespect—I love her very much—but my mother is nuts," he said forcefully. "She eats and drinks more than her share. That's how she gets through her days. Now that I think of it, maybe she always did. She's not exactly your typical type-A personality."

Whitney laughed. "I guess not."

"The bottom line is, this won't be easy for you. Other than a few lapses, you've basically been uninvolved. That's going to change."

"Gabe, I said I'd stay for a week, not six months. You're making too much of this."

"I'm trying to warn you. You're obviously a decent woman, warm and kind and generous. I know you want to do the right thing, but in this case, you're a babe in the woods. You don't know what it's going to take out of you."

She considered telling him about Wiley Cane and what nine months of him had taken out of her, but she decided against it. It wasn't the right time. This wasn't about her. "I'm fairly intelligent, a college graduate, efficient, logical and I can cook," she said instead. "It won't be tamales and enchiladas, but fried chicken, catfish, hush puppies, chicken-fried steak and grits won't go over too badly. It's comfort food and meant to be cooked in large amounts. If worst comes to worst, I'll send for my mother. She makes the best pecan and sweet-potato pies anyone has ever tasted."

He stood and reached down to pull her up with him. "All right, Whitney. I can see there's no changing your mind. Consider yourself warned. I'm usually somewhere at the center during the day and in my office at night. Drop by anytime you want to complain. I'll understand, believe me. Feel free to ask if you need anything. There's an open account at the local market for food. I'll authorize you to charge on it. Otherwise, you're on your own. My mother has her own system. I have no idea what it is. No one will be offended if you want to try something different. God knows I'm grateful to you. I don't think I've said that, have I?"

"Not yet."

Again he grinned. Ten years faded from his face, and once again, Whitney's breath caught.

"Consider it said. I'm very grateful you're doing this for us."

Slowly, so he wouldn't notice, she inhaled. "You're welcome."

"If you don't mind keeping Claire with you, I'll be on my way to the hospital. All the phone numbers you'll need, including my cell, are posted in the kitchen next to the refrigerator. I'll call when I get a chance."

"Don't worry about a thing."

He looked as if he would have liked to say something else, but decided against it. Whitney watched him walk to his truck, wave once and drive away. Only then did she pick up her bags and turn back to the house.

Thirteen

After carrying her luggage back to the room she had recently vacated, Whitney made her way down to the kitchen. Claire sat at the table drinking a glass of milk.

"Well," Whitney said bracingly. "What should we do now?"

Claire didn't respond. She kept her eyes downcast.

"Is there anything I can help you with? Homework, maybe?"

Still no response. Whitney suppressed a wave of panic. Would Claire choose this time to slip into one of her spells? She desperately wanted her computer and its world of information available at the touch of her fingertips. Could she leave the little girl alone? She made an instant decision.

"I'll be right back," she said, and ran up the stairs to her room. Grabbing her computer bag, she dashed back to the kitchen. Claire hadn't moved.

"Thank goodness I didn't leave this at home," she said conversationally, not expecting an answer. "I had no idea I'd be staying this long." Quickly, she plugged in the computer and touched the power button. Immediately, the familiar Windows icon glowed from the screen. She located her browser and had just finished typing in the word *autism* when the phone rang. Whitney picked up the receiver. "Hello?"

An unfamiliar voice asked for Mercedes Mendoza.

"She's not available right now. This is Whitney Benedict. May I help you?"

"I'm Amy Patterson. My mother and I have reservations for two nights," the voice said. "I thought I'd let you know we'll be there about six o'clock."

Whitney's heart sank. "Thank you for calling." A thought occurred to her. "Do you have any food preferences?"

"I think I mentioned that my mother is elderly. She has trouble with anything spicy. But other than that…"

"Great," Whitney replied. "We'll expect you at six. I hope you enjoy your stay here."

"We're here for a funeral, Ms. Benedict. I thought Mrs. Mendoza knew that."

"I'm so sorry." Embarrassed, Whitney vowed in the future to say only what was necessary. She hung up the phone. "I blew that one," she said to the stoic Claire.

She looked at her watch. "Maybe you could do your homework down here with me while I work on the computer. Or else, we could check out the refrigerator and see if we need anything at the store. If not, we could visit the horses at the dressage center. What do you think?"

Was that the merest flicker of an eyelash? Was there something going on behind that expressionless little face? Whitney decided to allow the options she'd offered to percolate while she did a little research of her own.

She chose a Web site that offered definitions of autism, and began reading. Immediately her interest was piqued. Apparently there were different degrees of the condition, and different approaches to treatment and no true biological test, although heredity played an important role. Whitney glanced at Claire. She had finished her milk. There was no indication she was aware anyone else was in the room.

Once again Whitney focused on the computer screen. The first description offered up by the autism Web site certainly didn't fit Claire. She'd never seen the child mouth objects or throw tantrums, but then, she'd only been here a few days shy of a week. Scrolling down to the next section, the words *Asberger's syndrome* caught her eye. Now, this was more like it. Children with Asberger's didn't function normally in social situations, although they appeared to act and speak normally in familiar surroundings. *They were insensitive to the feelings of others, lacking compassion,* the article said, *focusing on compulsive behaviors. School settings were particularly disastrous, causing regressive, sometimes dangerous behaviors.* Whitney had seen Claire pull into herself, refusing to communicate or socialize, but her behavior wasn't dangerous. She was a little girl, for heaven's sake. How *dangerous* could she be?

The article did say there were degrees of the disease and that some children responded remarkably well to a diet without gluten, dairy products and corn. Whitney winced, recalling the glass of milk Claire had just consumed and the rich carbohydrate bounty Mercedes served her family several times a day. Had Gabriel or his mother ever considered limiting Claire's diet?

She glanced at the child's bowed head. Did she dare try it or was she presuming too much? Maybe if she spoke to Gabriel, he would agree to an experiment. Whitney turned off the computer and stored it away in its bag. Then she opened the pantry door and began examining the shelves. Corn meal, sugar, flour, white and whole wheat, raw beans, rice and baking ingredients were stored on the top shelves. Canned goods and condiments, soups, tomatoes, artichokes, olives and every imaginable oil and vinegar were at eye level. Just below these, a plethora of spices, coffee, tea, dried fruit and nuts had been labeled and arranged in alphabetical order. When it came to food, Mercedes was organized and practical. Whitney was intrigued. Could her true personality be hidden among these shelves? The food wasn't terribly promising for what she had in mind, but it certainly wasn't impossible. She would stick to the refrigerator and fresh produce: vegetables, meat, chicken and fish, rice and fruit, healthy food, diet food, certainly not the menu most people would expect at an established bed-and-breakfast.

She turned to find Claire directly behind her. "I want to see Lorelei," the child said.

Slowly, Whitney released her breath. "I think that can be arranged. Run upstairs and change your clothes while I check on the guest rooms. I'll meet you down here in fifteen minutes."

She was both rewarded and puzzled by Claire's flashing smile. It was almost as if the little girl was blocked, unable to show her emotions at certain times and not others. There was certainly nothing wrong with her reaction now.

Whitney wandered through the guest rooms. Four were available. The two at the back of the house had adjoining balconies overlooking the patio. The sheets were crisply laundered and crystal vases filled with fresh flowers and stalks of lavender lent a subtle scent to the air. Mercedes must have prepared for her guests early this morning. The rooms shared a bath, but they were also the most private. She had no idea who had reserved the remaining two bedrooms. A thought occurred to her. Maybe Mercedes had counted on having all of her rooms available, even the one Whitney hadn't vacated.

She fluffed the pillows, cracked a window and resolved not to worry until the problem actually existed. She had yet to stock the refrigerator with food she knew how to cook, call her office and her mother, in that order, and supervise Claire in the dressage ring. Glancing at her watch, she decided against disturbing Gabriel. He would call with an update when he had a chance.

After pulling on her own boots, she met Claire, dressed in riding breeches and a helmet, at the foot of the stairs. Their walk through the field to the center wasn't filled with conversation, but the silence was neither unusual nor uncomfortable. The minute they reached the parking lot, Claire broke away and raced to Lorelei's stall. Juan was slipping the halter over the mare's head.

"You're just in time, *niña*," he said. "She's already groomed. I'll saddle her for you. Your papa said you might be here this morning." He smiled at Whitney. "Gabriel called. How are you managing?"

"I haven't done anything yet," confessed Whitney. "I thought Claire might like a little reward before lunch."

Juan nodded. "I've seen you in action. If you want to ride, we can find a mount for you. The lower ring is empty."

"Thanks, but not today. I'll take Claire out for about an hour or so."

He handed the child the lead rope. "She's all yours. I'll get the saddle."

Claire beamed. She rubbed the mare's forehead and

leaned against her flank. Then she pulled a carrot from the feed bag hanging on the door and, leaving it flat on the palm of her hand, held it under the animal's velvety mouth. It disappeared immediately. "I'll give you another one when we're through," she promised.

Juan returned with the saddle and pad. After he'd tightened the girth, he clasped his hands and offered Claire a leg up. Without hesitation, Claire picked up the reins with her left hand, grabbed the withers and placed her knee in the human grip. She nodded at the groom. "I'm ready."

He lifted her to the saddle, waited for her to settle in and then adjusted the stirrup leathers, rechecked the girth and stepped back. "Well done. Don't overdue it, now. Start slow."

"I will." She grinned at Whitney. "Let's go."

Whitney stepped back. "After you."

Permission was all Claire needed. Expertly, she guided the mare out of the barn and down the path to the exercise ring. Whitney followed. She leaned against the fence and watched approvingly. Her own preference had been the hunt seat. She had jumped horses, never attempting the ballet movements of dressage, but that didn't mean she wasn't familiar with them. She recognized the straight back and deep-seat requirements of modern dressage. Claire had them down, even to the animal's self-carriage and well-rounded outline. Gabriel had chosen well for his daughter's mount. The horse was beautifully trained and the little girl was obviously an able student. Whitney wondered if she would respond to animals other than horses. The Mendozas had no house pets, and yet Claire spent most of her time at home. It was something she would bring up with Gabriel.

Her cell phone rang, and reluctantly Whitney pulled

it from her pocket. This time, Everett Sloane wouldn't be appeased.

"What's going on, Whitney?"

Somehow, Mercedes's fall and the plight of her family sounded weaker over the phone than it had in Whitney's mind when she'd volunteered to stay and help out. "This has been a difficult decision for the Mendozas. The least I can do is stay for a few more days."

"It escapes me how the two are related."

"It's difficult to explain over the phone. You'll have to trust me."

The silence on the other end of the open line made her nervous. "Everett, are you still there?"

"You are telling me everything, aren't you, Whitney?"

"What do you mean?"

"That's better. For a while there you didn't sound like a lawyer."

"Give me one more week."

"What in the hell am I supposed to tell Kincaid? And what about the conference call?"

"Tell them the sale is in the bag and I'm taking a much deserved vacation. One week can't make that much difference."

"It is in the bag, isn't it, Whitney?"

She drew a deep breath and closed her eyes. "Yes," she said, and punched the off button.

Before she could talk herself out of it, she called her mother. "In for a penny, in for a pound," she muttered under her breath.

Pryor Benedict stared at the phone in disbelief. She couldn't believe what she'd just heard from her daughter's mouth. Whitney wasn't coming home. She wasn't coming home because the woman she'd been staying with had *broken a bone*. What on earth was going on? Carefully, Pryor replaced the receiver and fanned her face with her hand. She made a mental note to open the windows in the front room. But not now. First, Boone needed to hear this.

She let herself out the front door, walking across the grass to the stables. Her husband was deep in conversation with Lewis Markham, the previous owner of Turkish Delight, a three-year-old Thoroughbred Boone had picked up for a song because of the Markhams' nasty divorce. Normally Pryor would have returned to the house, but not tonight. Tonight, she was not in the mood to wait. She tapped her foot impatiently.

Boone waved her over. "Hi, hon. I was just telling Lew I'd like to give Turk here another year before racing him."

"You do what you think best, Boone."

"He'll be four by then," the man protested. "You'll lose millions, and so will I, if he misses out on the Derby."

Boone chuckled. "I wouldn't go so far as to say millions, son. Thousands, possibly, but I'd just as soon not race an untried, California-trained horse. He can't run in mud and he doesn't know the tracks. Our turf is different. So are our winters. I mean no offense, but he's not Kentucky bred. Others will have the advantage. We can't rush him. He'll make plenty of money without the Derby."

Tight-lipped with anger, Markham turned away.

Boone looked at his wife. She raised her eyebrows significantly. He shrugged and went after him. Pryor flushed.

"Listen, Lew," she heard her husband say. "I know something's not sitting right with you. Think about it, sleep on it and we'll talk it over in the morning." He held out his hand. "Fair enough?"

Grudgingly, the younger man accepted the olive branch. He nodded at Pryor before walking away.

"Poor kid," Boone said, his voice laced with sympathy. "It's hard giving up control but—."

Pryor interrupted him. "Whitney called."

Her husband's face lit up. "What did she have to say?"

"She's not coming home."

"Why not?"

"That Mendoza woman broke a bone."

Boone frowned. "What's that got to do with Whitney?"

"My point exactly. I don't know what's gotten into her. I'm beginning to think she's relocating to California."

"Nonsense. Her life is here."

"What if it isn't? What if she's gotten herself into something she'll regret?"

Their eyes met and the name *Wiley Cane,* unspoken but very much there, rose up between them.

Boone was the first to regain his good sense. "Whitney's not a kid anymore, Pryor. She's a grown woman, a sensible woman. We both want her to be happy. If she's met someone, he'll be worthy of her."

"What if it's Gabriel Mendoza?"

"Then he must be a hell of a guy."

Pryor could barely speak. "You can't mean that. He's divorced. He lives with his mother and he has custody of three children, two of whom aren't even his, and the one who is has been diagnosed with autism."

Boone attempted to console his wife by wrapping his arm around her shoulders. She shrugged him off.

"How do you know all this?" he asked.

"How do you think? Whitney told me."

"If she told you all that, she's not interested in him," Boone said flatly.

"What's that supposed to mean?"

"Stop and think a minute, Pryor. Has Whitney ever come clean with us about anyone she's seeing?" He used the diplomatic *us* on purpose.

"Your point, please?"

This time he took her hand and she did not pull away. "Whitney would rather chug rubbing alcohol than have us give her the third-degree about who she's dating. She's been that way ever since she was a kid. She knows we don't approve easily."

Pryor sniffed. "She can hardly blame us, not after Wiley."

"Maybe not," Boone agreed. "Still, it can't be easy on her having to get her parents' approval. She's thirty-seven years old, honey. If she doesn't know what she wants now, she never will. All we're doing is making her tighten up like a rat in a chokehold. You know what I think?"

"No, Boone," she said. "What do you think?"

He ignored her tone. "It's like this. Whitney's like one of those catfish down there in the creek. They won't have anything to do with you if you try too hard, no matter what kind of bait you offer up. But if you pretend you aren't looking, and your line is floating easy in the water, they'll snap so fast your head'll spin."

Pryor looked steadily at the man she'd been married to for nearly forty years. She could tell him that his analogy was absurd, that Whitney was no more a catfish than she was a polar bear, but there would be no point. Once Boone settled on an idea, it was as hard to part him from it as it was to separate a fly from a honey stick. She'd been foolish to think she would get satisfaction from sharing this new information with him. He was only a man. Men always wanted a quick fix.

Pryor didn't want resolution. She wanted to discuss

and analyze, inspect her daughter's every little word, turn every nuance inside and out. Whitney's phone call had pushed her into irrational behavior, namely searching out the first human in the vicinity. She should have known better than to ask her husband to satisfy the insatiable need she had for examination. What she needed was a woman's ear, a woman's voice, the sensible, sane advice of a kindred spirit. She would call Lila Rae. Lila Rae was her godmother and her aunt, and a font of wisdom—if Pryor reached her before she dipped too deeply into the sherry.

She patted her husband on the shoulder and turned back to the house. "Never mind, honey," she said over her shoulder. "I'll go back inside now. Take your time. I haven't started dinner yet and I still have a phone call to make."

Fourteen

Gabe called just as Whitney lugged the last bag of groceries in from the car.

"There's nothing wrong with her leg," he said. "Nothing more than a sprain, not even a bad one, but they want to keep her overnight, anyway. Her cholesterol and blood pressure are off the charts. Apparently she hasn't seen a doctor since Pilar was born."

"You're joking."

"I wish I was. Maybe this fall saved her life." He sounded more angry than worried. "Her eating habits are out of control and she drinks too much."

Whitney didn't know how to respond. It didn't seem appropriate to agree with him. She couldn't very well vilify the woman who'd been so good to her. "Will you be staying with her?" she ventured.

"I'll stay until I've talked to her doctor, then I'll buy her a few magazines and make sure she's comfortable. I should be home for dinner. How's Claire?"

"You can ask her yourself." Whitney handed the phone to Claire. "It's your dad. He wants to talk to you."

"Hi, Daddy," she said. "I rode Lorelei today. Whitney took me and then we went out to lunch. She was just perfect, Daddy. You should have seen her." Claire pinched off a cluster of grapes, tucked the phone against her shoulder and disappeared into the living room.

Whitney wondered if Gabe would make the leap in subject from horse to woman and back to horse again as easily as his daughter had. She began unloading food from the bags. The back door opened and slammed shut.

Eric appeared at the entrance to the kitchen with Emma close behind. He saw Whitney first. "I thought you were leaving today."

"I was, but your grandmother had an accident."

He paled. "Is she okay?"

"Actually, yes. She sprained her ankle, but it's not serious. The doctor wants to keep her in the hospital overnight for tests. Your dad should be home early this evening."

Emma peered over his shoulder. "Why are you still here?"

"Your grandmother has rented out her rooms. I volunteered to stay and help out until she's back."

"That's really nice of you," Eric said, "but we can help. You shouldn't have to stay because of us or the B and B. Emma and I can handle it." He looked at his sister. "Right, Emma?"

Surprisingly, she agreed with him. "Right. It's not exactly rocket science."

"Maybe there's more to it than you think," Whitney said gently. "After all, you have school."

"If they're only keeping her overnight, what's the big deal?" asked Eric.

"The tests might reveal something more serious. Your dad needs a little time to figure things out. Your grandmother has hurt her leg. She may not be able to get around very well."

Emma's eyes narrowed. "I suppose you're just the one to help Dad out, aren't you?"

Eric flushed. "Knock it off, Emma. She's just trying to be nice."

"Oh, is that what you call it?"

"Excuse me," Whitney interrupted. "I have no idea what you're imagining, Emma, but it sounds ridiculous. Now, if either of you wants to talk to your dad, he's on the phone with Claire right now. When you're finished, I could use some help with dinner and the dishes. Two ladies are arriving at six o'clock tonight for a funeral tomorrow. I'd like one of you to explain the routine to me. Will they expect anything tonight other than their rooms or am I off the hook until breakfast?"

Emma looked mutinous.

Eric spoke up. "Gran usually invites people to the patio for appetizers if the weather's nice, otherwise it's tea in the living room in front of the fire."

Whitney folded her arms. "Well, which is it today, nice or not?" It had to be about seventy degrees, but Calfornians wore Ugg boots and wool long after the rest of the world had gratefully shed their winter clothes.

"I'd say it's a little cold," he replied. "I'll lay a fire in the fireplace while Emma talks to Dad on the phone. I'll show you where everything is."

"I bought some pastries from the bakery in town. Will that be okay? I'm not much of a cook."

"Pastries sound great." He nudged his sister. "Don't they, Emma?"

Emma turned on her heel. "I'm going to talk to Dad," she said over her shoulder.

Eric shook his head. "I apologize, Ms. Benedict. Emma's been…different, lately."

"What's going on? Is there something I should know?"

"I'm not sure. I think she misses my mom. I could be wrong. She doesn't say anything to me. We're not exactly close. I don't think anybody's close to Emma."

Whitney saw a look of anguish flash across his expression. A look like that had no business showing up on the face of a sixteen-year-old boy.

"If you'll show me where I can find a teapot and cups, I'll be eternally grateful," she said gently.

He pulled out that and more: serving plates, delicate silver spoons and knives, dessert forks, lacy white napkins and bone china. "This is what Gran normally uses for tea. If you think you can handle it from here, I'll go over to the dressage center. It's my day to help Juan."

It wasn't the first time Eric had surprised her. He was giving her a whole new perspective on the word *teenager.* "Go ahead," she urged him. "I'll manage. I might even be able to recruit Emma."

He rolled his eyes. "Good luck. Even Gran can't make her do what she doesn't want to do."

Whitney laughed. "It doesn't matter. I'll be fine. Do whatever you need to do."

He grinned, obviously relieved. "Good luck. I'll be back around six."

She heard his footsteps clatter on the stairs. Turning to the task at hand, she mentally organized the next hour. After filling the sugar bowl and creamer, she arranged the pastries on the smaller platter and began chopping strawberries, kiwi, grapes and bananas for a fruit salad. After the perishables had been refrigerated and the pastries covered, she started on dinner: broccoli, pan-roasted chicken, rice and a green salad, a simple meal that fit the dietary restrictions she'd read about on the Asberger's syndrome Web page.

It was satisfying cooking for a family. She'd never done it before. At home, Pryor was in complete control of the kitchen. Whitney had never made more than a snack for herself when her mother was around.

She decided that the family would eat dinner in the dining room thirty minutes after the ladies were served their tea in the living room. The couch and chair near the fire were cozy and private.

Humming to herself, Whitney called the girls from the bottom of the stairwell. "Claire and Emma, I need help setting the table." After waiting for what she considered to be a reasonable amount of time with no response, she climbed the stairs. Emma's bedroom door was closed. She knocked. "Emma, I need your help setting the table."

Still, no response. Whitney cracked the door and peeked in. Emma was lying on the bed. She wore earphones and her eyes were closed. The steady beat of a bass drum rattled the wood floors.

"Hello," Whitney shouted.

Emma's opened her eyes, looked at Whitney and closed them again.

Whitney considered her options. Deciding against physical violence, she located the plug and pulled it.

Emma sat up and tore the earphones off her head. "What do you think you're doing?"

"Please come downstairs and set the table," Whitney said calmly.

"I'm busy."

"So am I."

"No."

"Excuse me?" Whitney's eyes flashed dangerously.

"I said no. I'm not hungry and I'm not going to set the table."

"I see. Does that mean you won't be joining us for dinner?"

"That's what it means."

"All right," Whitney said. "Since you're not eating, I won't ask you to help clean up, but I still need your help with the table. You and Claire know where everything is. I don't."

"You should have thought of that before you volunteered to stay here."

Maintaining eye contact, Whitney walked across the room and sat down on the bed beside Emma. Keeping her voice steady and low, she spoke carefully. "I'm not asking you, Emma. I'm telling you to come downstairs and set the table. Your dad has had a tough day and your brother can't do everything on his own. If you don't have enough shame to treat your family better than you do, that's your problem. I'm leaving soon. Your appalling manners and selfishness don't matter to me in the least. But I will tell you this. Don't underestimate me. I can be a very scary enemy. Consider this a threat. If you aren't downstairs in three minutes, you'll be very, very sorry."

With that she left the room. Claire stood at the top of the stairs looking down. Whitney held her breath. Slowly the child turned, saw Whitney and smiled. Breathing a sigh of relief, she reached for Claire's hand and led her into the kitchen. "Can you find everything to set the table?" she asked.

Claire nodded. "I always set the table."

"Good. What does Emma do?"

"Whatever Gran tells her."

"Tonight she's going to help you." *If she comes downstairs,* Whitney thought to herself. She had absolutely no idea what to do if Emma called her bluff and stayed in her room. How did mothers do it? Whitney's respect for Pryor rose several notches.

"The plates we use are up there." Claire pointed to a cupboard near the refrigerator.

Whitney pulled out five plates and set them on the island. "What about glasses and salad plates?"

"I'll get those." Claire pulled out a stepping stool, climbed on it and opened another cupboard. She picked out six glasses, one at a time, thought a minute and put one back.

Whitney turned away. She would help if she was asked, but not until then. Busying herself with chopping the salad vegetables, she didn't hear Emma slink into the room. Suddenly she was beside Claire, silently folding napkins and filling glasses with water. Deliberately, she avoided meeting Whitney's eyes.

"How was Mrs. Cook today, Claire?" she asked her sister.

"Okay."

"What did she read to you?"

"We started a new book. *Island of the Blue Dolphins.*"

"That's a good one. I'll read you a chapter later."

"I'll read a page and you read one," Claire negotiated.

"Sounds good."

Whitney set the water to boil for the tea. Maybe she was too hard on Emma. The girl had a heart after all, or maybe the whole family had a soft spot for Claire.

The doorbell rang. Whitney wiped her hands on the dish towel and left the kitchen to answer the door. Expecting two women, she was surprised to see a uniformed officer of the county sheriff's department. He held an envelope in his hand. She recognized it immediately. "May I help you?" she asked.

"I'm here to see Gabriel Mendoza. Is he around?"

"I'm afraid not."

"Do you happen to know where I might find him?"

"Not at the moment."

"Are you aware of the penalty for lying to a police officer?"

She stiffened. She'd heard the question a thousand times before, but this time it raised her hackles. "As a matter of fact, I am," she said crisply. "I'm an attorney. Now, if you'll excuse me, I'll take your card and tell Gabriel that you stopped by. I'm sure he'll call you as soon as possible."

"Do that." He handed her his card. "I'll be in touch."

Whitney closed the door and leaned against it. Who would be sending Gabriel a summons? Maybe someone had been injured at the dressage center. From the window she watched the squad car drive away.

"Who was that?" Emma's voice was near her ear.

Whitney turned quickly. "A police officer."

The girl's eyes widened. "What did he want?"

"To see your dad."

Emma's nervousness seemed out of the ordinary.

"Is something wrong?" Whitney asked.

"No," Emma said quickly. "Other than the other night, nothing at all."

Whitney decided not to pursue it. Emma was not her responsibility.

"The table's set," the girl said. "Is there anything else?"

"Thanks. That's it, I think, unless you want to take care of waiting for the Pattersons and helping with their luggage."

Emma shrugged. "Whatever. I'll listen for the bell upstairs."

"Good." Whitney smiled. "I'll finish dinner and set

out everything for tea if you think you can handle it alone."

"Gran usually sets out the stuff and invites them down. If they show up, she brings a pot of tea. That's all there is to it."

"I'll keep that in mind."

Emma rolled her eyes. "Like I said before, it's not exactly rocket science."

Whitney looked around. "Where's Claire?"

"Upstairs. I'm going to help her with her times tables."

"That's very nice of you."

"Who else does she have?" Emma replied scathingly. "No Dad, no Mom, no Gran, no Eric." She ticked them off on her fingers, then looked at Whitney. "I guess I forgot about you, didn't I?"

"That's not really fair, is it, Emma?" Whitney asked gently, ignoring the reference to her. "Accidents happen."

"I know that. And they usually happen to us."

Whitney turned back to the kitchen. She wondered what Pryor would make of this worldly teenager with her sullen disposition and her scornful perspective of the world. Maybe it would make her rethink her position on grandchildren. Now, if she could just get the food on the table all at the same time, while it was still reasonably warm, she would consider her first day in charge a success.

Gabriel arrived at the same time as the Patterson ladies. He carried in their luggage, answered their questions, smiled politely and disappeared into his room. Emma, true to her word and dressed more conservatively than usual in a jeans skirt and sweater, showed them to the living room and poured tea.

Eric stuck his head into the kitchen. "Do you need anything or can I clean up before dinner?"

"Go ahead," replied Whitney. "I'll dish everything up in fifteen minutes."

Somehow it all fell into place. Whitney, with Claire's help, carried the food to the table and all the Mendozas, Emma included, slid into their seats at approximately six o'clock.

"This is great," said Eric. He reached for the chicken. "What is it?"

"Pan-roasted chicken breasts with mushrooms. It's a staple of my mother's, her impossible-to-mess-up recipe."

"I don't how to thank you, Whitney," Gabriel said. "You've made everything much easier."

The glow she felt in her cheeks disappeared with Emma's snort. She ignored her. "Thank you," she replied, "but it's the least I can do. Your mother's been very gracious to me."

"She wants to marry Dad off and you're here," Emma said under her breath.

Gabriel's eyes narrowed. "Is there something you want to say, Emma?"

Emma pushed the food around on her plate. "A cop came by today."

Gabriel finished chewing. His voice was deliberately calm. "Any particular reason?"

Emma shrugged. "Not that I know of. Ask her." She jerked a thumb at Whitney. "She's the one who talked to him."

"Is that so?" He glanced at Whitney. "I'm sure if it was important, she would tell me."

Whitney dabbed at the corners of her mouth with her napkin. "Actually, I have no idea what he wanted, other than to talk to you. When I told him you weren't here, he said he'd come back."

Gabriel nodded. "It doesn't sound like there's anything we can do about it now, so I'm for enjoying this delicious meal." He looked around the table. "Eat up, everybody, and be grateful. If Gran can't cook for a while, and when Whitney goes home, you'll be stuck with my cooking."

Collectively, all three children groaned. Gabe grinned. "I guess that means you're hired, Whitney."

She laughed. "I'm flattered."

Later, after the older children had gone upstairs and Gabe had tucked Claire into bed, he came back down to the kitchen to help Whitney with the last of the dishes. "Tell me about our visitor," he said.

Whitney hung up the towel and turned to him. "He had a summons."

"Are you sure?"

"Absolutely. He had the attitude and the envelope."

"Damn. I didn't think she'd do it."

Whitney tilted her head. "Are you in trouble, Gabe?"

"You might say that. It's Lynne, my mother-in-law. She wants to take the two older kids away from me."

"Why?"

"It's not personal. Lynne has nothing against me. My guess is she's feeling guilty since Kristen deserted us. She's stepping up to the plate because Eric and Emma aren't mine. She's trying to do the right thing."

"How do the kids feel about it?"

"Eric wants to stay. No one ever knows what Emma wants."

"How far will the woman go?"

"About as far as she has to, I guess." Gabe ran his hand through his hair. "She's got great timing. I'll say that for her. I sure didn't need this right now."

Personally Whitney agreed with him. She didn't remind him of the obvious: the proceeds from the sale of his horses would more than pay for the best family law attorney in Ventura County.

Fifteen

"Knock, knock." Ramona, holding one baby on her hip and another by the hand, poked her head inside the back door of the kitchen. "Is anyone home?"

Whitney laughed. "Where else would I be at eight o'clock in the morning? The kids just left for school, Mrs. Cook is with Claire and there are two women upstairs who asked to have breakfast served at 9:00 a.m. sharp."

Ramona looked at the cluttered counter. "My goodness. What are you attempting to make?"

"I thought about scrambled eggs, some bacon, toast and fruit."

Ramona shook her head. "There's an easier way." She handed Whitney the baby in her arm and picked up the other one. "Wait a minute and I'll get the playpen from the car. I know it's not politically correct nowadays to cage your children, but sometimes, difficult circumstances require extreme measures. I'll be right back."

After she'd gone, Whitney stared into the chubby little face close to her own. The baby stared back, his eyes round and curious. Tentatively, she smiled. The toddler smiled, too. "Hi," she said.

"Hi," he parroted.

A wave of pleasure surged through her. "What a cutie pie you are. What's your name?"

"That's a little beyond him," Ramona said from behind her. She clutched her son around the middle with one arm and with the other dragged the folded playpen behind her. "I'll set this up and then help you with breakfast and any other meals you need."

"Thank goodness," Whitney said feelingly.

Ramona deposited the baby on the floor, opened the playpen, threw some toys inside and stabilized the frame. Then she set both boys inside. "That should take care of them for a while."

"I really appreciate this," said Whitney.

Ramona glanced at her. "I should be thanking you. This is my family. What you're doing for us is probably the most generous act I've heard of in a long time. It's the least I can do."

Whitney smiled. "Frankly, I'm enjoying it. It's a completely different kind of challenge than I'm used to." She changed the subject. "What's wrong with bacon and eggs?"

"The timing is too important. People have to be ready and waiting and everything has to be hot at the same time. I'd go for strata, croissants, coffee cake, sausage and fruit. Ma has chafing dishes for the strata and sausage. Everything else can be set right on the table ahead of time along with the juice. Don't forget dry cereal, the milk pitcher and coffee."

Whitney hesitated. "I'm not sure about strata. I've never made one before."

Ramona grinned, suddenly looking very like Gabriel. "That's where I come in. Chef's school comes in handy. Let's see what you've got in the refrigerator." She opened the door and pulled out cheese, eggs, green onions, peppers, fresh herbs and ham. "So far, so good. See if there's any focaccia bread in the pantry. If not, just pull out some chewy sourdough. That works just as well."

Sooner than Whitney expected, the strata was in the oven, the fruit chopped and arranged, sausage sizzling in a skillet and Ramona was sifting ingredients for the coffee cake.

"You're amazing," Whitney said. "It's beautiful and elegant. I could never have come up with anything like this."

Ramona stirred the wet ingredients into a well in the flour mixture. "You're a lawyer, not a cook." She poured the batter into a greased pan, tapped it on the counter and stuck it into the preheated convection oven. "Where's Gabriel?"

"At the dressage center. He didn't go in at all yesterday."

"Has he told you what he's going to do about Lynne?"

Whitney kept her eyes on the counter she was wiping down. "Lynne?"

"The children's other grandmother."

"No."

Ramona sighed. "It's a shame, really. Lynne has no idea what she's getting into. I almost wish she *would* take the kids. They'd be right back here within a month."

"Do you really think so?"

Ramona shrugged. "Who knows? She's stubborn. It's possible she'd have a hard time admitting she couldn't handle them."

"I guess Gabriel loves them very much," Whitney ventured, not quite comfortable with discussing the situation with Ramona, but curious enough to continue the conversation.

"He's had them since they were babies. Kristen's ex-husband has never been in the picture. Gabriel is the only father they've known. It worked out well for a while, until Claire was about two and it was obvious something was wrong." She washed her hands and dried them on a towel. "She's improved tremendously because she was diagnosed early. Still, Kristen couldn't handle her alone. That's when Gabe moved them in here, hoping Ma could help when Kristen couldn't take any more. We all thought things were better. I guess they weren't. Kristen left and Emma's been acting up ever since. She's always in trouble." Ramona sighed. "It might be the best thing for Gabe if Lynne took her."

"She's asking for Eric, too."

"That would be a shame. Eric and Gabe are close."

"Eric is sixteen," Whitney said carefully. "That's old enough to choose who he wants to live with."

Ramona poured two cups of coffee and carried them to the table. "Come on. We deserve a break and I don't know how much longer the twins will last." She looked at her watch. "Your ladies are due down here shortly. We'll hear them on the stairs."

Whitney joined her at one corner of the sunlit table. She busied herself with the mindless, homey tasks of pouring cream and stirring sugar.

Ramona continued the conversation. "California courts usually side with blood relatives, even when it seems ridiculous. Besides, lawyers and court battles are expensive. Danny's brother has been trying to win a fair custody and child support settlement for two years. He's spent tens of thousands of dollars and not much has changed."

"Gabriel could have tens of thousands of dollars," Whitney reminded her, "and we're not talking about giving the children to a mother who's been the major caregiver. A woman in her seventies may not be considered the best guardian for two teenagers."

Ramona looked at her with Gabriel's blue-green eyes. "May I ask you a personal question?"

"Of course."

"Please don't be offended. I'm just curious."

"Go on."

"Are you interested in my brother for personal reasons? Is that why you're here?"

Whitney opened her mouth to deny the preposterous allegation, but Ramona cut her off before she could speak. Her words were rushed, embarrassed, and obviously sincere.

"It's ridiculous, I know, for me to think someone like you would even look twice at a man with Gabe's baggage. But if you are interested, even a little, I want you to know that he's a quality person. He's educated and sensitive and loyal. He has so many interests outside of horses and the dressage center. You haven't had any time to get to know him properly, away from all these other distractions, but if there's even the slightest chance, I wanted to put in a good word." She smiled shyly at Whitney. "You're a quality person, too. I think it would give my brother such a boost of confidence to know someone like you is attracted to him, even if it didn't come to anything." Her smile faded. "As long as he doesn't get hurt. I couldn't bear it if Gabriel was hurt again."

Whitney was speechless. She stared at the dark-haired woman for a long minute. Then she smiled. "I'm flattered," she said. "You've given me a tremendous compliment."

"But?"

Whitney laughed and gave herself some time by sipping her coffee. "Has anyone ever told you that you're incredibly direct?"

"All the time," Ramona said candidly. "You're not answering the question."

"I don't know how to answer it," Whitney said slowly. "I've never even considered Gabe in those terms." That was an outright lie. She was ashamed of herself in the face of the other woman's blunt honesty, but ethically she couldn't answer any other way. "Gabe is attractive and intelligent," she continued, "but I live in Kentucky and I may be representing a client in a transaction that involves him."

"And yet you're here, cooking and cleaning in his kitchen and caring for his children. How do you explain that?"

"I don't know," Whitney answered, looking around. "There's something about this place. I wanted to help out." She shrugged. "It's nice to be needed in ways no one's ever expected of me before. Does that make sense?"

"Not entirely."

"I'll try to explain. At home, I'm my mother's daughter. When I visit my parents, I fall into the role of the child-come-home. My mother feeds me, asks questions about my job, my love life, my prospects, my health. My dad talks horses with me and asks more questions about my job, my love life, my prospects and my health. I live in a town house with two bedrooms, a small yard and very little in the refrigerator except a bottle of wine, tomato juice and a tub of cottage cheese. At my office, I diplomatically work at bringing people of vastly different cultures, ethnicities and experiences together and politely coerce them into agreeing with one another and then cementing those agreements with a written contract. Do you see where I'm going with this?"

"Vaguely."

"This—" she waved her hand to encompass the room "—is a completely different world for me. No one has preconceived notions of who I am or how I'm supposed to behave. No one expects me to be Whitney Benedict, international relations attorney. It's restful. An entirely different part of my brain is being used. Here, I'm working on a timetable with different consequences if I don't pan out. I'm enjoying your family, Gabe's family." She wet her lips. What was it about this young woman who inspired such confidences? "My mother's desperate to have grandchildren," she continued. "Until now I thought I didn't want what she wanted. I'm giving myself this opportunity, a short one, I admit, to see if I might want it after all."

"In other words, you're using Gabe and his immediate family to see if you might want one of your own, a different one?"

"I guess so, although it isn't as cold-blooded as it sounds and there are circumstances I'd rather not discuss at the moment." She looked directly at Ramona. "Gabe does need help right now. Are you offended?"

Ramona searched her face. Whitney held her breath until she saw the woman's smile.

"Be careful, Whitney," she warned. "You might become emotionally involved with a man, three children and a custody battle."

"I don't think it will come to that."

"How can you be so sure?"

"For one thing, Gabe doesn't appear to be the least bit interested in me romantically."

Ramona's eyes were very blue in the perfect oval of

her face. "If you say so." She jumped up. "I've got to get the boys home. Do you need me to stay or can you manage on your own?"

"I'll be fine," said Whitney. "Thanks again."

"No problem. Call if you get stuck. I'll check on you later with a few suggestions for dinner."

Whitney helped her pack up. She watched while each toddler was strapped into his car seat.

Ramona spoke to her twins in a singsong baby voice. "Say bye-bye to Whitney."

They drove away in a harmony of waves and good-byes and Whitney turned back to the kitchen.

Gabriel waved the horse and rider in. He waited by the gate until the woman was close enough to hear. "You're not focusing, Shelly," he began. "When you turn you need to remember to adjust your position. Your weight has to be on the inside. Press down on the inside stirrup. Your leg must stay active by the girth to encourage the bend through the body. Otherwise, impulsion won't be maintained. Your outside leg stays passive, unless the quarters start to fall out." He smiled to take the sting out of his words. "I'm preaching to the choir. You know all this. Something's up. What is it?"

She slid off the horse, a petite redhead in her forties who looked ten years younger. Keeping hold of the reins, she approached him. "I'm just not into this today, I guess. The open house was last night. I thought you were going to drop by."

Gabe stared at her blankly. Open house? What in the hell was she talking about? Then it hit him. "Shelly, I'm sorry. My mother had an accident. I spent the whole day with her at the hospital."

She avoided his eyes. "That's okay. Under the circumstances, there isn't anything else you could have done."

"I could have called. I'm sorry," he said again.

"No problem."

But it was. He knew it, by her face and what she didn't say. Shelly Sims was nice enough. Her checks were always on time and she rarely missed a day at the center. But lately, Gabe was beginning to wonder if he was as much of an attraction as Miss Mollie, her horse. Shelly was single, attractive and close enough to his own age to be interested. She insisted, in the nicest way possible, that it be Gabriel who instructed her. He acquiesced, although he didn't normally take on students, because he couldn't afford to lose her business. She'd invited him to the opening of her third real estate office in Calabasas, a community of single-family homes priced in the millions. He'd actually been looking forward to it, a night of mingling with adults, a world far away from horses.

He'd used his mother's accident as an excuse, but he knew that wasn't the reason for his lapse of memory. He hadn't given Shelly Sims a single thought since Whitney Benedict had stepped out of her rented Chevy Impala, mostly because every moment he wasn't spending working through the twisted tapestry of his life was spent thinking about her.

He remembered the first time he saw her, looking like no one had ever looked before, deliciously cool, at ease, serenely confident. He remembered that the breeze ruffled her slitted skirt and that she wore high heels. Her blouse was silk and wrapped around her breasts and waist, completely feminine, subtly defining her, the entire package appearing attractively in charge and professional. She had silvery-blond hair and a fudgy, back-throated laugh. She spoke to Claire as if she were an adult, and she knew horses.

He felt like a boy in the throes of his first crush and he didn't particularly like the feeling. He didn't *want* the feeling. His insecurities made him curt, nearly rude. He wanted…he didn't know what he wanted. *What is love? 'Tis not hereafter, present mirth hath present laughter. What's to come is still unsure.*

He wouldn't go there. It was impossible. *She* was impossible, even though she made it seem as if they were on level playing fields.

Shelly pulled him back to the present. "You can make it up to me."

"What?"

"Where are you, Gabe? Have you heard anything I said?"

"Sorry. I've got things on my mind."

"I said you can make it up to me. I'm free for dinner."

He groaned inwardly. He didn't have time for this. He didn't know the moves. He wasn't quick enough.

"That's nice of you," he said, "but I've got to get back to Ventura to check on my mother."

"I didn't mean tonight."

"Oh?"

"I'm free this weekend and all next week."

Caught in his own tangled web.

"Will you call me?"

Reprieve, albeit briefly. He nodded. "I'll do that."

"I look forward to it."

He watched her lead the horse away. The weight was back on his shoulders, heavier than ever.

Sixteen

Gabriel punched in the code for home on the keypad of his cell phone and then tucked it under his ear while maneuvering his truck into the middle lane. Whitney answered on the third ring. "How are you?" he asked. "Are you okay or regretting you ever heard of the place? C'mon, be honest."

He held his breath, expecting what he believed to be the inevitable, that Whitney would throw up her hands and tell him she'd bitten off far more than she could chew.

Unbelievably, she laughed that low, sultry laugh that should not have belonged to a cool, blond lawyer representing the Austrian government. "I have to admit that it's a challenge, but I think I'm handling it," she said. "Ramona helped. Your mother's two paying guests left this afternoon and two more are due tomorrow. The kids just came home from school. Eric is on his way to the dressage center with Emma and Claire and I'm in the middle of trying to reproduce Ramona's chicken marinade. How are you?"

"Right now, extremely grateful. I can't tell you how

helpful you've been. I have no way of making this up to you."

"I'm fine, really," she said quickly, brushing off his thanks. "Are you in the car?"

"Yes. I'm on my way to visit my mother. That's why I called. I wonder if you could meet me in town tonight. I have a few legal questions to ask you and I'd like to do it away from the house."

"What a sad and safe way to ask me for a date," she teased.

Suddenly he felt as lighthearted as if he were sixteen again. "I'll try anything that works." One second passed, then another and a few more after that. "Is it working?"

"What about the kids and dinner?"

"Eric is old enough to handle the girls for a few hours. They've managed soup and sandwiches before. Put the chicken in the refrigerator and meet me."

Sandwiches weren't what she had in mind for Claire's diet, but she could work around it. "All right. Is casual okay?"

"It'll have to be. I'm in my work clothes."

"Then I'll stay in mine. Where shall we meet?"

"There's an Italian place called Donatelli's on Fifth and Main in Ventura. It's not fancy, but the food's good. Is six o'clock too soon?"

"I'll be there."

Gabriel replaced the phone. It had been a long time since he'd felt so optimistic. Nothing had changed for the better. In fact, a great deal was worse. His mother wasn't well and he faced a child-custody lawsuit, neither of which he could do anything about at the moment. He knew his emotions were short-lived and had everything to do with Whitney and the dinner ahead of him. It was temporary, but so was life. So much of what he'd once believed would be forever really wasn't. He would take what was offered, as it was offered, and not worry about how long it would last.

Mercedes looked unusually helpless lying in the hospital bed shrouded in blankets, an IV attached to her arm. The tray of food by her side was untouched.

Gabriel entered the room and sat down beside her. "You aren't eating, Ma," he said gently.

She fixed her black eyes on him. "This isn't food, Gabriel. A dog shouldn't have to eat this food."

"You have to eat something. The broth looks okay and so does the Jell-O. Nobody can do much damage to those."

"Jell-O is a child's dessert," she pouted. "Adults don't eat Jell-O, and I don't like broth. Why eat anything at all?"

"You won't get anything else," he warned her.

Her eyes turned hopeful. "Maybe you could bring me something, some nice lasagna or a pizza. Casa Consuelo's is open until five. You could bring me some enchiladas or chili *rellenos.*"

"I can't bring food like that into the hospital, Ma," he said patiently. "Besides, it's not good for you."

She struggled to sit up. Her eyes flashed dangerously. "Who are you to tell me what's good for me? I'm seventy-six years old. I've lived longer than anyone in my family. If I hadn't tripped, I wouldn't be in here and this nonsense wouldn't be happening."

He ignored her. "Has Pilar been to see you?"

"I sent her away."

"Why?"

"She's like you, too full of her own advice."

He tried to change the subject. "Ramona came to the house today to help Whitney."

"She called this morning. I told her not to bother to come here. I'll be home before she figures out what to do with the boys."

Gabe nodded. When his mother was in a mood, it was best to humor her. "Has the doctor been here?"

"He was in this afternoon, but he wants to talk to you." She tightened her lips stubbornly. "I told him I wouldn't take that cholesterol medication, *mijito*."

Gabriel mentally counted to ten. "Why not?" he asked pleasantly.

"I don't like taking pills. They make me gag."

"You take vitamins."

"Those aren't pills, and I don't swallow them whole. I pound them with my mortar and pestle, mix them up with orange juice and drink them. I never could take pills."

"Did he say what might be contributing to your high cholesterol?"

"No." She wouldn't look at him. "But I told him I was too old to go on a diet."

"You're right."

She glared at him suspiciously. "What does that mean?"

"It's hard to change lifelong habits, which is probably the reason the doctor suggested cholesterol medication. It's one or the other, Ma. You can't keep going like this. One of the kids is going to come home and find you on the floor. Do you want that?"

"Of course not."

He leaned forward and took her hands in his. "Will you think about this? For me? Please?"

Her eyes filled. "There isn't anything I wouldn't do for you, *mijito*. You know that."

"Take the pills, Ma. We don't want to lose you anytime soon."

She pulled one hand away and reached for the spoon on her tray. "Pull the lid off the broth, Gabriel. Maybe I will try it, and the Jell-O, too. Next time ask them to bring a little chicken and potatoes. I don't like over-cooked beef, unless it's inside a tortilla." She pushed the meat around on her plate. "Maybe you could bring me some homemade salsa. I should be able to eat salsa. You know how to make it, don't you, *mijito?* I could give Whitney the recipe if you don't have time."

"Whitney's done enough for us," he said quickly. "It isn't good to get so dependent on her."

"Why not?"

"Because she's going home."

"Oh."

He didn't like the sound of his mother's response. "You do understand that she has to go home, Ma. She's got a job, a good job, one that takes years of schooling. We can't expect her to work as an unpaid housekeeper forever."

Mercedes picked at the lint on her blanket. "I wasn't thinking of forever."

"What were you thinking of?"

"A month. Maybe she could stay for a month and you two could get to know each other better. She's a lovely woman, Gabriel. You couldn't do better if you placed an order."

He stared at his mother, wondering if she could really be so naive. "I want you to promise me something, Ma," he said carefully.

"Anything, *mijito.*"

"Promise me you won't ask Whitney to stay any longer than this week."

His mother's eyebrows rose.

Gabriel felt the edges of his temper curl and sizzle.

He stood and walked to the window. It overlooked the parking lot. "You may not understand this, but I want you to listen. If you interfere in this, you won't be helping. There are some things people have to figure out for themselves. This is one of them."

"You do like her, don't you, Gabriel?"

"Very much," he acknowledged, turning in time to see the satisfied smile lurking on his mother's lips. "That isn't the point. If there is even the slightest possibility of something happening between us, it will be completely impossible if you suggest that she do anything else for us beyond this week."

"But why, Gabriel?"

He tried to explain, knowing it wouldn't make a difference. Mercedes Mendoza heard only what she wanted to hear. He'd spent a lifetime trying to reach her and here he was, still trying. "I don't want to be under obligation to her. Our circumstances are far enough apart as it is. Leave me a little pride."

"Your pride might be all you're left with."

"I'll handle it."

Mercedes leaned back against the pillow, her food forgotten for the first time in her life. "Why do you have so little confidence in yourself, my son?" she asked softly. "Who or what gave you the idea that you don't deserve a woman like Whitney Benedict?"

"No one." He was clearly exasperated. "It's plain enough. Whitney is a lawyer. She comes from a well-known, well-established family and she has no children."

"So, you're not a lawyer. You have your own business. Everyone's family is well known somewhere, and, as far as having children, you make it sound as if that's a liability. I don't see it that way. I don't think she does, either."

He sighed. "Just promise, Ma. That's all I ask. Let me do this my way."

She waited a full minute before answering. "All right, Gabriel," she said at last. "I promise, but I won't let you hang yourself. If it looks like you'll lose it all, I'm going to act. You know I never interfere, but I won't watch you drown. I'm your mother, after all."

He knew it was nothing more than a reprieve, but maybe Whitney would be on her way home before his mother could do any real damage.

She was already seated at a small table in the corner when he entered the restaurant. He saw that she'd dressed up after all, not so that she stood out, but enough to know that she'd gone to some trouble. He approved of her narrow slacks and the long-sleeved, scoop-necked sweater, both in a seaweed-green that changed the color of her eyes. Her hair was pulled away from her face and allowed to fall across her shoulders in two pale, silvery curves.

She smiled when she saw him.

"Thanks for coming," he said. "Have you been here long?"

"Just a few minutes. I'd like a glass of wine, but I waited to see if there was anything you preferred."

"We have a great pinot noir in this corner of the world. If you like, we could give it a try."

She nodded, a curious smile on her face.

"What?" he asked.

"Do you know a lot about wine, Gabriel?"

He nodded. "My dad was Austrian. He knew his wines and his food. I don't mind taking after him in that way."

"Your mother told me you were close."

"Very." He waved the waitress over and ordered a bottle of Cedar Creek pinot noir, the 1998 Reserve.

"Is it hard for you to talk about him?"

"Not really. It helps me remember him." He smiled. "How about you? What are your parents like?"

"They're young," she said. "My mother's fifty-eight and my dad just turned sixty."

"Which one do you take after?"

"My mother," she said without hesitating, "if you're referring to appearance. We look exactly alike. If you're curious as to what I'll be like in twenty years, come home with me and I'll introduce you to my mother."

"You don't sound very pleased about that."

She shrugged. "It isn't her appearance I object to."

The waitress brought the bottle of wine, uncorked it and poured a small amount into Gabriel's glass. He tasted it and motioned for her to fill both glasses.

"The linguini with clam sauce and the walnut gorgonzola tortellini are both excellent tonight," the woman said.

Gabriel looked at Whitney. "Shall we go for it?"

She nodded. "Yes, please. They sound delicious. If we get one of each, we can share."

"What bothers you about your mother?" he asked when they were alone again.

"She's relentless," Whitney said immediately. "She chips away until there's nothing a person can do except crumble."

"And your dad?"

"Daddy doesn't have a chance." She sipped her wine. "This is delicious."

"Are they happy together?"

Whitney looked surprised. "I have no idea," she said after a minute. "No one's ever asked me that question before. I've always thought of them as my parents rather than people who need to be happily married."

He refilled her glass. "Do you mind if I ask the million-dollar question?"

"Is it going to be, 'Why aren't you married?'"

"No."

"All right. Ask away."

"How has a beautiful, intelligent and generous woman like you managed to avoid marriage for as long as you have?"

"That isn't fair."

"Is that one of the rules?"

She laughed, but he could see that it was forced. She didn't answer right away. Finally she spoke. "If I tell you, you'll owe me. It means that you have to answer one of my questions, even if it's one you'd rather not. Agreed?"

"Agreed."

"I was married, briefly, a long time ago. Because of him I became a lawyer."

"What happened?"

She looked directly at him. "His name was Wiley Cane. It still is, actually, but I prefer to think of him in the past tense. He was dirt poor, two years older than me and very southern, a real good old boy. I met him my last year in high school. He'd come back after a stint in the Youth Authority. He showed up at school that first day steeped in an aura of forbidden danger. He smoked cigarettes, drank beer and was good with his hands. He lifted machine parts and laid pipe. He had an awful reputation. It was irresistible. I succumbed to the secret desire of every girl who sees a gorgeous, well-muscled, unattainable young animal. I believed I could tame him and that all he needed was a good woman to bring him around." Her smile was brittle. "I was wrong. I nearly killed my parents before I realized just how wrong I was, but it wasn't before Wiley almost killed me." She left out the other part, the part that really counted, the part she had no intention of revealing to anyone this side of heaven. Pity wasn't the emotion she wanted to evoke in anyone, least of all Gabriel Mendoza. "I was so grateful to the lawyer who arranged my annulment that for a while I ranked him right up there with God. He inspired me to follow in his footsteps." She drained her glass. "That's my story. I'm sure you never imagined it would be so sordid."

"I admit, you don't look the part of someone who could be taken in by anyone."

"Give me a little credit. I was seventeen years old."

"Yet you're still alone."

"I believe it's my turn to ask a question."

"Shoot."

She set down her glass, folded her arms and leaned forward. Deliberately, Gabriel kept his eyes on her face. "This may seem ridiculous, but humor me."

"All right."

"Are you attracted to me?"

For the first time since he'd sat down, Gabriel doubted himself. Which was the answer that would settle everything down again and allow them to eat their meal without embarrassment? He settled on the truth. "Yes."

"Was it there from the beginning, or did I grow on you?"

His lips twitched. She'd only had two glasses of wine. Maybe she was one of those people who couldn't hold alcohol. "I'd have to say from the beginning."

Her forehead furrowed. "What was it that attracted you?"

He paused. "'Her voice was ever soft, gentle and low, an excellent thing in woman.'"

"A man who quotes Shakespeare. Are you trying to impress me?"

"Is it working?"

"Yes, but you don't have to."

"Why not?"

"I'm already sold."

His eyes narrowed. "Don't play games with me, Whitney. What's going on here?"

She wet her lips. "I'm leaving soon. Under the circumstances, we don't have much time to get to know each other."

He wouldn't help her. She'd have to spell it out clearly so he knew there was no going back.

"I thought we might skip a few steps in the usual courting ritual."

"Which steps might those be?"

She sat back in her chair. Her cheeks were very pink. "Damn it, Gabriel, leave me a little pride."

He leaned forward. "You'll have to say it, Whitney, loud and clear, because I'm having a hard time believing this is really happening."

"I can't say it."

"Why not?"

"Because of who I represent. It isn't ethical."

"Then why are we having this conversation?"

"I won't always be in this position. I have to know if there is any possibility of us going beyond where we are now."

"You live in Kentucky."

She nodded. "Do you have anything against long-distance relationships?"

His slow grin deepened the grooves in his cheeks and squared his chin. "Do you always call the shots?"

"Yes."

"Thanks for the warning. I've never been to Kentucky."

"That's going to change very quickly."

He laughed. "I've never even kissed you."

"That's going to change, too, even more quickly, I hope."

"You can count on it."

"Tonight?"

"No."

She stared at him. "Why not?"

"Because you're still a lawyer representing the Austrian government, and because I'd like to be the one calling some of the shots."

Seventeen

Emma stared sullenly at her PE teacher, tuning out the lecture she'd heard once a week since school started in September. She knew better than to interrupt or even answer. Miss Sinclair was happiest listening to herself talk, and as far as Emma was concerned, she had nothing new to offer.

"Are you listening to me, Emma?"

Emma barely nodded.

The woman sighed. "I don't know what to do with you. I've never seen anyone so resistant. Believe it or not, I want to help you. If there's a problem, please tell me."

This time Emma didn't even bother to nod.

"All right, Emma." The woman's tone had changed. "I'll give it to you straight. The next time you come to class without your gym clothes, I'll fail you. You'll have to take PE again if you want to graduate. Is that clear?"

Emma looked at her feet. Anything could happen in four years. It was a lifetime away. She had better things to think about.

"Consider yourself warned," the teacher said, turning away.

Taking her words as a dismissal, Emma walked out of the gym and into the main building. A group of girls she recognized stood in a small group, directly in front of her locker. Tracy Davenport, the acknowledged leader, hissed a warning as Emma approached. The dead silence was a giveaway. Obviously she had been their topic of conversation. She reached through their tight circle to dial the combination on her locker. They separated, allowing her access. The sooner she could be away from here, the better. Tracy, once her best friend, now treated her as if she had the plague. Not that it mattered. She wanted nothing to do with Tracy and her rah-rah club of wannabe cheerleaders.

"Hi, Emma," Tracy ventured. "How are you?"

"Give me a break, Tracy," Emma replied scathingly. Why wasn't her stupid locker cooperating?

Tracy's brown eyes flashed. "What is your problem? Why are you acting this way?"

Finally, the lock clicked open. Emma opened the door and stuffed her book bag inside. Slamming it shut again, she turned to Tracy. "What way?"

Tracy linked her arm through Emma's and dragged her away from the group. "Go on without me," she called back.

Emma pulled her arm away. "Get lost, Tracy. I don't have anything to say to you."

"I'm not going anywhere until you tell me what's going on. We've been friends since kindergarten. What is it? I have a right to know."

Emma's lip quivered. She could feel herself losing it. "Go away."

"Not until you tell me why."

"Why are you being so stubborn?" Emma shouted. "I don't want to be friends anymore, that's all. We aren't the same. I don't want to hang out with the people you hang with."

"Those people are your friends."

"Then why are they talking about me behind my back? Why are *you* talking behind my back?"

Tracy looked wounded. "I'm not saying anything behind your back that I haven't said to your face. What's wrong, Emma? You can tell me." Her eyes flickered over Emma's exposed midriff and low-cut jeans. "Why are you being so weird? Does it have to do with your mom?"

"No." Close to tears, Emma brushed past Tracy and ran down the hall toward the exit. Blindly, she pushed open the doors and ran down the steps across the wide green lawn. Her heart slammed against her chest and her breath came in gasps. She hated Tracy Davenport. She hated her teachers. Nothing was going right. Nothing had gone right since her mother left.

Emma stopped at the side of the 7-Eleven on the corner to catch her breath. She heard someone called her name. At first she thought it was Tracy. Without turning around, she started walking again, quickening her pace. The call came again. This time she recognized the voice. A bubble of hope and joy welled in her heart. She turned, inhaled and started to run toward the woman coming toward her. "Mom," she shouted. "Mom. You came back."

Kristen Mendoza hadn't intended to do more than cash in what was left of her investment account, call on her children and her mother and leave town the same day. She hadn't counted on the look on Emma's face when the child hurled herself into her arms. "There, there, baby," she crooned, cradling the unfamiliar dark head against her shoulder. What on earth had Emma done to her hair? Circling the school, scouting out what seemed like hundreds of fourteen-year-old girls Emma's size with blond hair, she hadn't recognized her daughter at first. If she hadn't spotted Tracy, she would never have known where to look.

After a minute, she pulled back, setting Emma at arm's length to look at her. It wasn't that the clothes were shocking in themselves. Kristen was used to seeing skimpy clothes and bare skin, but she'd never seen them on Emma. What was Gabriel thinking to allow her to dress this way? She had the grace to flush. She had no right to criticize Gabriel. He was holding it together all alone, if you discounted Mercedes, and Kristen was more than happy to do that.

She had never warmed to her mother-in-law. Not that she didn't admire her. Mercedes was the kind of person she longed to be—dramatic, unselfconscious, flamboyant, colorfully and ethnically exotic. Kristen, with her pale hair and eyes and her thin features, could never compete, not in that arena. Why she ever felt she had to was a mystery that was never resolved to her own satisfaction. Maybe it had something to do with Gabriel. She realized, only recently, that everything significant in her life began and ended with Gabriel. She was trying to change that.

Kristen brushed Emma's hair from her forehead. Her daughter's face was grimy with tears and running mascara. "Oh, Emma. I've missed you so."

The child's eyes widened eagerly. "Are you staying?"

Kristen shook her head. "No, sweetie. I can't do that. I need to work and my work is on the road."

"Can I come with you?"

Rather than answering, Kristen linked her arm through Emma's, leading her in the other direction.

"Let's get a bite to eat and I'll tell you everything," she suggested.

"I have to call home. Dad checks on me. He'll want to know where I am."

"I'll drive you home. We can talk on the way."

Emma hesitated. "I'd rather talk somewhere here."

"I'd like to see Eric and Claire, too."

"That's not a good idea," Emma said quickly.

"Why not?"

"Gran hurt herself. She's in the hospital for a few days. A friend of Dad's is there." Emma frowned. "She's not really a friend. She's a lawyer."

"A lawyer? Why does Dad need a lawyer?"

"Austria wants to buy the Lipizzaners."

Kristen's heartbeat quickened. "Really?"

"He doesn't want to sell," Emma explained. "Gran and the aunts do, I think. Anyway, Whitney stayed to help when Gran had her accident."

They had reached Kristen's car. She buckled herself in and waited until Emma was settled before resuming her questioning. "Let me get this straight. A lawyer representing Austria offered to buy Dad' horses. He doesn't want to, but she's staying, anyway."

Emma nodded.

Kristen stared straight ahead. "What's she like?"

"I don't like her."

"Why not?" Kristen pulled the car out into the line of traffic.

Emma shrugged and looked out the window. "I want to come with you. I don't like living with Dad and Grandma."

"That isn't possible."

Her question was nearly a whisper. "Why not?"

"Oh, Emma. It isn't that I don't want you with me."

How could she make her needs clear to this child without sounding as egocentric as a teenager? Maybe such a thing wasn't possible. Maybe all that was left was the truth. She swallowed. "I travel all the time. I live in a trailer. You have to go to school. Children need stability." Her daughter's silence smote her. "Honey, are you listening to me?"

"There's a boy at school who sailed around the world on a boat with his parents. He was gone for two years. If he can do it, why can't I?"

"It isn't the same."

"Why not?" Emma wailed. She was crying again.

Kristen sighed. "His mother and father were there, in the boat, with him. They had time to teach him his lessons and correct his papers. I'm gone all the time, rehearsing or driving or performing."

"You don't have to do that. Why can't you just come home? Dad can take care of you, like he did before."

Kristen shook her head. "It doesn't work that way. Dad and I are divorced. He doesn't want to take care of me. I don't want it, either. I like supporting myself. It makes me feel good about myself."

"What about me?" Emma asked. "Does it make you feel good to leave me?"

Kristen winced, feeling the familiar wave of guilt rise up all over again. Emma hit the nail on the head. In order to spread her wings and leave the stranglehold of her life with Gabriel, Kristen had sacrificed her children. No one had ever said it, not in so many words, but it was there on all their faces, Gabriel's, Mercedes's, her mother's, and now Emma's. "No," she said, her voice low. "Leaving you is the price I had to pay. Someday, when you're older, you'll understand."

"When I have kids, I'm never leaving them," Emma

said fiercely, her hands clenched. "Eric doesn't want to see you. He hates you, and Claire's worse than she was before. In case you're wondering why I don't like Whitney, it's because Gran's trying to marry Dad off to her."

For a minute Kristen held on to the words, trying them out, weighing the idea of Gabriel with someone else in her mind. "How does your dad feel about that?" she asked carefully.

Emma glared at her mother. "She's gorgeous. How do you think he feels?"

Kristen refused to rise to the bait. "I'm sure when Dad remarries, he'll choose someone that loves you, even if she isn't gorgeous."

Emma grunted.

"We're not getting back together, Emma," her mother said slowly. "I know that's what you want. Dad and I don't love each other anymore. We don't want to be together. We just weren't right."

"You were right enough for twelve years." Emma folded her arms. "You can't just keep divorcing people, Mom. If you get married again, it'll be the third time. Isn't it embarrassing to say you've been married so many times? You're like that old actress, Elizabeth Taylor."

Kristen's mouth twisted. "Hardly that, but point taken."

"Are you seeing anybody?"

"No." She didn't add *not now*. Emma didn't need to know that.

"You loved Dad before. I bet, if you tried, you could again."

"It doesn't work that way, Emma. Can't you see how hard this is for me?"

"You're not the only one who's having a hard time."

When had she become so cynical? Kristen wondered.

Was it all because of the divorce? Were the kids really so unhappy living with Gabe?

They traveled the rest of the way in silence. She stopped the car at the end of the road, out of sight of the house. "I probably should have called your dad first. He might not like my dropping in like this."

"Since when have you cared what he liked?"

"Since when have you become such a brat?" Kristen returned sharply. Her hand flew to her mouth. She turned stricken eyes to her daughter. "I'm sorry, Emma. You're hurting. I'm just not used to hearing you talk like that."

Emma's lips tightened mutinously. "Let's go. No one will be there but Whitney and Claire. You can meet your competition."

"I'm more inclined to apologize for your manners," Kristen said under her breath.

Emma was right. Whitney Benedict *was* gorgeous. She was blond and slim and she moved in the loping, long-legged way of a colt in slow motion. No wonder Gabriel was attracted to her. Kristen hadn't counted on liking her, but it wasn't possible not to. Her smile was genuine, and her voice, sweet and very southern, would melt snow cones in January. Somehow, Kristen found herself seated beside Emma at the table with a cup of tea and a plate of warm cookies in front of her. A woman after Mercedes's own heart. She felt like a long-awaited, warmly welcomed guest. That would change when Gabriel arrived.

"I'd hoped to see Eric and Claire," she began.

"They're with their dad at the dressage center," Whitney explained.

"Of course." Kristen hadn't been gone that long, but already she'd forgotten routines. "Maybe I'll meet them there." She smiled at Emma. "Would you like to come with me, sweetie?"

"No," Emma said bluntly. "You can have your family reunion on your own."

Kristen's cheeks burned. "That's enough, young lady. In case you've forgotten, you're my family, too."

"That's a good one, Mom. Listen to yourself." She stood. "I'm going upstairs. I have work to do."

"I didn't see your book bag," said Whitney.

"I left it at school."

"What about your homework?"

"I have everything I need here."

"How *are* you doing in school, Emma?" her mother asked.

"Great. I'm doing great, just like always." Her smile was brittle. "See ya."

"Can we go out to dinner?" her mother asked.

Emma shrugged. "Whatever."

Kristen waited until she'd left the room. "Is she always this way?"

"I think she's going through a tough time right now."

"What about Eric and Claire?"

"I think the children miss you," Whitney said gently. "It's an adjustment to be without their mother."

Kristen met her glance squarely. "Do you think I'm awful for what I did?"

Whitney hesitated.

"Go ahead. I can take it."

"I'm not in a position to judge you. I don't know you."

"You know what I did."

"I don't know how you felt or what your reasons were. I've been here a week."

"Emma says you're a lawyer."

"That's right."

"You're here to buy Gabe's horses."

"I represent the potential buyer."

"How much money will Gabe get?"

Something flickered behind Whitney's eyes. "I can't really discuss that with you."

Kristen nodded. "Fair enough. What do you think of Mercedes?"

Whitney laughed. "She's a character. I like her very much."

Kristen stood and rubbed her arms. "That makes one of us. We never did get along."

Whitney changed the subject. "Tell me about Claire. I'm not familiar with her type of autism."

Kristen closed her eyes in an attempt to compose herself. Her lovely, precious little girl, the child she so wanted to have with Gabriel, had proved, in the end, to be her nemesis, the straw that broke the camel's back. She leaned back in her chair and crossed her arms against her chest. "Claire is the most difficult challenge I've ever faced," she said bluntly. "I wasn't up to it. I never will be. I'm not the mother a child like Claire should have. I don't require perfection by any means, but I can't deal with a handicap of that magnitude. She consumed me. I had nothing left for anyone else. Ironically, she made it possible for me to leave. That's as honest as I've been with anyone. I have no idea why you should be the one to bring that quality out in me. Maybe it's because Emma told me that Mercedes chose you as my successor. I feel a responsibility to warn you about what you're getting into."

"I've been here a week," Whitney reminded her again.

"Are you attracted to Gabe?"

Whitney remained silent.

"I guess that's my answer." Kristen continued. "He is very attractive, a study in opposites—well-read, physically active, masculine but still sensitive. He's really rather sort of amazing."

"If you feel that way, how could you leave him?"

"It just didn't work. I already told you. I couldn't manage Claire and he couldn't forgive that. Gabe has impossible expectations. I couldn't live up to them. I was tired of disappointing him and ended up resenting him terribly. Nothing is worth that. I wish you luck with him."

"It's a little early for that."

"I should go," Kristen said. "I never intended to actually see anyone, but I couldn't help myself. Emma looks awful. Don't tell her I said that."

"Will you see the others?"

Kristen shook her head. "I don't think so. There's nothing for me here."

"Listen." Whitney pitched her voice at its most persuasive. "I really think you should see Eric and Claire. They're your children. They need to see you, even if it's just for an hour or two. Take them somewhere. They'll live on it for a long time. It's the least you can do."

"What difference does it make? Look at Emma. How has she benefited from seeing me?"

"Just because she's trying to punish you right now doesn't mean she isn't better for having seen you."

Kristen sighed. "All right, Whitney. You win. God knows I don't need another strike against me. I'll see the kids."

The relief on Whitney's face was obvious.

Kristen laughed. "They won't thank you for protecting them, you know, and unless Gabe's a completely different person, he'll be furious that you've interfered."

"You're probably right."

Kristen felt a strong surge of compassion for Whitney Benedict. She was a kind woman. Under different circumstances, they might have been friends.

Eighteen

Gabriel finished up the last of his paperwork, swept the pile into a semblance of organized chaos and pulled down the top of the antique desk he'd acquired at an estate sale. It was a splurge, solid mahogany, well out of his price range and completely inappropriate for the dusty office of a horse stable. Yet, he'd never once regretted it. Whenever he wheeled his chair up to the enormous desk and rolled back the pleated top, he felt different somehow, elevated, as if he'd traveled back to another time, another world, where men and women dressed for dinner, ate and drank from cut crystal and fine china, where children were cared for by competent nannies, and heavy bedroom drapes weren't pulled back to let the sun in until noon. In other words, a world as far away from the dirt and the barns and the dawn-until-midnight legacy his father had bequeathed him without once bothering to ask whether it was what Gabriel wanted.

The truth was, he hadn't wanted it, not at first. Gabriel loved language, specifically the English language. The words of the classic poets, usually British, weighed on his mind, rolled off his tongue, flitted through his consciousness at the oddest times. His library of books, all hardcover, were worn, spine-battered, the gilt edges dimmed and dog-eared, favorite passages marked, notes etched in the white spaces of the margins.

Long ago, while lying on a warm green lawn at the University of Santa Cruz, half dozing in the warmth of a benevolent sun, listening to one of his professors read a passage from Yeats, he'd entertained the notion of teaching English at one of those campuses where ivy crept up the walls of graceful brick buildings that had proudly stood for two hundred years. He closed his eyes and imagined lecturing behind a podium to a hushed classroom, his senses steeped in the scent of old books, the gleam of seasoned wood and the subtle haze of chalk dust swirling around his head.

It hadn't happened. Even though Gabriel graduated with a degree in English literature and a minor in mathematics, he'd done nothing with either discipline. He'd spent his junior year and the summer after his graduation in England, but, too soon, his father needed him. He'd intended his return home to be temporary, but one year rolled into the next and, before he knew it, he was married with two stepchildren and a daughter of his own. Gabriel, raised in the tradition of family first, buckled down for the good of everyone except himself. And then a funny thing happened. The trade of his ancestors, the Austrian horsemasters and the Spanish vaqueros, grew on him.

"Hey, Dad." Eric leaned against the doorjamb. "I finished spreading fresh hay in the foaling barn. It doesn't look like anything'll happen with Tiny Dancer tonight. She's too mellow."

Gabriel nodded. "I agree. Why don't you collect your sister and we'll go home."

"When is Gran leaving the hospital?"

"They want to do an angiogram," Gabriel replied.

"What's that?"

"They send a monitor through the arteries and the chambers of the heart to be sure there isn't any blockage."

Eric blanched. "That doesn't sound good. Are you going to let them do it?"

Gabriel raised his eyebrows. "Since when do I have the last word when it comes to Gran?"

"Do you *want* them to do it?"

"I'd rather they wait until she's up and around. They have other tests that aren't as invasive. She's still complaining of serious pain in her ankle. I wonder—"

"What?"

Gabriel blinked and looked at his stepson. "Never mind. It doesn't matter. I'm hungry. Let's go home."

"You might have to convince Claire. She's joined at the hip with Lorelei."

A smile tugged at the corners of Gabe's mouth. At first he wasn't sure about setting Claire up with a spirited Lipizzaner, but she'd wanted it so badly. "Good," he said.

Eric's flashing grin warmed his face. "I've got a few things to finish up in the tack room and then I'll warm up the truck. I'll meet you outside."

Gabe turned out the light, locked up the office and took an indirect route down the dirt path into the third barn where the Lipizzan mares were stabled. One had foaled last week. He stopped in front of her stall. The colt was a beauty, smoke-colored, with the delicate molded head and wide-spaced dark eyes typical of the breed. This one's fuzzy coat would thicken and his splayed legs straighten when he was a few weeks older. "Hey, fella," Gabe said softly, "get some sleep. Your mom needs turnout time and you'll have to keep up with her starting tomorrow."

"Hello, Gabriel."

The voice came out of nowhere. Bracing himself for the painful wrench in his gut that Kristen never failed to bring, he turned. She was more hollow-eyed than he remembered, her figure backlit by the warm glow of the lamplight. Seconds passed. Nothing happened, nothing more than a twinge. Relief flooded through him. "Hello, Kristen. What brings you here?"

"My children."

"You're kidding." The words were out before he could stop them.

Her mouth twisted. "I guess it's too much to hope that we can be civil with each other."

"Not at all. I can do civility. Eric and Claire are here. I'll go back to the house and leave you with them. You can drop them off later when you see Emma."

"That's big of you."

"What did you expect?"

She shrugged. "A greeting, maybe. Something along the lines of *How have you been, Kristen. You're looking well.*"

Gabriel nodded. "I can do that, too. You're looking well, Kristen. How have you been?"

"I miss the kids," she said. "Other than that, I'm fine."

"Good." He started to walk past her.

"Wait." She reached for his arm and changed her mind. The distaste on his face was obvious. "Could we talk for a minute?"

He shook his head. "The kids are ready to go home. This isn't the time."

"When?"

His brows knitted together. "What's the point?"

"I need money," she said simply. "I'm not making it."

He stared at her. "Why not get a job?"

She flushed. "I'm not exactly skilled labor, Gabriel."

"You're the one who left."

"Does that mean I'm supposed to be destitute?"

"You know I don't have money to throw around. You cleaned out half of everything we had when you left. What happened to all that?"

"It's expensive to travel."

"Don't they pay you anything?"

She lost her temper. "Why are you being so brutal? I'm not making enough. If I was, I wouldn't be telling you this. I'm not a spender, but I have to live."

"I'm not sure what you want," he said evenly. "You have three children whose support you're not contributing to. Two of them aren't mine. What about that?"

She ignored him. "What about the house?"

He sighed. "Don't be stupid, Kristen. It belongs to my mother. It always has."

"The horses don't belong to your mother."

"She owns a percentage. So do my sisters and I. It was ours before I married you. Separate property stays that way."

"Not if it's co-mingled. The proceeds from this business supported our family for years."

"I don't have money to support two households. You knew that when you left. We've already agreed on a property settlement."

"I kept the right to collect spousal support."

What had he ever seen in her? "Go ahead. Try to collect. You might find yourself with fifty percent custody of three children or else having to pay a hefty amount in child support."

"And you might find yourself splitting the proceeds of the money from the Austrian government."

His breath caught. "May I ask how you know about that?"

"Emma told me. I picked her up at school."

"Did she also tell you that I have no intention of accepting the offer?"

Kristen crossed her arms and leaned back against the door. "You might have to."

"Mom?" Eric's voice cut through the tension.

She turned, mustered a smile and held out her arms. "Hi, honey."

He didn't move. "What are you doing here?"

She lowered her arms. "I had a little break and thought I'd swing by and see you and your sisters."

"How long are you staying?"

"Just tonight."

Eric nodded. "How are you?"

"I'm fine. And you?"

"Great."

The silence lengthened.

Gabe and Kristen spoke at once. "I guess—"

"I think—" Kristen stopped.

Gabe continued. "Your mother would like to spend some time with the three of you. Why don't you grab something to eat together?"

"What about Whitney?" Eric asked. "She's expecting us."

"I don't think she'll mind," Kristen offered. "After I dropped Emma off, Whitney talked me into coming here."

Too late, she realized her mistake. "I would have come, anyway," she said. Her voice was barely audible.

Gabriel looked away in disgust.

"It's okay, Mom," Eric said quickly. "I have homework. Maybe you can spend some time with Claire and Emma."

Kristen wet her lips. "Emma has homework, too. I don't think—"

A small, silent figure slipped under Kristen's arm, ran to her father and leaned against him.

"Hi, honey," Kristen said softly. "How are you?"

Claire looked at her mother and burrowed deeper into Gabe's side.

Kristen inched forward. "You've grown so much, Claire. I wouldn't have recognized you." She held out her arms. "Come on, baby. Give Mama a kiss. I've missed you. I brought you a present." Slowly she reached into her purse, pulled out a folded piece of cloth and shook it open. It was a T-shirt with a logo on the front. "See? It's from Las Vegas. That's where I've been the last few weeks. Do you like it?"

Claire stared at her mother.

Defeated, Kristen's arm dropped. "I'll leave it for you."

Despite his personal antipathy, Gabe hurt for Kristen. She was still a mother and these were her children. "You and Emma can finish your homework later," he said to Eric. "I'll drive Claire home to get her sweater and then the four of you can go out."

"Really, Gabe," Kristen protested. "If they don't want to come, it's okay. I understand."

"Eric, take your sister to the truck. I'll be there in a minute." He waited until the children were out of the barn. "You're not getting off so easily, Kristen. You can damn well take your kids out for a meal. It's been six months since you've seen them."

"When did you get to be such an asshole, Gabriel?"

"When my wife deserted her family for an adolescent fantasy."

"Do you ever think you might have had something to do with it?"

All the pent-up fury of the last eighteen months exploded and he lashed out at the cause. "I might have, if it was only me you'd left. It's the kids I ache for, Kristen. I got over you long ago. A man can have more than one wife, but your kids have only one mother. You're what they're stuck with. I blame myself every day for giving Claire a mother like you."

She gasped and lifted both hands to her cheeks.

Gabe strode past her out of the barn, well aware he'd crossed a line.

Pulling open the door of the truck, he nodded at Eric. "Your mother's waiting for you."

"I'd rather drive back with you."

He slanted a long, hard look at the boy he couldn't have loved more if he'd been his own flesh and blood. "I'd like you to do this for me, Eric. I want your mother to be with her children tonight."

"Why?"

He wanted to shout *to remind her of what she's missing,* but he knew better. "It's important to her and to all of you," he said instead.

Eric sighed. "Okay, Dad. Whatever you say."

They were nearly home when Claire spoke for the first time since seeing her mother. "Are you mad at me, Daddy?"

"No, sweetheart."

"Who are you mad at?"

"No one."

"Why is Mommy here?"

"She came to see you, Emma and Eric." He reached over and took his daughter's hand. "She's taking you out to dinner. You'll like that, won't you?"

"I guess so." Claire was quiet for a minute. "Will she bring us back home?"

Good Lord! He'd never understand what went on in her mind. "Yes," he said emphatically. "She'll bring you back right after you eat. This is your home. You're not leaving it."

"Will Eric and Emma come home, too?"

"Yes. They'll come home with you."

"Will they ever leave?"

Gabriel looked at his daughter. The reassuring denial was on the tip of his tongue, but he couldn't bring himself to utter the word. It was a promise he might have to break. Damn Lynne Chamberlain and damn her daughter. He made a mental note to call a family law attorney first thing in the morning.

The delicious, comforting aroma of cooking meat and onions wafted through the air when he opened the door to the hacienda. *Whitney.* He'd nearly forgotten Whitney. What would she make of all this? He tugged on a lock of Claire's hair. "Run upstairs and get a jacket. You can wait for your mom in the kitchen. Tell Emma to be ready in ten minutes."

Claire disappeared up the stairs and Gabe walked into the kitchen. A half-empty glass of wine sat on the counter. The table was set for six and Whitney was pulling something from the oven. She glanced at him and smiled. "I hope you like pot roast."

"I like it," he said, "but we'll be the only ones eating it."

She frowned. "Oh?"

"The kids are going out with their mother."

She thought a minute, then smiled sunnily. "Would you mind if I asked the young couple who checked in today if they want to join us? It's short notice, but they might not have any plans."

He stared at her. Just like that she'd adjusted, no complaints, no recriminations, no long-suffering sighs, just acceptance and a sensible, generous suggestion.

"I don't mind at all," he said. "In fact, I'll ask them myself."

She smiled. "They couldn't possibly refuse."

He almost kissed her. She was so appealing standing there, her nose flushed from oven heat and wine, her makeup rubbed off, her pleased-as-punch smile and her wheat-gold hair pulled back and secured with a wooden skewer she'd probably found in the flatware drawer. But Kristen was due any minute with Eric and he wasn't sure how Whitney felt about public displays of affection. It occurred to him that he hadn't done anything spontaneous for a very long time.

"How do I go about finding a family law attorney?" he asked abruptly.

She looked surprised. "I suppose you could go online to the American Bar Association. You should be able to get several referrals. I wish I could help, but I'm not licensed in California."

"Aren't you going to ask why?"

"I know why."

"There's more. Kristen knows about the offer for my horses."

Whitney nodded. "She mentioned it when she brought Emma home from school. I told her where to find you."

A muscle jumped along his jaw. "I may be in some trouble here, Whitney. You might think twice before getting involved with me."

"Okay," she said, looking at him steadily. "I've thought twice."

"And?"

"I'm still here."

This time he did kiss her, a brief, warm, unsatisfying brush of lips against lips. It was over before the back door opened and Eric bounded through the kitchen and up the stairs to wash his hands. Apparently Kristen had decided to wait outside in the car.

Nineteen

Pryor Benedict replaced the phone carefully in its cradle, smoothed the nonexistent creases from her gray wool slacks and considered her black, exquisitely crafted, flat-heeled Brazilian leather boots. Deciding they would do, she gathered her purse and coat from the hall closet and set out on her mission. She didn't look in the mirror. Pryor never looked in the mirror. She didn't have to. Her morning ritual was enough. She never left her bathroom until she was completely satisfied with her appearance and then she never thought about it again, other than to reapply lipstick after each meal.

Settling herself in the car, she set the radio to her favorite classical music station, buckled her seat belt, adjusted the mirror and swung by the foaling barn to tell Boone she was leaving for the afternoon.

At the barn door, she called out the window. "Boone, are you in there?"

He came out immediately. "Where are you off to, honey?"

"Lila Rae invited me for tea."

Boone kissed her cheek. "Give her my love. You girls have a good time, now."

"We will. Don't forget we have the Lesters coming for dinner at seven."

Boone nodded. "Be careful."

Pryor nodded and drove off, intent on her errand but not so intent that she didn't notice what everyone involved in the delicate cycle of the equine industry noticed. As she drove, she scanned the landscape for the odd tuft of toxic fescue or white clover in the pasture, or black fences indicating a farm's declining profits, or—thankfully absent this year—the dreaded line of trucks bearing dead foals lined up in front of the equine autopsy lab, casualties of the baffling plague that left Lexington's five hundred breeding farms empty of more than three thousand foals.

Whitney Downs, like most of the breeding farms here in Kentucky, was a working farm. No fancy chandeliers lit the sheds. No oil or real estate money filtered down for owners to play with. Every penny made was from breeding, boarding and selling horses. Baby-making was what Pryor's family had always done. It was what they knew. Far more than training or racing, the mating, foaling and auctioning of the season's offspring consumed a manager's days and put bread and butter on the table. Without babies, a farm was dead.

So was a family, reflected Pryor bitterly. Without new blood, the Whitney-Benedicts would fade into oblivion. The future rested on the shoulders of her only daughter. Pryor didn't blame Whitney entirely for her lack of interest in continuing the family legacy. It was her fault, too. Hers and Boone's. If only they'd had more children, or if Whitney had been a boy, maybe things would be different. Not that Pryor would have traded Whitney for a boy, but more children would have spread out the responsibility, improved the odds.

It was with this in mind that she'd called Lila Rae and weaseled an invitation for tea. Lila Rae was her mother's only sister and something of a recluse now that she was well into her eighties. But age hadn't dimmed her faculties, and her advice on everything from babies to marriage to the society pages was pure gold. Pryor couldn't remember a time when the woman had led her astray.

She hadn't troubled Lila Rae with family difficulties for a number of years, not since the Wiley Cane incident. It seemed to Pryor that she owed the woman a respite and the assurance that her visits weren't always predicated by a family crisis.

Tallulah, her aunt's housekeeper, who was nearly as old as Lila Rae, answered the door. She took Pryor's coat and purse and sniffed disapprovingly. "Ol' miss is waitin' in the parlor," she said. "Don' be keepin' her too long. She needs her afternoon nap."

"How are you, Tallulah?" Pryor asked. She was not put off by the woman's greeting.

"If people wouldn' call up and ask ol' miss if they could come for tea, I'd be a whole lot better."

"Aunt Lila Rae likes company."

"She don' need company after lunch."

"I'll try to remember that," Pryor said dryly.

"You do that."

"Thank you, Tallulah. I'll find my own way to the parlor."

Lila Rae Whitney sat upright in a straight-backed chair, pearls at her throat, her silver-blue hair immaculately groomed in tight, even waves around her head. She wore hose and a navy St. John knit with white piping around the lapel and collar of the jacket. She didn't rise, but held out both hands. "How lovely to see you, dear."

Pryor kissed both cheeks and settled down across from her aunt in a stuffed wing chair. "Shouldn't Tallulah be retiring?" she asked.

"Probably," Lila Rae admitted. "But it would kill her. What would she do all day?"

"The same thing you do."

Lila Rae laughed. "Don't be ridiculous."

Pryor sighed and changed the subject. "How are you?"

"I'm on the wrong side of eighty, Pryor. How do you think I am?"

"Full of vim and vinegar, as usual. I'm betting you live to be a hundred."

The gray eyes widened in pretended shock. "Ladies never bet, dearest."

Pryor knew she was pleased. "I have a problem, Aunt Lila Rae. I need your help."

"Let's have our tea first. Tea is so healing. It dissipates unpleasantness."

As if on cue, Tallulah walked through the door bearing a tray complete with a teapot, porcelain cups and saucers, a sugar and creamer, lemon slices, spoons and forks with the initials *EW* delicately engraved on the handles, and two slices of a pale yellow cake studded with poppy seeds.

Lila Rae smiled. "Thank you, Tallulah."

As usual, the woman's surliness disappeared around her employer. So did her speech patterns. "You're welcome, Miss Lila." She switched on the ceiling fan. "Are you comfortable or do you want me to turn on the air conditioner?"

"We're fine, aren't we, Pryor?"

"Yes, just fine."

"You can run along now, Tallulah. Miss Pryor and I want to be private."

"Yes, miss."

Pryor watched her aunt pour the tea. The blue-veined, paper-thin hands added a slice of lemon to both cups and two cubes of sugar to one. It was a ritual the old woman loved. She never forgot who took what in her tea. Pryor accepted the sugarless cup.

"How are Boone and Whitney?"

Pryor understood the routine. Everyone they had in common would be commented upon before the real purpose of her visit was allowed to come up. She didn't think she could wait for all that. "They're fine, Auntie," she said impatiently.

"That nasty horse business of last year hasn't resurrected itself, has it?"

"Not this season."

"I surely hope not."

"Whitney is in Los Angeles…well, not exactly in Los Angeles," she amended, "but close by."

"That girl certainly does get around."

"The firm sent her."

"I assumed as much."

Pryor cut to the chase. "It's about Whitney that I've come today."

"I hope that's not the only reason, dear."

"Of course not," Pryor said, embarrassed by her gaffe. "You know better than that. When's the last time I've come to you to complain about something?"

"Now, now, Pryor." Lila Rae shook her immaculately coiffed head. "There's no need to be so defensive. You know you're always welcome, no matter what the reason."

"I know that, Auntie."

"Now, then, tell me about Whitney."

Pryor leaned forward, determined not to indulge in Tallulah's lemon cake. She knew from sneaking a peak at the recipe that it contained a full cup of butter and another of heavy cream. The woman had never heard of margarine or Splenda. The fat content alone would be more than Pryor allowed herself in a week. "I told you Whitney was somewhere close to Los Angeles."

"You said the firm sent her."

"Yes, well, I don't think she's there now because of the firm." In less than five minutes Pryor had informed her aunt of Austria's offer for Gabriel's horses, Mercedes's accident and Whitney's decision to stay and help out.

Lila Rae stirred her tea thoughtfully. "You're not going to like this, Pryor."

"Why not?"

"The child's in love."

Pryor groaned and leaned back in her chair, tea and lemon cake forgotten. "I thought so. I didn't want to admit it, even to myself, but I knew it had to be that."

Lila Rae nodded. "Your instincts always were good."

"But he's got three children and an ex-wife."

"Whitney's no spring chicken, dearest. If you want to see her married, you'll have to make a few compromises."

"But he lives in California. I want my grandchildren nearby, not thousands of miles away."

Lila Rae hesitated. Her eyes were cast down in apparent contemplation of her tea.

"What is it, Auntie?" Pryor demanded. "I know you're not through yet."

The lovely gray eyes, so like Whitney's, focused on Pryor's face. "You're not facing facts," she said bluntly. "Whitney is thirty-six years old. Chances are good that she won't have children of her own."

"Thirty-seven," Pryor said automatically. "Whitney is thirty-seven."

"My point exactly."

"Women her age and older have children all the time."

"With difficulty," the woman said. "I may be ancient, but I do keep up on the news."

"She could still have them."

"Yes, she could, and the sooner she tries, the better her chances are. Obviously this young man is fertile, if he has three children."

"Only one is his."

"One or three," Lila Rae said matter-of-factly. "Either way, he's proved himself." She leaned forward and took her niece's hand in her own. "You know that his virility isn't really the most important question."

Pryor's lip trembled. "Yes. I know. What should I do, Lila Rae?"

A small smile curved the old woman's lips. "If it were me, I'd have a heart-to-heart talk with the girl."

Pryor's mouth dropped. "You know how hard it is to get anything out of Whitney. She's a very private person."

"Sugar her up a bit," her aunt suggested. "Drop in on her. Compliment her. You're good at that, Pryor. Why can't you behave that way with your daughter?"

"I can't just drop in, Auntie. I have to give her some warning."

"For pity's sake, Pryor. You're her mother. What's the worst that can happen? She'll say she's busy and you'll try again. Or else you could go somewhere together, you know, for the weekend, to one of those spas everybody's talking about."

"I'm afraid," Pryor said honestly.

"My dear child, Whitney won't throw you out. She's

a good girl, in spite of that streak of stubbornness that appears to run in our family."

Pryor stared at the thin sliver of lemon floating in the amber pool of her tea. She couldn't pick up and leave with Whitney for a weekend. It wasn't just Whitney who would look at her as if she'd grown horns. Boone wouldn't like it, either. He couldn't manage on his own. Without her, his diet would be potato chips and macaroni and cheese. She'd come home to a husband who needed bypass surgery. She looked at Lila Rae. "What about Boone?"

"What about him?"

"He doesn't know how to cook."

"Have him eat out."

"His cholesterol is high."

"Make up his meals and freeze them."

"He won't eat them without me."

"Boone isn't a child, Pryor. He can be left alone for a few days. Women leave their husbands all the time."

"I suppose so." Pryor wasn't convinced.

"Of course, there's another way to look at it."

"What's that?"

"The unmarried state isn't the worst thing in the world. I'm not married."

"You're eighty-six, Lila Rae, and you've had three husbands."

"Your mind is going, Pryor. I'm eighty-two."

She was eighty-six if she was a day, but Pryor knew better than to argue. "I want Whitney to be happy."

"Then talk to her. If she's serious about this young man, you'll meet him. She can't exactly hide him away forever. You have an obligation to your daughter to give him a chance." Lila Rae shuddered delicately. "She made a dreadful mistake last time. I attribute it to her extreme youth. She won't make that mistake again."

The very thought of Wiley Cane stiffened Pryor's resolve. "I'll do it," she said, her mind made up. "When Whitney comes home, I'll figure out a way to have a long private talk with her. I'll make her tell me the truth."

"Good for you." Lila Rae picked up Pryor's untouched plate of lemon cake and offered it to her. "Here, darling, eat your cake. You don't want Tallulah mad at you. She worked all morning over this dessert."

Sighing, Pryor sampled a forkful of cake. The tart sweetness was everything she'd imagined it would be. Her fork went down for another bite, and then, throwing caution and saturated fat to the wind, yet another.

Lila Rae smiled. "It's so lovely to have you here. You really should come more often."

She told Boone while they were dressing, in preparation for the Lesters. She'd deliberately dallied while preparing the food, but now the salad was in the refrigerator and the Parmesan cheese sprinkled over the chicken divan. She mentioned it casually, after she'd screwed the backs of her diamond studs into place behind her ears and just before slipping her feet into her favorite suede ballet slippers. Pryor was tall, she had no need of heels, especially not at home with friends.

"I'm thinking of going away for a few days with Whitney."

Boone stopped in the act of tying his shoes. "Is she home?"

"Not yet. But Lila Rae told me I should talk to her about Gabriel Mendoza. She suggested we go somewhere together for a weekend, you know, a mother-daughter thing?"

"What is your purpose, Pryor?"

"I just want the truth out of her, that's all. She's fallen in love with Gabriel Mendoza. I think we should know her plans."

"What we *should* do is wait until she introduces him to us. Besides, how do you know she's in love with him?"

"Lila Rae told me."

"That's wonderful, Pryor, just wonderful. Since when does Lila Rae have the inside track on Whitney?"

"You know she's never wrong."

"I don't know any such thing."

Pryor sat down beside her husband. "I wish you'd stop combing that strand of hair across your bald spot, Boone. It's so vain and it doesn't fool anyone."

"We're not talking about my hair. We're discussing our daughter."

Pryor wet her lips. "I have a bad feeling about this, Boone. I went to Lila Rae because I truly believe Whitney needs me. My intuition tells me she's fallen for someone inappropriate again. I can't live through another Wiley Cane. I just can't."

Boone left his shoe untied and took his wife's hands in his own. "Whitney isn't seventeen anymore, honey. She's a thirty-seven-year-old woman. We can trust her to fall in love. She doesn't need her mother's approval. If you want to spend a weekend with her, I'm all for it. But do it because you miss her. She's smart enough to figure out your motives, and then who knows when we'll see her again."

"I have to do something, Boone. I can't just sit still while she makes another mistake. The man has three children. She can't know what she's getting into."

Boone sighed. Never in thirty-eight years had he won an argument with Pryor. He would leave it to Whitney to upset her mother's plans. The thing was, he couldn't bear to see Pryor hurt. She wanted so badly to be part of their daughter's life, but she hadn't the faintest idea of how to go about it. "I wish you would listen to me, Pryor, just once."

She was silent.

He shook his head, dropped her hands and resumed tying his shoes, evening out the loops, securing the knot with just the right degree of tightness. "I guess there's no point in continuing with this discussion."

"Are you mad at me, Boone?"

"I am."

"Do you love me?"

She'd done it again, disarmed him completely. She knew by his answer.

"Always, honey. You know that."

Pulling down his head, she kissed the spot where his hair no longer grew. "Thank you, Boone. I love you, too."

Twenty

Gabriel signed the last of the hospital paperwork, nodded at the nurse and rested his hand on his mother's shoulder. "I'll meet you downstairs."

"I don't need a wheelchair," Mercedes said emphatically.

The nurse soothed her. "It's policy, Mrs. Mendoza. You'll be out of it soon enough."

Gabriel watched his mother visibly restrain herself. He hid a smile. Maybe this stint in the hospital had been good for her—and, if not for her, for everyone else.

"Do you want to stop for something to eat?" he asked when they were alone in the car.

"All I want is to go home, sleep in my own bed and cook my own food."

Gabriel hesitated. "The doctor talked to me about your diet. He told me he discussed it with you, too."

"I'm not going on a diet."

He changed the subject. "Whitney's been doing some research on Asberger's."

Mercedes's face lit up. "She's a sweet girl. Imagine, going to such trouble for us."

"She told me that certain foods trigger spells, and by eliminating them completely, symptoms disappear."

"Hmm. That's nice." Mercedes looked out the window.

"Ma, did you hear what I said?"

"I heard you, *mijito*."

"It's going to take some time, three months or so, but she believes we can help Claire if we cook the right way."

"I always cook the right way."

"You aren't cooking with the right foods."

She glared at him. "What are you talking about?"

"Corn, dairy products and glutens have to go."

"What are glutens?"

"They're found in wheat and processed foods."

Mercedes looked thoughtful. "Wheat and corn are staples, *mijito*. How will we eat if I can't use those?"

Encouraged that she would go so far as to even continue the subject, Gabriel explained. "It isn't as hard as it sounds. Food is just more basic, that's all. Meat, chicken, fish, potatoes, vegetables, salads are all okay."

"What about milk? Claire is a little girl. She needs strong bones. How can we not give her milk?"

"There are substitutes. She can take supplements. Dark green vegetables are full of calcium."

"What about desserts, cookies and ice cream? It doesn't seem right to punish her for something she can't help."

Gabriel sighed. "Food isn't a reward, Ma, and healthy food isn't a punishment. Claire likes Popsicles and sorbet. There's also gluten-free flour. We'd all be better off with a diet like that. I'm actually enjoying it."

Mercedes sniffed. "How scientific is this diet? Why haven't any of the doctors you've taken her to mentioned it?"

"Because most doctors don't think in terms of nutrition. This isn't a quick fix. It's part of a lifestyle that

Claire will have to assume for as long as she lives. We should give it a try. Even if doesn't help, it can't hurt."

Mercedes was quiet for several minutes. "I suppose if Whitney believes this will work, we *should* try it."

Gabriel stared at his mother.

"Don't look at me like that," she said huffily. "The woman is smart. She knows things. Besides, I won't be able to manage on my own for a while. Whitney should be able to cook the way she wants."

"Hold on a minute." His hands tightened on the wheel. "She's going home as agreed, Ma. We'll manage without her. We have to."

His mother's lips tightened stubbornly.

Again Gabriel changed the subject. It was the only way to avoid an argument. "Lynne's suing me for custody of Eric and Emma. I have to find a lawyer right away. The court date is set for three weeks from now."

"I don't believe she'd really do that."

"Believe it. There's more. Kristen is back, temporarily. She wants money from the Lipizzaner sale."

Mercedes stared at her son's profile until he looked at her. "I thought you weren't selling."

"I may have to."

"Not for her, *mijito*. I'll scrub floors for the rest of my life before I see that woman get one penny of our money."

Gabriel smiled. "It won't come to that."

"Whitney's a lawyer. What does she say?"

"Her specialty isn't family law and she doesn't practice in California. I have to find someone here."

"She must have an opinion," his mother persisted.

Gabe nodded. "She believes that because the business was mine before my marriage and because Kristen left me to support her children, I won't get hit too badly."

"Good."

"She does think Kristen will be entitled to something, Ma. She'll have to pay child support because she's responsible for the kids, too, but she's entitled to spousal support. We'll probably have to settle."

"What's the matter with you, *mijito?* Are you afraid to fight?"

"It isn't a fight, Ma," he said wearily. "It's about what's fair and legal. The average divorce in this state costs each partner eighteen thousand dollars. This one could end up costing a lot more, after the fact. I don't want to go through all that again. It's emotionally as well as financially draining."

"Why doesn't she just drive herself off the nearest cliff?" Mercedes muttered. "No one would be the worse for it."

"The kids need their mother," Gabriel said tersely. "Even a part-time mother."

Mercedes didn't comment. They drove the rest of the way in silence. The door opened as they pulled into the lot and Whitney stepped out onto the porch. Claire was with her.

Gabriel helped his mother climb out of the car and then handed over her crutches. She stood, balancing awkwardly. "I've missed you, *mijita*," she said to Claire. "Come and kiss me." Obediently the little girl walked to her grandmother and slipped her arms around her ample middle. Mercedes kissed the dark little head. "My goodness, you've grown in only a few days." She smiled at Whitney. "I don't know how to thank you."

"You're welcome. We're all so glad to have you back. Ramona and Pilar are coming later today. Luz called this morning. I told her about your accident. She's flying home tomorrow."

"That isn't necessary," Mercedes clucked. "My girls are good girls, but they worry too much. What's to worry when we have you?"

"Whitney is leaving tomorrow, Ma," Gabriel reminded her. "I told you in the car."

"Tomorrow?" Mercedes's brow wrinkled. "I don't think—"

"Tomorrow," Gabriel said firmly.

Whitney's eyes twinkled. "It sounds like he wants to get rid of me, doesn't it?"

"I didn't mean—" he began, and then stopped when he realized she was teasing.

"I have to go home," Whitney admitted. "I'd like to stay longer, but it isn't possible. You don't have anyone scheduled to rent the rooms until next weekend. Ramona and Pilar said they'd be here on Friday to get everything ready."

"I'd like you to stay longer as our guest," replied Mercedes. "It was never my intention to use you as unpaid help."

"I know that," Whitney assured her. "Let's go inside. Eric and Emma will be home soon, and since this is my last night to cook, I'll make something special."

Mercedes limped past her. "Thank goodness my room is downstairs. I think I'll have a little something to drink and take a nap."

"Let me get it for you," said Whitney. "I have sodas and lemonade. If you'd like something hot, I can make tea."

Mercedes waited until Gabriel had disappeared into her room with her overnight bag. "I want a little something more," she whispered. "Maybe a glass of sangria or a lavender margarita."

"I'm afraid both of those are beyond me."

Gabriel reappeared. "Tea, Ma. You can have tea or a

diet soda. Later, at dinner, you can have a glass of red wine. No sangria and no margaritas."

Without answering him, Mercedes, on her crutches, lurched into her room and shut the door.

Whitney raised her eyebrows.

Gabriel's face was grim. "She's not winning this one."

Twenty-One

Whitney's suitcase was packed and her clothes laid out for tomorrow. After checking the bathroom and the closet to see if she'd missed anything, she looked at her watch. If she wanted to serve dinner early, she would have to begin cooking now. She started down the hall. The door to the bathroom shared by the children was closed. Something wasn't right. Whitney couldn't put her finger on it, but the stillness disturbed her. The hacienda felt silent, sleepy, as if the energy within had been temporarily suspended.

Mentally, she checked off the whereabouts of the family. Mercedes was napping. Eric, Claire and Gabe were at the stables. That left Emma. Whitney knew she'd come home a while ago. Where was she?

Backing up, she peeked into Emma's room. No human presence there. Stopping at the bathroom, she knocked on the door. "Emma, are you all right?"

"Go away." The girl's voice was muffled.

Whitney was about to do just that when her conscience smote her. She knocked again. "Emma, let me in."

"No."

There was no doubt about it. Emma was crying.

"Please, open the door. Maybe I can help."

"Nobody can."

"I'll tell you what. If I can't, I'll go away and you can lock the door again."

Whitney heard the click of the lock and then the door was open. Emma stood over the sink, a towel draped over her shoulders. She was staring into the mirror. Anguish distorted her face. Her hair was a startling snow white.

"It's awful," she cried. "I can't go to school like this. I can't go anywhere. Why did I do this?" She rested her head on the sink and sobbed.

Whitney crossed her arms and leaned against the jamb. "Calm down, Emma. It's only hair. It can be colored again."

"No, it can't. It says on the box that if I do it again before three weeks, it will fall out."

Whitney, who had been coloring her hair since the first strands of silver appeared in her early thirties, moved forward, resting her hands on the girl's shoulders. "Stand up," she ordered. "Let's see the damage. I might be able to fix this."

Emma's hiccupping tears stopped immediately. Her eyes met Whitney's in the mirror. "Do you think so?"

"Possibly. Show me the box."

Emma pointed to the trash.

Whitney fished it out and began reading the disclaimer on the back. "What color were you intending to get?"

"That one." Emma pointed to the front of the box where a woman with hair the color of sunlight smiled back at her.

Whitney pulled a small container from the inside. "I think I know what the problem is. You've applied the bleach to take out your color but you didn't shampoo in the dye to put it back in. Didn't you read the directions?"

Emma shook her head. "I read some of them. It was easy the last time. There was only one bottle and I just washed it in."

"That's because you were going from light to dark. This is different."

"You mean I didn't do anything wrong?" Emma asked warily.

Whitney looked at the girl's pale, nearly nonexistent eyebrows. "What color is your hair naturally?"

"The same as the woman on the box."

"I thought so. Why did you dye it in the first place?"

Emma shrugged. "I wanted a change."

"That was your first mistake," Whitney said. "You probably had lovely, silky blond hair. Why you would dye it an unnatural black is beyond me. Bleached hair won't ever look like the real thing, not until it grows back. The texture is all wrong. But you'll be blond again, if that's what you want."

Emma nodded.

Whitney looked around. "Are there plastic gloves around here anywhere?"

Emma pulled two pieces of wrinkled latex from the trash and handed them to Whitney.

She tugged them on. "Tuck the towel into the neckline of your blouse and sit down on the toilet seat while I attempt to remedy the damage."

Emma sat down. "You're a lawyer, not a hairdresser. What if you do something wrong?"

"Could it be any worse?"

"How do you know how to do this?"

"The directions are on the box. Close your eyes."

Emma closed them. "Is your hair natural?"

"Sort of."

"What does that mean?"

"It means I color it to cover the gray. Otherwise, this is as close as I can come to the color I was born with."

"Yours is the color I want."

Whitney placed her forefinger over the tip of the bottle and shook it. Then she began massaging the dye into Emma's bleached hair. "I'll do my best."

"You're really pretty, for someone your age."

Whitney's heart warmed to this pathetic little waif. "Thank you, I think."

"I wish I looked like you."

"That's a lovely compliment. If you stop destroying your looks, you'll probably turn out to be gorgeous."

"Did you ever do anything that destroyed your looks?"

"No." *Just my soul.*

Emma sighed. "I guess you were always perfect."

Whitney relented. "I wasn't perfect at all. I was stubborn and rebellious and sometimes I had a smart mouth that could have used a bar of soap. Not that my mother would ever have done such a thing. People don't nowadays. But, I'd say I was a fairly typical child. My parents always said they wished they had three more like me."

Emma's eyes opened. "Really?"

"Close your eyes, Emma. If this stuff gets into one of them, you'll be in trouble."

Emma closed them again. "Did your parents only have one kid?"

"Yes."

"How come?"

Whitney applied the last of the dye to Emma's part. "Sometimes it just works out that way."

"If you ask me, there are too many people in our family."

"Really?" Whitney smiled. "Three children doesn't seem like a huge number."

"I'm not talking about Eric and Claire and me. I mean all of us, all the Mendozas. A person can get lost in a family like ours."

"You can open your eyes now."

Emma's eyes flickered open. "Am I finished?"

"Not yet. You have to wait twenty minutes or so. Then I'll rinse you out and we'll see how it turns out."

"Thank you," Emma said suddenly. "You're really pretty nice."

"My pleasure, but I think you should wait to see the results before thanking me."

"At least you tried."

For a minute, standing here in the bathroom with this blue-eyed girl whose wisps of hair around her forehead and ears were beginning to take on the shade of harvested wheat, the years rolled back, twenty-five or so, and Whitney was in another bathroom with Pryor who was soothing her while she cried over the disaster that was her first and only perm.

"Yes," Whitney said softly, "I tried."

Emma's hair turned out after all. It was by no means the color that would have grown naturally from her head, but, considering what she had to start with, Whitney congratulated herself on a job well done.

Later that day, during dinner, she waited for other reactions. Emma came downstairs and took her place at the table. Her grandmother, distracted by pain, said nothing. Neither did Gabriel or Eric, fresh from the stables. Whitney set her teeth. What was wrong with these people? Didn't they notice the child at all? No wonder she was dyeing her hair black and wearing ridiculous clothing. She was about to clear her throat and remark on Emma's improved hair color, when Claire spoke up.

"Your hair is blond again, like Mommy's."

Emma tossed her head. "I was sick of it. I wanted a change."

Mercedes clapped her hand to her mouth. "I thought something was different. It looks beautiful, *mijita*. Don't ever change it."

Gabriel cleared his throat. "You look great, Emma. I'm glad you did it. I'm sorry I didn't notice. I've been preoccupied lately."

"Whitney helped me."

"Really?" Gabriel glanced at Whitney.

She laughed. "I happened to be here when she was dyeing it back. Together we averted a major disaster."

Eric said nothing. He made his way through his meal, sneaking furtive looks at his sister.

"Well?" she said, addressing her brother. "Aren't you going to say anything?"

He shrugged.

"C'mon, Eric. Do you hate it? Was I better as a brunette?"

"It's cool, Emma. The blond is better."

"What's the matter?" she demanded.

"It's nothing, except now that it's blond, and so short—" He hesitated.

"What?"

"You look like Mom."

Emma looked stricken. Eric looked down at his plate. No one said anything for a full minute. Then Gabriel spoke bracingly. "That's a compliment, sweetheart. Your mom was a pretty girl. She's still pretty. Isn't she coming today to pick you up?"

"It's tomorrow, Dad," said Eric.

Over the rim of her water glass, Whitney looked thoughtfully at Gabriel.

It was cold and dark at six o'clock the following morning. Whitney stood beside her rental car, rubbing circulation into her arms. Gabriel, hands thrust into his jacket pockets, stood beside her.

"So," he said, his breath condensing in the frigid air, "I guess this is it."

She looked at him. "I guess so."

"You're probably wondering what I'm going to do about the horses."

"The thought has crossed my mind. I need to give my client a definite answer, Gabe. I've put it off every time I've been directly asked, but I can't stall them any longer. If you're really going to refuse, I need to know. It could be a real problem for my firm."

"I'm sorry I'm taking so long. It can't be easy for you."

"Or you," she added, thinking of his custody suit. "Can we decide on a deadline?"

"Give me two days."

"All right."

"How will I know if it's me you want, or all that money?"

She was looking directly at him, and saw the twinkle in his eyes. "You'll have to take your chances."

He tipped her chin up and studied her face. "You're probably the prettiest lawyer I'll ever encounter."

"Flattery will get you everywhere."

His hand dropped to his side. "I want to thank you, Whitney."

"Your entire family has thanked me profusely. I consider myself well thanked."

"I certainly owe you a great deal for helping out this week, but that isn't it."

"What else could you possibly be grateful for?"

"For telling me how you felt."

She blushed. "That was a little unusual, wasn't it?"

"I'm incredibly flattered and more than a little surprised that you think I'm worthy of your regard."

"Gabriel—"

"No. Listen to me. If this never goes any further than right here and now, I want you to know what it means to me to have someone so smart, so decent and so damn beautiful show a romantic interest in me. My confidence was in the dumps. It isn't anymore. So, if you go home and decide this isn't what you want, I'll understand. You'll still have done me a favor."

"Are you brushing me off, Gabriel?"

Instead of answering, he pulled her into his arms and kissed her. "Not a chance," he muttered when he could speak again.

"Don't say another thing," she whispered, laying her finger against his lips. "I don't want to remember anything else just now, only this."

Nodding, he stepped back.

The last thing she saw before she turned the car out on the road was the rangy length of him standing tall in a pool of early sunlight, his arm lifted in a final farewell.

"Please, don't let this be the end," she said out loud. "Please let me see him again."

Twenty-Two

Whitney threw her suitcase into her trunk and breathed in the warm, humid air of her home state. It wasn't bad, not by southern standards, but the temperate climate of California had spoiled her. She turned on the air conditioner and waited while the engine warmed up. There was no reason to hurry. She didn't want to go home to her stark town house and empty refrigerator, not just yet. Maybe she would drop in on her parents.

The broken white line of the two-lane highway divided blue-green hills and rolling flatlands. Whitney felt something tight inside herself unfurl as she traveled the road studded with white wooden churches and brick school buildings, faded farmhouses and red barns, children riding bikes, and this year, because the temperature was unseasonably warm for Kentucky, men and women rocking and chatting on wraparound porches.

Miles went by unnoticed as the land rose up and fell away. White-trunked aspen and liquid amber maples sported new growth, heralding the height of the season. As she traveled deeper into horse country, split-railed fences and signs indicated the Thoroughbred farms for which the region was famous.

She found Boone where she always found him, in his office in the barn.

He greeted her warmly. "You're home. It's about time."

"Hi, Daddy," she said wearily, sinking into the shabby sofa her mother had relegated to Goodwill long ago and Boone had rescued. "I thought you and Mama might like some company."

"You can bet on that. Does she know you're home?"

"Not yet. I wanted you all to myself first."

Boone rubbed his forehead in a futile attempt to erase the frown in the middle. "Is everything all right, sugar?"

"Of course. Why would you ask that?"

"You've been gone two weeks. Your mama was worried. I hope your trip was successful."

"It was all right. I'm not sure you could call it a success, professionally speaking, that is."

"What about not professionally?"

Whitney sat up. "Spit it out, Daddy."

"Your mama thinks you've got something going with Gabriel Mendoza."

Whitney blushed. "That's ridiculous."

"That's what I told her. Lila Rae concocted some fool idea of you and your mother going away together for a weekend."

Whitney stared unseeing at her father. She was thinking of Kristen Mendoza and her unnatural desire to rid herself of her children. "That's not a bad idea," she said slowly. "Maybe Mama and I *should* take a weekend for just the two of us. We could both use a vacation."

Boone frowned. "Something happened to you out there in California."

"People change, Daddy," Whitney said gently. "How

long has it been since you and Mama have taken a trip together?"

Boone was silent for a long minute. "To tell you the truth," he admitted, "I don't think we've been away alone together since before you were born."

"That's terrible," she said flatly.

"I guess it is."

"Maybe you should plan a real vacation."

"I can't leave just like that. What about the horses?"

"The horses will always be here, Daddy. If you keep telling yourself you can't go because of a horse, you'll never go."

"I never have seen Santa Anita," he admitted. "I'd like that."

"Racing season has already started. You better hurry."

"Yes, sir." Boone rubbed his chin. "I'd really like to see it. Just to walk the place where Seabiscuit won the Santa Anita Handicap would be really something. My daddy worked there for a while. Did you know that?"

Whitney shook her head.

"Oh, yes, he sure did." Boone leaned back in his chair. He loved relaying a good story. "He told me about that track—'the best in the West' he called it—right up there against the San Gabriel Mountains. He was there when it reopened after the war in 1945. Did you happen to visit it when you were there?"

"No. California's a big state." She knew she sounded defensive.

"It's not that big, honey. Arcadia can't be that far from Ventura, no more than an hour and a half. I checked."

Whitney sighed. "You're the one who loves the track, Daddy, not me. It's always been just the horses for me. Besides, I had other things on my mind." She rubbed her temples. "I'm sure Mama would be thrilled if you planned a trip with her."

"I'll think about it." Boone grinned, leaned back in his chair and crossed his arms behind his head. "So, sweetheart, tell me, why a spur-of-the-moment visit from my favorite daughter?"

Whitney shrugged. "I missed you." She looked around her father's office. "I missed all of this. In California, I found myself in the middle of the whole horse thing again. It's different, and yet it's not."

"Those Lipizzaners are spectacular horses. I'd like to see them."

Whitney nodded. "They're beautiful in their own way, not like Thoroughbreds, just different. Dressage is a far cry from racing." She looked pointedly at her father. "It's not as cruel."

Boone nodded. "That's true. I'm not proud of it. I wish it was different, but money is the bottom line. One slip on a wet track and a beautiful three-year-old is euthanized. It's not right, but it's the way it has to be."

"Why?"

"Because a million-dollar animal isn't a pet, Whitney. There's too much at stake. Unless he's a stallion and a winner, unless his owner can recoup his losses with stud fees, it's not worth keeping him alive."

"I hate that," she said vehemently. "It isn't right."

Boone sighed. "I know you hate it, honey. That's why I didn't try to convince you to stick it out with me in the business. I saw right away that you didn't have the stomach for it, and I mean that as a compliment. You're a softie at heart. That's why your profession of choice surprised me. I thought maybe you'd go into teaching or pediatric medicine." He shrugged. "Not that it matters, so long as you're happy. You are happy, aren't you, Whitney?"

"Sometimes." She remembered her first conversation with Mercedes. "No one is happy all the time."

"I'll settle for most of the time. Are you happy most of the time?"

"I think so." She frowned. "It isn't as though I ask myself that question on a regular basis. I just go on living."

"That's no answer, sweetie. If you're happy, you'd know it."

"Are *you* happy, Daddy?"

"You bet." His wide smile was genuine. "Every day of my life, I wake up believing I'm the luckiest man alive. I'm married to the only woman I've ever loved. I live in God's country. My bills are paid. I have a gorgeous, successful daughter and I get to do the only work I've ever wanted. What could be better than that?"

"Nothing, I guess," Whitney admitted. She'd always known that her father's expectations, unlike her mother's, weren't particularly high. On the hierarchy of personality types, from simple to the most complicated, Boone was very close to the bottom. She loved him, even envied him, for the basic person he was, but didn't for a minute compare herself, or her mother, to him. Pryor Benedict, despite her protestations otherwise, was a very sophisticated personality. Whitney knew she'd spent a good part of her early marriage in a state of seething frustration over what she perceived as her husband's lack of depth. Personally, Whitney believed she'd sold her father short. On occasion, when he was interested, he showed exceptional insight. It wasn't often enough to suit Pryor, but, even so, Whitney believed her mother was happier lately, since she'd reconciled to herself that Boone would always be Boone and if she wanted intellectual stimulation, she would have to find it with her friends.

"I guess I should go in and see Mama," Whitney said, but she didn't get up.

Her father looked at her and closed the ledger he was working on. "How about the three of us getting something to eat and you can tell me all about California."

She laughed. "You're just feeling sorry for me because I'm at loose ends."

"Not at all. Your mama and I need to eat. You need to eat. We all like company. I'll tell you what. Let me change out of these horse-smelling clothes and we'll go to that barbecue joint your mother refuses to let me see the inside of. I'll buy."

"It's a deal, as long as you order the chicken with a side of beans and a salad. No ribs, no cole slaw and no butter-drenched corn."

Boone groaned. "You get more and more like Pryor every day."

"We love you. We want you to be around for a long time."

Two hours later, Whitney and Pryor sat beside each other in the sitting room at Whitney Downs, drinking tea from cups of paper-thin china. "I missed you," her mother said.

Whitney smiled. "Me, too."

"I know you're an adult, and a very capable one, too, but I was worried about you," Pryor said honestly. "You've never behaved like this before."

"Like what?"

"Well, let's see." Pryor ticked off on her fingers what she believed to be her daughter's transgressions. "You took more than a week from your job. You accepted responsibility for a man, three children, an injured woman and a bed-and-breakfast. You neglected to check your e-mail. I know, because I sent you at least one message every day and you haven't mentioned or responded to any of them. When you spoke to me on the phone, your conversations were completely unlike yourself."

Whitney frowned. "What does that mean?"

Pryor laughed. "My darling girl. You are an extremely efficient, matter-of-fact young woman with one of the most organized minds I've ever been privileged to know. In California, you sounded scattered. You couldn't tell me when you were coming home. You had no answers when I asked you about the progress of the offer for which your firm sent you in the first place, and all you talked about with any rationality at all was that child's condition, which I can't remember the name of right now."

"Asberger's," Whitney replied. "Claire has Asberger's syndrome. I'm sorry I worried you, Mama."

"To tell you the truth, Whitney, at first I was worried, but when I really thought about it, I was relieved, too."

"Relieved?"

"Yes. For the first time you sounded so…so… normal. It's normal to care about things outside of your job."

"Is that what you think? That all I care about is my job?"

Pryor nodded. "I have a confession to make. Sometimes, I feel incompetent around you and I wonder if you see me that way, too."

Whitney stared at her mother. "Never once has that crossed my mind."

Pryor sighed. "Thank goodness. You have no idea how relieved I am." Her forehead wrinkled. "Why are you so involved with those people? I was worried that you'd been brainwashed by some California cult."

"Don't be ridiculous."

"It happens, Whitney."

"Not to me. You know me better than that."

"I thought I did, until now."

Whitney's scowl took thirty years off her age. Pryor was reminded of the stubborn little girl with scraped knees and tangled hair who'd thrown herself into her arms and sobbed when her friends, tired of her unrelenting domination, requested that she go home. She bit back a smile. Now was not the time for reminiscing.

"Clearly, I haven't been taken in by a cult," Whitney said wearily.

"I realize that now and I realize something else, as well."

"What's that?"

"There isn't a darn thing I could do about it if you were."

Whitney laughed. "I don't think I've ever heard you admit such a thing."

"May I ask you a personal question?"

"If you must."

"Will you be honest with me?"

"I'll try."

"I think you're involved with Gabriel Mendoza."

Whitney stared at her.

"Am I right?"

"No."

Gray eyes met gray. The space between them sizzled with tension.

"I am not involved with Gabriel Mendoza," Whitney repeated.

"Would you like to be?"

Whitney hesitated.

Pryor wagged her finger at her daughter. "You said you would try."

"Oh, all right." Whitney set down her cup. "I'm attracted to him. He's intelligent, unassuming and hard working. He's also very unusual."

"He lives in California and he has three children," Pryor reminded her.

Whitney sighed. "I know. I thought that being there in the middle of his family would help me decide if I could handle it."

"And?"

"And, nothing. I was too busy to really get to know him. Besides, I went to California in a professional capacity. It would have been unethical to make it personal."

Pryor's eyes widened. "So you came home, just like that."

"Not exactly. I'll know more as soon as I get this offer sewn up. I'm beginning to believe it might not happen. Gabriel doesn't want to sell his horses."

"Why not?"

"It has something to do with his father." She shrugged. "I'm still trying to figure out what kind of man turns down millions of dollars to keep a legacy alive."

"Maybe that's his allure for you."

"Maybe." She looked at her mother. "I thought you wanted me to get married to someone with prospects."

"Of course I do."

"But?"

"Are we talking marriage, Whitney? Can you really think seriously about this man given all of his obligations and the geographical distance between you? Money isn't everything, you know. In fact, if there's too great a disparity in what each partner brings to a marriage, that can cause problems, too. You can't be thinking of relocating to California!"

"No. I don't think so. I don't know. I'm confused. How will I ever know if I rule him out immediately?"

"Sweetheart." Pryor took Whitney's hands in her own. "This isn't something to try out, not with a man like Gabriel Mendoza. Think about this. His children are vulnerable. The very fact that he has them, and his ex-wife doesn't, says a great deal. He's been hurt. This isn't your ordinary corporate type whose profile has been matched up with yours, and forty others, in some vague Internet database. This is a good man with three children and a widowed mother. I'm sure the family is lovely, but they won't be if you play with him."

"That's not fair."

"Fair or not, it's an accurate assessment of the situation," Pryor said flatly. "You don't have to admit it to me, but if you're honest with yourself, you'll know what to do."

Whitney changed the subject. "I have to go home and think of what I'm going to tell Everett tomorrow. He won't be pleased." She stood and kissed her mother's cheek. "I'm leaving now. Sleep well."

"Whitney?"

"Yes?"

"You aren't *that* involved with Gabriel, are you? I mean—that is—you haven't…" She left the sentence unfinished.

For an instant, Whitney was confused. Then she understood. "No, of course not. This isn't a movie. I was there two weeks and we were surrounded by children."

Pryor held her glance for a long minute. Satisfied, she stood. "Daddy and I will walk you to your car."

Inside the door of her town house, she dropped her bags in the entry and switched on lights as she moved from room to room. The button on her answer machine blinked demandingly. The number to the right indicated thirty-four messages. She pressed the button and walked back to her suitcases, where she rummaged in her carry-on for the bottle of wine she'd brought back with her. It was the same wine Gabriel had chosen on their one and only date.

Suddenly his voice was in the room with her, on the tape. Snapping into attention mode, she ran back into the kitchen, stopped the tape and rewound it. "Hello, Whitney. It's Gabe. Obviously, you're not home yet, but I couldn't wait any longer. This place feels strange without you. What a difference two weeks makes." He laughed. "I hope your flight went well." He paused for a minute. "No pressure, but I'd sure like to hear from you. Take care."

Her cheeks burned. She listened to the message once again, and then again after she'd poured herself a glass of wine. What did it mean? How much did it mean? He'd stepped out on a limb calling her so soon. He deserved to be called back immediately. She wanted to call him. She'd planned on calling him in a day or two, even if he hadn't called her. But once she did, once she continued the connection, she knew there was only one way to move, and that was irrevocably forward. Women her age were either serious about finding someone or they removed themselves from the game. Which was she? What did she want?

Her mother was right. Gabriel had gone through enough. He wasn't a man to be toyed with. A return call would mean she understood and accepted the rules. It meant she was in for the duration. In California, her mind had been so clearly made up. The pull of his family and all that she was missing was strong. The idea of such a commitment and all that it entailed was terrifying.

Whitney mulled over her mother's words. Now she wasn't at all clear. To call or not to call, that was the question. How appropriate that Shakespeare should come to mind when she thought of Gabe.

Mercedes washed her hands in the kitchen sink and smiled at Claire, who stood beside her. "*Mijita,* go into the pantry for your grandma and see if the avocados are ripe. I want to make some guacamole for your daddy."

"For me, too?"

Mercedes looked surprised. "You don't like guacamole."

The little girl tilted her head. "Yes, I do."

"All right. I'll make some for you, too. Bring three avocados. That should be enough."

Obediently, Claire opened the pantry door and disappeared inside. Soon she was back with three soft black avocados. "Here." She handed them to her grandmother.

"Do you want to help me?" Mercedes asked.

Claire nodded.

"First, find a glass bowl. I'll cut and peel and you can mash."

"I like mashing," Claire said slowly.

Mercedes slid a knife into the dark skin, cutting through the buttery flesh and severing the fruit in half. Then she scraped the yellow insides into the bowl. "Now," she said, "it's your turn."

Carefully, Claire pressed the tines of her fork into the meat until it oozed out from under the metal.

"Good," Mercedes encouraged her. "Keep doing that until it's smooth. Then we'll add jalapeños and lemon."

With the tip of her tongue curling against the corner of her mouth, Claire continued her task while her grandmother squeezed the juice from a lemon, chopped the chili pepper and added both to the mixing bowl.

"There now," she said. "A little salt and pepper and we have the best guacamole there is."

Claire dipped a tentative finger into the mix and tasted it. She nodded solemnly. "Daddy will like it."

"Yes, he will."

Claire frowned. "Gran? Why did Whitney go away?"

"Do you miss her, *mijita?*"

Claire nodded.

Sitting down heavily, Mercedes pulled the little girl onto her lap. "Whitney had to go home. She lives in Kentucky."

"Will she come back?"

Mercedes looked down into the fragile, earnest face of Gabriel's daughter and wondered which answer would be the least damaging. "Maybe," she said. "In fact, I think it might be quite possible, but I can't say for sure." A thought occurred to her. "Do you want her to come back?"

Claire nodded.

"You must like her very much."

Again Claire nodded. "She took me to ride Lorelei and she played with me on the swing set." She met her grandmother's black eyes. "I don't feel different with her, Gran. Everybody else makes me feel different."

Mercedes pulled her into a fierce hug. "I know, *mijita,* I know." Once, in another lifetime, someone she couldn't remember told her that grandchildren were all joy and no worry. *All pleasure and no pain,* she'd said. The woman was a fool.

Twenty-Three

Gabe struggled to keep his roiling emotions from showing on his face. The retainer alone wasn't impossible, but the rest of it… His hand shook as he removed his checkbook from the inside of his coat pocket.

Adam Winchester, Ventura County's family law expert, leaned back in his leather chair. His unruly gray eyebrows, thick neck and craggy face reminded Gabe of a mountain man rather than a high-powered attorney. "I'm sorry, Gabe. This will be tough on you."

"It was inevitable," Gabriel said briefly. "I can pay you the retainer upfront, but as for the rest of it, you'll have to bill me. I'll do the best I can." He looked across the enormous desk at the wily old lawyer. "I'm good for every penny of your money. You don't have to worry about that."

"The thought never crossed my mind."

Gabe nodded, satisfied.

"Why don't you go home and think about this before you pay me anything," the lawyer suggested.

"What's the point? I have no choice."

Winchester leaned forward. "Actually, you do."

"How?"

"The money that will go to your ex-wife is a given. We don't even have to litigate. In California, spousal and child support are formulas. Other than that, Kristen has no claim to your business. The trust was set up so she can't benefit from any proceeds should your family sell it. I'll be completely honest with you, Gabe. I believe we can win with your own daughter, but the custody case regarding your stepchildren is a lost cause. You won't get them and you'll piss away a fortune in legal fees in the process."

A thin white line appeared around Gabriel's mouth. "I have to try," he said, his voice low.

"Take my advice. Work this out with your ex-wife outside the courtroom. It's in both of your interests."

"I don't think that's possible."

"There is another alternative."

Gabe's eyes lit up with a wary hope. "What's that?"

"You could give her a substantial sum of money and absolve her of child support. Agree to lenient visitation with no responsibility on her part. In other words, you share custody and pay for everything, and then some."

Gabriel laughed. "I'll definitely think about that." He laid the check on the desk. "Meanwhile, take this."

Winchester rose and held out his hand. "I'll give it my best."

Gabe shook it and nodded. "I'm counting on that." Alone, in the elevator, he leaned against the wall and closed his eyes. He'd never felt such overwhelming despair. He couldn't face going home, not yet, when he was still raw and reeling from the money he'd spent and the sad prospect that it probably wouldn't do anything for him.

In his idealistic youth, he'd never once considered a

career in law, or any other money-making endeavor. Now that choice amazed him. Why hadn't someone warned him just how much adulthood cost? High schools should have classes that included job hunting and money managing. Holding down a job wasn't enough. Teenagers should have ninety percent of their net income withheld so that real life, whenever it happened, wasn't such a shock.

Outside, the noonday sun was hot on his bare head. Slipping on his sunglasses, he turned down the busier side of the street, hoping for a sidewalk café that wasn't too crowded. Intent on his mission, he would have missed the small, red-haired woman walking past him if she hadn't turned around, given him a second glance and called out his name.

He recognized her voice immediately. Turning, he forced a smile. "Shelly. How are you?"

"I'm great. What are you doing in this neck of the woods?"

"I had an appointment," he said. "What about you?"

She pointed to a glass-front commercial space across the street. "That's my office. I was heading out to lunch. Will you join me? My treat. You owe me one," she said before he could refuse.

He hesitated.

"C'mon, Gabe," she coaxed him. "You have to eat."

He smiled. "I'd love to have lunch with you, Shelly, and I do owe you. Lunch is on me."

She relaxed. "How about Russell's? They have about everything anyone could want."

Gabe didn't care what he ate. All he wanted was to get through this, find his car and drive home, alone.

Shelly chattered away beside him, apparently not requiring a response, which was preferable to a real conversation where he had to think and pay attention. The restaurant was at the end of the block. There was no outside seating, but the hostess found them a table by the window.

"I'll have iced tea and a barbecue chicken salad," Shelly said to the waitress.

Gabe closed his menu. "I'll have the same."

"So," Shelly said when they were alone, "what appointment brought you downtown?"

He drained his water glass and avoided her eyes. "A legal matter."

She studied his face for a minute and then changed the subject. "I was out to see Miss Mollie early this morning. I think she'll be ready to advance a level in the Santa Barbara show. What do you think?"

Grateful for her tact, he answered honestly. "I think you need a little more experience. You might be okay, but why risk it?"

"Why not?" she asked. "What do I have to lose?"

"Confidence."

She laughed. "I've got plenty of that. One bad set of scores won't faze me."

He stared at her, realizing that what she said was true. Shelly Sims was a woman who took chances, rolled with the punches and didn't take setbacks personally. Her line of work required it. Was she born with the ability to shrug things off, or had she acquired the talent along the way? "Does anything throw you?" he asked.

Her eyes widened. "I'm assuming you don't mean literally."

He shook his head. "You know what I'm talking about. Frankly, I'd like some of your attitude."

"I'm flattered."

"How do you do it?"

A flush rose in her cheeks. She twisted her water glass around on the table with perfectly manicured fingers. He noticed that her nails were squared off with those whiter-than-white tips that looked like bleached bone. "I don't have as much at stake as you do," she said.

"What does that mean?"

"I'm not married and I have no children. I don't have to weigh decisions all that carefully. If I end up destitute, I won't be taking anyone down with me."

"You're exaggerating."

"To a degree," she acknowledged, "but not entirely."

The waitress set their salads in front of them.

Gabriel picked up his fork, suddenly hungry. He didn't want Shelly Sim's solitary life, but he didn't want his own, either. Surely there was something in the middle. Once, he thought he had it. Then Kristen left.

"How long have you been divorced?"

Her question startled him. "Legally, about six months, but we've been apart nearly two years."

"What happened?"

Gabe wasn't a proponent of full disclosure, especially when it came to personal information. He was about to suggest another topic of conversation when it occurred to him that this might be the first step toward desensitizing himself to the bleaker aspects of his situation. "She left me," he admitted. "It came out of the blue. I didn't even know she was unhappy."

"Has she said anything since?"

"No, not to me, but she's implied a few things to the kids."

Shelly raised an auburn eyebrow. "Such as?"

Gabriel fought against the resistance knotting his stomach. "I wasn't there for her, whatever that means. Our daughter, Claire, was born with a condition called

Asberger's syndrome. She would have been difficult for anyone to manage, but for Kristen, it was impossible."

"Why?"

"Claire doesn't relate like other kids. She doesn't react with compassion or appreciation. She can't understand concepts like fairness or sharing. We—Kristen had the other two kids as well. I moved us in with my mother, thinking it would take some of the housekeeping pressure off. That was a disaster. It was too much for Kristen. She threw in the towel." He drew a deep breath. "And I inherited the whole mess."

"I'm sorry, Gabriel. You've been through a great deal. I think it's commendable of you to take on your stepchildren."

"I appreciate that, Shelly. I wish everyone saw it that way."

"Meaning?"

Gabriel shook his head. "I'm through. It's your turn. You haven't told me anything about yourself. How have you managed to avoid the domestic life so far?"

"I was married for a while," she said slowly. "Fortunately, there were no children. He's gone for good. I don't even know what happened to him."

"Why didn't it work out?"

"I'm not sure, really. We were young and wanted different things. I don't remember being particularly devastated when he told me he was leaving. I watched him go with a sense of relief." She smiled. "That was ten years ago. There have been a few possibilities since then, but nothing panned out. I'm beginning to think I'm not the marrying kind."

Personally, he agreed with her. She wasn't a natural, comfortable kind of woman, certainly not the kind who appealed to him. "What about kids?" he asked.

She shook her head emphatically. "Not for me. Children are a different species. I can't even talk to them."

"C'mon, I've seen you talk to Eric."

"He's nearly grown up. I'm talking about *children,* anyone under the age of twelve. You know, the ones who get into movies at reduced prices and order off a different menu. They're the ones I don't get."

This time Gabe's laugh was genuine. "I know exactly what you mean."

Her eyes met his over the rim of her iced tea glass. "I'm glad we understand each other," she said. "That way there won't be any misunderstandings or expectations."

It took him a full minute to get it. Normally, women didn't come on to him. The fact that he was married with three children kept even the most persistent at bay. "Look, Shelly," he began. "I like you and I've enjoyed our conversation."

"But?"

He wasn't any good at this. "I'm sorry. It's no reflection on you. You're a lovely woman, but I'm not ready for more than friendship."

"I've heard that before. When men say they're not ready, it really means they're not interested."

He didn't contradict her. The minute dragged out into two and then three. He couldn't think of anything more to say.

Apparently, she'd had enough. Gathering her purse, she stood. Her smile was brittle. "See you around."

Leaning back in his chair, Gabe loosened his tie and released his breath. He'd walked into that one with eyes wide open. It wasn't entirely unexpected, not quite a disaster, but close enough. What next, he thought? What else could possibly happen?

Dropping two twenties on the table, he left the restaurant, climbed into his truck and headed south on the 101. Passing his own exit, he turned off on the road leading to Ramona's. Today was her day off. With any luck, she would be home.

She answered the door immediately. With a finger against her lips, she ushered him inside. "I just put the boys down for their nap. If they don't hear you, we'll have peace and quiet for about an hour."

"I won't stay that long," Gabe assured her. "I came by to run something by you."

"Come into the kitchen. We can talk while I make us something to eat."

Gabe followed her to the back of what looked like an enormous great room. The house, a restored old barn in the middle of renovation, was in the roughest stage of its remodeling. Only the structure remained intact. Inside, every wall had been demolished. Open beams exposed new insulation and the staircase had no railing. Only the kitchen, Ramona's office, was complete, with a Wolf oven, stainless-steel appliances, a sub-zero refrigerator, a convection oven, double sinks and enough counter space for four people to work comfortably.

He pulled up a chair and sat down at the oak table, marveling, not for the first time, at how Ramona had managed to inherit the best characteristics of both parents, their mother's creativity and their father's pragmatic, no-nonsense ability to sift through the peripheral and expose the core of what was important. It was the latter quality he needed today. "I've decided to sell the horses."

She nodded. With a swift slash of her knife, she sliced through two heirloom tomatoes. "I thought you would. It makes sense, doesn't it? I mean, it's such an enormous amount of money."

"Why don't I feel good about it?"

Wedging whole basil leaves and fresh mozzarella between the tomatoes, Ramona scooped up the two stacks, arranged them on a toasted baguette and drizzled olive oil over the top. Then she poured two glasses of bottled water, added slices of lemon and set everything on the table. "You will if you think about it."

"I could use some direction."

She set two plates and forks on the table and sat down across from him. "Okay. First of all, this money will benefit everyone, including you."

"Go on."

"Luz is okay, and so am I, but Pilar could use some help and Ma is getting older. Running a B and B is hard for her." She lifted a forkful of tomatoes and cheese to her lips and nibbled delicately. "I think you could use the money, too," she said between swallows, "and not only because of the kids."

"What do you mean?"

Ramona's blue eyes clouded. "You need a challenge, Gabe. I'm not sure you realize it, but you've been in a rut for quite some time now. Nothing excites you. Your eyes don't light up anymore. Starting up a business of your own, one that isn't Dad's, would do you a world of good."

"I appreciate the counseling, Ramona, but I was asking about Pilar."

"Pilar?"

"You said Pilar could use some help. What's going on?"

"Essentially, she's not making it."

"Why not?"

Ramona chewed thoughtfully. "Some of it comes from her lifestyle, but there's more to it. Her asthma prescriptions cost money. That isn't her fault. When Dad died, you and Luz were on your own. Your education was paid for. Danny and I were settling down. Pilar was still in college. She wasn't able to finish. She has loan debt and she can't go back to school until that's cleared up. It would help a lot if she could finish. Luz helps her out."

Gabe stared at her, stricken. It never occurred to him that his pretty baby sister, with her wild butterscotch hair, honey-gold skin and dark eyes, hadn't been provided for. He'd forgotten all about her asthma. He'd been so caught up with his own family problems that he wasn't there for his sisters when they needed him. And now, when he'd been offered this windfall, they were standing by him willing to abide by his decision. "Christ, I'm a selfish bastard."

Ramona reached across the table and squeezed his hand. "You're no such thing. What could you have done, Gabe? You're up to your ears with your own problems."

But now you can help. The unspoken words hung there in the space between them.

"Don't beat yourself up too much," his sister said. "You came here to tell me you were selling the horses. At some point you must have realized that was the right thing to do."

Gabe finished his tomatoes, stood and kissed her forehead. "Promise me something."

"What?"

"Tell me when one of us is in trouble. Okay?"

"Okay. I promise."

Driving home through the buttery afternoon sunlight, Gabe found himself at loose ends. He didn't want to go home and he didn't want to go back to work. He missed Whitney, her rich laugh and the tiny vee between her eyebrows that meant she was thinking. He missed her voice, the simplicity of her meals and the careful, complete way she had of answering questions. She was so sensible, so grounded. Seeing her working in the kitchen, quizzing the kids about their lessons, carrying in the tea tray for guests, gave him a glimpse of a world he'd only dreamed of, a graceful, ordered world as far away from the pulsing, scattered chaos of the hacienda as one could possibly be.

An idea occurred to him and gathered momentum in his mind. The more he thought, the more possible it became.

Twenty-Four

"Hello, Whitney."

"Gabe." Her hand clenched the telephone so tightly the knuckles strained white beneath her skin. "How are you?"

"I miss you."

Her stomach flipped over. She'd started this upfront, no games relationship. Now the question was, could she handle it? "Me, too," she whispered, keeping her voice low so her secretary wouldn't hear.

"I need to see you." There was an urgency to his voice.

"Is anything wrong?"

"No. I made a plane reservation. I'm flying in this week."

"Flying?"

"To you. To Kentucky."

She swallowed and leaned against her desk. The edge bit into her hip. One word, one hint of hesitation, and it would all be over. "That's wonderful," she said, keeping her voice warm, her anxiety under wraps. "When will you be here?"

"It's all right, then? You haven't changed your mind?"

She could feel his relief and her own stomach settled.

"No, Gabe. Nothing's changed." She closed her office door. "You can stay with me." A thought occurred to her. She drew a long, silent breath. "It's Derby weekend. Bring the kids. You can stay at Whitney Downs."

He was silent for a minute. "That's a huge imposition for your family. We couldn't do that."

"My parents will love it. Truly."

He hesitated.

"I'd like you to meet my family, Gabe."

He hesitated. "Okay. You're on. We'll be there Friday afternoon."

"E-mail your flight information to me. I'll pick you up at the airport."

"I've reserved a car."

"Have you come to a decision about the horses?"

"I'm selling. It's a go."

Amazingly, she managed to sound normal. "Fine. Call when you get in and I'll meet you at my office."

She replaced the phone and pressed her palms, bloodlessly cold, against her hot cheeks. He was coming here to Lexington to stay with her and he was selling the horses.

Again the phone rang. It was Everett Sloane. "I'm about to return Ambassador Moser's call, Whitney. What am I supposed to tell him?"

"It's a go."

Silence. "Are you positive?"

"Gabriel is flying in Friday afternoon. We'll finalize everything then."

"Congratulations. I have to tell you, I honestly didn't think it would happen."

She refrained from telling him she didn't, either.

He changed the subject. "If you're free tonight, Wendy and I are having a few friends over to see the New Zealand pictures. How about it?"

"I'll have to take a rain check. I have things to organize at home."

Everett laughed. "I know the feeling. Another time. Let me know if you think we can take on the Razavi claim. It looks interesting."

"Definitely," she fibbed, and hung up the phone, grateful that she'd been spared the photographic details of yet another Sloane family vacation.

Pulling her hair away from her face, she let the silky-fine strands sift through her fingers, mentally noting that she needed a trim. Maybe she could fit one in before Friday. Then she sat down at her desk and flipped through the file she'd been given earlier this morning. Her potential client was an American student of Iranian descent, conscripted against his will to serve in the Iraqi army during the Gulf War, captured by American troops and detained for two years at Guantánamo Bay on terrorist charges. His parents, nationalized Americans, were putting up the money for his defense, but so far there had been no takers. Either the facts didn't hold up, or no one wanted to take on the federal government. Whitney wasn't sure it was even possible. The *terrorist* label was still new enough that precedent hadn't been set. The case could go all the way to the Supreme Court. Part of what she liked about her job was the variety. Taking on a precedent-setting lawsuit meant doing nothing else until it was settled, and settlement could take years. Still, someone had to take it on. A man couldn't vegetate in a military prison forever without a trial, not an American.

She flicked on her lamp, slid one long, nylon-clad leg over the other, picked up a yellow highlighter and began attacking the first page of the document in front of her.

* * *

Carefully, Claire Mendoza pulled the curry brush down Lorelei's left flank. A cloud of dust billowed around her head. Repeating the motion, she attended to her task steadily, talking as she worked. "You like this, don't you, girl?"

The mare flicked her tail.

"When I'm old enough, I'll ride you in the Grand Prix. You're already good enough, but I'm not. Daddy says I'm coming along, but I saw the videos and I have a long way to go."

Lorelei blinked and buried her head in the mash pail.

"I wish I could ride you by myself, without Juan or Daddy beside me." Claire thought a minute. "I sort of did when Whitney was here. She sat on the fence and let us ride. It was only in the ring, but we still did it. Didn't we, girl?"

The horse continued to eat and the little girl continued to brush. "I love it when no one else is here except us. I guess it's okay when Daddy and Eric are here, but that's all. I don't like it when it's noisy. I can't think." Claire poked her head inside the tack room, found a hoof pick and a stool and returned to Lorelei's side. She positioned the stool so the horse could see her, sat down and picked up the mare's back left leg. "I'm not going to hurt you, girl," she said gently. "Just keep eating. I'll clean you out and everything will be just fine. You like being clean, don't you, girl? I like being clean, too, but I don't think I'd like it if someone was touching my toes. I'm ticklish." She pushed her tongue between the gap where her front teeth should have been.

"Mommy used to clean between my toes and I didn't like it. You remember Mommy, don't you? Sometimes, I have a hard time. I have to think really hard to remember her face. Daddy put away all her pictures. Maybe you don't remember her. It's okay. She's gone now. She told me she wasn't coming back, except to visit. I guess she didn't like it here." Claire pulled a strand of hair from her mouth. "You like it here, don't you, girl? I do, too. Daddy likes it here and Eric likes it here and Gran likes it here and Emma—" she stopped. "Maybe Emma doesn't like it here, but Whitney does. She told me she did before she went away."

The mare shifted her weight, lifted her nose out of the mash pail, snorted and buried it again. Claire smiled and pressed her cheek against the animal's warm, muscled flank.

Gabe stood outside the stall and watched his daughter minister to the mare. He held his breath, afraid to mar the scene's perfection, the horse's white coat, the little girl's dark, loose hair, the chatty, confident innocence of her words, the careful movements of her small, tanned hands and, the part that stung the insides of Gabriel's throat with its unconscious purity, the obvious love emitted by the child for the horse she considered her own.

Her own. The phrase threw him when he realized its implications. Lorelei was part of the Lipizzaner package, a middle-aged brood mare with good reproductive years ahead of her. He'd given Claire the mare before he even knew about the damned offer. He couldn't break her heart. Hell would freeze over before he'd make his daughter give up her horse. He would have to make Whitney understand. Lorelei wasn't part of the deal.

"Hi, sweetheart," he said softly.

Claire tensed, but she didn't look up. "Hi."

"How are you doing in here?"

"Okay."

"Lorelei sure looks good. She's so clean. She looks like silver."

No answer.

"Are you hungry, sweetie?"

Claire shook her head.

"It's about time to clean up."

Claire's small face assumed a rigidity that Gabe knew only too well. What did the experts say? *Allow the situation to defuse. Give your child time to solve her own problem.*

Gabe stepped back. "I'll finish up in the office. When you're done, I want you to find me there. Okay, Claire?"

Nothing.

He frowned. "Please answer me, Claire. Just say yes or no. I want—I need to hear your words."

Her lips tightened. Minutes ticked by.

"All right, sweetheart. I'll be in the office." He turned to go. He was nearly out of the barn when he heard her voice again, talking to the horse, not to him.

"I have to go in a few minutes," she said. "I have to eat my dinner, just like you, only with Gran and Daddy and Eric and Emma. I wish I could eat here with you."

Gabe's mood lightened. She sounded almost normal, like any other little girl with her favorite pet. No matter what else he gave up, he would keep Lorelei for Claire.

Pryor sat out on the porch, a glass of lemonade in her hand. Lila Rae sat across from her, holding an identical drink. Between them was a half-empty pitcher and a plate of sugar cookies, another recipe of Tallulah's so heavily laden with butter it was sure to bring on a heart attack.

"I love this weather," said Pryor, her head lolling

against the high-backed lounge chair. "Late spring and fall are the only decent seasons we have."

Lila Rae nodded. "Speaking of fall, I'm thinking of going away for Thanksgiving."

Pryor sat up. "You're joking."

"No, I'm not. I looked through those cruise brochures you showed me. I'm not getting any younger, Pryor. I'd like to see the Greek islands before I die."

"But it's a family holiday," Pryor wailed. "We hardly have any family as it is."

"Whose fault is that? You should have had more children."

"That isn't fair." Pryor's hands trembled. She set down her lemonade glass on the side table.

Lila Rae frowned. "I didn't mean to upset you, sugar. Obviously, I hit a nerve. We've been down this road before. Don't you think it's time to talk about it? I can bring out the sherry."

"I don't need alcohol."

Lila Rae wisely remained silent.

"Oh, all right." Pryor tilted her glass to get the last delicious drop of sugary liquid. Her head was feeling strange. She stared defiantly at her aunt. "Boone wasn't up to it." She started to laugh and then stopped immediately. "No pun intended." She lifted her hand to her forehead. "Did I really say that?"

"Whatever you say is safe with me," Lila Rae assured her. "You know nothing goes beyond this porch. It's vulgar to gossip about family."

"The thing is," Pryor continued, "Boone has this problem." She stared into her glass. "At first, I thought it was me. I felt inadequate, undesirable. My friends were complaining because their husbands wouldn't leave them alone, and here I was, hardly getting lucky at all. After a year or so it wasn't unusual for two or three weeks to go by with nothing." She looked at the older woman. "You do know what I'm talking about?"

"It happens to all of us, eventually."

Pryor refilled her glass. "But not for a long, long time. Not until middle age when you're used to each other and it doesn't matter as much."

"It always matters."

"Not like it does when you're twenty-five. I was too hurt and insecure to wonder if the problem was his. For years we went on that way, stepping around each other, never really addressing the problem." She shrugged. "Now we've leveled out. At some point I woke up and realized sexual frequency had nothing to do with love. I learned to appreciate my husband." The corners of her mouth tilted up. "Better late than never. Menopause helped and so did all those Viagra ads. I mean, if Bob Dole could appear on national television and talk about erectile dysfunction, then I definitely wasn't alone. If Elizabeth can tolerate having the world know her husband couldn't get it up, then I suppose it's something lots of women go through." Pryor looked up, embarrassed by her honesty. "Everything's fine now, except that we have only Whitney. Not that Whitney isn't a wonderful, wonderful daughter. I wouldn't give her up for the world. I don't want you to think I'm not happy with my daughter. It's just that I wish there were a few more of her."

Lila Rae stared off into the distance as if deep in thought. "Maybe I'll take the cruise in September instead of Thanksgiving." She smiled at her niece. "I wouldn't worry about Whitney if I were you. She's a smart girl."

"She's invited Gabriel Mendoza and his children for Derby weekend."

"My goodness." Lila Rae's gray eyes widened. "She sounds serious."

"That's what I'm afraid of."

"Pryor, honey, make up your mind. I thought you wanted a family. Seems to me if Whitney marries this Mendoza fellow, you'll have a ready-made one."

"California is a long way from here, Lila Rae."

"It'll give you an excuse to travel."

"Boone doesn't like to travel."

Lila Rae sighed. "He'll learn to like it. People make do, Pryor. You can't have everything the way you want it."

"Promise me you'll be here for Thanksgiving."

"I promise."

Twenty-Five

Fayette County, Kentucky, the heart of bluegrass country, was about as different from Southern California as Gabe's solid warmbloods were from the long-legged, high-strung Thoroughbreds he saw munching on grass and chasing one another in the pastures and paddocks all around him. This was horse country at its best, and the gleaming coats, muscled flanks and flaring nostrils of the well-cared-for animals proclaimed it more than anything else he'd seen. He'd read about the stillbirths and aborted fetuses in central Kentucky, but there was no evidence of it here. These were the princes of the equine world, household names worth millions, whose owners spent even more millions in stud fees, training, entry charges and maintenance for that one-in-a-million chance of beating the odds in three races, the Derby, the Belmont and the Preakness, the famous Triple Crown. Even Gabriel, whose preferences lay in showing instead of racing, felt his chest tighten at the thought of bringing home such a prize.

He drove easily, a map open beside him on the passenger seat, his eyes on the road, his peripheral vision filled with rolling green hills, white split-rail fences, large wood-and-brick homes, and more spindle-legged Thoroughbreds than he'd ever seen in one place in his life. Claire in the back seat and Emma, beside him in the front, had their noses glued to the windows. Eric had elected to stay home with Mercedes. His junior prom was this weekend. Gabe would figure out some way to make it up to him.

It was too early to call Whitney away from her job, but not too early to stop in at her family home. He had to admit he was more than a little curious to see where she had acquired her horse sense, as well as her antipathy for the industry.

According to the map, he should be approaching Madison, the town closest to Whitney Downs. Sure enough, an elegantly engraved sign in gothic script swung gently from two posts, indicating the turn. The road leading to the house was dirt-packed, winding and lined with enormous oaks.

"Wow!" Emma said reverently. "This is some place."

Gabe pulled his rented Taurus close to the house, climbed out and stretched his legs. The house, seasoned by time, was colonial in style, with a huge wraparound porch. The girls clamored out after him. Together they approached the entrance.

An older version of Whitney opened the door. She held out her hand and smiled warmly. "Welcome, welcome, Gabriel. I'm so pleased to meet you."

Gabe shook it. "You must be Whitney's mother. Thank you for the invitation. I'm grateful that you're having us on such short notice."

"It's no trouble at all. I love company."

Gabe believed her. He hadn't expected such blatant enthusiasm. Her accent was lovely, more pronounced than Whitney's. He rested his hands on the girls' shoulders. "These are my daughters, Emma and Claire."

Pryor reached out her hands to the girls and led them inside. "We'll go upstairs right away and I'll show you around. Then I'll fix y'all something to eat." She looked over her shoulder at Gabe. "Why don't you go over to the barns and find Boone. He's anxious to meet you."

"I'll do that."

Gabe crossed the rich green grass to the working heart of the stud farm. The barns were immaculate, as if from a *National Velvet* picture book.

"Damn it, Reese," he heard someone yell from inside, "we're gonna lose this one, too. Where in the hell is that vet?"

"Easy does it, Boone. She's not finished yet," another voice said.

"I need another pair of hands, and quick. She's going crazy on me."

Gabe swung into action and ran toward the sound. Inside the foaling barn, two men grappled with a mare in the last frenzied stages of giving birth. She was on her side. Her eyes were wild and flecks of foam escaped from her mouth. Underneath her belly one tiny leg and hoof had punctured the amniotic sac and hung free, a breeder's nightmare. "What can I do?" he asked calmly.

The smaller man looked up. "Who are you?"

"It doesn't matter," the other man, who was obviously Boone Benedict said. "Come here, son. Take my place and try to keep her still until I get the hypodermic."

Gabe stepped through the flailing legs and squatted down. "You'll lose the foal if you shoot her now."

"I'll lose her if I don't," Boone replied tersely. "If we can quiet the mare down long enough so she doesn't roll over, we might save both of them."

Gabe ran his hands expertly down the mare's belly. He knew the foal was in the right position. Otherwise, the head would be exposed. "Who's worth more?" he asked.

"It's a toss-up. I'm gonna go get the needle. Whatever you do, keep the foal's leg free. We're not the goddamn Irish National Stud. We can't afford a crippled colt."

Gabriel nodded. "I've got her." Speaking soothingly to the frightened animal, he eased his hand inside the mare's vagina and searched for the other leg. It was twisted. "I think I know what the problem is," he said to the man who remained behind. "If we can get the mare to stand, I can fix it."

"I don't know." Reese wasn't convinced. "If something goes wrong, we'll be in a hell of a fix with Boone."

Ignoring him, Gabe worked on the mare, urging her up on her feet when he knew all her instincts told her to lie down, to succumb to the numbing pain and incredible pressure pulsing through her body. Finally, he succeeded. The mare stumbled to her feet in the throes of another powerful contraction. Gabe waited it out, keeping his grip on the twisted leg. His brow was wet with sweat. Gradually, the pressure retracted and the mare settled down just as Boone returned with the hypodermic and a towel.

"How's she doing?" he asked.

Gabe nodded at the needle. "She won't need that. The foal's leg is twisted and his rib cage is large, but if you give me a few minutes, I can pull it free."

Boone hesitated, afraid to hope, watching the young man relax the mare with his voice and, with his hands, ease the foal through the birth canal, pulling free the other leg, then the chest and the head. Finally the rest of the body fell into his arms.

Tearing the remains of the amniotic sac away from

the small wet newborn, Gabe sat back on his heels and grinned. "A happy ending after all. It's a girl."

Boone slapped him on the back and tossed him the towel. "Well, I'll be damned. Who are you, son? If you need a job, you've got one."

Gabe chuckled and wiped his hands on the towel. "I'm Gabriel Mendoza. Pryor sent me. I'm here to see Whitney."

"I guess you don't need a job, but how about a drink and a clean shirt?" Boone looked at Reese. "What about you, ol' buddy? Are you up for a tall one?"

Reese shook his head. "I'm bushed. You go on without me. I'll finish here, clean up these two, give 'em their antibiotics and then take off."

"If you're sure, I'll play host to our guest and come back later to check on our new arrival. You can tell our vet he's fired."

"She's a good-looking filly," Gabriel said on their walk back to the house.

"She ought to be. That was Dante's Lady you had your hands buried up to the elbows in. She was bred to Narragansett. The filly's got best bloodlines in the state of Kentucky." He looked speculatively at Gabe. "But you know something about bloodlines, don't you, son?"

"I guess Whitney told you."

"Hell, Whitney didn't have to say anything. I'm in the business. Anybody who knows horses knows the Franz Kohnle story."

"Most people don't put two and two together. After all, my name isn't Kohnle."

"Why is that?"

Gabe shrugged. "My father's memories of Europe weren't good ones. He wanted his children to start over with no links to his past, so we took our mother's name, in the Spanish tradition."

Boone nodded. "Nothing wrong with that, nothing at all. Whitney carries her mother's family name. It's a southern tradition. I'm the same way. Boone is a family name, too." He opened the door and stepped back to allow Gabe to precede him. "I'll show you to a bathroom where you can wash up. There's antibacterial soap in the medicine cabinet, and I'll see if I can find you a shirt. When you're finished, I'll meet you in the living room, first door on your right."

Gabe took off his blood-stained shirt, then scrubbed his hands and dried them thoroughly. Carrying the shirt, he went in search of Boone. Framed photos in the hallway stopped him. The Benedict family gallery depicted Whitney at various stages of her life: baby Whitney, bald as a chicken egg, held proudly in a young Pryor's arms; infant Whitney's first Christmas; toddler Whitney with a head of sunny curls, her hands in a birthday cake; Whitney and her first pony; Whitney's first day of school; Whitney and her father standing beside a long-legged, chestnut Thoroughbred; Whitney showing the first signs of puberty, dressed in breeches, jacket and boots, exhibition clothes; Whitney holding a first-prize blue ribbon; a grown-up Whitney, slim and straight in a formal gown, her shoulders sculpted and brown; and the most recent, the woman he knew, a smiling Whitney in a cap and gown holding a diploma. A wall of pictures, testimony to a young, successful woman's life, evidence of her parents' pride.

Boone came up behind him, carrying a clean shirt. "She's something, isn't she?"

Gabe pulled it over his head. "Yes, she is."

"I suppose everyone feels that way about their children," Boone acknowledged.

"Probably, but in your case it's well deserved."

"Pryor thinks you two are an item."

"Not yet," Gabe said honestly.

Boone laughed. "That's an optimistic answer."

"It doesn't hurt to hope."

"No, son, it doesn't. It was that way for me, too."

"Really?"

"Leave your shirt in the bathroom and come with me. I don't know where my wife has gone with your kids, but I'll pour you a drink and tell you about it. Is bourbon and branch okay with you, or would you prefer whiskey?"

"Don't waste either on me. I'll have a beer."

The house was decorated much more formally than the hacienda, yet it wasn't at all sterile. An aging, obviously expensive, Persian carpet covered warm oak floors. Long windows looked out on a deep lawn shaded by giant, green-leafed maples. On opposite sides of the fireplace, cream-colored couches flanked a wide, low table. The walls were the same color as the couches, but every available surface was covered with original oils, their subjects a mix of horse races, pastoral Kentucky and covered bridges. Above the fireplace was a life-size portrait of a spectacularly muscled Thoroughbred painted in a style that Gabriel recalled was popular a hundred years ago. On the opposite wall were ceiling-to-floor shelves entirely filled with books. Gabriel had never seen so many books in his life. His estimation of the Benedicts, already high, rose. "You have quite a library," he said.

Boone handed him his drink. "Impressive, isn't it? It's all Pryor. She's the reader in the family—along with Whitney, of course, but Whitney took her books with her. I'm a periodical man myself. Nothing longer than the daily newspaper or an occasional magazine article for me. I'm not apologizing for it, mind you, but I can't take credit for the books. Pryor never finished college, mostly because she married me. Women didn't do that in those days, go to school after they got married. Still, she managed to squeeze in quite an education on her own."

Noting works by German philosophers, Russian playwrights, Irish poets, contemporary biographies and classic American novelists, Gabe agreed with him. If Pryor Benedict had read these books, she had a liberal arts education equal to anyone. He sat down on the couch across from Boone. "You were going to tell me something."

Boone's face softened. "Am I right in assuming you're taken with my daughter?"

"Are you surprised?"

"Not at all. Whitney has been collecting men all her life."

"I believe you, especially now that I've seen her pictures. Is that what you were going to tell me?"

"No. That goes without saying. What I wanted to tell you is that I felt the same way about her mother. Forty years ago, I didn't think I had a chance in a million with Pryor Whitney." He lifted his glass of bourbon. "Just goes to show you, anything can happen. 'Course it isn't the same, Pryor and me, you and Whitney. I didn't have two nickels to rub together. Whitney has a high-paying profession and you have a business that could make you a multimillionaire."

"So do you."

Boone shook his head. "Only if I get lucky. So far, that hasn't happened. We make a decent living, Pryor and me, don't get me wrong. But we're not millionaires by a long shot. Breeding racehorses is never a sure thing. Every year is a new challenge."

Gabe had the fleeting thought that he'd been invited into the living room of a female version of Mercedes Mendoza. Apparently no topic was off limits for Boone. No wonder Whitney was so comfortable at the hacienda. "Anything involving the performance of animals is a challenge and a long shot."

"Are you here to sell?"

"Yes."

Boone leaned forward. "That's a big step, son. Will you go out of the business entirely?"

"No, sir. It's all I know. I'm thinking of starting over with different stock."

"I see. Well, you're here on a good weekend. The Derby is something to see."

"Actually, I flew out here to see your daughter."

Boone leaned back again. "Listen, Gabe. You seem like a real nice guy. Just remember, Whitney's been on her own for a long time. It might be hard for her to change her ways." He scratched his head. "For some reason, she's not the domestic type."

Gabe grinned. "Like you said, anything's possible."

Boone was well into another Whitney story and his third bourbon and branch when the telephone rang. He picked it up. "Hi, honey. Yep, he sure is. We're having quite a time out here. I think this guy's a keeper. He delivered a foal for me." He frowned. "Okay. I'll fill your mother in. She was hoping you'd all stay here tonight and eat supper. Uh-huh. Don't worry. I'll calm her down."

Gabe kept his expression blank.

"Oh, sure, hon. I understand. I'll send him on his way." Boone replaced the phone. "She wants to meet you at her office. Apparently she has plans for the two of you to have dinner out." He grinned sheepishly.

"Sorry about the time. I guess I got carried away. You go on now. I'll break the news to Pryor."

Gabe rose. "I'll tell your wife and the girls that I'm leaving."

Thirty minutes later he pulled into an underground parking lot in Lexington, locked the car and ran up the ramp to the elevator. The doors opened to an opulent lobby with a hunter-green carpet, a marble counter and a polished mahogany desk. It was empty. Several hallways branched from the lobby, like spokes in a wheel. There was nowhere to sit.

Unsure of what to do next, Gabe chose one of the hallways and wandered through it, reading the names on the doors as he walked. So far, none of the offices appeared to belong to Whitney.

"Are you looking for me?" Her voice, low and perfectly pitched, called out from behind him.

He turned and smiled. She looked exactly as she had the first day she showed up in his yard, with her mile-long legs, straight wheat-colored hair and business attire. He swallowed.

"Hi," she said.

He walked toward her. It was late. He hoped no one else was in the office, but it made no difference. He wasn't going to spend another minute without holding Whitney Benedict in his arms.

She came easily, willingly, as if she knew his intent and it matched her own. He was conscious of the scent of her, fresh, crisp, citrusy, definitely not floral. Whitney would never be floral.

All coherent thought left him when her mouth met his and opened. He sank into a well of sensation, softness under his lips, smoothness under his fingers, heat rising in his chest and down through his groin. He deepened his kiss. A low moan sounded in the back of her throat. She pushed against his chest. Reluctantly, he lifted his head.

Her cheeks flamed and she stepped back, out of his arms. Her voice was air-filled, breathy. "That was quite a welcome."

"I missed you."

"Obviously."

His eyes narrowed. "Did you miss me?"

"Yes," she said without hesitation.

He relaxed. She didn't play games. It was one of the qualities that attracted him. "Sorry I'm late."

She laughed. "I know what it's like trying to get away from either of my parents. I can't blame you."

"Are you hungry?"

"Yes."

He grinned. "For food?"

She blushed. "Yes," she said again. "That, too. I made reservations at one of my favorite restaurants. It's not fancy, but the food is delicious. I hope you like ribs and French fries."

"I do."

She linked her arm through his. "This place makes the best barbecue sauce you've ever eaten. It also has a pretty good wine list. I remember that you know something about wine."

Gabe didn't tell her that tonight her favorite restaurant would be wasted on him. All he wanted to do was touch her and look at her, in that order. Later, maybe, food would matter to him again. "Lead the way," he said instead.

Twenty-Six

The restaurant offered the kind of local, down-home food that Whitney loved. It was informal enough for patrons to feel comfortable, but upscale, too, so that it had a full bar and a decent wine list. The hostess led them to a corner table, covered in a red-and-white checked cloth.

"Tell me what you think of Kentucky," she said, after they were settled with a bottle of French Burgundy and a basket of squaw bread. She looked at him hungrily, paying careful attention to the tiny details that took him from good-looking to unique: the tight pull of skin over the blades of his cheeks, the square of his chin, the arched bridge of his nose, that olive skin paired with slate-blue eyes and the flashing white of his smile. Conscious that she was staring, she looked away.

"Kentucky's clean," he said, "easy to navigate and incredibly green. This really is horse country."

She nodded, forcing herself to focus. "Yes, it is."

"Whitney Downs is quite a place." He grinned. "I like your dad. He's a character. He reminds me of my mother."

The clear, rain-colored eyes widened in surprise. "Really? In what way?"

"What you see is what you get."

She laughed. "That's true."

"Your mother's great, too."

Whitney frowned. "My mother's terrific. She really is, but she's different." She hesitated. "She's more demanding than my dad."

"Why do you say that?"

She couldn't remember if anyone had ever been so tuned into her. He was truly interested, not just making conversation. He deserved a careful answer. "She doesn't take disappointment well, and if she senses defeat, she becomes relentless until she gets her way. And yet, everything she does, she does for me."

"Are you referring to anything in particular?"

Whitney shrugged. "Law school was a problem and so was my marriage. She was right in that instance, but I think if she'd been less controlling, as far as Wiley was concerned, I might have found that out before I went the distance."

"Did she break up your marriage?"

"No. It was doomed from the start. In fact, she picked up the pieces." Whitney twisted her wineglass on the table. "It's hard to explain. Something changed for me in California. Before, I would have said that my mother has tunnel vision. She's like a racehorse with blinders on and the finish line in the distance." Her eyes met his. "Don't get me wrong. I love my mother. I don't know what I'd do without her, but sometimes the only recourse was to remove myself or else I'd never have any independence."

"And now?"

"Now it's easier to see her point of view."

"Why do you think that is?"

The vee in her forehead was very pronounced. He wanted to rub it away.

She spoke softly. "Watching you with your children, seeing how much they mean to you, meeting your ex-wife, made me understand how lucky I've been. My mother has always been there for me. Your children haven't been as fortunate." She looked at him. "I hope this isn't painful for you."

"No. Not anymore. I regret Kristen. I wish I'd never met her, but that's all."

Whitney leaned forward. The wine on her empty stomach was doing double duty. "Maybe it would have turned out differently if you hadn't come back to live with Mercedes."

"That wasn't my first mistake."

"What made you do it?"

His eyes never left her face. "There was Claire to consider. Kristen couldn't cope. She was close to a breakdown. I had to make a living. The way I saw it at the time was, I had no choice."

"What else do you regret?"

"Marrying her, for one. Leaving Europe early to come home and work with my father. Giving up a discipline I loved to breed and train horses."

"But you love that, too."

"I grew to love it." He reached across the table to refill her glass. "Maybe I'm not particular."

She was conscious of his hands. They were brown and strong, the fingers long with clean, blunt nails. A wave of desire, so strong it made her dizzy, rose in her chest. Her stomach coiled.

"I think you're very particular," she said softly.

The tone of her voice had changed. He looked at her,

the heat in his eyes unmistakable. "Maybe we could postpone dinner."

"Or, I could throw something together, later."

"I'll tell our waiter we'll be back tomorrow."

She could barely get the words out. "Good idea."

Whitney never could remember the details of the ride back to her town house. For the most part, she leaned back against the headrest and closed her eyes, opening them only to indicate where Gabe should turn. When she led him through the door and flipped on the hall light, she was embarrassed by the starkness of the spacious rooms. "I don't spend much time here," she confessed. "I keep telling myself that I'll figure out the walls and furniture at some point, but it hasn't happened."

His eyes twinkled in amusement. "It isn't a deal breaker."

She realized that somewhere along the way the tables had turned. She, who'd started out so coolly confident, was swimming beyond her limits, while somewhere he'd taken the junior-lifeguard course. "What is a deal breaker, Gabe?"

He never answered and it didn't matter. Her question drowned in the wave of emotion that propelled them toward each other, in the tangle of limbs and the frantic shedding of clothes, the connecting of flesh against flesh, silk and steel, angle and curve, the heat of racing pulses and seeking mouths and searching hands, the rise and leap of hot blood, and finally, when it seemed as if every sense was saturated and there was nothing left to be said or heard or touched, she was lifted and shaken with the shattering, tension-rich peaking, and the long, slow slide into lethargy.

Gabe recovered first. He propped himself up with his

elbow. "Christ," he said when he could speak again. "Looking at you, who would have thought?"

She knew exactly what he meant. "So much for maintaining a professional distance." The idea struck her as funny and she laughed. The bubble of humor expanded in her chest and she couldn't stop. Tears came to her eyes and rolled down her cheeks and still she laughed. Gasping, Whitney buried her head in his chest, closed her eyes and gave herself up to the delicious tickle of happiness filling her throat.

He waited her out, holding her tenderly. When she collapsed against him, he kissed her ear. "I guess that means you liked it."

She sniffed. "I need a tissue."

He reached across the bed for his shirt and offered her the sleeve.

She stared at it and then at him. "You must really love me if you're going to let me blow my nose on your shirt."

"Actually," he said, "it's your dad's shirt. I was going to wait a few days before confessing my feelings, but there you have it."

She smiled and pressed the sleeve of his shirt to her nose.

"I was hoping you'd tell me you feel the same," he said after a minute.

"I think I do, Gabe. I really think I do. I'm not sure how it happened. I haven't known you for very long."

"We're not kids, Whitney. We're of an age where we should know what we want."

"Do you want to get married?"

"Are you proposing?"

She sat up and pulled the sheet around her breasts. "First, I have something to tell you."

"Is it good news or bad?"

"It's bad." She shook her tousled head. "Very bad."

"In that case I'll prepare myself. But first, I have to tell you something, too. I'm keeping Claire's horse, Lorelei. She's attached to her. I can't separate them. I wouldn't want to even if Claire was normal."

"I know. I don't think that will be a problem."

"There's something else, too," he continued. "I've seen a lawyer about the kids. We have a plan. We're going to assume that Kristen wants money. I'm going to give it to her, within reason."

"I hope it works for you, Gabe."

"I need to know that you'll be okay with this," he said earnestly. "Taking on three kids is a huge challenge, and Emma and Claire aren't the easiest kids. The money will help. I wouldn't even be asking you to do this if it wasn't for the money. We'll have a good life. I promise not to burden you, too much. I'd like to say we'll take it slowly, but I don't want to. We can have more kids if you're agreeable." He shook his head. "I can't believe I'm saying this. I know it's too soon. Tell me what you want, Whitney."

Her face felt frozen in its expression. *More kids. Did he really want more kids?* "Isn't three kids enough for you, Gabe?"

"Wouldn't you like to have one or two of your own? Our own?"

She struggled to pull in air, one painful, stabbing breath, and then to expel the words she hadn't ever spoken out loud to a living soul. "I can't have children. I lost a baby once, and I can't ever have another. No one knows, not even my parents."

His hand reached out and cupped her cheek. She closed her eyes against the compassion she knew she would see on his face. Her pride was strong. She couldn't bear pity. She didn't want sympathy or even understanding. She wanted acceptance, no more than that.

"What happened?" It was a question, gently asked, nothing more.

She opened her eyes. "I was pregnant. Wiley came home drunk and used me for a punching bag. It only happened once. I left right away. But once was all it took. With my parents' help, I pressed charges. He was already on parole. They put him away for five more years." She bit her lip. "Can you believe what a fool I was? What a stupid, ignorant fool?" She shook her head to erase the memory.

"Why wouldn't you tell your parents?"

"Are you kidding?" Her eyes were wide and clear and her hair fell across her shoulders like pale silk. "My mother's dream is to have a huge family. News like that would kill her. She couldn't handle it. It's better just to let her believe it's possible."

"You're kidding yourself with that kind of thinking, Whitney. Your mother is an adult. She'll accept the truth, and after the initial disappointment, both your lives will be easier. Surely you can't enjoy having her grill you about your marriage prospects every time she sees you?"

"Of course I don't. But I've waited too long. You have no idea what my mother is like when she's wounded."

"I'll be there to pick up the pieces."

She looked at him. "Will you, Gabe? Will you really? What about you? Do you want more children of your own?"

"Like you said, three is enough."

"But you may not have three. You may end up with only one."

"I don't think so, but if it happens, I'll deal with it.

At least we don't have to worry about the grandchildren thing with my mother. She has plenty, and Pilar isn't even married yet."

"Are you sure, Gabe?"

"Yes," he said, so emphatically that she was convinced.

She settled back into his arms and pressed her lips against his chest. "Maybe this will work out after all."

"It had better work out. Do you have any idea how awkward it's going to be telling your mother I'll see her tomorrow morning?"

Whitney winced. "Ouch. I forgot about the kids."

"It was your idea." He pulled at a strand of her hair. "Under the circumstances, I would have been happy to leave them at home."

Whitney groaned. "Even at my age, I'm still afraid of my mother's disapproval."

Gabriel shifted her in his arms so that they lay facing each other. "I don't think it has anything to do with being afraid. It's the conflict you're avoiding." He grinned. "I guess this means you're kicking me out."

"No. I'm going home with you. In the morning we'll all eat together and then head over to Churchill Downs."

At seven the following morning, Pryor stood in the doorway of the kitchen, her eyes wide with surprise. "Whatever have you done, Whitney? It smells delicious."

"I've made breakfast. You can call everybody down while it's hot."

"The children will be exhausted. It's three hours earlier for them."

Whitney stood back and surveyed her handiwork. Ramona's strata sat in a chafing dish in the middle of the table. Beside it were platters of bacon, fruit, sausage and grits with gravy. The table was set with shining silver, a pitcher of orange juice and a French press filled with rich, steaming coffee. "They can handle it. They're young and they won't want to miss the race. Go wake them. I'll call Daddy in from the barn. He's been awake for hours."

"Nerves, probably," Pryor said. "It's been a long time since Whitney Downs has entered two horses in the Derby."

She turned back to the stairs and met Gabe and the girls on the way down. "Good morning," she said. "I thought I'd have to drag you out."

"Not a chance," replied Gabe. "This is a once-in-a-lifetime experience. How many people can say they sat in a box seat at the Kentucky Derby with the Benedicts of Whitney Downs?"

Pryor laughed. "I suppose that's true. C'mon down and eat. Whitney has cooked up quite a spread."

Boone walked through the back door and washed his hands at the sink while the others settled into chairs around the table.

"What this?" Emma scooped up a forkful of grits and watched it drip through the tines. "It looks gross."

"It's no such thing," said Pryor. "This is a southern dish, sort of like your hash browns. I do think it's an acquired taste, though. Don't be surprised if you don't fall in love with it all at once."

"I'm not even going to eat it," Emma announced.

"Emma," Gabe said sternly.

"Eat whatever you want, Emma," replied Whitney, "there's plenty of food. But don't take anything you aren't going to eat. It's wasteful." Lord, she sounded just like Pryor. Quickly she glanced across the table. Was that a twinkle she saw in her mother's eye?

"Sure smells good, honey," said Boone.

"I had nothing to do with it," announced his wife. "Your daughter did the cooking."

"Is that so?" Boone looked surprised. "What's this?" He poked at the strata.

"It's an egg dish. Gabe's sister taught me how to make it."

He sampled a mouthful and his face lit up. "Mighty good. Time well spent. Pass me some of that sausage."

"Just take one, Boone," his wife suggested. "Eat the fruit." She looked around the table and smiled. "I'm so pleased y'all are here. It's just lovely to have children in the house."

Whitney rolled her eyes.

Emma spoke up. "It's the coolest place, Dad. Claire and I are staying in a room with a four-poster bed."

Gabe nodded. "My room is pretty nice, too."

"That's a wonderful compliment coming from someone whose mother runs a bed-and-breakfast."

Claire perked up. "My room at home is pink," she announced.

Pryor smiled. "Pink was always my favorite color. I wanted Whitney to have a pink room."

"Why didn't she?" asked Gabe.

"Are you kidding? Whitney with a pink room?" Pryor shook her head. "I don't think so. She had to have red or fuchsia or lime-green."

Whitney interrupted. "I think we'd all better eat up or we'll be late for the race. I'd like Gabe and the girls to meet the jockeys before they mount.

"Hear, hear," said Boone. "We don't want to miss that."

The Kentucky Derby held at Churchill Downs on the first Saturday in May had been a Whitney-Benedict family tradition since the turn of the century. Everyone even slightly affiliated with the family attended the race that began the countdown to the Triple Crown. The series of three races, beginning with the Derby and the Preakness and ending with the Belmont determined which Thoroughbred would go down in American racing history as the winner of the most prestigious purse in the racing world.

For the humans involved, it was a dress-up occasion as worthy of the right clothing as a wedding or graduation. Pryor and Whitney were slim and lovely in linen skirts and sleeveless blouses with wide-brimmed straw hats. They sat in the Benedict owners' box sipping iced tea, scanning the crowd and pointing out familiar faces, men in white suits and bucks, women with tanned shoulders, elegant hats and high-heeled sandals.

Churchill Downs had opened at eight that morning to a sea of thousands in Lycra pantsuits, short-shorts, T-shirts, halter tops and straw hats. They flowed in steadily to the sound of rock music, cheers and hawkers offering everything from popcorn to deep-fried Twinkies.

It was nearly time. Horses were coming through the tunnel. Television cameras focused on the tanbark ring. Owners and trainers met on the paddock, searching for their own colors. Jockeys in bright silks walked down the stairs. Crowds of spectators lined the fence.

Whitney caught up with her father and his jockeys in the mounting circle. She introduced Gabe and the girls to the small, self-contained men, giants of the equine world.

"Mount up," boomed from the loudspeakers. Strains of "My Old Kentucky Home" brought the crowd to its feet.

"Good luck," Emma called out.

The jockey dipped his head. "Thank you, miss."

They watched as the jockeys led their mounts around

the clubhouse and down the long stretch to the starting gate. The gates slammed shut behind them.

"I'll stay here," said Boone. "Y'all go on up to the box and watch with Pryor. Hurry now. You don't want to miss the start."

They settled into their seats just as the shot rang out. Horses and riders surged forward around the first turn.

Whitney grabbed Gabe's hand and leaned forward. In three minutes, it would all be over. The horses were head to head. No one had taken the lead. Burlington Stables was ahead now, with Claiborne advancing. Cinnamon Stride and Night Journey, the contenders from Whitney Downs, were still together in third place. Another Claiborne colt moved up a position, from third to second around the bend.

Whitney's grip tightened. If someone didn't make a move soon, their hopes for a win would be history. Then it happened. Cinnamon Stride took the bit in his mouth and moved forward from third to second position, nudging out the hard-running Claiborne colt. The line was thinning out. Slowly, Cinnamon Stride switched leads, left to right, his hooves flying over the ground, leaving the second Claiborne and Night Journey breathing dust. Like magic, the horse leaped forward, narrowing the distance between himself and Winged Hermes, now in first place.

Whitney stood and removed her hat, her heart in her throat. The crowd roared as the two horses raced through the top of the straight. The jockey flashed his stick. The horses were neck and neck. Slowly, purposefully, Cinnamon Stride pulled ahead.

Claire's arm stole around Whitney's waist, her eyes intent on the drama before her. Cinnamon Stride pounded the turf furiously, his jockey pumping and urging and flashing his whip. And then it was over. Cinnamon Stride opened one length and then two, sailing across the finish line by a good three-and-a-half lengths.

The crowd howled with glee.

"Oh, my God, we won," shrieked Emma. "We won."

"My, my." Pryor waved her hat in front of her face. "There won't be any living with your father. I never wanted to buy that colt, but he insisted."

Whitney looked at Gabe. "Well, what did you think?"

He released his breath "I think your father has an iron stomach. I couldn't do it."

"Not many can," agreed Pryor. She gathered Claire and Emma in her arms. "Shall we join Boone in the winner's circle?"

"What happens now?" Emma asked Pryor.

"Now, my darling child, the parties begin. However, I think those are better left to the adults. I'll take you home while Boone enjoys himself for a bit. Your dad and Whitney can catch up with us later."

"Can we go riding?" asked Claire.

"You bet, honey. That's exactly what I had in mind."

Twenty-Seven

Pryor pointed to the new filly pressed up against her mother in the stall. "She's just one day old," she said to Emma and Claire. "See how alert she is? Can you imagine being able to walk when you're only one day old? It always amazes me."

"She's beautiful," Emma said reverently. "What will you name her?"

"I don't know yet," Pryor replied. "We have to apply to the Jockey Club to be sure the name we choose hasn't already been used. It's a rule with racehorses."

Emma looked around at the blue-green grass and tall trees, at the split-rail fences, the neat layout of the barns and the wide lawn leading to the house. "I like it here," she said. "I can see why you stayed."

Pryor's eyebrows rose. "There was never any choice in the matter. Where else would we go? My family has lived here for a hundred years."

"That's a long time." Claire spoke for the first time. She looked at her sister. "You said Kentucky would be boring."

"Really?" Pryor laughed. "Any place can be boring. It's attitude that makes all the difference."

Emma flushed. "I didn't exactly *say* it would be boring. I said it wouldn't be like California."

"It isn't like California," agreed Pryor. "It has its own kind of beauty." She wrapped an arm around Emma. "I forgive you for jumping to conclusions. You're a child and children rarely have open minds."

Emma didn't know whether to be flattered or insulted. She resolved her problem by changing the subject. "Eric would have loved this. Too bad he didn't come."

"Next time," Pryor promised. "Right now, I bet I could convince Reese to find some horses you could ride."

"Not me," Emma said hastily. "I don't ride."

"Nonsense. You don't want your little sister to show you up, do you? Besides, I'll stay right beside you."

Claire clapped her hands, in a rare show of emotion. "Please ride with me, Emma."

Emma swallowed. The truth was, horses terrified her. She didn't mind brushing them or cleaning up after them, or even leading them around, but the thought of hauling herself up on top of a thousand-pound animal with long legs meant for running and a relatively small brain appealed to her about as much as sitting on the train tracks waiting for the Amtrak to squash her flat.

She looked at Claire. The little girl's cheeks glowed. "I'll watch you," she suggested. "You go with Mrs. Benedict and I'll stay here and watch."

Claire's lips turned down. "I want *you* to go with me. Please, Emma."

"Maybe Emma just wants to watch for a while." Pryor's voice was gentle. "She might decide to ride later."

Emma felt small and embarrassed. Claire rarely asked for anything. "Oh, all right," she said. "But I haven't done much riding. I'd need a western saddle."

Pryor laughed. "Saved by style. I don't think we have a western saddle. Let's check with Reese."

They found him down another aisle of the foaling barn applying a poultice to a dark gray mare.

"What happened?" Pryor asked.

"She's got herself a sizable cut right here on the left foreleg."

Pryor squatted down and eyed the leg. "Have you given her some antibiotic?"

The man nodded and pushed his hat back away from his forehead. "Yes, ma'am. She should be right as rain in a few days." He grinned at the girls. "What can I do for these lovely ladies?"

"We need two calm horses and one western saddle," Pryor said.

"How about Pretty Woman and Prime Suspect? They've been out in the paddock for two days now, which should've gentled 'em some." He finished wrapping the mare's leg. "Give me a minute and I'll see if I can scrounge up a saddle."

"It's okay if you can't find one," Emma cut in quickly. "I'm really not all that excited about riding today."

"No problem at all, young lady. We'll figure something out."

Emma bit her lip. "I'd really like to be here when Whitney and my dad show up," she tried.

"Why is that?" Pryor asked.

Emma shrugged. "It's personal."

Pryor turned away quickly, but not before Emma saw the smile tugging at her mouth. "You do whatever you feel is best, Emma."

Emma sighed. "I guess it'll be all right, as long as we don't stay out too long."

"Not long at all," Pryor agreed. "You can be the one to tell me when to call it quits."

Still only partially satisfied, Emma allowed Reese to saddle up a black horse that looked way too frisky to ever be described as calm. "Are you s-sure this is the right horse?" she stammered, staring down at the top of Reese's head while he adjusted her stirrups.

"You don't have to worry about a thing with Prime Suspect," he assured her. "He knows what he's doing. Just don't confuse him."

Great, thought Emma, *whatever that means.*

Pryor mounted her gelding and moved forward so that she was beside Emma. "These horses are well trained," she explained. "They won't do anything unexpected, as long as you don't give them more than one command at a time. Do you understand?"

Emma nodded. "As long as the commands are the same for all horses."

"Coming from a dressage center, you probably have horses who know more than ours. Take it easy and do what comes naturally. I'll be right beside you."

"What about Claire?"

Pryor glanced at the little girl, already on a small, red-brown mare. She held the reins in her right hand and her seat was relaxed and deep in the saddle. "I don't think we have to worry about Claire." She smiled at Emma. "Are you ready?"

"For what?"

"Bring your knees in, sit forward and, if you feel unsteady, grab the horn."

Pryor made a small clucking noise with her tongue. Emma's gelding broke into a trot. She clutched the pommel and tightened her legs around the animal's middle.

"Loosen up those legs, honey, or he'll run," Pryor called out. "Pull back on the reins if he's going too fast."

Run! That was the last thing Emma wanted a horse to do when she was on his back. Relaxing her legs was an exercise of sheer will, but she did it. Then she pulled gently on the reins. The gelding slowed. Pleased and relieved, Emma eased her grip on the horn and she followed Claire out into the ring.

Pryor followed behind. "We'll take a few turns around here and then we'll ride out to the track and I'll show you where we train our horses."

Emma glanced at her sister resentfully. Claire looked as natural and comfortable as if she was born to the breed, which in fact she was. Emma didn't like to admit it, but it appeared that her biology teacher, the one who said genes mattered more than environment, was probably right. After all, she'd been brought up in the same environment as Claire and she had no talent at all when it came to horses.

"That's it, honey," Pryor called out. "Keep her steady. There's plenty of room. You don't need to hug the wall."

Claire moved to the left. She leaned forward and loosened the reins. The horse broke into a smooth canter. They looked joined together as they flew around the exercise ring. Emma experienced a twinge of envy. Claire made it look so easy. Then she saw that her sister was laughing. Claire, who never laughed. She looked like any normal kid having a good time. Emma's heart hurt. She swallowed and looked away.

Pryor rode beside her. "Claire's doing really well. I didn't expect her to be this good."

"She's crazy about horses. She's had one since she was tiny. Dad gave her Lorelei, one of the Lipizzaner mares, after her pony died."

"What happened?"

Emma shrugged. "I'm not sure. I don't pay attention to things like that."

"What do you pay attention to?"

"Nothing you'd be interested in."

Pryor refused to be diverted. "Try me."

"I like music, mostly rap and hard rock."

"What else?"

"Clothes, movies, my friends. Stuff like that."

"I like those things, too."

Emma almost smiled. Whitney's mom was nice, even though she tried too hard. "Thanks for inviting us here," she said. "When I first met Whitney, I wanted to come here."

"What made you want to come to Kentucky?"

Emma was adjusting to the steady rocking of her horse's gait. "It was a bad time for me. I just wanted a change, that's all."

"From what I understand, you could have one if you wanted to."

Emma looked at her sideways. "How's that?"

"I heard that your other grandmother wants you to live with her."

"That wouldn't work at all," Emma said emphatically. "Besides, I didn't mean a permanent change. At the time, things weren't working out at school."

"Are they working out now?"

Emma thought a minute. "Sort of."

"What does that mean?"

"I guess things don't seem so drastic now. A few weeks ago it seemed like nothing was going right. Since then, my mom came back to visit and she says she'll come more often, and now Dad will have money from the horses." She shrugged, embarrassed. "I'm not explaining it very well."

"On the contrary," Pryor assured her. "I understand completely. At your age life has lots of ebbs and flows. Anyway, it looks like you got what you wanted, a temporary change."

"I wonder how long Dad will let us stay."

The frown line deepened in Pryor's forehead. "I'm hoping he won't take you away too soon."

"Really?" Emma was shocked. "You *like* having all of us here?"

"Two children isn't exactly a crowd, Emma, and to answer your question, I love having you here."

Emma was pleased. She smiled at Pryor and would have said something, but a white compact pulling up in front of the ring diverted her attention. Her father and Whitney climbed out at the same time. Together they walked to the fence. Whitney leaned her arms on the top rail while her dad squinted in disbelief.

"Emma?" he called out. "Is that really you up on a horse?"

"What does it look like?" she called back.

"Hi, Daddy," Claire called out. "Look at me."

"I'm looking, sweetie. You're doing great."

His eyes kept moving to Emma. She'd straightened her back and let go of the saddle horn. She kept her eyes straight ahead.

"Well done, Emma," Whitney called out.

Emma didn't answer, but a small, satisfied smile curled the corners of her mouth.

"I'm taking the girls out to the track for about an hour," Pryor called out to them. "Make yourselves at home." She nodded at Emma. "Are you ready?"

Swallowing, Emma nodded. The sooner they went, the sooner it would all be over. Without looking back, she followed Pryor and Claire out of the ring.

* * *

That evening as they sat around the dining room table with Boone at one end and Pryor at the other, Whitney noticed the table was set with the special-occasion china and silver. In the flickering candlelight, her mother's face glowed. She looked young and happy.

"Isn't this nice?" Pryor said, clasping her hands together. "Boone, please say the blessing."

Claire stared straight ahead and Emma looked embarrassed.

"Bow your head, dear," Pryor said to Claire. "Like this." She demonstrated.

Claire bowed her head.

After the mercifully short prayer, the serving bowls were passed around.

"When did you have time to make pot roast?" Whitney asked her mother.

"Pot roast isn't any trouble if you have a Crock-Pot. There's Derby pie and sherbet for dessert."

"What's Derby pie?" asked Emma.

"It's like a chocolate chip cookie, only in a pie," Boone explained. "It's a Kentucky specialty and very appropriate for today's dessert."

"Whenever someone asks the governor's wife for her favorite recipe, she sends that one," Pryor added.

"Who would do that?" Emma asked.

"Children who do their homework," her father replied.

Emma choked.

"Now, Gabe, I'm sure Emma does her homework," Pryor chided him. "I'm so impressed with your girls. They worked hard this afternoon and not a complaint from either of them." She beamed. "You're very lucky to have two such charming daughters."

"Very lucky," Gabe agreed.

Boone spoke up. "Pryor makes the best pot roast in Kentucky. Dish me up a big plate, sugar. I'd like twice as much of that meat and half as many vegetables."

"You know what the doctor said," his wife reminded him. "Eight servings of fruit and vegetables every day and only six ounces of meat. You can't have anymore, unless you give up dessert."

He rubbed his hands. "Bring on the dessert."

"You and I will have rainbow sherbet."

Boone groaned. "I like ice cream with my pie, not sherbet."

"That won't be a problem because you and I aren't having pie," Pryor said firmly. "I'm sure everyone would rather have ice cream, but because no one wants to make you feel deprived, we're all exercising some discipline. You should be grateful."

"I am grateful, but I'd rather have ice cream and pie, and today I'm gonna have it. It's not every day a man's horse wins the Kentucky Derby."

Across the table, Whitney's eyes met Emma's and her lips twitched. The girl's napkin was pressed against her lips in a Herculean effort to stifle her laughter. Whitney took pity on her and looked away. Had her parents always been like this and she hadn't noticed, or were their flaws more obvious in front of strangers?

"I'll have sherbet, too," Claire announced. "I'm not supposed to have pie."

"Bless you, darling child," said Pryor. "I appreciate the support. Do you see, Boone? We're all trying our best to keep you healthy, even the children. If Claire can exercise discipline at her age, so can you."

Boone winked at Claire. "Today, I'm gonna have Derby pie. Tomorrow, I'll worry about my heart."

* * *

Later, when Whitney and Gabe took over the sitting room to discuss the counter terms she would be presenting to the Austrian ambassador, Pryor climbed the stairs to look in on the sleeping children. Boone, fresh from his shower, walked down the hall to lay a hand on her shoulder.

"They're really very nice children, aren't they?" his wife whispered.

"Very nice."

"Whitney says that Claire's diet seems to be helping her condition."

"That's good."

"They're so happy here."

Boone grunted.

"They *are* happy here," she repeated.

"Of course they are. Who wouldn't be?"

"You're getting at something. I know you, Boone Benedict. You pretend to agree with me, but you won't actually say it, and that means you don't agree."

"I can't figure you out, Pryor. You're the most confusing woman on the planet."

"Why did you say what you did?"

"I didn't say anything."

"But you were thinking," she insisted stubbornly. "I know you're thinking something."

He sighed. "What I'm thinking is, they're nice, happy children. But they're Gabriel Mendoza's children, Pryor, and that means no matter how much you want to, you can't keep them."

She shrugged his hand from her shoulder. "I know perfectly well I can't keep them, but you don't have to be mean about it."

With that she disappeared into the bedroom, leaving

him to shake his head and wonder, once again, if he shouldn't read that book about men and women being from different planets.

Twenty-Eight

Sunday passed too quickly. Even Emma acknowledged that a barbecue ending with Boone's homemade ice cream, of which he only had a single serving, was an excellent way to spend an afternoon. Later that evening Pryor taught the two girls how to crochet. After giving them two crochet hooks, she invited them to choose a skein of yarn from her own collection to take back on the plane. As a grand finale, she astonished Boone by promising to bake her famous cholesterol-rich cinnamon rolls, the ones that won first prize at the state fair for tomorrow's breakfast.

While the girls were occupied with Pryor, Whitney and Gabe spent a great deal of time working out the details of Gabe's counteroffer. She would present it by telephone to the Austrian ambassador the following morning.

"I'm not supposed to be advising you, you know," she told him. "Technically, I'm representing the other side."

"There is no other side. I've decided to sell and accepted their price. All I want is one horse."

"The slightest hint of conflicting interests can be a problem. I'm hoping no one sees it that way."

"Have you met him?" Gabe asked. They'd found a rare moment alone and were sitting side by side on the porch swing.

"Who?"

"The Austrian ambassador."

She shook her head, acutely aware of his hand on her thigh. "No. But I think you will when this goes through."

"Maybe."

"You can count on it. Your father is a legend among these people. He performed a dangerous and difficult task for them and he was successful. They'll want to meet Franz Kohnle's son."

"Do you think I'll have any trouble keeping Lorelei?"

"I can't imagine that one middle-aged mare would make a difference."

In her office the following morning, while on the phone with the ambassador, she wished she could retract her words, or, at the very least, been less definitive in her assumption. "May I ask why it's so important to attain *all* the horses?" she asked. "Mr. Mendoza will want to know the answer to that question."

"I'm not at liberty to go into details," said the smooth voice with its slight German accent. "You may relay to Mr. Mendoza that our reasons are sound and not the least bit arbitrary."

"What if your answer isn't good enough?" Whitney asked. "What if your stipulation is a deal breaker?"

The silence stretched out to the breaking point. Finally, the Austrian spoke. "Please don't allow that to happen, Ms. Benedict. We aren't playing games. We've offered him a generous amount of money."

She wasn't intimidated. "Neither is Mr. Mendoza.

His daughter is very attached to her horse. The child has a rare form of autism. This isn't only about the money."

Again the silence was palpable. Whitney heard the murmur of voices in the background. Her source spoke again. "Please present our terms, and then arrange a meeting with Mr. Mendoza."

"In California?"

For the first time the arctic voice warmed. "By all means, in California."

"I want to be perfectly clear, Mr. Ambassador. If your offer isn't accepted, will the meeting still be necessary?"

He answered without hesitation. "Yes."

"I can't guarantee that Mr. Mendoza will agree to a meeting."

"I understand. Please try, Ms. Benedict."

She hung up the phone and rubbed her temples. Would Gabe accept the offer once he knew Claire's horse was part of the package? She sighed. There was nothing to do now but ask him. Once again she picked up the phone.

He answered on the first ring. "How does it look?"

"There's a problem. Can you meet me?"

"I'll be right there."

Whitney picked up the sheaf of papers in front of her and walked down the hall to Everett Sloane's office. "Is he available?" she asked his secretary.

The woman smiled. "I'll check for you." She picked up the phone and pressed a button. "Whitney Benedict is here to see you." She hung up. "Lucky you. Apparently he's been waiting to hear from you all morning."

Whitney groaned and opened the door, careful to close it behind her.

Sloane was seated behind his desk. He rose to greet her. "So," he began without preamble. "I hear that Mendoza may not bite."

She swallowed. "News travels fast."

"Is he an idiot? They're offering a fortune."

"There's a glitch."

He motioned her to a chair. "What's so special about this horse?"

Whitney sat. "It belongs to his daughter, Claire. She's eight years old and she has an unusual form of autism. She acts normally when she's around her horse."

"With that kind of money, he can get her another one."

Whitney's hands tightened on the arms of her chair. "Some things are difficult to replace."

"For Christ's sake, Whitney. It's a horse. How different can one be from another?"

"With all due respect, Everett, that is hardly the sentiment of a man from Kentucky horse country. Horses are as different as people. They have personalities and abilities and temperaments. This isn't a racehorse. She wasn't bred and raised to be a commodity. Lorelei is a family pet."

He stared at her. "You haven't become personally involved in this, have you, Whitney?"

She looked down at her hands, embarrassed.

"Shall I take over for you?"

"No." It came out too quickly. She wet her lips. "I'll finish it, Everett. Don't worry. I'll do everything in my power to make sure Gabriel accepts the offer. It's in his own best interests to do so, on all fronts."

"Stay professional, Whitney. We're in a bind here. This has gone on too long for us to accept defeat."

"I realize that."

"Good." He stood. "I think that covers it. Keep me informed."

"Of course." She handed him the sheaf of papers. "This is a copy of the counteroffer. Why don't you look it over?"

"I'll do that."

Back in her own office, Whitney threw her notes into her briefcase and closed the door behind her. "I'll be out for the rest of the day," she told her secretary. "You can reach me on my cell phone."

Without waiting for an answer, she took the stairs down to the lobby, walked through the glass doors and sat down on the bench under the elm tree to wait for Gabe. The sun soothed her. She closed her eyes and forced herself to breathe evenly. When Gabe drove up, she was completely relaxed and in control of herself again.

He climbed out of the car and sat down beside her. She ignored the rush of pleasure that warmed her cheeks.

"It doesn't look good, does it?" he asked immediately.

"That depends on your interpretation."

"What's going on?"

"They won't allow you to keep Lorelei."

"Why?"

She shrugged. "I don't know. The ambassador would like to arrange a meeting with you."

He frowned. "That makes no sense, Whitney. I don't believe they'd give up all the horses just because they can't have one. Lorelei isn't even prime breeding stock anymore. She's an older mare."

"Maybe you'll have your explanation when they meet with you."

"Who'll be at this meeting?"

"The Austrian ambassador and the director of the Spanish Riding School."

Gabriel thought a minute. "I'm calling their bluff. We'll have our meeting but I'm not giving up Lorelei." He stared straight ahead. "Tell them that."

"Fair enough." She bit her lip. "I have to ask you something, Gabe."

"Shoot."

She turned to face him. "What if it isn't a bluff? What if they won't buy the horses without Lorelei? Can you afford not to sell? Won't it be horrible for your family?"

For a long time he didn't answer. When she'd given up, thinking she'd gone too far, he spoke. "Claire is my family. She's here because of me. Maybe she's the way she is because of something she inherited from me. I'm responsible for her, more than anyone else. The rest of them will manage with or without the money."

Whitney felt the sting of his words, searing and clean and completely without compromise. She felt defeated. She'd had such high hopes for this day, the one day they would be completely alone without parents or children. He didn't suggest lunch or spending the afternoon together, and given his mood, she didn't mention it, either.

It wasn't until she was in her own car, on the way back to her parents' home, did she recognize the root of her emotion. There wasn't a soul on the planet who inspired in her the kind of feelings Gabriel had for his daughter, and there wasn't ever likely to be.

Pryor had outdone herself once again. Lunch was her mouth-watering fried chicken and potato salad. Boone took one look at the repast spread out on the picnic table in the back of the house and visibly brightened.

He sat down across from Claire and Emma and poured himself a tall glass of liberally sweetened iced tea. "I can't tell you how much better I'm feeling with a little fat in my diet," he said to his wife. "I read somewhere that if you don't eat some fat, you always feel hungry and you end up eating more."

"Really?" Pryor raised her perfectly arched eyebrows. "I'd like to see that. Be sure and find it for me."

Emma considered the chicken. "Did Whitney eat food like this when she lived here?"

"She sure did," Boone replied, "and she still does when we're lucky enough to have it. It didn't hurt her, either."

"Whitney understands portion control," Pryor cut in, "and she was always on the go. You couldn't find a more active child than Whitney was. Now she hardly eats a thing."

"She ate a lot when she was at my house," Emma said. "I think she likes Mexican food."

"Most people eat more when they're on vacation." Pryor turned to her husband. "Now, Boone, if you took just a bite of that potato salad and only one piece of chicken and loaded up on green salad and watermelon, your cholesterol levels wouldn't be off the charts and we wouldn't be having this conversation. If you'd just realize that I feed you the way I do because I don't want to lose you, maybe you'd be more cooperative."

"I know, honey." Boone was halfway through an enormous chicken breast. "I'll keep that in mind."

"Are we going home today?" Claire asked her sister. "I think so."

Pryor set down her fork. Suddenly, she'd lost her appetite. "I'd hoped you could stay a few more days."

"We still have school," Emma reminded her. "Besides, Gran is probably missing us."

"That's true," Pryor admitted. She wasn't feeling at all reasonable. Having Gabe and his children and Whitney under one roof with her was a dream come true. She didn't want to see it end. "Maybe you'll come back sometime."

"I hope so," Emma said honestly. "You've been really nice to us." She grinned. "I'm almost to the point where I like riding."

Pryor managed a smile. "California is such a long way away."

Boone covered her hand with his. "It's only seven hours by plane. That's not too long when you have friends on the other side."

Emma sighed and pushed her salad around on her plate with her fork. "Life is easier here," she admitted. "I don't have to worry about the same things I do when I'm at home."

"That's because this isn't home," Boone said wisely. "If you settled here, it would be the same when you went back to California."

"I want you girls to consider this your second home," said Pryor. "I mean it. Don't you forget about us or I'll fly to California and kidnap you."

Claire spoke up. "Why don't you have any little girls?"

"I did," Pryor answered. "Whitney was my little girl. But she grew up."

"Why don't you have another one?"

Pryor looked at Boone helplessly. He shrugged. "I guess I was only meant to have one."

Her answer appeared to satisfy the little girl. Relieved, Pryor picked up her fork again. Then she heard the sound of a motor. "I think somebody's here." She looked at her husband. "Are you expecting anybody?"

He shook his head.

She folded her napkin and stood. "I'll go and check out in front."

She was nearly at the door when it opened and Whitney stepped inside, followed by Gabe. "My goodness,"

Pryor said. "I didn't expect you back so early. Is everything all right?"

"There's been a complication," Gabe replied. "Where are the girls?"

"Eating lunch in the back. There's plenty more if you're hungry. We're having chicken."

"You go ahead," Whitney said. "I'll go upstairs and change. I'm not going back to the office today."

Pryor waited until Gabe was seated beside his daughters. Then she followed Whitney upstairs. She knocked on her closed door. "Honey, it's me. May I come in?"

"I'll be down in a minute, Mom."

"I need to talk to you."

Whitney's sigh was audible through the closed door. Pryor heard her steps on the floor. The door opened. She had already exchanged her Armani suit for a cream-colored linen shift and sandals. "What is so important that it can't wait?"

Pryor pushed past her and sat on the bed. "I want to know what happened."

"Nothing happened. Gabe won't sell Claire's horse and the Austrians want her. I'm not sure why one horse makes the difference, but for some reason it does. I have to arrange a meeting between Gabe and the principals in California. That's all there is to it."

Pryor frowned. "Gabe is giving up millions for a single horse? Is he insane?"

Whitney's forehead wrinkled. "It's certainly odd. I asked him the same question. In a nutshell, he explained that Claire is the most important person in his world and he feels responsible for her condition. He's afraid that she'll regress if she suffers the disappointment of losing Lorelei."

"Hogwash."

"We don't know that, Mama," Whitney said wearily. "We haven't seen Claire at her worst. Maybe he's right. Maybe a child's health is worth millions. I don't know."

"Children adjust," Pryor said flatly. "Claire will adjust. She lost her mother, for Pete's sake. She can certainly stand to lose an animal."

"Maybe. Maybe not. The point is, neither of us really knows what will happen to Claire without her horse. It isn't our decision. She isn't our child. We don't have to live with the consequences."

Pryor reached out to smooth her daughter's hair. "Am I right in thinking this clarifies things for you?"

"In what way?"

"Gabe is a very nice young man and he's certainly attractive, but his first priority will always be his daughter. I think you deserve better than that. You deserve a husband who thinks of you first, and the children you'll have together."

"Please give this up, Mom."

"You can't mean that this doesn't matter to you," Pryor persisted. "Don't you see? It will always be Claire."

Whitney turned on her mother, tiny forks of strain at the corners of her eyes. "What's wrong with that? She's a little girl. He created her. Is it wrong for him to feel responsible for her?"

"Of course not. I admire him for his loyalty. I adore those children. I haven't had so much fun in years. But what about you? I'm concerned for you. You're a beautiful, intelligent woman. I want you to have the life you deserve with the right husband and your own children, not someone else's."

Whitney shook her head. "It isn't going to happen, Mama. I'm so sorry to have to tell you this. I've avoided it for years, but I can't do it any longer." She took her mother's face between her hands. "Look at me, and just this once, listen without interruption." She swallowed, shook her head and continued. "There won't be any children. Not ever. There was a baby, once, with Wiley. I lost it in the hospital after he hurt me. I can't have any more children."

Pryor stared at her, registering the words. Something didn't make sense. "That was nearly twenty years ago," she whispered. "Modern medicine has changed. There are ways—"

Whitney shook her head. "I'll never carry a child. I'm so sorry." Tears spilled down her cheeks. "I'm sorrier for you than for me. I can live without children of my own, but seeing you these last few days, I don't know if you can live without grandchildren. I feel so terrible about disappointing you. All my life I was such a good kid. I made one terrible mistake, only one, but it was *the* mistake. I ruined your life."

Through the shock and pain of her daughter's words, something clicked in Pryor's brain, an instinctive knowledge that something needed salvaging. She wet her lips. "You did no such thing," she said carefully.

"Of course I did. Look at you. You're miserable because of me. Your only daughter can't do the one thing you've asked her."

"Stop it," Pryor ordered. The fog was gone now. She was completely lucid. "It just isn't true, Whitney. You've been the most incredible gift. I wouldn't trade you for the world. A large part of the reason I was so set on your having children was because I hoped you'd have at least one just like you, and I could relive those wonderful years all over again with another little Whitney." She laughed. "The chances of that were ridiculous, anyway.

Most people have terrible problems with their children, far worse than anything you put me through. Don't you think, even for a minute, that I don't get down on my knees every day and thank God for giving you to me? I'm so sorry you didn't feel like you could tell me this long ago. I ache inside that you carried this burden all by yourself. I'm the one who failed you, my darling. I'm so ashamed." Now Pryor was crying, too.

Whitney laughed through her tears. "We're a pair, aren't we?"

"More than you know. You've never asked why we didn't have more children."

"It never occurred to me. I assumed it was a personal decision."

"It wasn't a decision. We just didn't have them. I wanted more. So did Daddy." She lifted her hands. "But it wasn't to be. In those days, people didn't talk about infertility. We didn't go to doctors or have treatments. It was just something we accepted. Maybe, if I'd never had you, I would have been more proactive. But you were just about the best there was. I'm so proud of you, Whitney. You've accomplished so much. I should have told you that long ago."

"Really?"

"Really."

Whitney wiped her eyes. "They'll be wondering what we're doing."

"I guess we should go downstairs."

"The chicken smells delicious."

Pryor nodded. "It is delicious."

"Daddy must be in heaven."

"He's probably eaten four pieces by now." Pryor sighed. "Oh, well. It won't hurt him this once. I'll put him right back on whole-grain breads and raw vegetables tomorrow."

Whitney's mouth trembled. "Gabe and the girls are leaving tonight."

"How's your heart?"

"This time I think it might be broken, Mama." She turned into her mother's outstretched arms. "I don't know what happened, but if he keeps his horses, I don't think I'll see him again. He won't let me in. Isn't it funny? I've spent my whole life running away from commitment, and now that I want it, I can't have it."

"Oh, sugar, of course you can. Don't you see? This is a breakthrough. Now that you know what you want, you won't push the opportunity away. You're such a lovely woman, Whitney. If Gabe doesn't realize what he has in you, then he isn't worth it. Trust me, sweetheart. His loss will be somebody else's gain." Personally, Pryor would have liked to give Gabriel Mendoza a piece of her mind and tell him what a fool he was to reject the best thing that would ever happen to him. But Whitney wasn't a little girl anymore. She could handle her own problems far better than her mother could handle them for her.

Pryor stroked her daughter's head. She was exhausted. They'd come a long way in the past twenty minutes.

Twenty-Nine

Eric's look of relief when his stepfather walked into the barn early the next evening would normally have made Gabe laugh, except that he wasn't in the mood for laughing.

"Hey, Dad." Eric hugged him awkwardly. "Did everything go okay?"

"That depends on your perspective. The reality is, the sale doesn't look good."

Eric groaned. "Gran's not gonna be happy."

Gabe nodded. "For some reason the Austrians won't give up a single horse, not even Lorelei."

Eric checked his watch, wrote the time down on the chart hanging in front of the stall, and then gave Gabe his full attention. "Do they know how old she is?"

"They know everything, down to the last time she was shod."

"That doesn't make sense," Eric said flatly.

"Tell them that."

Eric sat down on a bale of hay. "Is Lorelei the only reason you won't sell?"

"What else would it be?"

The boy shrugged. "You were cool on the idea in the first place. Maybe you're using her as an excuse."

"Since when have you become Dr. Phil?" Gabe said sharply.

"Dad." Eric wouldn't be put off. "Claire can cope. She's not as fragile as you think."

"She's lost enough."

"We all have."

"She doesn't have the coping skills you have."

"Maybe it's the other way around," Eric said carefully. "Maybe she has more because things don't bother her as much as they do the rest of us."

Gabe stared at his stepson. Could the boy be right? Was he using Claire's horse as an excuse to nix the deal because it wasn't what he wanted? He would have to think that one through. "Juan says you've done a terrific job the past few days, Eric. I'm proud of you." He rested his hand on the boy's shoulder. "How was the prom?"

"It was terrific. Gran took a bunch of pictures."

"Make sure I get copies."

"I'm done here. Are you coming home now?"

"I think I'll take a walk and mull over a few things."

As usual, when something weighed heavily on his mind, Gabe headed to the same place, down the lane bordered by weeping jacarandas, deep into the heart of his mother's lavender field where the pollen haze was thick as smoke and he saw the world through a violet lens. The drone of insects sounded like a passing train, and the pungent scent of the blooms was so strong and acrid one deep breath burned the sensitive lining of his nose.

For the first time since Whitney told him the sale was no longer in the bag, he allowed the full weight of his emotions to roll through him. The ache was so severe it pushed against him like a fierce wind. He staggered forward, determined to reach some kind of resolution. After a few minutes in the spicy, perfumed air, his breath came easier and his mind cleared enough to sort through his options.

Without the money from the sale of the Lipizzaners, everything that was important to him would be gone. Lynne would take Eric and Emma, and Whitney would disappear from his life. She wouldn't go willingly, but in the end, she would go. There was no other choice. He refused to ask a woman like Whitney to give up everything she'd worked for to settle down in his mother's house and run a dressage center that barely made ends meet. She deserved more than that. Even if she got another job in Los Angeles, she would still be starting over. Gabe knew something about guilt and resentment and he wanted no part of either. "At least Claire will benefit," he said out loud. "My fragile, vulnerable faery child won't lose her mare." The words sliding off his tongue sounded hollow to his ears. He couldn't ignore the tiny voice in his head that suggested she might be losing a great deal more.

"Whitney called," his mother said when Gabe walked into the kitchen an hour later. She was sitting on a bar stool with her leg elevated, chopping chili peppers. As usual, a tumbler filled with ice and a suspicious ruby-colored liquid sat at her elbow.

Gabe opened his mouth to remind her that wine for medicinal purposes was limited to four ounces a day. Then he thought of the news he would have to break to her and changed his mind. Let her enjoy her evening. "What time did she call?"

"About twenty minutes ago. She wants you to call her at home."

He picked up the phone and walked into the living

room, closing the doors behind him. Mercedes would eavesdrop without compunction if she was within listening range, but she wouldn't pick up the other phone. She had her scruples.

Whitney answered on the first ring. Her voice sounded breathy, unsure. "He wants to fly in tomorrow and meet you on Wednesday at the dressage center."

"He?"

"The ambassador."

"Alone?"

"It sounds that way."

"If this is another attempt to persuade me to sell, I don't think I'm up for it."

"I think he wants to explain why the terms are so inflexible. That alone should interest you, I think. Or do you not want to bother? I can call and tell him you're no longer interested."

Her voice had turned clipped and professional, as if she had no stake in what he decided. Gabe knew her well enough to recognize that her defenses were on full alert. "No," he said wearily. "I'll listen."

Her voice warmed. "Good. Let me know how it turns out."

He frowned. "You're not coming with him?"

The silence stretched out. "No," she said softly. "He specified that he wanted to meet with you alone. There really isn't any reason for me to be there, too. Besides, I think you've already made your…decision, haven't you?"

He knew what she was asking, but he also knew he couldn't give her the answer she deserved. He wanted to explain, to have her override him, to allow her to make the sacrifice and live on his terms. But as much as he loved Whitney Benedict, and he did love her, he knew without question that he couldn't subject her to the selfishness of such a suggestion, not after he'd seen her family home, not after she'd told him about Wiley Cane. His only hope was the small chance that the ambassador would agree to his terms. Then he would have something to offer her. "Do you think it's a done deal?" he asked.

Again, another long silence. "You see, Gabe—the thing is, it doesn't matter what I think. Not anymore."

The hurt was peeling away at his nerves. "Why not?"

Her voice was slow, the words carefully spoken. "I've done some thinking and I've decided that I want more than a conditional relationship. I want someone who wants me no matter what his circumstances. That isn't you. At least, that's not the impression I'm getting."

He hadn't heard more than the first sentence of her reply. So, this was it. They were done before they'd even begun. He didn't trust himself to answer.

"Good night, Gabe."

"Good night," he managed to say, and hung up the phone.

Whitney stared at the phone in her hand. She couldn't believe what had just happened. The conversation hadn't gone as she'd planned it. She'd given him every opportunity to contradict her, to ask what she was talking about. He was supposed to ask what she meant by a *conditional relationship*. She would have told him that she understood his responsibility for his children, but she refused to base the future of their relationship upon whether or not he could keep a horse. Then he was supposed to apologize for his absurd thinking and tell her he'd fallen in love with her and wanted to be with her, no matter what happened with the Austrian government. Instead, he accepted everything she said without a single denial. Rarely had she predicted an outcome so poorly. She was a lawyer. The success of her job was based on her ability to foresee her clients' needs. This time, when it was so important, she'd failed miserably. Maybe she'd misread Gabe completely. Maybe his feelings didn't match hers. Maybe her mother was right. Maybe, with Gabe, she would never be a priority.

Suddenly, her energy left her. She kicked off her shoes and stretched out on her bed, fully clothed in her expensive linen suit. Only four short weeks ago she'd never heard of Gabriel Mendoza. She'd been perfectly satisfied with her life. If only she'd gone on the singles' cruise Pryor had planned for her. If she had, everything would be different. Her heart wouldn't hurt and she wouldn't have this pounding headache. She wouldn't be missing the jacarandas raining purple blossoms, or the sharp smell of lavender, or Mercedes and Ramona and the children, and she wouldn't be feeling so desperately and completely sorry for herself.

Gabe didn't know what he expected, but the man who stepped out of the town car looked like the quintessential European nobleman.

Eric, who'd been monitoring Claire and Lorelei in the turnout, had left his post to tell his father that the ambassador had arrived. "He looks like Count Dracula," the boy said, "except for his clothes."

Gabe laughed, pushed himself away from his desk in the office and walked outside to greet his visitor. Eric had described him perfectly. The ambassador was very tall with carved cheeks over a stern mouth, a full head of silvery hair, well-muscled arms and a tight stomach. He was thin and his eyes were ice blue. He was dressed casually, in creased khaki slacks and a polo shirt. He held out his hand. Gabe shook the hand he extended.

"Good day, Mr. Mendoza. I am Werner Pohl, the director of Vienna's Spanish Riding School."

Gabriel's eyebrows rose. "You're very welcome, Dr. Pohl." He nodded at Eric. "This is my son, Eric."

Pohl shook Eric's hand. "Please, call me Werner."

"Did I misunderstand?" Gabe asked. "I was expecting Peter Moser, the ambassador."

The man grinned and his entire demeanor changed. "I pulled rank, as you Americans say, and prevailed upon our ambassador to allow me to come instead. You see, I was a boy when your father left Austria, but I remember him well. I wanted very much to come and explain our situation to you."

Eric spoke. "It looks like Claire is finishing up. I'll get back to work. It was a pleasure meeting you, sir."

"Thank you, Eric."

They watched Eric walk away.

"His manners are refreshing. You are to be commended."

Gabe nodded. "Thank you. He's a good boy."

"Is that your daughter I see on the Lipizzaner mare you wish to keep?"

Gabe looked surprised. "Yes. How did you know?"

"We know a great deal about Franz's Lipizzaners. Am I correct in believing that she is the oldest breeding mare in your stock?"

"Lorelei is fourteen. Some would say she's too old to breed."

"Perhaps." He stroked his chin. "Lorelei. An interesting choice for a name. Are you an appreciator of the romantic poets, Gabriel?"

"You might say that."

"And what of the German philosophers?"

Gabe laughed. "Philosophy isn't one of my strengths."

"A pity," the Austrian said. "Still, if you read poetry, we may find some common ground."

Gabriel remembered his manners. "May I offer you something to drink?" he asked, "or would you like to see the horses?"

"Horses first, and then a drink."

An hour later, Gabe knew why Werner Pohl had been sent in place of the ambassador. This was a man who knew horses. He was also very similar in temperament to Franz Kohnle. As their tour progressed, Gabe found himself reluctantly drawn to this elderly horsemaster who spoke with the same cadence and accent as his father.

Their final stop was Macbeth's stall. The albino gazed back at them calmly, a prince whose bloodlines could not be mistaken, his skin translucent, the texture of softest silk, muscle and sinew so taut that a faint pink emanated from within the flesh and bone.

Pohl stared at him for a long time. When he looked away, his eyes were wet. "I was but a boy, but I remember it well, those dark days before Austria fell. When the air raids signaled, the horses would calmly file out of their stalls ready to take shelter in the passageway alongside the riding hall. A bomb would come down—crash—in the Michaelerplatz. The glass would fall around us like hail, and the Lipizzaners would crouch down, down, down, like this—" he held his palms out flat "—until the attack was over, and then they would just get up. They shivered, but they never panicked. They behaved like the veterans they were." He smiled at Gabe. "Did your father tell you?"

Gabe shook his head. "No. He didn't."

"He should have."

Later, seated across from the director amid the lush plants and hot color of his mother's patio, Gabe brought up the issue they'd avoided all afternoon. He leaned forward, searching for the right words, words that would explain without offending. "Your offer is a generous one," he began. "I'd like to accept it, but we've hit a snag over Lorelei, my daughter's mare. I feel that I have to keep her."

The old man nodded. "I wish that were possible, Gabriel. I've come a long way to explain why it isn't. Naturally, I hope that you will keep the information I relay to you confidential. May I count on you to do so?"

"Of course."

Pohl stared into his glass of ale. Then he looked at Gabe. "This is difficult for me."

"Can I help you?"

Werner Pohl smiled and shook his head. "Not unless you are a magician. Have you heard of navicular disease?"

Gabe frowned. "I haven't had too much experience with it, but I've heard it happens to horses who are confined to stalls or have strong physical demands made upon them."

"Precisely. It is a gradual progression of lameness in the front legs, rarely terminal but always debilitating. It doesn't happen to all confined, hard-working horses. We don't really understand the cause."

Gabriel waited. He knew the European aversion to reaching the point too quickly.

The horsemaster continued. "It isn't discovered until the disease is advanced, somewhere between the ages of ten and thirteen years." His mouth tightened. "Every Lipizzaner ten years and older at the Riding School is in the throes of this disease."

Gabe stared at him in disbelief.

"I don't have to tell you that this means the end of a centuries' old tradition," he continued. "Should anything happen to the school, and the thin line of continuity with the past be snapped, more would be lost than the livelihood of a few score of horses and riders. An art form of great subtlety and power, as abstract and as moving as the ballet, would vanish from the world's cultural heritage. Quite simply, we can't work lame horses. We can keep them comfortable with the proper shoes, exercise and drugs, even surgery, but those are temporary measures. We must have healthy animals."

Suddenly Gabe understood. "You want *my* healthy horses."

The old man nodded. "We must breed new stock. It is possible that the disease is hereditary. The horses sent with your father were from the line of Vilano, out of the Arab, Siglavy. They were selected because they were the strongest, the healthiest breeders, with the longest life spans. It was believed they could withstand the journey and breed on foreign soil. We need them returned. It was never intended that they would stay away permanently. In short, without your horses the school will cease to exist. I don't believe Franz would have wanted that."

"No," Gabe agreed. "He wouldn't. I'm happy to sell you my horses. But Lorelei is old for breeding purposes. Why not leave her?"

"Under the proper conditions, she can be bred for at least several more seasons. Her healthy foals may be the difference between survival and extinction for us. There is another reason, as well. Because of her age, we know she does not carry navicular disease."

"None of my horses have it," Gabe pronounced firmly.

"We have a board of directors," Pohl said sadly. "They want guarantees."

"You'll have fifteen mares."

"They're too young to be accurately diagnosed."

"That's crazy," Gabe protested. "Navicular-diseased horses have symptoms, a short stride, stumbling gait, unevenness on turns, reluctance to go forward, irritability. My horses don't show any of those."

"Neither do ours, until we've gone through the trouble to train them. None of your mares, with the exception of Lorelei, has reached the age when we can be sure she won't be a carrier. She is vital to our experiment."

Gabe was silent for a long time. "I assume you know about my daughter."

The Austrian did not look away. His eyes were kind. "Most unfortunate. I'm so sorry. I suppose it isn't possible to divert her with a mare whose bloodlines are not those of Vilano and Siglavy, a mare who is not a Lipizzaner." He looked at the brooding expression on Gabriel's face and sighed. "No. Of course not."

"My family and I own the horses together," Gabe explained. "My share will be a little over six million dollars. I've done the numbers. Starting over will cost me at least that much. For everyone else it would be a windfall. Ironic, isn't it? I'll be the only one who doesn't profit, unless I cash it all in and do something else."

"I understand."

"May I ask you a question?"

"Of course."

"What if I keep Lorelei? Are all bets off?"

The older man hesitated. "No," he said honestly. "We need the others, with or without Lorelei, but our chances will improve with her."

Gabe nodded.

"Will you return the favor and now answer my question?"

"Yes."

"If I had answered differently, would you have given her up?"

"Yes," Gabe replied. "You've convinced me."

Pohl nodded. "Then my visit had purpose. I'm glad I came." He smiled. "Don't look so despondent, my friend. Your horses were bred to perform. If you've trained them the way Franz was taught, they will live out their lives in disciplined luxury. The Spanish Riding School is their destiny. Do not deny Lorelei what you have given the others." Pohl stood. "I thank you for your time, Gabriel. You know where to reach me should you have any questions. I'm sure you understand that time is of the essence. I will go inside now and bid goodbye to your charming mother."

Gabe watched him disappear through the French doors. He leaned back in the patio chair and stared out over the lavender field. The situation had escalated beyond the personal and, therefore, was out of his hands. Except for breaking the news to Claire and signing the papers, the deal was as good as done. He wanted desperately to call Whitney, but maybe it was too late for that.

Thirty

Mercedes sighed. She tapped her index finger against the glass of wine that was now half empty. Normally, she would have replenished it, but Gabriel showed no signs of leaving the room and she didn't feel like arguing with him. He was standing by the window staring out at the darkening sky. He'd been there for a long time. Something was definitely wrong. She didn't like to interfere. No one would ever call her an interfering woman, but when her children needed her, Mercedes set her scruples aside.

She sighed. Gabriel was so sensitive. He looked weary to the bone. It was time to take the offensive. "What is it, *mijito?* How can I help you?"

He looked surprised, as if he'd forgotten he wasn't alone. "Nothing, Ma. I'm fine."

"No, you're not. Tell me what has you so troubled."

"I'm not troubled," he said, much too quickly.

"You're a terrible liar. Did you tell that man you're not selling him our horses?"

Gabe shook his head. "No. He'll get his horses."

Mercedes released her breath. She'd been worried. "It's the right thing to do, Gabriel."

"I know."

"If it isn't the horses, what is it?" she persisted.

"Please, Ma. Leave it alone. I'm fine."

"Is it Whitney? Did you have a fight?"

"Whitney and I don't fight."

Mercedes's eyes gleamed. "You should fight, *mijito*. Passion is good for a marriage. If you don't fight, you don't get scared, and if you don't get scared, you don't make up and if you don't make up, you don't appreciate what you have." She shook her finger at him. "Do you hear what I'm telling you, Gabriel?"

"I hear you, Ma. If we don't fight, we won't appreciate each other," he paraphrased.

"That's right. Next time something bothers you, you should fight."

"There won't be a next time."

"What did you say?"

He turned, exhaustion evident in every line of his face. "I said, there won't be a next time."

"Why not?"

"We won't be seeing her anymore."

"What did you do?" she demanded.

"What did *I* do?" He laughed bitterly. "Why are you assuming it was me?"

"Because I know you," she said flatly. "The woman is crazy about you."

"Not crazy enough."

"I know you better than you think, *mijito*. What did you tell her?"

"I didn't tell her anything. She's the one who said she didn't want any part of a conditional relationship. What in the hell does that mean? All relationships are conditional. Would she put up with me if I cheated, or drank or gambled, or if I stopped loving her?"

"That's not the point," said Mercedes.

"What is the point? I didn't want her to give up what she has if I could only offer her less. That kind of resentment can kill a marriage. I've been there, done that. Excuse me if I don't want to repeat the past. No, thank you."

"Oh, Gabriel," Mercedes said sadly. "I've raised a foolish son."

He didn't answer.

"You're not giving her the benefit of the doubt," Mercedes continued. "She isn't Kristen. The woman deserves to make her own choices. She's not twenty, *mijito*. Maybe she's had all the things she thought she wanted. Maybe she wants something else. By deciding for her, you've insulted her. Besides, you're selling the horses. She won't be giving up anything."

"She's done with me, Ma. She said it herself. It doesn't matter whether I sell or not."

"Talk to her, Gabriel. Change her mind."

He was silent. Mercedes hoped he was thinking. Like a good stew, there were times when words should sit on the mind. She stretched out her injured leg and stood carefully. "I'll finish dinner," she said.

Gabriel didn't answer.

Claire sat up in her bed, leaning against her pillows. Her knees were pulled close to her chest and she was flipping through the pages of a book. At the doorway of her room, Gabe hesitated. He would have given anything to avoid the news that he brought to his daughter. Lately, she seemed so much better, almost normal, as long as he ignored the occasional vacant look in her eyes. Having Eric and Emma around helped to distract him from her silences.

"Hi, honey," he said softly.

She looked up. "Hi, Daddy."

"What are you reading?"

She held up the book. He smiled. What little girl, crazy about horses, hadn't read *Misty of Chincoteague?*

"Emma started reading it to me and I'm finishing it."

He sat down beside her on the bed. "Smile for me, Claire."

Obediently the seam of her lips separated over her missing front teeth.

"I have to tell you something sad," he began.

She waited expectantly, staring at him with Kristen's blue eyes.

He swallowed. *Come away, O human child! To the waters and the wild, with a faery, hand in hand, for the world's more full of weeping than you can understand.* "Do you remember the story I told you about how Granddad brought our horses from Austria?"

She nodded.

"He never planned on keeping them here forever."

Again she nodded.

He swallowed. "It's time for them to go back to Austria."

She thought a minute. "Why?"

Gabriel considered his promise of silence to Werner Pohl and decided it didn't apply to Claire. "The Spanish Riding School needs our horses. Theirs are sick and can't perform anymore."

"How did they get sick?"

"Nobody really knows. They have a disease that makes their front legs lame."

"Will they get well after ours come?"

"No. It isn't the kind of sickness that gets better."

"Will our horses get sick?"

Sometimes it amazed him the way her mind leaped. "No," he said gently. "Ours won't get sick."

"What will we do if we don't have any more horses?"

"We'll have the stable and the dressage center. We'll keep all the horses who aren't Lipizzaners."

"Lorelei is a Lipizzaner."

He nodded. "I'm sorry, Claire. Lorelei has to go, too."

She slipped her small hand into his. "When?"

He frowned. This couldn't be as easy as it seemed. "Soon. Do you understand what I'm saying, Claire? Lorelei has to go to Austria. She won't be here with us anymore."

"She has to go, Daddy. She wouldn't be happy with all her foals and the rest of her friends gone."

"She wouldn't?"

"No. If we kept Lorelei, she'd be like Mommy."

Gabe was thoroughly confused. "How would she be like Mommy?"

"She'd be away from her family and it would make her sad, like Mommy's sad now."

"How do you know she's sad?"

Claire's eyes widened. "Every time I see her, she looks sad. She says she misses us."

Gabe tucked a curl behind his daughter's ear. "What do you think we should do so that Mommy isn't sad?"

She shrugged and resumed reading her book. Gabe understood the signs. Claire's attention had wandered. The discussion was finished. He was surprised it had lasted as long as it had. He kissed her cheek and stood. "I'll come back and turn out the light when it's time for bed."

Claire, absorbed in *Misty*, didn't reply.

Gabe left a message on Whitney's voice mail the following morning telling her he would accept the terms of the original contract. He didn't expect a reply. By noon a copy of the contract had been faxed back to him and by three o'clock he'd returned it with the necessary signatures. At four o'clock he was seated with Eric and Emma beside Adam Winchester in the lawyer's conference room. Kristen, her mother and their attorney sat on the other side of the table.

Lynne spoke first. "I don't think it was necessary to bring the children, Gabriel."

"They aren't babies and this concerns them," Gabe replied.

"Still, I don't think—"

Kristen interrupted. "They're already here, Mom. Let's just move on, shall we?"

Adam Winchester leaned forward. "It was my suggestion that Eric and Emma be here. It's customary to have teenage children give their parents input on how they're feeling about decisions that are made for them."

Lynne pursed her lips and settled back in her chair.

Her lawyer, Jim Thatcher, spoke next. "Mrs. Chamberlain feels that the children should be with a blood relative, preferably their mother. Given Mrs. Mendoza's schedule, however, that isn't possible. Therefore, as their maternal grandmother, she is willing to take the children into her custody until their mother's situation changes."

"Jim, that's the most interesting custody interpretation I've ever heard," said Winchester. "Where in the hell did you study family law?"

"I see no reason to get personal, Mr. Winchester," said the lawyer stiffly.

"You can't possibly think you can win this one in court."

"I certainly do."

Winchester hooted. "Let's see, now." He scratched his head. "We've got a mother who abandoned her children. We've got a widowed grandmother too old to handle active teenagers. We've got a stepfather, the only father the children have ever known, who picked up the ball and who works within walking distance of the family home. You have two teenagers who want to stay right where they are. I wonder who the court will decide for?" His smile disappeared. "Get real, Thatcher. They obviously don't pay you enough, or you wouldn't have taken this one."

Jim Thatcher frowned. "Mr. Mendoza may be the only father they've known, but the fact remains that he isn't their biological father. He didn't even adopt them."

"Only because their late father's social security benefits would cease—benefits, by the way, that Kristen Mendoza is still collecting, even though the children no longer live with her."

Thatcher protested. "I don't see the relevance—"

"It doesn't matter whether you see it," interrupted Winchester. "The point is, it's illegal to collect money for the support of children who are not dependents. The IRS frowns on fraud. Be assured they will be notified."

Kristen's cheeks burned. She swallowed, ignored the attorney and looked at her children. "Is it true that you want to stay with your dad?"

"Yes," said Eric forcefully.

Emma looked down at her hands.

"What about you, Emma? Do you want to stay with Dad, too?"

She sniffed. "I don't know. I don't want to leave Eric and Claire. I guess I want both of you to be together, like it was."

Kristen shook her head. "That isn't going to happen, honey."

"Then I want to live with both of you, half the time with Dad and half with you."

"That isn't possible, either."

Emma looked at her grandmother and her eyes filled. "I'm sorry, Grandma. I don't want to hurt your feelings, but I don't want to live at your house unless Mom lives there, too."

Gabe spoke up. "Kristen, if it's a matter of money, we can work something out."

"It has nothing to do with money," she said fiercely. "Don't you see, I have to do this for myself. I don't want to go back to the way it was, living in someone else's house, always walking on eggshells."

Gabe couldn't believe his ears. "What are you talking about?"

"My sentiments exactly," said Lynne. "What do you mean by walking on eggshells? When have I ever made you feel like that?"

Kristen clenched her fists. "Of course you don't know. Why would you? It wasn't happening to you."

"We're digressing," Thatcher said.

Adam Winchester held up his hand. "Hold on, Jim. We may be on to something here."

Six pairs of eyes stared at him.

"We can resolve this," he said easily. "Gabe wants the kids. Emma wants to live with both parents. Mrs. Mendoza doesn't want to move back into someone else's home." He looked at Kristen. "What if you had your own home close enough so the kids could stay with you when you're not touring?"

"I don't know when that will be," replied Kristen. "My schedule changes. It might not work with their school."

"If you're close to where they go to school, they won't need much notice."

"I don't have the money to buy a house," Kristen said stiffly.

"That's where Gabe comes in. I think he could be convinced to buy you a place where you could be with the kids." He nodded at Gabe. "How does that sound to you, Gabe?"

"It might work," Gabe said slowly, "with certain conditions."

Kristen bristled. "What conditions?"

"I'd like you to choose a house that's close enough for the kids to go back and forth between us on their own."

"Is that all?"

"You have to agree not to sell the place until all three of them are grown. I want the money to go for a home where they can be with you, nothing else."

Her lower lip trembled. "You don't think much of me, do you?"

Her mother broke in. "Let's not get into that." She looked thoughtful. "Housing has appreciated tremendously. It might be very expensive to buy a house outright."

"Since the children are primarily in Gabe's care, child support won't be an issue," Winchester interjected smoothly. "Naturally, the house will be Mrs. Mendoza's settlement. She will have to pay her own property taxes and waive all rights to spousal support."

"Now, just a minute," said Jim Thatcher.

Kristen spoke up. "It's all right. I'm not interested in being supported. The house is more than generous. I do have a question, though."

"Go ahead," said Gabe.

"When the kids are grown, is it mine to sell?"

Gabriel nodded. "Yes."

Kristen relaxed. "All right. It's a deal."

Events moved forward swiftly. The sale of the Lipizzaners was finalized without a hitch and the horses moved to Austria with incredible speed. Quarantines were lifted, duties paid, documents of sale and bills of lading prepared for the ocean voyage. Gabe had personally inspected the hold of the cargo ship where the horses would be confined during their week at sea. Two grooms had been sent from the Spanish Riding School to feed and exercise the horses throughout the voyage. Gabe had politely refused Werner Pohl's invitation to see the Lipizzaners installed in their new home. He didn't think he was emotionally up to seeing his father's legacy come full circle. Instead, he'd sent Juan and Eric, payback for missing the Kentucky Derby.

Except for dealing with Emma, whose nose was out of joint at what she saw as blatant favoritism toward her brother, Gabe's routine hadn't changed much. With his proceeds, he'd added another turnout, replaced the fencing on two of the rings and bought a badly needed late-model truck. Other than that, the major advantage to having money in the bank was peace of mind. If something broke, he could fix it. If he wanted to make a purchase, he didn't have to juggle his finances. He looked forward to replenishing his breeding stock at an upcoming auction in the bay area. Two Thoroughbreds he was particularly interested in were up for sale. He would have liked to discuss their merits with Whitney, but he hadn't heard from her. He didn't expect to, although he couldn't help taking a second look whenever he happened upon a slender woman with hair the color of ripe wheat.

Not a day went by that his mother didn't bring up her name. When he didn't respond, she shook her head and muttered under her breath. Maybe Mercedes was right. Maybe he *was* a fool. What he knew for sure was that he didn't want to hear Whitney say in words he couldn't misunderstand that it was completely over. This way, at least he could hold on to a slender hope.

Three weeks after the horses had sailed, Gabe locked up his office and reviewed the following day's itinerary before making his way home through the lavender field. He loved walking home toward the setting sun, across the packed-dirt road shadowed by olive trees that had seen the first Mendoza shape the adobe bricks for the base of the hacienda. Soon the lavender would be ready for harvest. The plants, minus their blooms, would look bare and blue-gray instead of the vibrant purple.

As usual, Mercedes would recruit the women in her family to gather her crop. Gabriel had grown up watching his mother, his sisters and, more recently, his daughters and their friends, swathed in gloves and bamboo hats, hacking systematically through the aisles. The blooms were gathered, tied and hung upside down from the rafters in the hay barn. After the entire crop was in, Mercedes would host an enormous barbecue for everyone who'd helped. If he closed his eyes, he could almost smell wood smoke. His mouth watered. Even if it wasn't barbecue, whatever his mother had planned for dinner was sure to be good, and he was hungry.

Gabe narrowed his eyes. A large truck pulling a silver horse trailer was parked in front of the house. The doors were open and the ramp was down. His mother, Emma and Claire were watching someone back out a horse. But it wasn't the horse that caught Gabe's attention. It was the slim blond woman in gray slacks, a white shirt and black riding boots. His heart pumped painfully. Whitney.

As if she could feel his eyes on her, she turned, her hand shading her forehead against the sun. Then she handed the reins to Claire and began walking toward him, slowly at first and then faster and faster until she was running loosely, easily, as if jogging across an area the size of a football field in riding boots was something she did every day. He must have run, too. They came together in the middle of the field. He reached out, lifted her off the ground and swung her around and around until she was flushed with laughter, and the urge to hold her close overpowered him. In full view of his mother and daughters, he bent his head and kissed her until he couldn't breathe.

Keeping his hands on her shoulders, he pulled away to look at her. "You changed your mind."

She laughed her warm, back-throated laugh. "I've come to give you a second chance."

He looked confused. "A second chance?"

"You're probably confused. I'm going to explain it to you."

He *was* confused. "Explain what?"

"What you're supposed to say when the woman you love tells you she wants to be with you, no matter what your circumstances."

Relief, like the surge that follows a rush of caffeine, flowed through him. He grinned. "The woman I love?"

She nodded. "Yes. The woman you love, who loves you back."

"I'm listening."

She tucked her arm through his and pulled him gently toward the house. "First, let me show you my present."

"Your present?"

"Actually, it's Claire's present."

"Claire's present?"

"Really, Gabe," she teased him. "You're going to have to stop repeating everything I say. It makes you sound positively henpecked."

He felt like a kid again. "Give me a break, Whitney. I'm still in a state of shock. Tell me about Claire's present."

"It's a mare. She's a four-year-old Thoroughbred from my parents' stable, compliments of Werner Pohl and the Austrian government."

Gabe stopped and stared at her. "Are you serious?"

"Completely." She spoke quickly, excitedly. "Her name is Firelight and her bloodlines are excellent. She took third place in the Derby last year, but didn't do well at Saratoga. She's fast but gentle, and because she's been handled with kid gloves, she isn't the least bit temperamental. In other words, she's perfect for Claire."

His euphoria faded. "I don't know what to say."

"*Thank you* would be a good place to start."

He shook his head.

Before he could speak, she turned on him, her words coming so fast they fell over each other. "Don't you dare say you can't accept her, or that she's too valuable, or any other nonsense coming into your head. You've given up your Lipizzaners and they're far more valuable."

"It's not the same, Whitney. I was paid for them."

"If I remember correctly, you were going to refuse that payment. It wasn't until Werner Pohl told you about the situation at the school that you agreed. He wanted to show his appreciation for your sacrifice. I suggested another mare. Is that so terrible?"

He didn't look convinced. "An animal like that is worth a fortune. How much of this is your doing?"

"Gabriel," she said sadly, dropping her arm. "If you don't do something about that pride of yours, it's going to make you very miserable." She started to walk away.

Come live with me and be my love, and we will all the pleasures prove. "Where are you going?"

"I need a minute," she said, without turning around. "This time the ball's in your court."

He watched her leave, the ring of truth in her words rendering him immobile. Why did it always come down to this between them? He wasn't a chest-pounding Neanderthal. What was it about this woman that brought out the machismo in his personality?

By the time he reached the porch, Whitney had gone inside with Emma. Claire and his mother waited for him.

"Look, Daddy." Claire was smiling. "Whitney brought her. Her name is Firelight and she's from Dr. Pohl. Can I ride her now?"

Gabe took a long look at his daughter's animated little face and knew he couldn't deny her this gift. He swallowed. "She's beautiful," he said, running his hands over her back and flanks. "Let's settle her in first and talk about riding in the morning."

When he returned to the house, Whitney was nowhere to be found. He sent Claire upstairs to wash her hands. His mother was in the kitchen drinking yet another suspicious glass of purple liquid. She shook her head when she saw him. "Gabriel, *mijito,* why do you keep shooting yourself in the foot?"

"Believe me, it isn't intentional."

"You know I'm not an interfering woman, but just this once I'll make an exception."

Gabe sighed and sat down at the table across from her. "What is it, Ma?"

"You're ruining your life," she said bluntly. "This wonderful woman has come three thousand miles bringing a gift for your daughter and this is how you treat her."

"I suppose it looks that way, doesn't it?"

She ignored him. "You should be kissing her feet,

The Lavender Field   369

promising her the moon, and what do you do?" She shook her head.

He gave up. "I know, Ma. I blew it."

"You go upstairs right now, knock on her door and tell her you're sorry that you've been such a fool. Tell her it will never happen again."

"I don't know if I can do that."

Exasperated, she glared at him. "Don't be an idiot. Read between the lines, *mijito*. Do I have to do this for you?"

Without thinking, he picked up the glass at his mother's elbow and drained it. The alcohol hit him immediately. Whatever she was drinking was potent. He shook his head to clear it, then pushed himself away from the table and stood. "No," he said firmly. "I'll do it myself. I'll give it all I have, but I can't be something I'm not. If it isn't right, it's better to know now, not later. This time it has to work, Ma. I have to know that this time it's forever."

Mercedes took his face in her hands. "Gabriel, my son, my own. You are so fierce, so intense. No one can see forever. All we have is what we know right now. Go with that, *mijito*. Follow your heart. Take happiness where you find it. If this woman makes you happy, don't push her away."

Gabriel focused on the familiar lines of his mother's face. Except for the thudding of his heart the kitchen was completely silent. Could it really be so simple? He stood. "Wish me luck," he said lightly.

"You won't need luck," his mother promised. "The woman loves you. She's in the red room."

With his heart in his throat, he climbed the stairs. Emma was in Claire's bedroom. They were seated across from each other on the floor, playing cards. He stood in the doorway for a minute, watching them. Emma held her thumb up and winked at him. "Go for it, Dad."

Immediately he felt better. The door to Whitney's room was closed. He knocked softly. No answer. He turned the knob. It wasn't locked. Cautiously, he opened the door. She was lying on the bed with one arm slung across her face. The rise and fall of her chest was slow and even. Closing the door behind him, he sat down on the bed and waited.

A minute passed. Her breathing changed. Then her arm moved away from her face. Slowly, she opened her eyes. They were luminous, the pupils large and dark. His breath caught. She smiled and he relaxed.

"What took you so long?" she asked.

"My mother was giving me advice."

"You, too?"

He nodded. "And you?"

"Yes."

"I'm a fool."

"She uses that word quite a bit," Whitney observed.

"You, too?"

"Yes."

"What do you think about going back to the beginning?"

"Where exactly is the beginning?"

"Let's take it from where we are right now."

She thought a minute, her eyes never leaving his face. "Where does that leave us?"

He picked up her hand and laced his fingers through hers. "I like what I do. I love what I do. I've grown to love it. Do you like what you do?"

"Sometimes."

"Do you think you might like to do it in California?"

"No."

He frowned. This wasn't going in the direction he'd hoped. "No?"

"I think I'd like to do something else."

"Like what?"

"I think I'd like to get back into the horse business."

He couldn't read her. Was she serious? "In what capacity?"

She sat up. "I'd like to handle the sales and breeding side of your business. I'd like it to be ours, equally."

The smile that started inside of his chest spread to his face. "I could go for that. What changed your mind?"

"You did. You love your horses. You treat them like children. I like that. Dressage is kind. It's for people who love horses. I've had an epiphany."

"Care to share it?"

"You bet. The way I see it is, I've been running from two things for most of my adult life. One of them is love and the other is horses. For me, they go hand in hand, my two loves. Finding you was finding my way back to my center. I won't give that up again."

"Thank God. Ma's right. I've been a fool. I promise it won't happen again."

She smiled. "There's something else, too. I'd like to buy an interest in the business."

"I don't need the money."

"I want to contribute. That way I'll feel the business is mine, too. I'd like our job descriptions to be specific, so we don't overlap."

"You're the attorney. Draw up a contract."

"You have a lot of money, Gabe. Would you feel better if your interest was larger? We could set up some kind of agreement, sort of a prenuptial?"

He didn't like the sound of that at all. "Absolutely not."

"I didn't think so." She smiled and sat up. "Shall we tell your mother?"

Her studied her face for a long minute, taking in the pale eyebrows and golden skin, the sculpted cheeks and wide, lash-rimmed eyes. Suddenly his heart felt tight and unsure. "What will we tell her?" he asked softly.

The gray eyes widened. "We'll tell her we're getting married and that we're going into business together. What else?"

He relaxed. It was going to be okay after all. "Just checking."

This time they found Mercedes on the patio. She was seated in a wicker chair, her eyes staring out over the lavender field, its stalks heavy with blooms.

"Ma," Gabe began. "We have something to tell you."

"I certainly hope so."

"Whitney and I have decided to go into business together."

Mercedes's face clouded. "What?"

Whitney couldn't bear the woman's obvious disappointment. "And we're getting married."

"Thank God!" Mercedes pressed both hands against her heart and beamed at Whitney. "I knew you were right for my Gabriel the minute I saw you. I'm so happy, so very, very happy." She clapped her hands. "We need champagne. *Mijito,* go down to the cellar and bring up a few bottles. I'll call your sisters."

She waited until Gabriel disappeared into the house. Then she turned to Whitney and patted the chair beside her. "Sit beside me. Have you decided on a date?"

Whitney sat down and shook her head. "Not yet. We wanted to tell you right away." She leaned forward, her eyes twinkling. "I think you should probably take Gabe's name out of the Matchmaker.com database."

Mercedes patted her cheek. "I did that long ago, right after you first came to us." She smiled happily. "Of course, you'll decide these things on your own, but if I might make a suggestion?"

"Please do."

"I was thinking that nothing would be lovelier than a wedding in the lavender field? Were you thinking the same thing?"

Whitney thought of her mother and her father and her great-aunt Lila Rae, and the lovely old house where every female in her mother's family had been launched for five generations. She opened her mouth to explain that she would probably have to be married in Kentucky.

"Look, *mijita,*" Mercedes said softly, nodding in the direction of the purple field, thick with blooms. "Look at my lavender field. Look. Close your eyes and smell."

Whitney looked, turned back to Mercedes, and then, as if pulled by an irresistible force, she looked again, closed her eyes and drew a long, slow breath. Sure enough, an image formed in her mind, an image of herself in a white dress on her father's arm, Gabe in a dark suit waiting at the end of a beaten path canopied with olive trees, Emma and Claire in purple satin, her mother slim and stunning in lavender lace, sunlight streaming through a sea of purple blooms, white wicker chairs, a bouquet studded with stalks of lavender, Mercedes and her three beautiful daughters tossing waterfalls of lavender seeds. All at once it seemed so clear and right.

Whitney smiled. "You know, Mercedes, you're right. I can't think of anything lovelier than having our wedding right here in the lavender field."

Mercedes sighed happily, leaned back in her chair and closed her eyes. "Whatever you think is best, *mijita*. It shall be exactly as you wish. You know, of course, that I would never interfere. My children will tell you, I have never been an interfering woman."

Epilogue

Vienna, Austria, two years later

Emma looks around at the gold-and-ivory riding hall, at the brilliance of the multifaceted chandeliers, snow cones of dripping ice, at the Austrian flags hanging from the red velvet balustrades and the portrait of Charles VI gazing down upon the spectators who wait in anticipation for Bizet's violins to announce the opening of the great double doors. She is impressed.

Her brother whispers into her ear. "It takes two years to teach a Lipizzaner to walk."

"I know that," she tells him scornfully. "Where do you think I've been living all my life?"

Eric grins. "Just making sure you appreciate what you're going to see. We have the best seats in the house, thanks to Dr. Pohl."

She glances at Whitney sitting beside her. "He thinks I'm stupid," she whispers.

"He doesn't think any such thing," replies her step-mother. Two years have honed her ability for employing diversionary tactics in potentially explosive situations. "Look at Claire. Her eyes are so big they've swallowed up her face."

It's true. Claire sits beside her father, her hands perfectly still in her lap. Her eyes focus on the double doors.

Gabe looks behind the heads of his children and winks at Whitney just as the lights dim and the first notes of L'Arlésienne Suite pierce the din of the crowd. A hush falls over the room. At the end of the hall the double doors slowly swing open and the first horse and rider move into the expectant arena.

Werner Pohl, perfectly composed, a vision in cinnamon livery, a two-corner hat and gleaming boots, leads seven other riders into the room. Under him, his neck perfectly arched, knees high and head proud, is Macbeth, the albino stallion, bred, born and trained in Ventura, California.

Perfectly synchronized, the horses move as if in a dream—the regal vertical carriage of the head, the slight downward thrust of the haunches, the precise and delicate placing of the feet—straight to the portrait of Charles VI, imperial patron of the Spanish Riding School. There, in a majestic gesture of homage, the riders doff their hats in a wide and sweeping salute.

The audience bursts into applause. Emma's worldly demeanor cracks and she claps along with them. "How do the horses know what to do?" she asks Whitney. "I don't see them using their heels or reins or anything."

Whitney smiles. "That's the whole point. Your attention is supposed to slip away from the rider so that he disappears and your focus is only on the fluid movement of the horse."

Eric grips her hand. His face glows with excitement. "Watch this, Emma."

She watches. The white horses move from walking and cantering to the *piaffe,* a sophisticated trotting on the spot, to the Spanish Step, pirouettes, half pirouettes, the mincing cross-steps of the plié, the weaving of the quadrille and pas de trois.

Emma knows what comes next, the most dramatic of all steps, the *courbette,* the *levade* and the capriole, the true "airs above the ground" where the stallion leaps into the air and, at the height of elevation, kicks out violently with his hind legs. Not every horse is up to it.

Emma holds her breath, praying that Macbeth doesn't disgrace her family. Even though the Mendoza Lipizzaners have been preparing for their debut for two long years, it isn't usually long enough to master the capriole. If Macbeth succeeds, it will be because of her father's training.

Collectively, the Mendozas lean forward. Whitney, keeping her eyes on the arena, reaches across her step-children to grip Gabriel's hand. She watches Macbeth slowly, gracefully, effortlessly, leap into the air and kick backward with his hind legs.

For an instant, the silence is complete. And then the room bursts into applause. Row after row stands in ovation. Werner Pohl leaves the conformation and walks Macbeth across the arena to where Gabriel and his family are seated. Doffing his hat with a flourish, he bows to the Mendozas. Gabriel stands and bows back. The audience roars its approval.

Behind Whitney's eyelids, tears burn. Four-hundred and twenty-five years ago, the Spanish Riding School opened its doors. Now, because of Gabriel, it will continue.

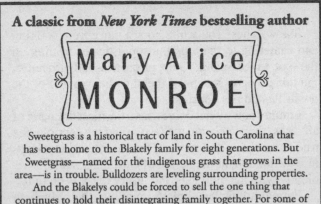

New York Times **bestselling author**

KAREN HARPER

Julie Minton thought nothing of her fourteen-year-old daughter, Randi, leaving home earlier that morning to go Jet Ski riding with Thad Brockman. But now Randi and Thad are missing—and the hurricane that hours ago was just another routine warning has turned toward shore.

With the help of Zack Brockman, Thad's father, Julie begins a race against time to find their children—but first, they must battle not only Mother Nature, but an enemy willing to use the danger and devastation of the storm for their own evil end.

HURRICANE

"Harper has a fantastic flair for creating and sustaining suspense."
—*Publishers Weekly* on *The Falls*

It was an affair…to regret

Laura Caldwell

Rachel Blakely's charmed life is
significantly tarnished after her husband
Nick's infidelity, but she wants to give
her marriage a second chance. Then a
business trip to Rome leads to a night
of passion with a stranger. Rachel
returns home, determined to put the
past behind her, and at first, life seems
golden again. Nick is more loving than
ever and, following his promotion, the
couple is welcomed into Chicago's high
society, where beautiful people live
beautiful lives. But there's a dark side…
one that sends Rachel's life spiraling
into a nightmare.

It's clear everyone is guilty of something.
But whose secrets will lead to murder?

THE ROME
AF︎ꟻAIR

**"A fabulous, hypnotic psychological
thriller. This book blew me away, and
Caldwell is a force we can't ignore."**
—*New York Times* bestselling
author Stella Cameron

*Available the first week of June 2006
wherever paperbacks are sold!*

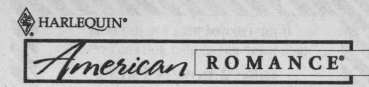

HARLEQUIN®

American ROMANCE®

IS PROUD TO PRESENT A GUEST APPEARANCE BY

QUILL
BOOK
AWARD
WINNING
AUTHOR

NEW YORK TIMES bestselling author

DEBBIE MACOMBER

The Wyoming Kid

The story of an ex–rodeo cowboy,
a schoolteacher and their journey to the altar.

"Best-selling Macomber, with more than
100 romances and women's fiction titles
to her credit, sure has a way of pleasing readers."
—*Booklist* on *Between Friends*

The Wyoming Kid is available from
Harlequin American Romance in July 2006.